Enjoy!

The Impotent Avenger

by

T. S. Farley

aka "TODD"

@TSFARLEY17

Copyright 2018 by T.S.Farley

First edition 2018

ISBN: 978-0-9989007-8-0

Kick-ass cover design by Justin Kauffmann
(www.justink.com)

For my sons. Everything for my sons.

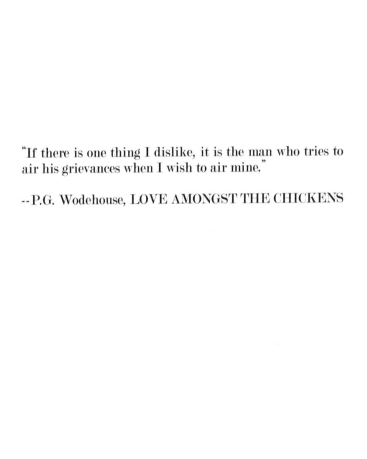

"If there is one thing I dislike, it is the man who tries to air his grievances when I wish to air mine."

--P.G. Wodehouse, LOVE AMONGST THE CHICKENS

Contents

I.

Role Play (Monday, 2013)

While conceding that his perspective might be skewed from a daily diet of way too much online porn, Finn Riley still couldn't shake the idea that any two young women he saw together on the streets of Manhattan had just been giving head. The same head, that is. Finn figured one of the girls had been tongue-tickling the top of some idiot's dong, the other ball-blowing the bottom of it, before those two little Lolitas had laid themselves down to get themselves laid but good. "High-five!" Finn imagined those Millennials shouting at the end.

In the forty-something Finn's day it hadn't been that easy to get any one woman into bed, let alone a matching pair of them, so he wasn't sure how he felt about this whole two girl/one cock phenomenon. On the one hand, when viewing said sexy scenarios on the Internet with his pants around his ankles Finn was universally in favor— consider him a "pro" vote right then, for sure. On the other hand, Finn himself still wasn't managing to get any of the sexy siren sandwiches that every teenaged boy in America now seemed to regularly revel in, so he could admit there might be a bit of envy there. Maybe a smidge of bitterness. Perhaps even the tiniest bit of bubbling, boiling, poisonous rage.

Nah, not really "rage," he thought. That was just his hard-on talking.

Finn smiled, strolling down Broadway on a warm May Monday, his hands tightly gripping the ankles of the toddler son sitting atop his shoulders. The "Prince of New York" he called the boy, now three years old, who was jabbering up there and leaning his head down and around to try to get himself right into his father's face. He giggled every time he managed to do so, especially as Finn— each time— feigned surprise to see him. His son laughed even more when Finn shook him, bucking the little boy around his shoulders like a rider atop a bronco, the child simultaneously laughing and telling his dad to stop.

Many of the women rushing up the Great White Way couldn't help but notice the bouncing boy, and on female faces young and old alike smiles appeared. Some were faint and some wide, but the laughing child regularly had an effect. Not every woman smiled, of course, and especially not those staring at their iPhones. Those women saw no boy. They saw no Finn either, he noticed with gritted teeth. Meanwhile, the men walking up the street— those pricks— remained unmoved, mostly stone-faced at the sight of father carrying son. One hirsute fat guy, himself certainly with kids at home, did notice, breaking into a great grin at the site of Finn and his boy. Still, Finn had to temper his appreciation for this dude's seeming decency because the look he directed at Finn was one of such saccharine sincerity that it made Finn want to just about puke. Pussy, Finn thought. Probably some kind of stay-at-home dad.

This daily commute was the best part of Finn's day, whether the boy was on his shoulders or walking beside him, hand in hand. From the pre-school on Central Park West to Columbus Circle they travelled— with regular sidebars to either the playgrounds of Central Park or the cookie section of the Time Warner Center's Whole Foods— before picking up Broadway and heading to their Midtown home. Finn loved the immediacy of the task, delivering his son from the safety of his pre-school to the safety of his apartment. There was no doubt about his purpose, no questions about the meaning of life. It was just "get the boy home." Finn also loved that during that trek he was absolutely free, untethered to modern society. He carried no cell phone so couldn't be reached, even by his wife. Not even by his wife! He carried no computer gadgetry of any kind, so neither could he check his e-mail, scan Facebook updates, or (again!) stare at the online version of the op-ed he'd managed to get published in the *New York Times* a couple years back. He couldn't troll through the newest listings of Craigslist's "Casual Encounters" or see what interesting might have recently transpired at his old standby, dirtyporn.com. No, for at least one glorious hour each weekday afternoon it was just Finn and his boy and New York City, the sun beginning a slow descent west over Manhattan as they walked home, the two of them alone and alive together, father and son.

"Fuck you!" Finn screamed, some a-hole in an Audi forcing his way through a crosswalk although the pedestrians clearly had the right of way. "You sonuvabitch..."

"Daddy," the Prince said, having heard those phrases enough times to know that Mommy didn't like them.

"Punk," Finn growled at the Audi's disappearing taillights. Standing in the middle of the crosswalk with his boy on his shoulders he stared after the car, hordes of Midtown pedestrians pushing past the unmoving father the way the Hudson and East Rivers lapped past the southern tip of indomitable Manhattan.

The Prince leaned down to his ear and whispered, "No swearing, Daddy."

"No swearing, people!" Finn spun around, addressing the crowd. "Think of the children!"

"Daddy...." The Prince was amused but not fooled.

Their apartment building at 54th and Broadway had class. The Albemarle she was called, a stone edifice eleven stories high and more than a hundred years old. Across Broadway, David Letterman held court every night at the Ed Sullivan Theatre, but the Albemarle's past was more impressive even than her present. Mae West had long called the building home, and though infamous 1919 World Series fixer Albert Rothstein hadn't been shot to death there he'd surely walked past on the way to getting fatally plugged next door. The building's basement, though, where a couple times each week Finn laundered his family's soiled dainties, had once been a speakeasy frequented by, among others, George

Herman "Babe" Ruth. Between the noted satyr Ruth and the nymph West, Finn figured, a whole lot of people at the Albemarle had gotten themselves fucked. Finn sure had.

Father and son were welcomed home in the building's lobby. "Gooooooooood afternooooooooon," Lexlhut, or "Lawrence," said, enunciating slowly and eerily in his normal voice, one that Finn's son would one day equate with a character from *The Hotel Transylvania* movie franchise ("Daddy, is 'Lawrence' a vampire?").

Lawrence, the building's primary doorman, had been working at the Albemarle for more than twenty years. Overnight shift, at first, but eventually earning the right to be the full-time, day-time doorman, a position that allowed him to sit idly at a desk on a high leather chair and lord his position and authority over anyone he felt his inferior (namely, all women and any foreigner other than himself, but especially blacks and Hispanics). Lawrence had been ensconced at the Albemarle for more than ten years before Finn first met his wife and starting sniffing around her building, at which point Lawrence had, naturally, opened the building's doors to Finn both literally and figuratively (really, what else could he have done, being hamstrung by the fact Finn was very white, very American, and very male). Hearing that Finn was at the Albemarle that first time to visit the woman Lawrence called "Danush," however, his face had lit up. As far as Lawrence was concerned, "Danush" was very, very pretty.

"Wellllccccccoooommmmeee," Lawrence had said (à la Count Dracula/Chocula), his wording and accent implying if not Transylvania at least some other largely-unknown and possibly no-longer existent Eastern European empire. In short order, as Finn visited the Albemarle with more and more regularity Lawrence had made clear that, although he would happily open the door for Finn, he was more than a doorman. Back home, in _____sylvania, it was stated/implied, Lawrence was someone else, someone important. He had been, maybe, a diplomat, a professor, an

historian? Lawrence had nodded and smiled at Finn back
then, knowing someone as wise as this youngish man would
surely understand.

But the real hoo-ha started when Lawrence found out
that Finn was a writer (*or, honestly, it might be more accurate to say that at that time Finn called himself a writer, as
this Omniscient Narrator refuses to sit idly by and let Finn
imply something about himself that was a bald-faced lie, because at the time Finn first met "Lawrence" and "Danush"
he'd written little more than a bunch of dirty e-mails and a
couple of lame travel journals*). At that point, in any case,
Finn could never darken the Albemarle's door ever again
without being offered one example or another of Lawrence's
oeuvre, because, come to find out, back in
_____sylvania the doorman had written and self-pub-
lished as many books about his country's forgotten history as
he'd opened New York City doors. Finn took those dozens of
proffered books, every single one, which he'd have been absolutely delighted to read if only he'd been able to understand
them in their native _____sylvanian.

Esteemed author or not, however, Lawrence didn't seem
all that bright to Finn. Every day it was the same thing. Finn
picked up his son at school, dragged him to Adventure playground on 68th street, or for a jaunt through Sheep Meadow
in Central Park, perhaps to the cannoli hut at the park entrance near Columbus Circle, and by the time they had lolly-
gagged home Lawrence welcomed Finn with the same
question.

"Daddy day?" he would query, apparently unaware that
every day— every *single* day— it was Finn that dropped the
Prince off at school, Finn who picked him up after, and Finn
who tended to the boy on the weekends. Lawrence knew that
"Danush" had been ailing, and he watched Finn bring his
son to and from school every *single* day, but his apparently
prehistoric Eastern European mind nonetheless seemed
unable to grasp the concept that Finn was both the child's
primary caretaker and that he had a dick. (Shiiiit, Finn

sometimes thought sympathetically, in truth that incongru-
ous idea— that one could be both a caretaker *and* penis-
carrier— was one that even a Westerner as forward-thinking
as Finn sometimes struggled with).

"Goooooooooood   afternoooooooooon," the   doorman
drawled the day of the obnoxious Audi. "Daddy day?"

"You bet!" Finn smiled madly, a little bit Jack
Nicholson's "Here's Johnny!" from *The Shining*, plowing
past. "It's that single, special day of the week where I pick up
my boy!"

Opening the door to 2A— where, although he didn't
know if either had ever actually been, Finn liked to imagine
the priapic Babe Ruth pounding the lubricious Mae West—
Finn heard nothing. Worse, he smelled nothing. Finn had
asked "Danush" to pop the fish in the oven if she was able,
but failing to see or smell any activity the husband was able
to surmise that his wife had not started dinner.

Finn wasn't much in favor of TV for children— and
don't even get him started on cell phones or computers— but
he set his son up in front of *Nick Jr.* and headed to the
kitchen. He set the oven to pre-heat and grabbed an apron
from the wall, pulling it over his head and tying it around
him although, in truth, his not particularly messy prep work
for dinner had already been done— there was no real reason,
other than the irony of it all, to wear such protection. Still
Finn found it funny, imagining himself a modern-day Betty
Crocker in a flowered apron (well, some days Finn found the
apron funny— other days its symbolism enraged him).

Finn pulled the salmon from the fridge, where it remained covered in Saran Wrap while marinating in what
Finn called his "sweet sauce": honey and bread crumbs. He
filled a bowl with blueberries and another with almonds and
considered the family meal. They would eat baked wild
salmon, wild Maine blueberries, and organic, roasted, unsalted almonds. Yes, the repast would be unusual— how
about a side dish, some potatoes, one might ask?— but on the

other hand Finn's family was about to sup on what he understood to be three of the world's five "superfoods". You added a pomegranate and a cup of green tea to the meal and they would all live forever!

The idea of death reminded Finn of his wife. The bedroom was dark, and from the doorway he saw Danielle sleeping on her side. The blankets were gathered around her legs, as if she'd tossed them off. Her black t-shirt was pulled slightly up her back and her black leggings pulled slightly down, so the tattoo on Danielle's lower back was visible. She may not have liked the word but Finn could see his wife's shapely "haunches." Finn loved his wife's haunches and, if he was being perfectly honest with himself, their existence was likely the very witches' brew that had led him into this mess: husband, father, stay-at-home dad.

But, frankly, Finn's problems were not the problem right then. Danielle seemed to moan quietly and seemed to arch her back. Finn wasn't sure what he was seeing until her hand slipped under the hem of her leggings and between her own two legs. In a voice throaty enough to have belonged to Ms. West and oddly sexy given its content, Danielle asked Finn a question.

"Did you get my chemo?"

Finn loved his wife, he really did, but he wasn't in the mood to talk shop. For the first time in what seemed forever, his once libidinous wife seemed horny. Finn slid on to the bed behind her and snuggled close, sliding one arm under her and the other over. He put his leg over hers. He readjusted and flattened his flowered apron so that he could align his crotch with his wife's ass and pulled her tight. His two hands gripped her two wrists.

"Did you get my medicine?" she repeated.

"I've got your medicine right here," Finn whispered into her ear.

"No," she said quietly, half-heartedly trying to free her hands.

"Just do what Daddy says," Finn whispered. "Just be a good girl and do what I say."

"No," she said quietly, struggling helplessly against her husband's grip. The combination of Finn's man-strength and his wife's cancer battle didn't make it much of a contest.

"No," she repeated softly, but it was Finn's favorite kind of no, the kind when she really meant yes.

"On your knees," he said, pushing her up, simultaneously trying to simulate the kind of forced sex his wife favored with a physicality that wouldn't hurt her. It was a delicate balance, Finn realized, trying to fake-rape a woman with a terminal disease.

Her leggings were quickly off and her ass up in the air, and the ease with which Finn entered his wife indicated that Finn had been right: Her "no" had absolutely not meant "no." In their world, wet meant "yes." His wife touched herself as Finn stroked her from behind, and looking at her haunches, at her bottom, at her naughty back tattoo, Finn found a rhythm that, although gentle, would finish him quick. He thought of the strip clubs they'd been to together, the swingers' clubs they'd visited, the Nevada brothel where the dopey whore (in Finn's defense, "whore" is what the woman had called *herself*) initially wouldn't share Finn's cock with his very own wife. She was the sexiest thing he'd ever known, Finn's wife, and he could never get enough of her. He fucked her harder, him (and, hopefully, her?) about to come, when the Prince of New York yelled excitedly from the living room.

"Arriba, Arriba!" the boy yelled at the TV as Finn banged his wife from behind.

"Arriba, Arriba!" the Prince continued, either egging Dora the Explorer on or perhaps encouraging his father to finish up fucking his mother.

"Arriba, Arriba!" the boy continued, nearly in unison to Finn's strokes as he bucked and came. Finn laughed and came. Danielle laughed and didn't come, but the husband and wife fell on the bed together, sated and amused.

"Arriba, arriba," they heard from the living room, and "arriba, arriba" the parents whispered together in reply.

"The medicine?" Danielle eventually asked.

"Got it."

"All of it?"

"Got the chemo but the Oxteller was only available in 150 mg pills. I have to go back Wednesday to get the 300s."

"They never get it right."

"A couple 150s should keep the seizures at bay."

"Never..."

"I'll get it, don't worry," Finn said, standing up from the bed to buckle his pants and straighten his apron. He leaned forward to kiss his wife gently on the lips.

"You can't stay in here for five minutes?" Danielle asked.

"I'd love to, honey, but—"

From the kitchen, the oven beeped. It was pre-heated to exactly 425 degrees.

"— duty calls," Finn said, heading out.

The Deflowering that Wasn't (1987)

In his defense, Finn had not started out so rape-y. In fact, if a "rape-i-ness quotient" existed— you know, the likelihood one might force him- or herself upon another sexually— the teenaged Finn would have been found firmly implanted... undeniably, unquestionably, irrefutably... way closer to the good end of the spectrum (with those people unlikely to rape anyone, e.g. eunuchs) than the bad end (among the obviously pro-rape folks, namely Bill Cosby and/or a huge swath of the Catholic priesthood). Rape someone? Force a girl to copulate with him against her will? Teenaged Finn? He couldn't get his hard cock into the willing cooch of his one true love.

For various shameful reasons, Finn remained a virgin until he was legally able to drink. Twenty-one years old! Teenaged Finn had been a handsome boy with a fine bushy head of hair, smart enough to get into the smart classes at Port Richards High School (if disinterested enough to then get booted out of them) and athletic enough to get his name festooned atop the sports pages of the local newspaper on more than one occasion. Finn's best friend was pretty much the most popular kid in school and his one or two erstwhile girlfriends were a couple of the prettiest girls around. It's not like our Finn wasn't trying to get laid. He most certainly was. He wasn't saving himself for marriage, or even the right girl either. Finn just wanted to dip his wick, to get it in somewhere, so much so that he'd likely have banged, à la the infamous *Portnoy*, his own cut of liver if only his Pilgrim parents had kept such a thing in the fridge.

Finn's lack of high school pussy may well have come down to those Pilgrim parents, a couple of staid New

Englanders (think of the couple from Grant Wood's "American Gothic" standing in front of a winter wonderland, a light coating of snowflakes in their hair) who were otherwise everything right in the world: earnest and conscientious citizens, kind and decent people, loving and supportive parents. Finn's paternal grandfather had arrived in Maine from merry (staid) old England after driving an ambulance for Great Britain during World War I (or was that Hemingway Finn was thinking of?), while his mother's people first appeared in Port Richards during the 1700's, the earliest-known ancestor a sea captain who must have come from Europe on, what, a Viking ship? A Boston whaler? The *Santa Maria*? In any case it had been a long time ago, back when there wasn't a lot of tomfoolery going on.

But Finn's parents, for all their attributes, were just a bit uptight. While doing the right thing might have been the most important goal in their life, not causing a scene was surely a close second. Once, the entire family— Finn, his parents, his three older brothers— were dining at an otherwise empty Greek restaurant in Tampa, Florida when unexpectedly, from the kitchen, out wooshed a half-naked belly dancer. Those six New Englanders, sober and alone, watched in frozen horror as that smiling sultry foreigner sashayed her assets in front of them until, unable to mask her embarrassment, the boys' mother bolted from her chair and scurried away, her sudden escape a release that immediately sent the male members of the family similarly a-fleeing in various directions, rats off a sinking ship. It was an event so uncomfortable that, to this day, so much as a mention of belly-dancing (or even Tampa) is enough to send various members of the Riley family rushing off, heads down, in different directions to different rooms.

But if those Pilgrim parents had saddled their boys with an unwavering need for decorum, so had they raised them right. The Riley boys were polite; they were conscientious; they were quiet and hard-working. They listened to

their elders, held doors for women, and helped little old ladies across the street. They said "please" and "thank you"
when the time was right, and never, ever, ever spoke out of
turn. More than anything, they did not cause a scene. Holy
Jesus, by all that is right in the world, if there was one thing
the Riley boys and their Pilgrim parents did not do, they did
not cause a scene. They kept to themselves and admitted no
weakness and did not cause a scene.

New Englanders they were, in other words, through and
through.

On top of this oppressive (read "loving") upbringing,
Finn was smart enough to see that in 1980s America, the
times they were a-changin'. Male heroes on TV or in the movies were no longer just the John Wayne-y, strong and silent
type. They weren't just cowboys or quarterbacks or fighter pi-
lots. No, men could be "sensitive." Male romantic leads could
be anyone— even (gulp) "men" like Alan Alda! That nebbish!
Meanwhile, newscasts and newspapers at the time were rife
with stories about the struggle to provide equal rights for the
long-oppressed minority that was the fairer sex ("ERA
Now!"). Plus, there was a lot of talk about not raping women
quite so much ("Take Back the Night!"). Our young hero,
Finn, in other words, reached sexual maturity— reached the
point of constant, persistent, unwavering, never-ending
cockal erection, in other words— during a time in this country's great history when the primary message seemed to be
that men should be more sensitive *and* fairer to women. Not
to mention: Enough with the raping of them! For Finn, in
other words, the quest for 1980s teenage sex was a minefield,
an honest-to-god god-damned minefield where he imagined
his hard-on as unwelcome a guest as Ronald Reagan in a San
Francisco bathhouse.

But those vexing times alone were not what kept Finn
from losing his virginity on the night in question (August 10,
1987). It was not some new definition of manhood that kept
Finn from finally getting laid that night, nor any changing

dynamic between the sexes. No, Finn didn't fuck Janie Flynn that night only because he was a big baby.

On the night in question (August 10, 1987), she called. She finally called. Finn's last year and a half of high school, Janie Flynn had been his erstwhile girlfriend. On their first date, they'd walked to the ice cream parlor in the center of town, the one next to the covered bridge and across the river from his parents' general store. They'd gone to his junior prom together (he in a white tuxedo with frilly blue shirt, her in a matching blue gown), played tennis every weekend and swam in her family's pool. And late at night, in the parking lot of the town's athletic fields, Finn and Janie would snuggle together in the front seat of his family's station wagon ("the Volare"), fogging up the windows in lengthy make-out sessions that thrilled Finn but never progressed past kissing. Finn wasn't exactly sure how to get to the next stage of "petting" because he was so inexperienced...and because he might have been subliminally worried he didn't have a lawyer on call in case Janie suddenly, unexpectedly, opted to take back her very own night: "Rape!" Stalled petting aside, Finn believed he and Janie would live happily ever after, which totally would have happened if only Janie hadn't been so young, so fickle, and so desired by every other dude in the local area.

On the night in question (August 10, 1987), however, things had changed. Time had passed. Janie was back from her first year in college and Finn his third, and though interaction between the two had been limited that summer (did Finn innocently driving the Volare past Janie's house a couple dozen times a day count as "interaction"?) Finn always held out hope. Janie actually lived right down the street from Finn and she truly was, both geographically and metaphorically, his "girl next door." So when Janie called, Finn answered.

"I'm naked," she said. "Wanna' come over?"

He did and she was. When Finn arrived through the Flynn's garage to Janie's downstairs bedroom, Janie was in bed, naked and alone. The room was dark, save the moonlight coming through the window, and while Janie kept herself covered with her sheets she held them up, inviting Finn in. Finn moved towards the bed but she stopped him.

"Get undressed," she said.

Finn did. He pulled his clothes off— the t-shirt, the soccer shorts, the socks and sneakers, leaving on only those 1980s-standard issue bikini briefs— and climbed quickly under the sheets, in a hurry not because he was ashamed of his athletic body but embarrassed because his hard, hard cock seemed as big as the moon.

For Finn, this moment with Janie was not just going to be the culmination of his thwarted quest for sex, an end to his benighted virginity, it was also going to be true love. It was. Janie Flynn was the girl he longed for, lusted after, loved. He had circled the neighborhood time and again that summer in the hope he might bump into her, nonchalantly ask what she was up to and then, perchance, walk her again down to the ice cream parlor. And if after a nice strawberry cone Finn had gotten Janie into bed and finally plowed her? All the better.

On the night in question (August 10, 1987), Finn and Janie immediately fell into each other like always, kissing wet and passionately. Finn squeezed Janie's supple breasts (she was an 19 year old athletic girl— they were supple!) and dragged his tongue over her bare, gum-drop nipples (had anything ever been so sweet?); he massaged her spectacular ass, round and equine, a bottom Finn would always believe was second to none (at least until that glorious night his wife unveiled her own spectacular rump); with his tongue in her mouth, Finn cupped his hand over Janie's vagina, the prickly hair there tickling the palm of his hand.

On the night in question (August 10, 1987), however, that was about the point when things went south— and not in any good way, either. Finn tried to slide a finger inside Janie, but his lack of experience with and thus limited understanding of the female genitalia— what the fuck was going on down there, he thought?!?!— meant Finn was stopped short. He felt heat; he felt hair; he felt wet; he felt lips; but Finn felt no hole. He was pretty sure there a hole down there somewhere— he'd read books! he was sure of it!— but Finn came up with nothing. It was a Rubik's Cube of pudendum, so far as Finn could tell, and he'd never had any luck with that puzzle either. Finn sure as hell wasn't going to just force his finger in ("Rape!"), but his probing, poking finger nonetheless came up with nothing.

"Ouch," Janie said, a comment that was both not unreasonable and that crushed Finn. He didn't like to screw up. Didn't like to not know what he was doing. Didn't want to cause a scene.

Neither did Finn want to be insensitive to Janie's needs. He didn't want to be too rough with her. He didn't want to be unfair.

Finn stopped kissing Janie and rolled onto his back, saying, of course, not a word. A New Englander through and through.

"I'm sorry," she said. She pulled Finn on top of her again and kissing him, she opened her legs. She slid her fingers into his bikini briefs and pulled them down. They kissed again, wet and heavy, Janie helping pull Finn's underwear down and him shimmying his hips to discard them.

Finn's cock was bigger than the sun and the moon and the stars.

The girl he loved lay below him, the girl he wanted more than anything else, willing, so so willing, but Finn knew it was done. He'd not been able to penetrate her with his finger, and his cock (not to brag or anything) put that finger to shame. Finn could either admit to this girl he loved that he was lost, a failure, a virgin, that he didn't know how to get his massive cock inside her without her help— or he could quit.

Finn quit. He didn't want to cause a scene. He rolled off Janie and sighed.

"Sorry," he said. "I'm just not feeling it."

It was a ridiculous comment, absolutely absurd, as both Finn and Janie were looking at his cock: It was throbbing like a tuning fork, vibrating, pulsing, pulsating, maniacally pumping blood. In the history of the world, no cock was ever "feeling it" more than Finn's cock right then. It was humming like a divining rod at Lake Superior, trying to bend itself against the laws of physics to point at Janie's vagina.

"It's okay," she said quietly. "My boyfriend in college sometimes can't perform when he drinks too much."

Finn nodded, pretending he'd not heard the phrase "boyfriend in college." His cock, meanwhile, was livid. Absolutely fucking livid! Although non-verbal, that cock really, really wanted to talk.

"Can't perform!?!" It would have screamed. "Can't bloody perform??? I'm the hardest cock in the history of the world here. I'm fucking ready for lift-off, a god-damned *Challenger* space shuttle aching to soar!" (*The Challenger, your Omniscient Narrator asks? Really? Had the talking cock not read a newspaper? Sheesh.*).

But it was over. Though the reasons had less to do with any ailing erection than some weird combination of propriety and expectation and fear, Finn could not perform and slunk out of Janie's home that night a failure. A tremendous, massive, epic failure. Wandering aimlessly around his neighborhood that night, with nowhere to go and knowing he'd never sleep, Finn tried to wish it all away.

"Take back that night," he laughed bitterly to himself. "Please take back that night."

But Finn knew the disappointment would be with him forever, the regret. He'd never forget that faced with his moment of truth, on what should have been a seminal night in his life (seminal it certainly was not), Finn had flinched. He'd balked. He'd not been able to perform.

A month later, back at college in Montreal, a gloriously fat-bottomed French-Canadian girl who wouldn't take "non" for an answer hauled Finn back to her dorm room and rode him like a horse-drawn calèche, putting an end to the stigma of the young man's virginity. That felt great, of course, though it didn't immediately temper Finn's regret or his view of himself as a tremendous, massive, epic failure. The passage of time helped, of course, as did a succession of charming girlfriends and then a wonderful wife, and eventually Finn could remember his childhood sweetheart with something other than shame.

Of course, even decades later Finn could never help thinking of that embarrassing event whenever he heard Eminem rap *Lose Yourself*— "You only get one shot, do not miss your chance to blow, This opportunity comes once in a lifetime, (yo)"— but for the most part Janie Flynn ended up a good memory for him, not a bad one. Plus, a mature Finn was actually able to see the silver lining in that dark cloud, too, as that humiliating night also proved pretty clearly that, as stated previously, if it ever came to a question of real rape, Finn Riley was definitely not your man.

A Hero is Born (Monday Night, 2013)

Finn had forgotten— or pretended he'd forgotten— that Monday was poker night. After serving his family that fine, fortifying dinner of fish and fruit and nuts— and after answering his wife's confused look regarding the odd make-up of the meal by smiling aggressively, saying "Not a restaurant, honey, not a restaurant!"— Finn was offered the night off. Danielle said she felt good enough to give the Prince a bath and put him to bed if Finn wanted to "go out." If she insisted, he said.

Finn opted for a post-prandial constitutional, a walk that began in Midtown but then ended up an hour later, unsurprisingly, in Finn's old stomping grounds of the East Village. He stopped first on Second Avenue, at one of his favorites: Moishe's Kosher Bakery. The Mainer Finn was as goy as a guy could be, so exactly what "kosher" meant was a conundrum to him (was one not supposed to eat kosher desserts after a dinner of pork chops? Fish? Chicken? Those Jews were some mystery, Finn thought). Inscrutable religion or not, ole' Moishe could cook some sweets, with Finn opting for his boy's favorites: rainbow cookies. How the Prince loved a rainbow cookie! Moishe, bedecked as always in a yarmulke and wearing a bushy beard and long side curls, the strings of his possibly magical undergarments sticking out from his black slacks, wrapped a pound's worth in a white cardboard box, tying it tight with long colored string. As was his custom, he then offered Finn a free taste of a freshly-baked dessert (and you thought the Jews were tight!), that night a warm cherry turnover.

"Fantastic," Finn smiled, chewing cherry as he headed out the door, tossing back as a good-bye the only Yiddish word he knew. "L'Chaim!"

Finn understood the word was more toast than salutation, but he figured it wouldn't matter since he'd just tossed the old Jew a couple of sheckles for the cookies.

"L'Chaim," Moishe smiled back, the phrase "goofy goy" surely flashing through his mind.

Down St. Mark's Place, Finn was pretty much gutted to see that the long-standing and legendary Yaffa Café was closing for good. He stopped at East Village Books, the tiny subterranean shop where he always searched for paperbacks. He rifled through the stacks in search of all his favorite authors: his favorite female author, Esmeralda Santiago; his favorite Latin author, Gabriel Garcia Marquez; and the usual collection of solipsistic and cock-o-centric male authors that Finn so adored (Fante & Bukowski, Hem & Fitzy, Hey Jack Kerouac, Hank Miller, John Irving, Tom Robbins, Tom Wolfe, Pete Hamill, Jay McInerney, anyone at all other than horribly depressing Bret Easton Ellis, whose morose books and joyless characters made Finn want to just about vodka himself to death). Eventually Finn stumbled upon an adequate buy, a well-worn copy of some Chuck Palahniuk (*Fight Club*).

Standing on St. Mark's Place in New York City on a warm spring evening, a newly-discovered used paperback in his back pocket and a pound of freshly-baked rainbow cookies for his son in his hands, all was good in Finn's world. Then, alas, the Boogie man appeared. The literal Boogie man.

"Finn!" Boogie shrieked, coming towards him from First Avenue. "I see you Finn!"

Watching Boogie approach, Finn felt both doom and delight. Boogie was a freaky-fro'ed African-American kid ("kid" being a relative term, Boogie's thirty-something age looking pretty grand to the forty-something Finn), a character well-known all around the East Village and pretty much the mascot of Finn's favorite bar. Boogie hobbled about with a cane and spoke in a shrill, high-pitched voice, injuries the result of a fight in London years earlier, someone purportedly having whacked Boogie over the head with a beer bottle and done some real damage. It was also reputed that Boogie was packing in his panties a pecker like a leviathan (as the legend goes, one fine eve a *New York Times* editrix named Lucy was riding back to the East Village from a pleasant trip to the titty bar "Scores" with Boogie, believing on the cab ride home that her hand rested gently on that young man's arm when, much to Lucy's surprise, she looked down to discover that her hand was gripping not Boogie's forearm but his frighteningly large schlong. The head of that enormous dong, she is said to have said, was reminiscent of a caveman's cudgel). Sober, Boogie was quiet, sweet, and charming, but when he drank— and how he drank!— shit went down. It went down hard. Finn, meanwhile, had the willpower of a heroin addict in a heroin store, so when Boogie was drinkin' and Finn came around: uh-oh!

They met outside East Village Books. "You downtown for poker?" Boogie asked.

Finn had forgotten— or pretended that he'd forgotten— that Monday was poker night at 7B. In the halcyon days of Finn's youth— five years prior, before the arrival of the wife and kid— Finn had frequented a bar called "7B," also known as "the Horseshoe Bar." Or "Vazacs." Or "The bar with no name" (ironic, no, for a bar with at least three names?). The place had been both Finn's muse and his nemesis; he loved it, but the next morning his head always hurt.

The bar, across the street from Tompkins Square Park on the corner of Seventh Street and Avenue B, didn't look particularly dangerous. In fact, in a six-story red brick building with an enormous, antique advertisement painted on the side and massive, multi-paned, Tudor windows, the establishment may well have looked like the prototypical NYC bar. It probably did because in recent years it had so often been used as a TV or movie set that 7B may have sub-consciously become part of the American psyche. The scene when Crocodile Dundee waves around a machete saying "*This* is a knife"? Filmed outside 7B. The scene where Frank Pentangelli nearly gets choked out with a piano wire by the Rosato brothers in *Godfather 2*? Inside 7B. When Carrie and Samantha meet some loser dudes who ultimately disappoint them in one of those insufferable/interchangeable "Sex in the City" episodes? At least one time it was in 7B.

But on quiet Monday nights when the bar had not been turned into a TV set or film location, 7B had long hosted a midnight poker game for the regulars, including Boogie; Ricky (the bar's huge Dominican doorman, who simultaneously sat in on the game and checked ID's at the door); Don (the greasy-haired weekend barkeep); Lucy (Don's big-busted and bigger-brained girlfriend and the aforementioned *New York Times* editrix); Jimmy (a chunky cheese peddler and loquacious sort); Sunil (an Indian guy from London who, it probably goes without saying, was super-smart); and, at least in the old days, Finn (a relative old guy without much affinity for or ability at cards).

But those games had started late, and they started on nights after the gang had been drinking and didn't intend to stop drinking. On one poker night, for example, Finn's eyes had come into focus to find himself, quite surprisingly at 4 AM, sitting at the counter of the all-night diner Odessa on Avenue A, Boogie and Don on either side of him and a huge spread of food in front, frankly a meal— syrupy pancakes, a side of liver and onions, a frosted mug of Busch Light beer— that obviated any need to ever wonder if Finn at that time was drinking maybe a little too much? Still, as much as Finn had always enjoyed those card games, he'd avoided them since the arrival of his wife and child. Returning home at 4 am— or 5, or 6— after nights of binge drinking when Finn had to take the Prince to school at 8 AM did not seem too bright an idea.

"You down here for the poker?" Boogie asked Finn again.

"Nuh-uh," Finn answered. "No way. Too late."

"We start at 8 these days," Boogie said.

"Uh-oh."

It had been half a decade since Finn had been to 7B, but given his history he imagined his return would engender a considerable hullaballoo. He couldn't help thinking, especially with Boogie at his side, that he'd be met as a conquering hero: The doorkeep Ricky would surely offer a warm nod of recognition and a shake of the hand, numerous regulars would likely wave or raise their glasses to him, at least one elated cry of "Finn!" would certainly echo through the place, and of course the punk bartendress Dita would come around to the front of the bar to hug Finn and console him about his wife. For at least a moment Finn would be home again in the bosom of his bar.

It didn't happen though. When Finn pushed through 7B's swinging front doors his entrance was met not with any excited clamor but with near complete silence. The place was a ghost town. There was no Ricky, no Dita, no regulars that he knew. Maybe one guy sitting alone at a table in the back was someone Finn might have recognized (Where was the dude from, Finn tried to recall. Kansas City? Chicago? What was he, a set designer? A voice-over actor? Finn couldn't exactly remember.)

When Finn had thought of 7B over the last five years, he'd imagined it the way he'd lived it, with the same cast of characters perched atop the same bar stools. But now he could see they were gone. All gone. Missing from his regular spot at one end of the horseshoe bar was Dr. Rocco, the grizzled psychologist who'd always been sipping vino and scribbling notes about the sex offender meetings he hosted every Monday and Tuesday nights, confabs during which "Rocco the Psycho" basically did his darnedest to convince all those creepy sex offenders to put an end to their creepy sex offending. A Herculean task, but Dr. Rocco tried.

Gone from his favorite spot at the other end of the bar was Barry the Angry Artist, a good-looking, grey-haired, fifty-something fellow who always had *The Daily News* spread open, a mixed drink in his hand, and an impression of his teeth imprinted into the ridge of the bar in front of him— late at night, when the liquor really kicked in and especially if the Yankees lost, Barry couldn't take any more of the buffoonish kids swarming his beloved East Village, so instead of punching someone Barry would chomp down on the bar in front of him. Aaaargh, he would roar, before unleashing a bitter bite.

Worse, too, was the unconfirmed scuttlebutt that Barry the Angry Artist might be gone for good. As in, really *gone*. Done for, kaput, dead. Though Boogie told Finn that Barry had moved farther downtown a couple years prior and had thus switched locals, a travelling liquor salesman who peddled his tasty if poisonous wares all over lower Manhattan kept tabs on the angry artist for everyone at 7B, and the most recent news about Barry had been ominous.

"The last time I saw him the guy was yellow," the liquor salesman spat, "*yellow*!" (Odd, people at the time were said to have thought, that a guy who made a living pandering booze seemed so disgusted by a guy drinking himself to death?)

Though no one said it, everyone knew what the color yellow meant: liver trouble. For a gang whose social life revolved around late nights at a bar, it was a sobering thought. Not "sobering" as in quitting drinking, of course, but the fact one of their drinking buddies might die of organ failure due to alcohol poisoning did disconcert at least one or two of them.

The poker game was actually gone from 7B, too. Although the East Village had at one time been Manhattan's Wild West— a place so out-of-control that cabbies wouldn't go there and cops rarely did, a neighborhood where the FDNY was reputed to have let a building or two burn right down— gentrification had changed it all. Suddenly rules ruled, and it was no longer legal in New York City to have a charming little card game in an establishment with a liquor license, not even in the East Village. Instead the 7B poker game had had to adjourn to Boogie's nearby apartment, a move which Finn would soon discover had turned the game, frankly, into a sad version of its formerly glorious self. While Boogie had a great pad, it lacked the allure of a bustling East Village bar, and in time many of the original players had faded away too: Finn was the first of them, of course, but then Ricky disappeared (no longer working at 7B he skulked back to Brooklyn for good) while Sunil had moved back to London and Jimmy to Denver. On the night of Finn's "triumphant return" to the East Village then, only Boogie, Don, Lucy and Finn sat down to play. It was the same poker game in theory, Finn thought, but nonetheless most certainly not the same.

Kindness was not the lingua franca of the 7B poker game, cynicism and sarcasm were, and though Finn had not lately played he still knew how to talk. When during his return to the game his old friends asked Finn about his new life— how was being a dad, or a stay-at-home dad for that matter?— he told 'em straight.

"All day, every day, I'm a full-time babysitter," he said, throwing a couple chips in the pot.

"I thought if they were your kids it wasn't babysitting?" Lucy asked, raising Finn's bet.

"Semantics," Finn grumbled, tossing his cards away and folding. "Call it what you will, at the end of the day I'm still wiping someone's ass."

"Isn't your son out of diapers?"

"He is, but just recently," Finn answered. "His IQ is apparently off the charts but the Prince of New York still likes his daddy to handle the poop."

"The Prince of New York?"

Finn smiled. "A while ago, when he first started talking, my son walked into the kitchen first thing one morning, butt naked, and looked around. He held his hands in the air, palms up, and said his first whole sentence. In a tiny little, lispy voice: 'Where'sh my toasth?'"

"Cutest thing I ever saw," Finn finished. "Never loved anything so much."

"Hey, what's in the box?" Boogie asked, nodding at the white cardboard next to Finn. "Treats?"

"Treats for the Prince."

"Understood," Boogie said. Even to that bunch of drunks, kids were sacred.

"But I'm up to my neck in shit all day," Finn said.

"Noooo," Boogie answered, his wide eyes an attempt at condolence as he pushed all his chips into the center of the table.

"Literal shit," Finn continued, folding the pair of cards in front of him. "My wife has a Yorkie, a teeny, tiny, fifteen-year-old, yapping, lap dog that wears a diaper. And suspenders to keep that diaper on! A couple times a day I have to walk him for her, a Yorkie in a diaper and suspenders, like that's not bad enough, but then out there, in the street...."

"...IN PUBLIC..."

"...I have to take off the dog's diaper full of piss and shit and then put on another. One time my wife asked me to wipe his ass to be sure he didn't get an infection........"

"...IN PUBLIC! ...a dog in a diaper...wipe his shitty ass...."

"Look, I love my wife," Finn continued, tossing a pile of chips into the pot, "but I'll tell you what, that dog's butt ain't getting wiped by me..."

"Respect," Boogie said.

"Respect," Don nodded, agreeing. Though Don was a white guy and Boogie black, Don liked to occasionally take on the language of the streets, if mostly to tease his pal Boogie.

"Yikes," Lucy said. "That ain't right."

"Ain't," Finn concurred.

Poker was not really Finn's game, not even that simplistic Texas Hold 'Em (where players made the best poker hand they could from their own personal pair of cards and the five shared cards turned up on the table). To succeed at the game one needed to be patient, logical, and mathematical, at least a couple attributes the rash and volatile Finn had lately been lacking. Plus, to really prosper at poker— even Texas Hold 'Em— one had to concentrate on the cards flipped up on the table, considering all the different hands they might make, not to mention pay attention to the other players' moves and possible maneuvers, an awareness that was definitely not our hero's forte. At poker, as in life, Finn really didn't care a great deal about what anyone else was up to; if he was being brutally honest with himself, Finn really only gave a shit about himself.

And his family, of course, he might have added! And his family!

"How's Danielle?" Boogie asked, the question that had quietly been hovering over the table finally asked.

"I'm all in, you asshole," Finn barked, pushing all his chips into the middle of an already pretty big pot. "Do you mean is my wife in diapers, asshole? Do you mean does she wear a colostomy bag? Is that what you're asking, Boogie? Do I have to wipe her ass, too?"

Finn glared, first at Boogie but then at all of them. No one would meet his gaze, and in the awkward silence that followed they each, one by one, silently tossed in their cards.

Finn smiled, flipping over the hand in front of him: The two of hearts and the seven of diamonds, the statistically worst starting hand in Texas Hold 'Em.

"Bluffed ya', bitches" Finn laughed, raking in the chips. "Bluffed ya'!"

The table roared, everyone glad that Finn didn't really seem to be mad, and relieved, too, that he most likely wasn't having to wipe his own wife's ass. Still, that was a new one even for Finn, using Danielle's fragile health to win a single hand of poker. How low could he go, one had to wonder? How low could he go?

"Oh snap!," Boogie laughed, seemingly very tickled to have been so duped by Finn.

"Snap!" Don echoed, himself perhaps just happy to be able to use that goofy term.

"Honestly, Danielle's okay at the moment," Finn began answering the earlier question. "Diagnosed three years ago at five months pregnant with Stage IV colon cancer. 6% survival rate. Six! A bunch of surgeries. Then a blood clot in her lungs. A bowel obstruction. Seizures resulting from the chemo. Cancer came back one time, but maybe now my bad-assed wife is beating it all...?"

(His "bad-assed" wife? Ironic, no, for a woman with colon cancer?)

"Respect," Boogie said, and all the players nodded.

"Of course," Finn continued, "she is on daily chemo pills these days, which tire her out, and her body is pretty well beaten down for good— she's had like seven surgeries, is missing organs, with scars all over her stomach. Her entire life seems to be visiting one doctor or another, just trying to survive. Plus, the seizures have blasted holes in her brain, so she has memory problems. She's not intellectually the same. Her personality is different...."

"Man," Boogie said to more nods.

"But she's not dead, meaning she was lucky, my son and I are lucky," Finn concluded, trying his best not to bring everyone down. "Still...."

Everyone at the table waited.

"...Still, now we're all living our lives in the shadow of another recurrence. Huge statistical chance of that happening, apparently, so we wait for it. We wait for cancer... and maybe death."

No one said anything until Lucy leaned forward and grabbed Finn's hand, squeezing it. "I'm sorry, hon" she whispered.

Finn squeezed back and tried to keep the tears from forming in his eyes. "What are you gonna' do?" he asked, shrugging his shoulders. "Smash shit? Jump off a bridge?"

The table was silent.

"But she ain't dead!" Finn tried to wrap it up happily. "Danielle's not dead yet."

"Thank god," Boogie agreed, trying himself to wrap it up happily.

Finn couldn't help himself though. "It's just that she'll never be the same. Even if she does live."

A couple hours and many beers later Finn had won the game, less due to any great skill on his part than the simple smiling of Lady Luck. After Lucy had been knocked out of the game— the woman was smarter than the rest of them, and a better poker player, so it might have been surmised that her early elimination simply meant she wanted to go home to bed— the five cards on the board were four clubs (including the Ace) and the Ace of Hearts. The remaining players each tried to play it cool but eventually dumped all their chips into the middle of the pot, each gleefully expecting to win but with Boogie's supposedly unbeatable (with the King of Clubs he held in his hand) Ace-high "nut flush" first losing out to Don's powerful Ace-high full house and then Don's seemingly invincible hand nonetheless then being crushed by Finn's almost unheard of straight flush.

"Four, five, six, seven, eight of clubs, boys!" Finn laughed. "Who's your daddy now, kids? Who's your daddy?"

("Who's your daddy?" Ironic, no, from a man newly defined by fatherhood?)

After the game Finn pocketed his winnings and dragged Boogie and Don to 7B to buy the losers a drink: "Cinnamon schnapps for all," Finn ordered, the collective groan of his pals being just the result he wanted. (Notably, however, it should be said that the more the boys drank those schnapps the more they liked the liquor. It was subtler than they'd originally appreciated perhaps, or more sophisticated, but definitely more efficacious. Plus, fresh breath!) Soon our three young heroes reached the point of the evening when they thought that every thought that flittered through their combined minds seemed like a good idea— nay, a *great*

idea!— until eventually the trio jumped into a cab and sent
it gunning towards the Lower East Side. Don had suggested
they head south to listen to the night's selections at the
"Happy Endings" reading series, a monthly performance of
literary prurience that Don promised would be "titillating,"
but that idea was certainly one of those drunken inspirations
not fully thought through given that the "Happy Ending" series happened but once a month, on a Wednesday at 9 pm,
while those three amigos were out adventurin' at what was 2
a.m. on a Monday "night." Plus, Boogie rejected Don's idea
outright.

"Fuck your 'titillating' reading," Boogie snarled. "Let's
see some titties!"

"Tits!" Don immediately agreed, his interest in hearing
about sex suddenly overwhelmed by his interest in looking at
it.

"Teats," Finn said, not enthusiastically but not unen-
thusiastically either.

"Boobies!" Boogie offered.

"Breast-eses!" Don agreed.

"Scores" was too far away, all the way on Manhattan's
west side, so Finn and his friends decided instead on "The
Slipper Room." If "Scores" was the city's stereotypical empo-
rium of ecdysiasts, the place full of fake-breasted, overly-
made-up, Eastern European dancers on the make, "The Slipper Room" was something else, a little bit of Gotham magic.
It wasn't a straight-out strip joint as much as a charming
burlesque show, with nightly entertainments that included
magicians and contortionists and genuine "strip tease art-
ists," mostly a bunch of artsy-type, big-bottomed girls who
would shake their behinds when taking it all off— all, of
course, being their entire wardrobe except for tassels and a
feather boa or two. Think Blaze Starr, in other words, more
than Nomi from *Showgirls*.

"Orchard and Rivington," Finn told the cabbie, apparently having enjoyed enough previous visits to the site that
its address was seared into his memory, even lo these many

years hence. Then, scrunched between Boogie and Don in the back of the taxi, an unopened white cardboard box of rainbow cookies nestled snugly in his lap, Finn stared silently out the window of the moving cab. The dark brick buildings slid past looking like the headstones of the graveyard his East Village had become.

"Yaffa's closing?" Finn asked.

"Yup. Like Life Café before it."

"And Café Pick-Me-Up."

"Second Avenue Deli."

"Mars Bar."

"CBGBs," Boogie said.

"CBGBs..." Don echoed, the pair of them bemoaning the loss of the venerable venue whose heyday had happened in the 70s, the decade in which the two of them had been born.

"You know Chloe Sevigny moved to Brooklyn?"

"Of course she did. But where is she gonna' get her frozen yogurt now?"

"Or her cupcakes?"

"You probably can't get smack in this neighborhood anymore," Finn said. "Probably couldn't get stabbed...

Boogie turned to Finn. "Wait, how's that not a good thing?"

"It's the principle of it," Finn growled. "That this is a place where, you know, better watch out, you just might get yourself shivved."

"Yeah," Boogie joked, "The sort of thing to keep the riff raff out."

"No," Finn corrected. "You wanna' keep the riff raff *in*. It's the frat guys you wanna' keep out."

"Isn't someone the grumpy old man," Don joked.

"You would be, too."

Boogie decided to fuck with Finn a little. "Well, at least we have Quidditch."

"Quidditch?" Finn asked. He knew he wasn't going to like the answer.

"Have you read Harry Potter?"

"I'm a grown man, Boogie."

"Have you read it?"

"As soon as I finish the Berenstain Bears."

"Anyways, Quidditch is the game from Harry Potter. The made-up, fictional schoolyard game out of Harry Potter. Sunday mornings at the basketball courts at Tompkins Square, the NYU kids get together to play a little Quidditch. Some co-ed Quidditch."

Finn muttered to himself.

"Non-contact, co-ed Quidditch," Don added, joining the fun.

Finn swore under his breath.

"Non-competitive, non-contact, co-ed Quidditch," Boogie continued.

"I don't think they even keep score," Don added.

"Of course they don't," Finn muttered, squeezing his eyes closed, wishing it all away. It had to be some kind of cosmic joke. "Where's a junkie when you need one?"

The Quidditch talk had soured Finn, but the night really turned dark when they arrived at Orchard and Rivington, at the intersection where "The Slipper Room" was supposed to have been but where it decidedly was *not*. Finn distinctly remembered that magical place being situated in a three-story brick building on the southwest corner of Orchard and Rivington, with a tiny pizzeria across the street at the northwest corner of the intersection. Finn had so many fond memories of visits to "The Slipper Room" first and then a nice slice of Sicilian after. They were the kinds of nights Finn was astute enough to realize would one day become fodder for tales to his young son about the glory of New York City's "good old days."

But disembarking from the cab with Boogie and Don, Finn found no "Slipper Room" on the southwest corner of Orchard and Rivington. Neither did he find the quaint pizzeria he regularly used to visit on the northwest corner. Instead, on the four corners of Orchard and Rivington, Finn and his friends found a high-end clothing store, a brand-new chain pizza restaurant with a stupid name meant to evoke New York's romantic past ("Goodfellas" or "Godfathers" or the like...), and a shop specializing not just in desserts, but tiny, tiny, cutesy cute desserts.

Most troubling of all for Finn, however, was that on the southwest corner of Orchard and Rivington— where Finn and his friends had historically ogled tasseled boobies and where they'd believed they would always ogle them!— stood not "The Slipper Room" in a three-story brick building but a brand-new, twelve story monstrosity made out of concrete and, mostly, glass: The top eleven floors were residences of some kind, either apartments or hotel rooms, Finn couldn't say and didn't care, while at street level stood, of course, a closed outpost (it was the middle of the night) of some previously unknown dessert mecca. Its glass walls were shiny and welcoming, its name painted colorfully on the sides of the building facing both Orchard and Rivington and in a smaller font of the front door.

"Funkiberry?" Finn asked.

"Frozen yogurt," Boogie offered. "It's like Red Mango... but funkier."

"Like Pinkberry but gayer," Don added.

"Like Berrywild but fruitier."

"Like Culture but less sophisticated."

Finn raised an eyebrow. "You're telling me there's a frozen yogurt shop named Culture?"

"Eighth Street in the West Village," Boogie explained.

"Isn't that cute?" Finn asked. "Isn't that just the fucking cutest thing you ever heard?"

Boogie and Don might have continued with their colorful quips about frozen yogurts spots forever but their conversation was interrupted when a pack of young toughs/teenagers came screaming around the corner on their skateboards, heading fast and east down Rivington. Although a pleasant spring night, Finn saw that the four skateboarders wore on their shaggy-haired heads various types of stupid, floppy knit hats, while in their wake he would soon enjoy a view of a whole bunch of droopy pants and flapping boxer shorts.

"Danger, Grampa!" one of the skaters yelled as he deftly dodged Finn, Finn's disgust with the disappearance of "The Slipper Room" being tempered just long enough for him to jump out of the way of the rolling child, leaping directly atop a number of overflowing black garbage bags piled near Funkiberry's side door. Bottles clanked, of course, and the pile of bags collapsed under Finn's weight, but he managed to stumble away without falling down. Regaining his balance, Finn saw coming out of the trash pile not (to the surprise of anyone who's ever lived in New York City) a skittering phalanx of rats but a rolling baseball. Without thinking Finn scooped the ball up quickly and raced into the street, getting ready to unleash the laser arm that had made him a famous outfielder (for at least a year or two in small-town New England), preparing to pelt one of those obnoxious skateboarders in the back of the head with a horsehide "hello!"

"Punks," Finn yelled, taking a crow's hop and motioning as if to throw the ball hard after the idiot skateboarders in their wind-swept Jockey shorts. Finn didn't throw the ball, however, although he did hurl more invective the teenagers' way.

"Losers!" he yelled. "Buffoons!"

Boogie and Don were laughing, having avoided the skateboarders entirely while nonetheless seeming to enjoy Finn's meltdown.

"Kids today," Don muttered, shaking his head, pretending to sympathize with Finn while pretty clearly not.

"Hey you!" Boogie yelled, shaking his fist after the skateboarders, trying to control his own uncontrolled laughter just long enough to mock Finn. "Hey, you kids stay off my lawn!"

"Curmudgeon," Don teased.

While Finn appreciated his friends' little jokes, he still wasn't amused: "The Slipper Room" was gone. So much of his

New York seemed to be going or gone. Finn stood in the middle of Orchard and Rivington and looked back at where "The Slipper Room" had once stood. Funkiberry, it said! Finn might have thrown the baseball though the plate glass window if only it hadn't felt so good in his hands. He opened his palm and balanced the ball there, holding it up to a streetlight.

"It's real," Finn said aloud. "Actual horsehide, you can tell. Not one of those bullshit, fake plastic balls. Not rubber. Not a kid-friendly ball. It's a ball that would feel like something if you made contact with a bat. It's a ball that would hurt if it hit you."

"It's got heft," Finn continued. "I'd forgotten that a baseball is hard and heavy."

Finn's friends were watching him in silence. The man's shoulders slumped, as if he were finally relaxing, maybe the weight of the world slipping away.

"Baseball," Finn sighed like a character from *Field of Dreams*, the movie based on the book *Shoeless Joe* that he'd first read in the 8th grade. "Baseball, apple pie, 1950s Americana. The good old days..."

"Uh, not to quibble..." Don started.

"...But your 'good old days' weren't so good for blacks," Boogie finished.

"Or women."

"The Jews."

"Gays."

"Not really so good for anyone but you white guys," Boogie concluded.

Finn stopped staring at the ball and turned to his friends. His eyes seemed to come back into focus. To Boogie he said, "What's up, my nigga'?"

Somewhere Teenaged Finn fainted away. Teenaged Finn had not just suffered from white guilt, he had basically been paralyzed from it. For pretty much unknown reasons—perhaps his liberal upbringing, perhaps his inherent supersensitivity to the plight of others, or perhaps his primary desire to never, ever, ever, for any reason, cause a scene— Finn grew up feeling the need to apologize to everyone, especially black people, for his whiteness and good fortune, even though one might have argued that Finn, born in the 1960s, was himself not actively responsible for either slavery or this country's long and storied history of racial prejudice.

Even Finn's youthful admiration for Boston Celtic legend Larry Bird was a cause for consternation for him, as supporting the oh-so-pale-white Bird while he dominated a historically black game was construed by some as a type of racism. By any objective measure, in the early 1980s Bird was— along with Magic Johnson— one of the two best basketball players on the face of the Earth, but Finn still felt the need to apologize every time he cheered for Bird's regular heroics. "Sorry," Finn would say to people in bars— especially black people!— as Bird heartlessly rained downed three-pointers and crushed the dreams of various teams and their fans. "Sorry," Finn would say again and again, shrugging like "what can ya' do?," internally celebrating the Celtic's sporting genius while outwardly apologizing for his own possibly-insensitive support of it. "Sorry, sorry..."

Teenaged Finn, in other words, not only had never uttered the word "nigga'," he'd never even allowed the word to form fully in his mind. "Sorry!" He would have said to anyone and everyone if the word had even tried to do so.

"What's the problem, my nigga'?" Finn had said to Boogie.

"Excuse me?" Boogie said, his eyes wide.

"It's okay," Finn answered with a quick smile. "I have black friends."

Don hooted in the background.

"One black friend that I know of," Boogie corrected. "You *had* one black friend."

Finn looked at Boogie and knew he didn't mean it. They'd drank together enough that some things just didn't matter. Still, a gesture needed to be made, so Finn dug a bill out of his pocket and handed it to his friend.

"What's this?"

"Ten bucks," Finn said to his friend. "Reparations. Saying 'nigga' was my bad, my boy."

"Your 'boy'?"

"Nuh-uh," Finn shook his head. "No way. That's not racist. My people have been saying 'my boy' forever."

"Your people?"

"The English," Finn explained. "Brits. Anglos."

"You mean whites?" Boogie asked.

"Honkies," Don helped. "Crackers."

Finn ignored him. "No, the Queen's English, like, 'Spot of tea, my boy?' Nothing racist about it."

"Course not," Boogie said, but his lack of enthusiasm made Finn reach into his pocket one more time, from where he pulled out a crumpled wad of cash: three one-dollar bills. He handed the money to Boogie.

"More reparations," he said. "Personally, I don't think 'my boy' is racist but here's three bucks to make it all right between us."

"A dollar per century of slavery," Boogie said. "Now we're even."

Finn grabbed Boogie's Afro'ed head and kissed him squarely atop it before walking back to the middle of the intersection. There were, at that hour of the night, no cars. Finn turned to face Funkiberry. He stood thirty feet from its front door and began an elaborate, old-timey baseball windup, standing up straight with the ball in his right hand and windmilling his arm around and around. He added high leg kicks to the windup and pretended again and again to throw the ball at the door. It was a bit of a baseball pantomime and Finn imagined he looked like a player from a silent movie, but when he started talking he took on the persona of the Negro League superstar, Satchel Paige, all slow and southern, pure molasses and corn pone.

"'I'se gonna throw 'em my bat dodger,'" Finn said as Satchel. "'Cain't no one hit my bat dodger.'"

"No, that's not racist," Boogie said, shaking his head. "Not racist at all."

Finn kept windmilling and high-kicking and pretending to pitch the ball at the frozen yogurt shop's glass front door, all the while spouting off famous Satchel Paige quotes that had somehow become embedded in his brain.

"'Nevuh' eat fried food,'" Finn said. "'It angries up the blood.'" Wind-up, high-kick, fake pitch.

"Throw it!" Don yelled.

"'Don't look back,'" Finn said as Paige. "'Sumthin' might be gainin' on you.'" Wind-up, high-kick, fake pitch.

"Do it," Boogie agreed.

"'You win some, you lose some, some get rained out,'" Finn continued, using the last Satchel Paige quote he knew in his best Satchel Paige voice. "'But you'se got to dress for all of 'em.'"

Wind-up, high-kick, real pitch.

Finn had been a pretty good high school baseball player in his day, and when he released the ball he had aimed it at the dot above the "i" in the word Funkiberry painted on the shop's front door. The dot, naturally, had been designed to look like a scoop of frozen yogurt, a last little bit of adorable that may have been the very thing that finally made Finn snap.

Finn's pitch, in fact, was perfect, slamming elegantly into that very scoop-shaped dot before completely shattering the entire front door. Finn was surprised to see that the door's glass did not spider-web like a broken car windshield might but that it actually exploded, falling into pieces. Anyone who wanted to could simply walk through the shop's front door at that point, which Finn and friends might have done if only a blaring alarm hadn't immediately gone off and a flashing white light hadn't begun illuminating the entire area.

Finn turned to Boogie and Don and smiled, an ecstatic look on his face that the friends hadn't seen for at least five

years. It was simple delight, pure joy. The weight of the
world really seemed to have been lifted off him.

Don threw his hands in the air, hooting anew, and began high-stepping in place like some kind of crazed clown.
With a little fiddle music to accompany his boot scraping,
Don could have been a redneck cheerleader of sorts. Boogie,
meanwhile, held his cane in the air and did a little jig.

"Oh snap," he laughed.

For all their festiveness the friends were still made
aware by the buzzing burglar alarm and blinking white light
that it was also time to scram, and the last Finn saw of Boogie and Don that night they were headed in the direction of
their East Village homes, laughing and high-stepping and
"snapping" just as fast as Boogie's hobbled legs could go.
Meanwhile, it was time (or well past time) for Finn to go
home, so he grabbed the box of rainbow cookies he'd previously placed atop a parked Land Rover and headed up
Orchard, northwards towards Midtown. Finn had, at that
point, a considerable bounce in his step, maybe even a sparkle
in his eye, but about halfway up the block he had to pause:
On the next corner Finn saw what looked like a vaguely familiar pizzeria and, across from that, a three-story brick
building that was eerily reminiscent of the one that had once
housed "The Slipper Room."

Approaching the intersection, Finn had an epiphany.
"Orchard and *Stanton*," he remembered. "Of course!"

Looking back to the corner of Orchard and Rivington,
where the Funkiberry burglar alarm was still blaring and its
obnoxious white light still flashing, Finn experienced a mo-
mentary pang of guilt: Although he had never come to any
conscious decision about his actions that night, Finn understood that in smashing that Funkiberry's front door he had
struck a blow for New York City. He had struck a blow for
America. All change was not progress, Finn had innately understood, and when he thought that little bit of Gotham
magic known as "The Slipper Room" had been replaced by yet

another fuckin' confectionery hut his violence against the Funkiberry had made perfect sense.

But with "The Slipper Room" still standing proudly on the corner of Orchard and Stanton, as it always had, was Finn's perfect strike, his baseball blow on behalf of New York and America, still the right thing to have done? Finn pondered that question briefly but he knew his answer: Fuck, yeah, it had been the right thing to do. Finn could imagine no world where smashing the glass front door of a forgettable, soulless dump named "Funkiberry" could ever be wrong. He knew that neither he nor any other person, living or dead, had ever moved to New York City because of its splendid array of dessert options, and so it was with complete confidence that Finn knew that rotten little joint had gotten just what was coming to it. Of that Finn was sure: That fuckin' little Funkiberry got exactly what it deserved.

And so was born the Curmudgeon Avenger.

Rat Attack! (Tuesday, 2013)

It wasn't exactly a pick-up line.

"My wife has cancer," Finn said to the mom sitting on the next bench over at Adventure Playground, at 68th street just off Central Park West. He nodded towards the Prince playing in the sandbox near the woman's daughter.

"I watch my son since she can't," he continued, a statement that wasn't exactly true but that Finn figured worked nonetheless.

The woman might not even have known Finn was sitting next to her, her attention previously alternating between her child in the sandbox and the iPhone in her hand. Finn's unbidden explanation of his wife's medical condition and his unforeseen presence in the playground had therefore caught the woman quite off-guard. On the one hand, she seemed sorry to hear about Finn's wife, but on the other she wasn't exactly sure why Finn had suddenly begun a conversation with *her*.

"I'm sorry," she said, questioning, looking around as if Alan Funt and the crew from *Candid Camera* might be lurking nearby (or maybe instead Ashton Kutcher and the gang from *Punk'd*, depending on the woman's exact age and cultural touchstones?).

"Not your fault," Finn said. "I just wanted you to know why a grizzled old man like myself might be skulking here amongst the children."

"Grizzled" was an exaggeration, Finn knew, and "old man" an outright lie. Yes, Finn was middle-aged, his youthful abdominal six-pack having turned into a pony keg and the stubble of his shorn head coming in silver, but Finn also knew he was not unattractive. He had blue eyes, white teeth, a good nose. His legs, draped in shorts, had been sculpted from a lifetime of soccer. His beautiful son, in addition, was only yards away. Combined, Finn knew, it was not a bad look. Not a bad look at all.

"Understood," she smiled, revealing her own set of clean, white teeth. The woman was otherwise not remarkable though, looking like many a Central Park mom: thirty-something, white, tanned, her hair pulled back into a loose ponytail and no make-up on her face. She wore a loose, white peasant blouse diaphanous enough to reveal a tan bra underneath, while her legs were clad in black yoga pants. Finn had to make a conscious effort not to leer, but if he'd known the woman well enough he'd probably have admitted that most of his current sexual fantasies involved thirty-something moms in yoga pants— those leggings just slid so easily down, didn't they? Those women's asses were so close to being bare. The sex was just so near.

"I'm Finn," Finn said.

"Maggie."

It was 10 A.M. on a sunny Tuesday morning on the day after the night the Curmudgeon Avenger was born. Finn had returned home that morning just before the alarm would blare at 7 A.M., figuring that his wife and son would still be sleeping. Imagine Finn's surprise then when he pushed quietly through the front door of apartment 2A, clad in the uniform of an NYPD traffic cop and wearing mirrored sunglasses (more on that later...), only to find his wife standing in the hallway, scrolling through e-mails on her phone. Over the course of the previous night Finn had texted Danielle to inform her that he would be back "late," then "later" and finally "later still," and Danielle knew Finn enough to understand that those "laters" could be any time up to 7 A.M., when her husband could always be counted on to get her son ready for school. He'd not ever missed that opening bell.

Inside his front door, Finn opted to play it cool, lifting a finger to his patrolman's cap and nodding. "Ma'am," he said to his wife.

The wife looked her husband up and down. "Do I even want to know?" she asked.

Wasn't she something, Finn marveled! Half the reason he'd married Danielle, he thought, was that she had such aplomb. When they were first dating, Danielle told Finn that after breaking up with a previous loser boyfriend that loser ex- wouldn't stop calling her and sending her angry, insulting e-mails. He eventually started threatening her though, which the feckless cad then came to find out was the very line over which Danielle wouldn't be pushed.

"You want to threaten me?" she had screamed at the ex- over the phone, "I'll be outside my apartment building in 30 minutes. I dare you to show up."

"I dare you!" she yelled into the phone, "Thirty minutes!", a half-hour during which Danielle had recovered from her front closet a silver-stocked, double-barreled shotgun that her father may or may not have been hiding from the authorities, a weapon she boldly lugged through the Albemarle's front lobby ("Danush?" one can imagine Lawrence saying...) into her father's SUV, parked out front. In the front seat of that vehicle Danielle then sat for the next hour, the loaded shotgun across her lap and a box of cartridges open at her feet. Fearlessly she waited, perhaps even willing the cowardly ex- to show his wussy face.

He didn't show, of course, as Danielle figured he wouldn't, but neither did he bother her again via telephone or computer.

Yes, his wife had considerable aplomb, Finn thought admiringly, a ton of aplomb, in fact, so much so that when her husband returned from an entire lost night on the streets of New York City, adorned in an outfit most reminiscent of the bad guy from *Terminator 2*, Danielle wasn't frazzled or jealous or scared; she wondered only if her husband's explanation would be worth the telling.

"Do I even want to know?"

"I was righting various wrongs," Finn explained.

"Great, but now it's time for school."

Finn quickly showered and dressed like a normal person before feeding his son a fine breakfast (Greek yogurt, organic strawberries, and granola layered into a beer glass and identified as a "Daddy Parfait") and packing him a fine lunch for school (leftover salmon, the Pilgrim grandmother's homemade applesauce, cornichons, a box of organic apple juice, and, of course, one of Moishe's well-travelled rainbow cookies). He dressed his gorgeous boy in miniature Converse high tops, little Levi jeans and a wee black leather jacket before strapping him into the stroller for the quick jaunt to school.

"Finn," Danielle asked as he headed out the door. "Are you going to be alright? Did you sleep?"

"Not a wink," he smiled, fully energized, apparently inspired by the previous night's escapades. "I'll sleep when I'm dead."

The stroller was outside the apartment door and Finn leaning back inside the apartment when he said it, but when he uttered the word "dead" Finn had lowered his voice to keep the Prince from hearing it. Death was a concept Finn didn't believe the boy yet needed to consider. He had forgotten, unfortunately, that the word "dead" might have an equally unsettling effect on his wife, especially on the day when she was making her regular three-month visits to the oncologist and the neurologist.

"Sorry," Finn winced.

"It's okay," Danielle said, but on her face was a look that said even a woman with such aplomb could only take so much.

At school Finn was surprised to discover that there was no school ("professional development day for the teachers" was the unsatisfying reason Finn was given at the front door), so it was to Central Park father and son went. There the Prince of New York played in a sandbox with a pretty blonde girl while his father talked to her pretty brunette mother. It was going pretty well between the kids until eventually, predictably, an imbroglio ensued: The ownership of toys was disputed; a struggle followed; words were exchanged; feelings were hurt; sand was thrown; retaliatory dirt was volleyed; slaps were leveled; blows were landed; tears were shed...

In such situations some parents come out swinging themselves, defending their little angels no matter how clearly the evidence points to their own innocent child's culpability, but Maggie was not one of those mothers.

"It had been going so well," she said to Finn as both parents made their way towards the sandbox donnybrook.

"My boy always has to have his way," Finn offered.

"And my daughter isn't a very good sharer," Maggie replied.

So Finn dragged his son, crying and kicking and screaming, from the sandbox back to his bench, while Maggie dragged her daughter, crying and kicking and screaming, back to her bench one bench away. When the Prince got too hot he had a tendency to overheat and throw a fit, so when Finn noticed his boy's red face he, as surreptitiously as possible, dumped a fair share of cold water over his son's unsuspecting head.

"Daaaa-aaaaady!" the boy screamed, his brow scrunched tight and his eyes staring daggers at his old man. "Why'd you do that? Whhhhhyyyy???" Screaming more, crying louder.

Just another day at the park, in other words.

"The joys of parenting," Maggie nodded to Finn as she held her wailing daughter in her lap.

"Bad Daddy!" the Prince was now yelling at his father. "Bad Daddy!"

"Satisfying on so many levels," Finn said to Maggie.

Finn loved his son— he *loved* him, in fact, not just wholeheartedly but perhaps even obsessively— but in truth he loved him less at moments like this. Finn had been born and bred to never, ever, ever cause a scene— not for *any* reason!— but somehow the Prince of New York had gone a different emotional route: He had no problem at all publicly shaming his father via a voluble verbal dressing down.

"Bad Daddy!" he continued to yell. "Bad Daddy!"

Without stereotyping those various "ethnics" all too much, the white guy Finn figured his boy's histrionics were surely inherited from his wife's family, a mixed mélange of Jewish-American and Italian-American Brooklynites who weren't just able to shamelessly scream at each other in public, they might actually have considered such intercourse the most preferable means of communication.

"Bad Daddy!" The Prince kept yelling. "Bad Daddy!"

Finn sighed. He may not have ever uttered the words aloud, but the fact was that he hated parenting. He haaaaaaaaaaated it. The ceaseless logistics of the job, the minutiae, the daily battles over every little thing from what to eat to what to wear to when it was time for bed, Finn would have preferred to be absolutely anywhere else in the world whenever those things went down.

Finn may have been diligent about feeding his son well, for instance, but some days the Prince just wasn't amenable.

"Eat your raspberries along with your cereal," Finn might say. "They're organic. And delicious!"

"No thanks," his son might reply, the father's blood immediately beginning to simmer and his fear growing exponentially.

"But you love raspberries, son. And they're so good for you. Yummy!"

"No thanks," his son might casually repeat, blankly staring up at *Nick Jr.* on the living room TV's big screen.

"So you don't eat raspberries anymore?" Finn might ask, feeling himself getting literally hot under the collar, suddenly worried that the nutritious organic fruits that for so long had been a staple of his son's diet were no longer being consumed by him. But those raspberries were a daily dose of vitamins and minerals, Finn thought! Eating them ensured his son would grow and flourish and prosper. It allowed him to have treats like rainbow cookies, too, so long as the boy was first eating well! Not eating the raspberries anymore, Finn thought on the other hand, would surely result in an undernourished Prince, leave him surviving only on junk food, nutrient-free processed foods like candy and cookies and chips, meaning Finn's beautiful boy would end up withering on the vine, as it were, no longer growing or developing or turning into the singularly spectacular little fellow Finn believed he was otherwise destined to be. In truth, as far as Finn was concerned, not eating those little red berries spelled almost certain doom for his son. It was suicide, Finn thought. Virtual suicide!

"Eat your raspberries!!!" the father would end up bellowing, his bass-voiced screaming resulting in his wife coming running and his boy bursting into tears.

"Eaaaaaat them!" Having dropped his voice to as deep a register as it would go, the demand sounded like it came from a monster. "Eaaaaaat them!"

Finn would end up frantic. "Eat them or you won't live!!!" The spectre of death again rearing its ugly head in their family home.

"Get out," Danielle would have to yell at her husband. "Get out of here right now," Finn allowing himself to be pushed out the front door and stomping angrily away, unsure how (again) the fine breakfast he'd whipped up for the child he loved so much had devolved into a terrible fight about the little boy's fleeting mortality.

For Finn, the worry was constant. If his son didn't concentrate on brushing his teeth, the father imagined them ending up yellowed, cracked, missing, greatly reducing the boy's chances at any real success out in the great big world. If the boy didn't go to sleep on time at night, the man imagined his brain's synapses not forming the connections they needed to, withering on the vine as it were, dooming his son to life as a retard. And while Finn personally espoused the worth of walking— for both its value as exercise and in helping one to really know New York City— for the first three years of his son's life Finn still nearly always transported him around with the Prince strapped firmly into a stroller. The idea of his beloved son walking unrestrained on Man-

hattan's busy streets otherwise terrified Finn, always resulting in him imagining the boy darting into traffic, a car
careening forward, a terrible scream...

Frankly, if he could have Finn would have liked to duct
tape his son into that stroller after he'd already buckled and
tightened all its straps. Maybe duct-taped and Super-glued
him right in there real snug, real good, Finn thought.

Still, Finn couldn't deny it: His days as a New York City
stay-at-home dad rearing a brilliant little boy were producing a lifetime's worth of memories. The first year the High
Line opened (before it took on its current function as con-
vention center for all the world's geriatric European
Unioners), father and son would regularly pick up snacks at
D'Auito's Bakery near Madison Square Garden— rainbow
cookies and milk for the boy, apple fritters and coffee for the
man— before enjoying long meanders over that empty, elevated city park; it was a jaunt Finn absolutely reveled in, for
both the spot's beauty and the fact it was completely safe,
thirty blocks of raised walkway enclosed on all sides and allowing only pedestrian traffic. In Soho, father and son would
grab Sicilian slices at Ben's Famous before adjourning to the
Vesuvio Playground to splash in the sprinklers or frolic in
the pool. And Central Park, of course, so close to their Midtown home, promised pleasures around every corner, whether
father and son were digging in the massive Hecksher sandbox or chasing bubbles in Sheep's Meadow or sliding down
the slide built into a hill at the Billy Johnson Playground
near the Central Park Zoo (Just don't think about who little
Billy Johnson might have been, Finn had to warn himself.
Don't think about what must surely have happened to that
poor child in order for a New York City playground to be
named after him!)

His son Finn adored. Finn loved and adored and wor-
shipped the little boy, often for reasons that were impossible
to explain. The first time Finn had fed his son cornichons,
for instance, he had included them on the Prince's dinner

plate without an explanation of what those tart French deli-cacies might be. Minutes later, the Prince had yelled to his father in the kitchen.

"Daddy," he hollered, "can I please have some more of those tiny, tiny pickles?"

"Tiny, tiny pickles!" Finn thought his heart would ex-plode, but in retelling the story no one— not even his wife— was ever as overcome with awe and love as Finn had been to hear his son's interpretation of that brand-new side dish. "Tiny, tiny pickles!" The words warmed Finn every time he thought them.

Recently Finn's son had come out of a warm bath all pink-cheeked and blue-eyed, his blonde hair wet and slicked straight back, and when he searched out his father in the living room to give him a kiss good-night the boy was wear-ing a fluffy, toddler-sized, white robe bearing the insignia of Montreal's Queen Elizabeth Hotel. It was spectacular. His son was, simply, the most beautiful thing Finn had ever seen. He had never loved anything so much.

But, to be perfectly honest, Finn might have loved the boy too much, in a way that wasn't altogether healthy. Before he'd impregnated her, Finn had told Danielle he maybe shouldn't have kids because it was likely he'd worry about them too damned much.

"I'm already obsessed with Big Momma and Junior," Finn said to Danielle about the two fat cats he lived with at the time. "I can't fathom how insane I might be about a child of my own."

The look Danielle had given Finn— the withering, dis-missive, contemptuous look— was one he'd never forget. It said Danielle had been wrong about Finn, that he was just another idiotic, self-absorbed New York City male, all cock but no balls. No *cojones!* Not really a man.

In looking at his boy that night after the bath, however, in all his youth and beauty, the child full of love and sur-rounded by love, a future unfolding in front of him that Finn prayed would be varying degrees of wonderful, that father realized he may have been right about the idea of his having kids. See, Finn didn't just feel love for his son that night; his head was also filled with darkly murderous thoughts. Finn loved that kid so much that he would have killed for him at that moment, probably without so much as blinking an eye. He would have throttled or stabbed or pole-axed or shot-gunned anyone who threatened his little boy. Finn felt that night, hugging that spectacular little person, not just emotions of warmth and devotion but the distinct impression that by god he'd knife the first sumbitch who ever tried to mess with his child.

He wasn't exaggerating either. The summer before, on a sunny Sunday morning Finn and Danielle had pushed the Prince in his stroller up 7ᵗʰ Avenue towards Central Park so the boy could dig in the sand at Hecksher playground. Other children were already there, and the parents sat on benches surrounding the sandbox, sipping takeout coffee, chatting idly while lazing the morning away.

Then the electricity in the park changed, and parental antennae prickled: Soon a thirty-something man appeared, his face unshaven and his hair matted, wearing unlaced work boots on his feet and carrying over his shoulder a back-pack jammed to overflowing. He looked all around Hecksher— at the swing sets, the climbing area, the water fountains, and the sandbox— before, as every parent had feared, opting for the huge sandbox. Without seeming to notice the half dozen or so kids playing there, the intruder dropped his backpack in the sand and sat beside it. Then he lay back, using the backpack as a pillow, and instantly closed his eyes.

The parents' response was immediate, with mothers hissing names— "Daphne, get over here Daphne!"— and swooping up kids. One father began barking into his cell phone after calling 911.

"Hecksher Playground, at the south end of Central Park," he growled.

Apparently he wasn't having a great deal of luck explaining either the situation or its urgency. "Central Park in *Manhattan!*" he screamed.

Finn's son was near the slide on the far end of the sandbox, about forty yards away from but oblivious to the interloper napping in the sand. His father was not oblivious, however, and by the time the bum had lain down his head Finn stood near his feet. In his right hand Finn held at his side a Maasai war club that he'd brought back from a visit to Tanzania, a weapon that Finn had secreted in the bottom of the family stroller as soon as they'd purchased it. It had accompanied him throughout the city for nearly three years, in effect waiting for a moment just like that.

The club was two feet long, carved to shiny, made of black and hard ebony wood, thin in the handle but with a baseball-sized orb at its end. At its swinging end. On that baseball-sized orb had been carved a hard, tiny nipple, a protrusion whose purpose was to penetrate the skull as a means to crack it open, literally. Maasai warriors used the clubs in battle. It was no joke.

Finn looked at the bum sleeping in the sand. He noticed the nearly-treadless boots, with their holes in the toes, and the ragged bottom of the pants. He noticed the stained t-shirt and the shredded jacket. He smelled the familiar stench of a New York City street dweller, of garbage cans picked through and clothes unchanged and a body unwashed. And Finn felt no sympathy for the man, none at all. He felt only that if the sleeping derelict awoke and made any motion in the direction of his son, Finn would smash him over the head with a two-foot long club carved to kill. It wouldn't have been that hard, Finn thought. With his family standing behind him and his wife's terrible diagnosis hanging over them, smashing that bum in the head would not have been any problem at all for Finn. The NYPD arrived shortly thereafter, eventually leading the handcuffed hobo away, so Finn did not have to crack anyone's skull that day. But he knew, nonetheless, that he would have done so. It would not have been hard.

That day in the Hecksher sandbox— when Finn had so quickly placed himself between his child and danger and when he'd been fully prepared to fight that homeless guy to the death— flashed back into his mind just as soon as he saw the rat at Adventure Playground.

After Finn and Maggie had separated their respective child combatants, calmed them down, and cooled them off, they'd fed the kids (healthy) lunches and sent them back out to play. Finn's son and Maggie's daughter had since resumed their sandbox games, now seemingly the best of friends, apparently in their minds nary a thought at all of the bawling and brawling they had just recently been so fully immersed in. Amazing, Finn thought, to see those two children express more emotion— more anger and rage and frustration— than he might have experienced in his entire life first be felt and then almost immediately forgotten. Was that healthy, Finn wondered of expressing one's emotions so freely, so honestly, so *loudly*? He couldn't be sure. He was sure only that that wasn't how he remembered doing things when he was a kid.

Meanwhile, Maggie had returned to trolling the Internet on her iPhone while Finn ate the lunch a nice Mexican kid had just biked over from the bodega on Broadway. What could you say about a city, Finn thought, where a guy sitting on a park bench can make a quick phone call and then, as if a miracle, a nice Mexican kid on a bike will appear bearing bacon, egg and cheese on a roll and a steaming cup of hot coffee? Nothing but good, Finn thought! You couldn't say anything but good about a city such as that!

But on the far side of the sandbox Finn saw, while chewing on his cheesy breakfast sandwich, a rustling of the leaves in the low shrubs outside the park's iron fence. His parental antennae prickled again, and then he saw it, one of New York City's Grimiest: Rat! New York City's downtown parents may perhaps be well familiar with those verminous rodents, as any early-morning or twilight visit to the playgrounds of Tompkins Square Park (among other places) is guaranteed to include numerous sightings of many a skulk-ing rat, but those disgusting little fuckers were less frequently seen all the way up north in Central Park. Worse, Finn knew no sensible rat would ever be caught dead out in the open around high noon, nor around humans for that matter, meaning the big ole' rat Finn could see approaching the kids in the sandbox in the middle of the day was likely either a young and stupid rat or— Christ!— a rabid one.

"Rat," Finn said aloud, putting down his sandwich and standing up.

Now Maggie— dear Maggie, who Finn had heretofore felt at least simpatico with, if not more honestly been quite attracted to— was so fully immersed in the electronic goings-on of her magical cell phone that she didn't hear Finn utter what, in retrospect, she would surely come to consider an even more pressing bit of news.

"Rat," Finn said again, now louder, starting first to-wards the sandbox at a brisk walk but then picking up speed.

"Rat!" he yelled as he started to sprint, covering the thirty yards between himself and the children at what seemed a pretty good pace for a middle-aged man but that was, nonetheless, a speed that absolutely paled in comparison to the swiftness with which that gnarly ole' rat had gotten to the kids. The rat, you see, had unfortunately (especially for Maggie) already arrived at the children, having settled on the left foot of the little girl, stopping there to first sniff her shoe but then sneaking a peek up the pink pant leg.

"Raaaaaat!" Finn screamed, leaping off the top step of the playground's floor, hanging briefly in the air there before gravity delivered him down into the sunken sand below, his final scream finally rousing the woman whose child she would soon discover was right then being mounted by a fat rat.

"EEUUDYAUIDUUDDDD..." Maggie screamed, mindlessly, pointlessly, having looked up from her phone long enough to finally register that her little baby was under disgusting attack.

"AAAICKEIELIIE," Maggie screamed inanely, in full panic mode, leaping up from her seat on the bench and dropping her phone on the ground (so she really did love her kid more!), rushing towards the sandbox as quick as her Lycra-clad legs would could carry her.

"BBLSIESBBBEISI," Maggie wailed, running just as fast as she could go but nonetheless probably still feeling that she'd never get to her beloved baby. "AIDUEIAIIDIIEISIIAA!"

By the time Maggie finally arrived, Finn had already saved the girl. He'd leapt off the top step of the playground floor and landed two feet away from her, his right foot planted firmly in the sand and his left foot swinging violently forward. As previously noted, Finn had once been an athlete of some repute (even if that had been three decades prior in only one small New England town), but for all his sporting successes it was at soccer that Finn really shined. And at soccer, for that matter, Finn had not been known for his plucky defensive work or his solid reputation as a selfless teammate— no, he'd been known for his propensity for winning games due to his wicked shooting ability, the blasting of left-footed and right-footed shots from all over the field that regularly rescued his team's chances. And whenever those booming shots would find their way into the back of the net— gooooooooaaaaallllllll!— Finn would throw his hands into the air, a huge smile covering his entire face, the cheers raining down from all around bathing him in the applause and acclaim of his teammates and fans.

Finn was in it for the glory, in other words. For the girls and the glory, in all honesty, and that day on Adventure Playground he pretty much got both. With his right foot planted firmly in the sand, Finn's left foot had swung violently forward towards the big rodent perched on the little girl, and though he had kicked powerfully he also kicked deftly; in one fell swooooosh Finn's swinging left instep plucked the nasty rat off the little girl's foot and sent it flying in a vicious line drive back from whence it came. The rat—

perhaps never believing the pasty white guy that had been rushing towards him posed any threat or possessed such skills— was nonetheless smashed into the iron pole of the playground's fence with a sickening thud, its head going one direction and its body another, a bloody shower spraying behind.

"Goooooooaaaaalllllll!" Finn might have wanted to yell, but he was too freaked out by the rat's terrible attack— not to mention its grisly demise— so he plucked up the Prince of New York in one arm and Maggie's young daughter in the other (foregoing his otherwise normal behavior of not touching/carrying off other people's little female children), spinning away from the sandbox to rush back towards the relative safety of the park's benches.

"EEUUDYAUIDUUDDDD," Maggie continued to wail as she finally arrived, grabbing her daughter from Finn's embrace and racing, while crying, back towards her own spot on the bench.

"AAAICKEIELIIE," Maggie yelled and "MWWAAAHHH" the little girl cried. Only the Prince of New York was not carrying on, although that was probably due less to any inherent bravery on his part than the simple fact that he'd mostly been oblivious (again?) to that most recent terror threat.

Carrying his boy, Finn reached for Maggie beside him, and the woman curled her crying face into him as she lugged her baby back to safety. Passersby who saw the foursome fleeing might have imagined they were refugees running from some terrible tragedy— and in their own way, of course, they were.

"Are you okay?" Maggie cried and asked her daughter. "Did it get you? Did it bite you?"

She was manhandling her daughter's little ankles, turning them forward and back, upside and down, looking for bite marks or scratches. She looked at her daughter's lips, praying that she wouldn't see a mouth going frothy. She patted down the legs of her girl's little pink jeans, praying that she didn't feel anything furry and creepy buried there.

"Are you okay?" Maggie asked her daughter again. "Are you alright? Are you okay?"

Eventually Maggie realized the rat attack had been little more than gross. The vermin had touched her daughter but not really attacked her. The rodent hadn't harmed her girl in any way. When Maggie finally figured that out, she stopped the wailing and started to cry. She wept and wept, holding her child in her arms, the little girl wrapped around her mother just as tight as could be.

"I'm sorry," Maggie said to her daughter, kissing her again and again through the tears. "I'm sorry, so sorry."

Finn stood next to Maggie with his hand on her shoulder, consoling her, while the Prince sat down to sip a juice box. Then Maggie looked up at Finn and started to cry again, tears of fear still but tears of joy and relief as well.

"Thank you," she stood and whispered into Finn's ear, kissing his cheeks as she still held her daughter in her arms. "Thank you, thank you."

"Of course."

"Thank you," she cried, folding into Finn's chest, kissing his cheeks and his neck. "Oh my god thank you."

With her daughter still wrapped tight around her, Maggie hugged Finn with one arm and covered his chest with kisses. "Thank you, thank you."

She held her cheek against his chest and pulled him tighter. She closed her eyes as hard as she could and squeezed him closer.

When she released Finn, Maggie looked up at him with the most open, honest face he'd ever seen. "Let me give you a blow job," she said.

Finn had to laugh. "Whhhaaaaa— ?"

It hadn't exactly been a pick-up line, but earlier that day when Finn had leaned towards the mom sitting on the bench next to him and said "My wife has cancer," he'd done so in the hopes of conversing with her and, in all honesty, you know, a long shot for sure, but perhaps, probably one in a million, yes, but maybe somehow also getting himself a little sumthin'-sumthin' out of the deal, too.

And here it was!

"I'll suck your cock," Maggie whispered in one of Finn's ears, trying to lean away from her clinging daughter to shield her from the illicit proposition the mother was offering.

"I owe you. Let me suck your cock."

"My god, no," Finn couldn't stop laughing. "You don't have to do that."

"It's okay," Maggie whispered again, reaching with her free hand down to grab Finn's as yet unmoving manhood. "Come on, I live right down 70th. I'll send the housekeeper home."

Finn was giggling like a schoolboy. "No, no, no. You don't have to do that."

"It's okay," Maggie insisted. "My husband will understand. My god he'll probably blow you too."

Now she'd gone too far! "It was just a little rat!" Finn argued.

"Please," she said, and it looked as if Maggie was going to cry.

So what was Finn supposed to do? He'd used his athletic skills to impress a woman, as he'd long dreamed of doing, with the end result being— as Finn had always wished!— that that woman wanted to, no, she was *desperate* to, sexually service him. It was almost literally the culmination of a life-long dream some three decades in the making. Still, of course, Finn did recognize that there was that whole other bullshit bit about his marriage, his vows, yadda yadda, his wife's endless struggle against a deadly disease and all. What a dilemma for the poor man! What a predicament!

Was this really happening, Finn wondered? Was an attractive woman really begging to suck his cock? Literally pleading for it?

It was true, although Finn saw in Maggie's eyes not lust but fear. He knew that the oral sex she offered was not a gift for him but a reprieve for her, something to take her mind off the horrors she had just seen or was imagining. Maggie would have done anything at all, even jamming a strange man's cock into her mouth, if only to get her back to where she'd been just minutes before— safe in a Central Park playground with her beloved daughter on a warm, sunny day— instead of dealing with everything now racing through her head, pretty much a parent's worst nightmare, that being her darling little daughter facing a literal rat attack and figuratively standing beside a dark precipice, a gloomy void offering nothing below but terror and dread, disease and death.

"It's okay," Finn said, pulling Maggie close to him. She still had her daughter wrapped in her arms, and Finn picked the Prince up from the bench to complete the group hug.

"It's okay," he said to her again, Maggie crying with her face in Finn's chest. "It's what we do for our children."

His eyes welled up. "It's what we do for our children," Finn repeated.

That Central Park tableau— a man and a woman and two little children huddled together on the playground, some with teary eyes and all hugging each other tight— was poignant enough that it would have surely moved any passersby who saw it, although less likely was that any witnesses walking by could ever have guessed the dynamic that had led to the tender scene: Specifically, that a random stranger saved a little girl from a savage attack by a revolting rodent, with that little girl's pretty mother so grateful for the stranger's brave aid that she offered a no-strings-attached blow job in thanks, that perpetually horny male stranger then even more surprisingly rebuffing the hot mom's kind offer of gratis oral sex because of his own marriage vows and/or his desire to use that unbelievable turn of events— my god, the horny husband had said "no" to a sexy woman's offer of free fellatio!— as a chit to ensure his own loving wife would be on her own knees that very night, with all that crazy cock-sucking talk really not yet even getting to the real heart of the matter, that being the bubbling over of the terrible undercurrent always present in any poor parent's head, the sickening realization that even for their own precious child there is no reprieve from the inevitable progress of inexorable Death Death Death...

Nah. Probably no one saw that coming.

But it was true. Finn never had any intention of accepting the frantic Maggie's generous offer, none at all, both because he didn't want to take advantage of the poor woman's desperate emotional straits but also because he endlessly desired only his very own wife, his Danielle, the one woman for whose throat Finn's cock had always been earmarked for that night.

His darling Danielle, Finn thought. He hoped her visits to the oncologist and neurologist were going okay.

Sporting Clichés (1987, Part Deux)

Let's not call the Hall of Fame just yet, however, regarding Finn's purportedly extraordinary athletic abilities. Yes, as a young man he'd been a decent high school baseball player and a pretty good college soccer player, while as a middle-aged man at Adventure Playground Finn had unleashed a kick that at least one mother would always believe more heroic, more important, than even any World-Cup winning goal. All of that was undeniably true, but it still didn't negate the fact that for the longest time even Finn himself characterized his own sporting career as a failure. A tremendous, massive, epic failure, in fact: All he could really remember about it was the time he dropped the ball(s).

Finn recognized that the whole thing was such a cliché, like something out of a YA novel for boys, but his last real soccer game really *was* his last chance at glory, one more shot to win the Quebec championship he'd been chasing for four years. Prior to the game, Finn was happy, confident, contented: He'd recently been relieved of his unfortunate virginity by the aforementioned gloriously fat-bottomed French-Canadian girl, and he was a starting forward on Canada's second-ranked college soccer team. All was right in his world.

It looked like that confidence was about to pay off just minutes into the big game. Finn saw his opponent's last defender dribbling the soccer ball with too much nonchalance, paying too little attention to Finn just twenty yards away. When that defender glanced in the other direction, Finn exploded forward, attacking like a shark to chum, poking the ball away from the unsuspecting defender and bursting in towards the opponent's net. Their goalie was tall and gangly but he rushed towards Finn with limbs akimbo, his four arms and legs seemingly everywhere, flapping around, looking less like the normal appendages of a human being than the eight arms of a vengeful squid. But Finn pushed the ball past the shambling goalie too— even if he kicked the ball a little harder than he might have wanted to, directing it a little more off towards his left than he'd hoped— and then chased it down, at that point seeing to his right nothing but the gaping, open goal. All Finn had to do was cut the ball back and roll it into that empty net and the glory would be his. The angle was a little tight but it was a shot Finn had made many times.

The entire thing had happened at breakneck speed— Finn's surveying of the situation, his theft of the ball from the last defender, his deft avoidance of the panicked goalie— but he instinctively understood that he only had a little time left, too. Both the goalie and defender, not to mention all their teammates, were certainly rushing back towards their own goal as fast as they could go, desperate to get there in time to stop what seemed Finn's certain goal, with our young hero's realization that they were coming— "They're coming! They're coming!" Finn was screaming in his head— convincing him to shoot the ball before he was really ready.

He panicked, in other words. And he missed, of course.

While the angle had been tight, Finn actually pulled the shot back too much, so after he hit it he watched the ball roll across the entire face of the empty goal before going out of bounds on the other side. Finn turned away from the failed shot to see his coaches and teammates on the bench and hundreds of fans on the sideline go from jumping up and down with certain joy into paroxysms of disbelief and despair.

Two hours later, with the game tied 1-1 (his team's goal having decidedly *not* been scored by Finn) and overtime completed, the match would be decided by penalty kicks. Finn was chosen by his coach to shoot fourth for his team, an opportunity to either right the wrong of his earlier snafu or to exacerbate what might have been turning out for Finn to be one significantly shitty day.

A penalty shot, Finn knew, was a Larry Bird moment, a chance to stand up when it counted and come through in the clutch. It was why Finn so admired Bird, not so much for his ability as his bravado: Finn remembered a playoff game the Celtics lost to the Cavaliers once when the Celtic great was sidelined with an injury, a victory the happy Cleveland fans celebrated by chanting "We want Bird! We want Bird!" The implication was that the Cleveland fans wanted Bird to return the next day so they could enjoy another Cavalier victory but that time one with Larry Legend in the line-up, their impassioned exhortations failing to consider, however, that at the time Bird was basically the baddest basketball player alive and one cold-hearted sumbitch.

"You look into Larry Bird's face," Charles Barkley once said, "You see the eyes of a killer."

"They want me, they got me," Bird said flatly before the game the next day, "I'm coming out with both guns blazing."

And he did, leading the Celtics not just to a victory over the Cavaliers but a massacre of them. It was annihilation that day, with the gloating Cleveland fans who a day before had been gleefully calling for Bird not just being chastened into silence by him but rather looking aghast at the athletic horrors he was perpetrating against their hometown team, fathers nearly having to shield their children from the emotional carnage the blonde Celtic was unleashing on the court. When it was over, Bird walked away nonchalantly though, almost disinterestedly, a contented if somewhat oblivious look on his face, basically the expression of a lion who'd just eaten a baby zebra in front of its distraught mom: "What are you gonna do about it?"

That's why Finn loved the guy so, not so much for his basketballing genius but because of his balls: Even with 18,000 angry fans screaming for his head, mocking and taunting him, Larry Bird never had any doubts. The pressure never touched him; the expectations had no effect. Larry Bird was Larry Bird and nothing else.

The problem was that Finn Riley knew exactly who he was too, and that was a guy whose impression of himself too often hinged on the way others viewed him. While Finn was a confident soccer player who some days took the field feeling invincible, other days he thought himself a fraud: It could take no more than one bad word by an opponent or a fan or one askance look from a coach to undermine him. Unlike Larry Bird, in other words, Finn Riley had doubts. Pressure didn't just touch him, it crushed him. Expectations had not a little effect on him but a big one. If you looked into Finn's face you saw not a killer but the killed.

Walking forward from midfield to take his shot at the penalty spot that day, in other words, Finn was a condemned man: He saw in front of him not any opportunity at greatness but only a chance to fuck up good. All he could think was that every person watching him trudge forward had seen how badly he'd botched his chance for glory at the beginning of the game. He figured they were whispering to each other about him, laughing, joking about his missing an open net that was almost impossible to miss. To make matters worse, the pressure Finn would have normally felt to score his penalty shot was intensified by the fact his team was losing the shootout, meaning they *needed* him to score right then. In fact, if Finn missed the shot his team would lose, so all that need and pressure and expectation resulted in the young man's head being flooded with one single idea: "Don't miss the net."

It should have been a crowning moment for him. He should have been proud, realizing he'd beaten out dozens of players to earn a spot on the team, that he was one of only eleven of the guys on the roster to take the field that day, one of only five who'd been selected to take a penalty shot. He should have been honored, but he had only one thought: "Don't miss the net."

And Finn was not just a good soccer player but a very good shooter of the ball, a specialist really, able to both blast shots powerfully and direct them delicately, to consistently curve and swerve them wherever he wanted the ball to go. He'd spent hundreds of hours the last years practicing soccer shots from all over the soccer field, and a penalty shot taken from only twelve yards in front of a goal protected by only one player should have been the easiest one of all, a cakewalk really, but that day a fraught Finn thought only one thing: "Don't miss the net."

Finn fixed the ball at the penalty spot and looked up at the goalie standing in front of him, the guy he once thought of as just tall and gangly having suddenly become enormous, gigantic, some mythical behemoth defending a magical cave. The goal behind him looked so small, absolutely tiny.

Finn stepped back from the soccer ball, preparing to kick it, looking up at the goal and the goalie one last time. "Do *not* miss the net," he warned himself.

He ran at the ball not really knowing what he was doing and not knowing where he intended to shoot it, later being told by a friend at the game that he'd approached his penalty shot like a drunk careening down the street, weaving first one way and then the other. Finn remembered none of it. He remembered only thinking "Don't miss the net."

Did he miss the net? Please. He missed the net, his sad little shot— struck entirely without conviction or belief— floating listlessly over the crossbar, way above it, eventually rolling its way down a hill behind the goal and out on to Sherbrooke Street beyond.

As the opposing team flooded the field in raucous celebration of Finn's failure, he fell to his knees in front of the empty goal. There he sat for minutes, his face blank, his eyes vacant. Eventually the young man felt a muss of his hair and a squeeze of his shoulder, and he was surprised to look up into the face of his aged coach. For four years that gruff old man had earnestly instructed Finn on the subtle nuances of improving as a soccer player, but between them had never passed so much as a single personal word. Finn wasn't sure the guy even knew his last name.

But the coach was reaching down to help him up. "Not your fault," the old man growled, even though player and coach both probably really felt differently.

Finn couldn't look at the man. It wasn't the loss itself—Finn got that it was just a game, just sports, life went on, etc. etc.— but he also recognized that when the chips were down, when his team really needed him, he'd flinched. He'd balked. He'd not been able to perform.

With tears pooling in his eyes, Finn had to ask. "Now what?" he said to the grizzled old man helping him stand. "Now what do I do?"

The old coach understood what the young man meant and tried his best to sympathize. The best the old man could do, however, was informed by an earlier era, less any touchy-feely Oprah-talk than the sort of hard-boiled advice that might have been spat out as part of some old-school, Vince Lombardi pep talk.

"What *can* you do?" the old coach grinned grimly. "Walk it off, son. Rub some dirt on it and walk it off…"

Finn couldn't believe it: "Walk it off"? He should just "rub some dirt" on his heartbreak and broken dreams and a crushing sense of failure and "walk it off"? That was all the coach had? The young man smiled bitterly at the old man's advice, thinking that so-called wisdom was useless enough that it might've been needle-pointed on a pillow for all the world to see.

Mirrored-Sunglass Traffic Cop
(Tuesday Morn, 2013)

The Curmudgeon Avenger's Tuesday pretty much planned itself.

After firing that first shot in what he would come to call his own personal "Battle for New York," Finn headed uptown, leaving in his wake at 3 a.m. a still-standing Slipper Room but a fucked-up Funkiberry, one now doubly illuminated by the alternating bright flashes of both white alarm lights and blue police lights. Finn had been about a block and a half away when he saw the police cruiser pull up, but he had no fear of the law: My god, he was a middle-aged white guy wearing khaki shorts and a Princeton t-shirt, lugging in his hand a wrapped white box of pastries. In the eyes of the NYPD Finn was, he knew, pretty much innocence incarnate. In that outfit, Finn figured he could have been standing outside the vandalized Funkiberry while licking a FroYo cone and he still wouldn't have been pegged as a suspect.

Not wanting to tempt fate though, Finn decided to skedaddle. With his liberation of the Lower East Side under way, however, Finn was way too jazzed to rush home, so he opted not to jump in a cab or hop the subway and instead began to walk uptown. While Finn was not the mystical type— he didn't really believe in fate or kismet or the like— in retrospect he had to think the route he chose that night/morning had always been destined for him. It's not like there was a big white star in the sky leading him to Baby Jesus or anything, but looking back Finn had to think his really-early-morning walk was always going to end in the same place.

Finn reached Houston Street, where off to the right he saw over a single-story brick building an illuminated sign, a vertical row of white blocks filled with the red letters K, A, T, Z, 'S. Katz's delicatessen, it was, one of Finn's favorites, an eatery known for serving to the masses massive mounds of hot pastrami and corned beef on rye. In its front window were pictures of U.S. Presidents eating sandwiches (Bill Clinton had noshed there, of course), dangling cuts of cured meats, and kitschy signs dating from as far back as World War II ("Send a salami to your son in the Army," for instance). The place was a New York landmark, a culinary mecca, and one was missing something if he or she knew Katz's only from that silly scene in *When Harry Met Sally* when Meg Ryan fakes the big "O" for Billy Crystal.

But as much as Finn loved Katz's, he was troubled by what he saw. Yes, Katz's was a New York institution, and the line of people waiting to eat there normally led out the front door and then down around the block, but it was still only a one-story building. Finn could see that newly constructed on one side of Katz's was a twenty-five story hotel. On the other side placards were already posted advertising what was about to be another twenty-story tower.

But above Katz's Finn saw a void, nothing at all, so much space really, all that emptiness worth millions as air rights and probably billions in real estate. Just imagine how many fat Midwestern tourists you could stuff into a hotel built high above Katz's, Finn thought. Imagine how many drunk Europeans. Imagine how many of those tiny little Japanese stacked like sardines into their little sleeping pods! Once you plowed under that historic delicatessen, Finn figured, there were twenty, thirty, forty stories worth of space up there. Imagine the room charges, the mini-bar fees, the in-room movies! Finn could see that emptiness above Katz's as nothing but a financial bonanza for some entrepreneurial type, and if Finn could see all those floating dollars, what must it look like to some greedy developer?

Finn loved Katz's, he really did, but in the end he couldn't help see it as another of New York City's little Alamos, a doomed institution surrounded by the conquering hordes; he figured it was only a matter of time.

Finn crossed Houston and headed west, along the way seeing the illuminated neon sign of "Russ and Daughter Appetizers," where the Lower East Side's Jews had long been buying their bagels and whitefish, latkes and lox. Finn had never once darkened their door, but he was still happy to see "Russ and Daughters" standing tall.

He was happier when further down the street he saw on the south side of Houston that Yonah Shimmel's knish bakery still lived. After Finn had moved to New York City and discovered what a knish was— basically, a heavily breaded pastry stuffed with mashed potato or cabbage, kasha or onions or cheese, sort of a Jewish calzone, if you thought about it, a Yiddish empanada, a Semitic Hot Pocket ™, as it were— it became a staple of his diet. He liked the hand-held food itself, Finn did, but he also liked the fact that Yonah Shimmel's had been in the same spot, selling the same food, since 1910. It was a link to New York City's romantic and multi-cultured past, an antithesis to the homogeny that Finn otherwise found all across a many-malled America, the very thing the unhappily-white-bread Finn had been looking for when he moved to Manhattan. That the knishery was still in business gave Finn hope, and he proudly raised his fist high in the air towards the restaurant across Houston Street.

"Solidarity!" he yelled, an image of Lech Walesa involuntarily flashing through his mind.

"Excuse me," interrupted a filthy old codger who didn't seem to have noticed our freedom fighter's impassioned shout. "But which way is the Bowery?"

Finn was charmed: a Bowery Bum! But he was also confused, because even if the guy was a derelict or a tramp— and he seemed to be, as his clothes were grubby, his teeth were gone, and just before he reached Finn the old man had stooped down to pick up off the sidewalk *a dime*— Finn figured the guy was decades late for the Bowery he was looking for. Long gone were those places where a wino might lay his head, all the homeless shelters and flophouses and SROs pretty much shut down or shuttered up for good. Instead the modern Bowery was home to art museums and million-dollar apartments and celebrity-infested hotels.

"I'm close, right?" The old man asked.

"Sure, right down there," Finn pointed, "just past the Whole Foods."

"What's Whole Foods?"

"You don't want to know," Finn told him.

Finn hung a right to head north on 2nd avenue, his favorite East Village thoroughfare, the street once known as the "Jewish Rialto" and home to the world's greatest vaudeville district. He was miffed at 1st street to see the filthy but wonderful Mars Bars had been replaced by the grotesque green of a TD Bank, but tickled at 7th to see Moishe's still selling pastries. At 9th Finn was annoyed anew with the redesigned Veselka, that Ukrainian diner having changed its décor from the traditional white Formica to what could only be described as "modern Barnes & Noble," its white tables having been replaced with boring browns of faux-wood, its walls redone in a bland and forgettable color scheme the likes of which could only be found in the breakfast nook of pretty much every Holiday Inn and Comfort Inn all across this great land. Worse, Veselka had taken to hanging cutesy signs on its wall, including one Finn had seen the past Christmas wishing all its customers "Happy Challah-Days!"

Finn shuddered to think of it. Surely all those fat Midwestern tourists and drunk Europeans and tiny Japanese loved the place now, just drank it up, but it was the old Veselka Finn pined for.

At 10th St. he had mixed feelings. On one hand Finn was saddened that the storied 2nd Avenue Deli was gone, having been run out of town by the neighborhood's skyrocketing rents, and he was doubly disturbed that that unique New York establishment had been replaced with the worst of the worst of the corporate monoliths: a Chase bank. On the other hand, even though it was then about 4 a.m. and Finn was supposedly heading home, he still had the feeling he needed money. Lots and lots of money, in fact. He might not have known why but Finn knew he needed cash. He was therefore certainly happy to have stumbled upon an outpost of his very own bank, because if there was one thing that really irked Finn— well, obviously there were many things that really irked Finn, but bear with us here...— it was having to pay bank fees to a massive, multinational corporation just to access his own money. His very own money! Frankly, Finn would walk whatever extra distance he had to in the city to avoid paying those fees, figuring the minor inconvenience of hiking an extra block or two (in Manhattan, a Chase bank is never more than that far away) was worth the dollars saved.

Finn withdrew from that Chase ATM his maximum daily allowance of cash— $500— and again headed north. He crossed over 14th, that normally busy cross-street not busy for what seemed the first time in Finn's New York life, and he strode past the pretty Stuyvesant Square at 18th. At 19th Finn started to get a feeling, at 20th there was a notion, and at 21st he had a hunch, so by the time he reached 22nd Street Finn knew exactly what he had to do: He took a left.

Halfway down the block there it was, Hector's Police Equipment, the 24-hour spot that sold supplies to the officers working out of the NYPD's 13th precinct house on 21st street and the recruits studying at the Police Academy next door. As soon as Finn saw the blinking blue lights lining the front window of Hector's, he understood it all, the Curmudgeon Avenger's ingenious plan appearing fully formed in his mind. He understood why he was going to Hector's (to purchase the police paraphernalia he would need to complete the morning's mission) and he knew why he needed all that cash (to grease the wheels of commerce).

That block of 22nd street between 2nd and 3rd avenues was one Finn walked regularly— on the corner, Rolfe's German restaurant made one mean schnitzel!— so he was familiar with Hector's. He was aware of the law enforcement caps that lined the shelves of its front window (historic NYPD hats but also headgear from the police departments in Boston and Philly, Chicago and Baltimore, even London and Paris, plus, for reasons unknown, what seemed to have been at least one Kaiser-era Kraut helmet, one of those angry little ones with a metal spike sticking straight up atop it). Plus, and of particular importance to his early morning visit that day, Finn remembered the sign posted clearly in the front window:

> "Most items in our store are restricted for sale to law enforcement personnel only.
>
> Law enforcement ID is required to purchase such items."

The money, Finn thought! He wasn't against trying to lie to buy what he wanted inside Hector's, but Finn figured it wasn't worth it. He was a doughy white guy carrying a box of cookies at four in the morning, from his every pore emanating the stink of cheap beer and the faintest essence of cinnamon liquor. He couldn't pretend he looked like any type of "law enforcement personnel," that Finn knew. He hoped only that whoever was working the cash register at Hector's that night could see him for what he was, not a crime lord or terrorist with evil designs on New York City but a slightly fucked-up father up to some mild no-good.

Plus, Finn knew, the late shift was different. What happened overnight, as they said, stayed overnight. Under the dark of a Manhattan moon, Finn knew, corners could be cut. Rules could be broken. Laws could be, if not ignored, at least interpreted broadly, which is why Finn brought $500 cash to a store where he only needed to buy a hundred or two dollars' worth of clothes. It was why Finn entered Hector's that morning not pretending to be police but with his money spread in front of him, twenty-five $20 bills fanned out in his hands like a new deck of cards at a Las Vegas blackjack table.

It was why, fifteen minutes later, Finn came marching right back out of Hector's, his money gone but now clad like a cop from head to toe: He wore his sneakers still, but over his shorts and t-shirt Finn had pulled standard-issue blue slacks and a short-sleeved blue shirt with NYPD Traffic Department decals sewn on each shoulder, the name Chen stenciled over the heart. He wore an official NYPD patrolman's cap perched jauntily on his head (official although circa 1999) and carried in his hand what seemed to be but was decidedly *not* a shiny NYPD badge, the metal brooch rather turning out to be some kind of eight-pointed "star" that looked like it might've once belonged to Wyatt Earp but that actually bore on it the words "Yorkshire Police Department." He also held a black leather notebook that resembled— and that Finn hoped would be misconstrued as— one of the ones wielded by New York City's meter maids.

Finn looked at his reflection in the front window of Hector's and liked what he saw. The outfit wasn't perfect but it would work, he thought. For the most part he looked like an officer. The whole traffic cop/meter maid aspect of the outfit had been an especially fortuitous turn, he thought, given the job in front of him. Finn was thinking maybe his look needed one more thing though, maybe one last little tweak, when from inside Hector's Police Equipment came the kid who'd just sold Finn his uniform The young Mexican— whose nationality Finn was able to surmise from the kid's red and green El Tri soccer jersey— stuck one hand out the front door, offering Finn what was, in effect, a parting gift.

"If you're gonna' do it, esé," the kid said, handing over a cheap pair of mirrored sunglasses. "Do it good."

Finn smiled his thanks and slid the shades on. He checked his reflection one last time: He looked good!

Although she may not have known it, the whole thing had been Ivy's idea. Ivy was a neighbor from the Albemarle, a gorgeous thirty-something Argentine with lustrous long black hair and a phenomenal physique, all ass and tits and womanly curves she was, basically a Jennifer Lopez doppelganger if J.Lo had been not from the block but Buenos Aires. Ivy never left her apartment without everything being just so, a smile on her face, her outfits impeccable, her tresses perfectly coiffed, all high heels and tight skirts and colorful blouses she was, sparkling earrings hanging from her ear lobes and dangling bracelets jangling on her wrists. "Hot" you could have certainly called Ivy, but "MILF" worked too, (she had a young son in 2013 and no one in their right mind would have been averse to banging her), even "spicy Latina" an apt description that in at least this one case proved to be more accurate than racist when it came to Ivy because the one time Finn and Danielle had co-licked the woman's nipples they both agreed that they detected far in the background what seemed to be the haziest trace of the taste of pablano peppers: Ivy was literally spicy.

Co-licked the woman's nipples, you might ask? It had been years prior, back in 2007, a year after Finn and Danielle had started dating, before the ugly spectre of her cancer had appeared and during a phase of their relationship that, frankly, was not for the faint of heart. A lot of things occurred— sexual things— that, well, were.... They made love, of course, Finn and Danielle, but they fucked too. They *fucked*. Missionary position sometimes, doggie-style, too, man on top and woman on top, cowgirl and reverse cowgirl, once even the double-reverse cowgirl (which, surprise!, brought the couple right back to cowgirl), occasionally even experimental efforts with awkward positions like the Pouncing Pederast (Finn: "Ouch.") or the Three-Legged Fawn (Danielle: "Ouch."). They did it all: There was role play and raping, oral sex and anal, visits to strip joints and massage parlors, the occasional paddling and cross-dressing (Finn claims no knowledge of any such thing), more than their fair share of figging and pegging (Slander, Finn swears! A bald-faced lie!).

One Sunday morning, the pair having fucked themselves tired all weekend and then read the Sunday *Times*, Finn suggested a golden shower. Danielle agreed without so much as looking up from the book review. "Why not?" she said. So that day Finn attempted to relieve himself all over the woman he loved, his efforts hindered only by the fact that even the grown-up Finn— sexually liberated at that point for certain, no longer scared of any damn thing— had a hard time getting away from that idea hard-wired into his head that, you know, women were people too. Those lessons learned in the 80s weren't easily forgotten, apparently, and there were really no rhetorical gymnastics Finn could come up with in his mind that made it okay to, well, piss on a dame. Plus, Finn's kidneys were absolutely not on board regarding that little Sunday perversion, absolutely refusing to release so much as a single drop of pee that day.

That Sunday was far from a loss though, as Danielle spent the entire day naked, walking around the apartment for the next six hours without even a stitch of clothing on in anticipation of her promised dousing. Nude, Danielle was, in a word, spectacular. She prowled like a panther, neither slight nor plump, beneath her skin an underlying structure of tight musculature. She had light blonde hair down to her shoulders and light blue eyes, a nose that if not pointed was at least angular, soft red lips that hid a tongue as long as Gene Simmons'. Her breasts were small but full, her belly firm and flat, her pussy tufted with soft golden hair. When she ambled away from him, Finn saw Danielle's strong shoulders, her straight spine, the sexy tattoo at the small of her back, and her bottom. That bottom! It was an ass that would have made Nina Hartley proud, high and round and firm. It was an ass for which odes were written. Novels, even.

But Finn's kidneys were heroic that day, absolutely heroic, valiantly fighting the good fight in defense of both feminism and common decency, steadfastly refusing to release from Finn's perverted Johnson so much as the tiniest little piddle. Finn had had a couple cups of coffee before he'd even broached the idea of the golden shower with Danielle, and after she'd agreed to it he took to gulping down glasses of water to expedite the process, but the kidneys held strong. All day long, as Finn sucked down first glasses of tap water and then cans of Coors Light beer, his kidneys were shut down, clamped closed just as tight as a drum. They gave up nothing at all.

But Nature, of course, eventually had to take its course, and by the time the sun had set Finn had drank...after all that coffee and water first!...an entire twelve-pack of beer (a dozen cans of 12 oz. Coors Lights, or 144 ounces of Colorado lager!)... his body at that point soundly defeated, pretty much destroyed really... no longer able to do anything but give up. His kidneys at last gave in, finally surrendering, at which point Finn suddenly realized he had to go— he really, really, really had to go, in fact— so he grabbed Danielle by the wrist and dragged her into the bathroom (giggling as she went), setting up his gorgeous girlfriend kneeling in the tub, before unleashing on his beloved what must have been the longest pee ever seen outside the elephant enclosure of the Bronx Zoo, a tremendous torrent of urine that began around the time "60 Minutes" started that evening and seemed to end about the time Andy Rooney came on to say good-night.

"Well," Danielle gamely said at the end of a golden shower that at one point seemed like it would never end but that eventually, mercifully, did. "We did that."

"We sure did," Finn agreed, both of them shaking their heads.

It was during this era of sexual fever that Finn first met Ivy, when she entered the Albemarle's lobby from 54th street one evening just as Finn and Danielle were heading out. Finn had only a moment to admire Ivy that night— the brown stiletto heels, the brown leather pants, the tight white Angora sweater softly surrounding a pair of great breasts so globular they immediately made materialize in Finn's mind, completely unbidden, the phrase "titty-fuck"— before she hurled herself at Danielle.

"Dani!" Ivy cried, throwing her arms around Finn's girl-friend before starting to cry. "Darren left me!"

Although Danielle sympathized with Ivy, hugging her and cooing into her ear, Finn was not impressed. Here we go again, he thought, another woman crying over some idiot man. Another one of those god-damn *Sex in the City* episodes come to life, he scoffed.

"And," Ivy sniffled, "after I just got my tits done!"

Hold on right there, Finn thought! Maybe this was one of those *Sex in the City* episodes featuring the spectacularly slutty Samantha, the only tales on that miserable show really worth 23 minutes of a "young" man's time.

"Do you want to see them?" Ivy asked.

The question had been directed at Danielle but Finn answered "yes." Ivy laughed through her tears and then, after the appropriate introductions were made, the next thing Finn knew the threesome were in the elevator, headed up to Ivy's place to get a good look at her brand-new tits. Standing in the elevator, Finn maintained a Zen-like calm, he was "in the zone," as they say, on one side of him his spectacular girl-friend— a woman in whose romantic, amorous, sexual thrall he faithfully remained— and on the other a big-boobed "chiquita" Finn found as "hot as a chile relleno." (*Yes, your Omniscient Narrator admits, those characterizations of Finn's were nonchalantly racist...*).

While Finn was managing to be a grown-up about it all— yeah, yeah, just heading upstairs with my spectacularly sexy girlfriend to have a gander at her spectacularly sexy girlfriend's huge breasts, no big deal— the teenage boy he had once been and his always chatty cock were besides themselves with glee. They were certain that the whole gang was on the verge of something big, an escapade so unusual as to not yet have made (as far as the imaginary kid and the talking cock knew) the pages of *Penthouse Forum*, Finn and Danielle sure as hell looking like they were about to succumb to the clever seductions of the emotional wreck Ivy and give her what she wanted: the exceedingly rare tag-team pity fuck (and with a neighborly twist to boot!)

"Ass! Boobies! Ass!" Teenaged Finn was yelling.

"Gonna' drown in pussy tonight!" The cock was blabbering.

Sheesh, Finn thought, could they act with some dignity? Still, even he had to admit it was something. What could you say about a city, he thought, where a regular guy like him could suddenly find himself so sandwiched between two gorgeous goddesses taking him up, up, up on the express elevator to Heaven? You couldn't say anything but good about a city like that. (Or, "Only in New York," as Cindy Adams liked to say in the *Post*.)

No sooner had they entered the apartment than Ivy pulled off her sweater, marching Finn and Danielle into her living room as she followed from behind. They turned around to see Ivy's fingers on the front clasp of her pink Agent Provocateur brassiere, and then, with a simple flick of her fingers that even the grown-up Finn had never mastered, her breasts were freed. As Danielle nodded with appreciation, Finn remembered a *Seinfeld* episode of old.

"They're fake," he said. "And they're spectacular."

Ivy laughed. "Feel them," she said, cupping each of her great breasts in her hands and handing them in the general direction of Danielle and Finn respectively. Like a scientist Finn cupped Ivy's big boob, pretending to be no more than an objective observer to all that was going on. He squeezed it gently, nodding approvingly himself.

"Feels real," he said.

"Right?" Ivy asked. "And you can't even see the scar."

"How's the sensation?" Finn asked, having become, apparently, some sort of expert in breast reconstruction.

"No problem at all," Ivy said. "Go ahead, lick my nipple."

Somewhere, Teenaged Finn fainted (again). Finn's grown-up cock, on the other hand, was operating at Code Red, doing absolute yeomen's work, urgently undertaking the many machinations needed to raise itself to fullest glory.

Finn looked at Ivy to be sure she was serious, and when he saw she was he nodded at his girlfriend. "Don't mind if I do," Finn said, before leaning down to take Ivy's delicious left boob into his mouth.

"Ooooh," Ivy moaned, closing her eyes.

"You, too, Dani," she whispered at her friend, Finn looking up with his mouth full to encourage his girlfriend to join him in what certainly seemed a most excellent idea, our hero being only slightly disappointed to see Danielle looking a little less enamored of the whole spectacle than he would've liked. She wore on her face a look he'd last seen when he peed on her for about an hour, an expression best described as game if not gung-ho. But Danielle then leaned down to take the second of Ivy's nipples into her mouth, the couple of lovers thus sucking in tandem on those couple of breasts.

"Ooooh," Ivy moaned.

"All hands of deck! All hands on deck!" Finn's cock was clamoring.

But covering Ivy's gorgeous left breast with soft kisses, Finn again looked up to see his girlfriend— herself with a biteful of boob— giving him what could only be construed as a dirty look. Flicking Ivy's right tit with her own soft tongue, Danielle held her index finger in the air and wagged it.

This is not happening.

Finn held his two palms up.

What are you talking about?

Danielle pointed to the apartment around them. While softly dragging her teeth on Ivy's erect nipple, she wagged her index finger at her boyfriend again.

You know I don't fuck around in this building. We aren't doing this with Ivy.

Circling Ivy's aureole with his tongue, Finn looked deep into Danielle's eyes and cupped his cock, at that point spectacularly hard. He wagged his index finger right back at Danielle.

Are you insane, woman? I'm as hard as a rock here. You can't say no to this. It's too good to be true! No way this isn't happening!

Danielle tried to look away from Finn but it wasn't easy, what with her oral orifice attached to her friend's chest and all. With a mouthful of nipple she tried her best to shake her head, and while she wagged her finger at Finn again she was less strident doing so that time.

Sorry, no, but we can't. We just can't.

Finn didn't take Ivy's breast from his mouth, but he stopped the tongue-tickling that he'd been at for a while. He looked straight at Danielle. He pressed his palms together and held them up, praying, pleading, as serious as any Sunday-morning supplicant.

Are you crazy??? Puuuuuuh-leeeeeeeeeezzzzzzzeeeeeeee.

But it was all a moot point, because as Finn was in the process of giving his girlfriend a petulant double thumbs-down Ivy's breast was suddenly wrested from his mouth, the woman's moaning quickly being replaced with some kind of high-pitched keening instead. Ivy turned her back to Finn and threw her shirtless self at Danielle for the second time that night, hugging her, sobbing, muttering something or other about "Darren, Darren, Darren," a verbal outburst that Finn took for the end of the sexy part of the night and the beginning of the whiny part, which just also happened to be the very moment Finn realized he had somewhere else to be. Anywhere else to be. Although Ivy didn't look up from Danielle's shoulders as Finn made his way to the apartment door, his girlfriend shot him a shrug and a look that implied she would be busy for the rest of the night, her plans to go out with her boyfriend having been replaced instead with what would likely be a long stretch of sisterhood, a bout of womanly commiseration, as it were, a whole bunch of bashing men and sipping peppermint tea as Finn figured it.

Although Danielle didn't get home until long after Finn had fallen asleep that night, the evening was far from a complete loss. To begin with, regardless of what Danielle

would later say happened in Ivy's apartment over the course
of the following hours— innocent girl-talk, she claimed—
Finn fantasized, with his pants around his ankles, that all
Ivy and Danielle's meaningful conversation that night had
quickly devolved into some sort of sordid Sapphic sex scene,
a wild pile of women as it were, nude girls everywhere, nothing but puckered lips, licked titties, and smooched cooches.
Was there maybe a strap-on involved? Finn couldn't say but
he sure liked to think so.

Plus, even more importantly, once Finn got over the initial disappointment of not consummating that tag-team pity
fuck with his girlfriend, he was proud to think of what had
happened: That incident with Ivy showed how strong Finn
and Danielle were as a twosome, how unique, not just being
another one of those silly couples blathering on and on all
their hokey bullshit about being able to "finish each other's
sentences"; rather, the thwarted threesome had revealed
something else about Finn and Danielle, something better,
namely that they were a pair of lovers who really understood
each other, who could truly communicate, who could talk to
each other without *saying* a thing, able to have entire wordless conversations when each of their mouths were filled to
the brim with a mouthful of mammary. Now *that* was a couple, as far as Finn Riley was concerned! *That* was true love.

While Finn saw Ivy occasionally over the next five or
six years, they never really had another significant interaction until the week before the Curmudgeon Avenger first
appeared, when Finn returned from delivering the Prince of
New York to pre-school one morning to find Ivy irate in the
lobby of the Albemarle. She'd just been to the 18th precinct
house down 54th street, she said, to complain about the obnoxious drivers who every morning nearly ran down her and
her son as she tried to put him on the school bus. Apparently
those drivers simply ignored the red stop signs flashing on
the side of the bus and sped right past, leaving in their wake
a frightened five-year old boy and his angry, angry mother.
Worse, it seemed to be some of the same drivers every day,

including one particular scumbag who usually led the illegal charge from the air-conditioned comfort of his shiny black Porsche SUV.

"Twice I've been to the police," Ivy fumed that day, "Two times! But they haven't done a thing."

While the NYPD's inaction was troubling to Finn, he might've understood why the cops didn't stop their assiduous pursuit of terrorists and hardened criminals to chase down the bunch of traffic scofflaws making Ivy miserable. But when he thought of it— the disinterested drivers nearly mowing down pretty Ivy and her special needs son just so they could race off to do their own thing— the whole thing just about made Finn sick.

Finn had bristled when he heard Ivy's story, and it troubled him for most of the day, but if he'd eventually put it out of this mind it was certainly not forgotten: In fact, the Curmudgeon Avenger had made a note. That was why the next Tuesday, at 6:30 AM, the line of cars that every morning had been selfishly and illegally blasting right past the school bus stopped outside the Albemarle— the school bus with its STOP signs activated and its red lights blinking!— were met on the other side of the vehicle by an unexpected sight: Standing at the intersection of 7th Avenue, blocking the 54th street traffic going forward, was a blue-clad police officer, his eyes covered with mirrored sunglasses and atop his head a blue patrolman's cap (official if circa 1999). In his right hand the officer held high a shiny star that one could only assume was an official badge of the New York City Police Department. With the huge orb of an orange sun beginning to rise over the East River visible behind him down 54th street, glinting off that silver star and off his mirrored sunglasses, it didn't take much to see that cop as some sort of Hollywood hero individually engaged in an epic battle against the endlessly rising tide of asshole drivers then flooding Manhattan's avenues (or so Finn thought at least.)

"Pull over," he barked at the first car that had snaked its oblivious way past the stopped school bus, that infamous shiny black Porsche SUV.

"Pull over, pull over, pull over," he said to the second, third, fourth, fifth and six cars that followed, an array of vehicles that covered pretty much the entire spectrum of automobiles, from a jalopy of a Chrysler mini-van to a well-used Toyota Corolla to a brand-new Lexus sedan.

"Pull over," he ordered, pointing all six of the vehicles to the empty southern side of the street.

"Engines off, licenses and registrations out," he yelled.

Finn wasn't fucking around. He hadn't fully thought his plan through, of course, and he wasn't outfitted in a way that would fool someone particularly familiar with the NYPD (Finn really hoped none of the drivers asked for his badge number, for instance), but he still wasn't fucking around. He figured at least some of those obnoxious drivers were harboring some guilt about what they'd done and he had right on his side, too, so Finn, as the Curmudgeon Avenger, would not be stopped.

He took out his cell-phone— a laughably archaic flip-phone, in fact, one that didn't even have a camera in it— and pretended to click a pic of the license plate on each of the guilty cars.

"Haven't started my shift today so I don't have the equipment to give you a ticket," he brusquely told each of the drivers. "Instead the NYPD will be sending you a gift in the mail. $250 fine for this first offense, $500 and revocation at the second."

Finn didn't know if that was true. He was making shit up, but it was shit, he hoped, that would scare those a-holes straight.

"What that means, remember," he told each of the drivers, "is that if you do this again, you lose your license."

Starting with the last car in the line of six cars, the jalopy of a Chrysler driven by a handsome 30-something

Latino man, Finn gave each driver a chance to speak. "Anything to say for yourself?"

"I only went when I saw everyone else go..."

"Uh huh, uh huh," Finn answered, not looking at the driver but looking down the street. "So it's your defense that you only broke the law because everyone else was breaking the law?"

"Uh, no, man, uh, I, uh..."

"So you're going with the asshole defense, huh?" Finn turned to look at him, knowing all the driver could see from Finn's eyes was a reflection of his own guilty face. "Everyone else was being an asshole so you thought you could be an asshole too?"

The handsome Latino said nothing. He looked like he thought it might be a trick question.

"Uh, no, Officer...."

"Young man," Finn began, "civilized society hinges upon the, uh, civilized actions of its, uh..."

Finn hadn't thought this little speech through, that was for sure.

"...its civilians..."

My god, how repetitive! How clichéd! Finn sure would have to clean that up before he got to the next car, that was for sure.

The next car was the new Lexus, and its blonde driver in her spiffy new suit was pretty sure she had a pretty good reason to have broken the law.

"I know, I know, Officer," she apologized to Finn. "I shouldn't have done it but I can't be late for work, I have a huge meeting this morning—"

"Oooooohhhh," Finn interrupted her. "No problem then. You have one of those meetings that's even more important than the lives of a bunch of developmentally disabled kids, I get it."

"No...." she said, dropping her head, her voice trailing off.

After he'd spoken to the driver of each of the last five cars in the line of six cars he'd pulled over— having reproached each of them, made them feel like the a-holes they were, sent them off expecting to get a $250 ticket in the mail and threatening them with license revocation if they ever pulled that bullshit move again— Finn happily watched each guilty driver pull slowly away from the curb, the bunch of them suddenly the most observant and conscientious of vehicle operators, all two-hands-on-the-wheel and yielding-to-pedestrians and even using-their-direction-lights-when-changing-lanes. It made Finn want to laugh to see them pull so meekly into traffic, but— and not funny at all— he also hoped they'd learned their respective lessons, too. He hoped those five drivers would never pass a stopped school bus again, and he hoped furthermore that they might've gleaned a more significant moral from the story: Namely, that maybe when driving in the future those five stopped motorists who'd met up with a shit-talking, mirrored-sunglass traffic cop might think twice about driving like a bunch of dicks.

But it was when Finn spoke with the driver of the final vehicle— the shiny black Porsche SUV, the car Ivy had seen speed past her son's bus nearly every morning— that the fun really began. The guy was youngish and handsome, his car and his suit dripping with wealth and his slicked-back black hair dripping with gel. He imagined himself, Finn was sure, some Master of the Universe.

"Please, Officer!" The guy had earlier yelled out his window towards Finn when Finn was speaking to the driver of the Toyota Corolla, the car closest to the Porsche.

He'd try to step out of his car but Finn, the epitome of calm, had held up a single finger to him. "Stay in the car," he said.

"But I was first in line!" he argued.

Finn excused himself from talking to the Corolla driver and ambled slowly up to this imagined big shot.

"You were first in line?"

"Yes, I was."

"You were first in the line of outlaws I pulled over for brazenly, heartlessly, illegally blasting past a school bus full of special needs students, risking all their lives just because you were in a hurry?"

"Uh...yes."

"You were first in line almost running down a bunch of mentally handicapped kids, so now you want better service? That's what you're saying? First in, first out, that sort of thing, special needs students be damned?"

"Uh, yeah, I guess so."

"Get in your car, you shmuck. Get in your car right now or I call for back-up."

"Shmuck" hadn't been the best word choice, Finn realized, and when he said it the guy tilted his head like a Newfoundland puppy trying to figure out his master's commands. Finn tried to backtrack.

"Get in your car, sir, and I'll be with you shortly."

The Porsche driver climbed back into his SUV, but as he did so he looked back at Finn. The guy was no dummy apparently, and about Finn he had his doubts. But Finn wasn't done at the Corolla, so he sidled back over there.

"Civilized society," Finn started again at the Toyota driver, "hinges on the civilized behavior of its civilians..." In the end it hadn't been such a bad speech, Finn realized. If you said it fast enough, he'd learned, and with enough conviction, it ended up sounding pretty good. It worked.

By the time he'd returned to the Porsche, however, its driver was ready. He looked at Finn's shirt.

"Chen? Your name is Chen?" he sneered. "I'm gonna need your badge number, Chen."

Finn stood beside the driver-side window of the Porsche SUV and looked at the man inside. He didn't say a word, but Finn also realized that at some point he'd have to put an end to this charade. The 18th precinct was all of a block away, and the streets in the area were often flooded with cops. The longer he stayed out there impersonating an officer, Finn knew, the greater the likelihood that the Curmudgeon Avenger would end up with his own legal troubles.

But the guy in the Porsche was such a dick! And so Finn couldn't let it go.

"Sure thing," Finn said, "No problem. As I stated previously, my shift hasn't officially started yet so I don't have my badge with me..."

"Didn't I see you waving it around before?"

Finn ignored him and continued, "...but given the special case you're turning out to be—"

"The special case?"

Finn ignored him and continued, "...I'm gonna' call the precinct for some help."

"I'm out," the greasy-haired Porsche driver muttered, starting his engine. "You're no cop."

"By all means, young man," Finn smiled behind his mirrored sunglasses. "Drive away! Let's add resisting arrest and fleeing the scene of a crime to the already obnoxious charge you're facing of failing to stop for a stopped school bus..."

The Porsche driver gritted his teeth.

"And a school bus," Finn whispered conspiratorially, leaning inside the Porsche's driver side window, "filled to the rafters with the retarded! That's the sort of story that plays so well on the news!"

"By all means, speed away, champ!" Finn continued, smiling, his eyes ever hidden behind those gloriously mirrored shades.

The Porsche driver scowled and then angrily turned off the purring engine.

"Porsche," Finn nodded, wondering if this young punk would get the reference to *Risky Business*. "'There is no substitute.'"

Finn flipped open his phone, laughing to himself at the idiocy of it all, before pretend-dialing.

"Sarge," he said into the cell phone. "It's Finn."

Finn? That might've been another mistake.

"Yes, Officer Finn Chen," he continued, wincing as he said it. "On the way to the precinct this morning I stumbled upon six perps illegally blasting past a stopped bus full of special needs kids..."

"Yeah, the short bus..."

"Five of the six were no problem, took their medicine like they should, they'll pay the fine, promised not to do it again, the usual, but one driver..."

Finn looked at the guy in the Porsche, who was listening to every word.

"Greasy-haired sort, imagines he's some sort of big deal, I think...."

The Porsche driver threw his hands in the air.

"He's gonna' be a problem, I can tell. Wants my badge number..."

"I know, I know, he's the asshole who almost mowed down the handicapped kids and I'm the bad guy, right?"

"Worse, I think he's a runner. He already started his car and threatened to take off..."

"What do I think we need?"

"I need back-up for sure. Guy thinks he's a hotshot. Stop signs aren't for him, it seems, so I imagine he doesn't think cops are either. Laws are for the other guys, this guy seems to think. I'd suggest you send me O'Reilly at least, maybe O'Sullivan too. The Irish guys, yeah."

"The paddy wagon? Up to you really. I can't imagine that O'Reilly and O'Sullivan can't drag this guy half a block to the precinct house, but whatever you think is best."

"No, he's not under arrest just yet, but he's impatient, I can tell. It's only a matter of time before we have ourselves a runner. Or a resister. A likely arrest in any case. The guy can't help himself, I can tell. He thinks he's too important."

Finn held his phone to his ear for a bit. He pointed his face directly at the driver of the Porsche, so even if the guy couldn't see Finn's eyes behind the mirrored glasses he understood he was being looked at.

"Definitely the tow truck. If we drag this guy in, as I'm sure we will, his sweet ride will be sitting here unattended. Have to be impounded for sure..."

The Porsche driver was gripping the wheel with white knuckles, shaking it back and forth.

"I got his license plate, Sarge, and his license, so he's not getting away but send the boys..."

"Just up the street, 54th and 7th. The Albemarle."

"You got it, Sarge."

Finn flipped his cell phone closed. He leaned on the front door of the Porsche SUV. He looked down the street, back to where the 18th precinct stood.

"I'm gonna' run down to the precinct," Finn told the guy. "Gotta' get my badge so I can give you the number. I imagine your lawyer's gonna' need that to make the case that you shouldn't have to stop for stopped school buses. Not *you.*"

The Porsche driver seethed, but he said nothing.

"You wait here," Finn said, patting good-bye the door of the shiny black Porsche. "The NYPD is coming for you, so I suggest you wait right here."

The Curmudgeon Avenger smiled at the punk. He adjusted his mirrored shades on his nose, nodded, and strode away. He crossed over to the north side of 54th street and headed west, taking a glance over his shoulder to see if he was being watched before plunging inside the Albemarle's front door, what with 7 AM approaching and it nearly being time for Finn to wake up his wife and son.

Forty-five minutes later, Finn came out of the Albemarle again, dressed like a dad and pushing his boy in the stroller. He glanced back at the intersection of 54th and 7th and was surprised to see the shiny black Porsche SUV still parked on the corner, its driver at that point out of the car and arguing with a NYPD meter maid (a real one, Finn knew) about the ticket she was writing him. At 7 AM the spot where the Porsche was parked had become a "No Parking" zone, meaning the dickish driver of that Nazi sports car was on the verge of getting his "second" ticket that morning.

"But I can't move!" he was whining. "Officer Chen told me to wait!"

The meter maid was a short, round African-American woman who Finn often saw around the neighborhood and who normally wore on her face a mask of imperturbable calm, being unfailingly oblivious (as stern and silent as the guard at Buckingham Palace she was) to the entreaties and threats of all those people who every day begged her not to give them the parking tickets she was most certainly still about to give them. But even that unflappable woman couldn't help herself when hearing about some mythical Chinese cop, and she broke out into a great, big grin.

"Officer Chen?!?" she laughed. "Never heard of him!"

Finn had to laugh, too, watching that douchebag driver being tortured by members of the NYPD both real and imagined.

The father turned the stroller towards Broadway, where he would push his beloved Prince of New York north towards pre-school. The warm sun was rising high into a blue sky over New York City, and Finn couldn't help but think it was looking like it was going to be a real good day— and, imagine, our hero made that rosy assessment about the upcoming morning not even knowing he was only a couple hours away from a nice lady in the park offering him some free fellatio!

Quite the good day indeed.

Daddy Dearest (Wednesday, 2013)

Finn didn't think there was a man alive (or one dead, for that matter) who could pull off the pram look. He thought if you put a stroller in front of John Holmes, that legendary cocksman would have looked neutered; if you put one in front of Mike Tyson, the "Baddest Man Alive" would've looked like a wuss. And on himself? Delivering his son to pre-school up Broadway most days, Finn was disgusted to see a reflection of himself in a hundred store windows: A grown man with a baby carriage. You prancing ninny, Finn thought. He got the feeling he should've been draped in a gauzy sundress for that daily constitutional, perhaps rocking a lacy bonnet or twirling a frilly parasol for all the world to see.

Finn remembered one winter afternoon pushing his son from the pre-school on Central Park West to the "frog park" on 11th Avenue where father and son liked to play, and cross-ing in front of a cement flower box at Lincoln Center Finn saw his reflection in the large windows of the Metropolitan Opera. The flower box blocked the view of Finn from his chest down, but from his chest up Finn liked what he saw: It was a brisk day, and a breezy one, so Finn had his U.S. Navy pea coat (a steal at only five bucks from the Salvation Army store on 46th street) buttoned tight and its collar flipped up. He had a black watch cap pulled low over his forehead and the beginning of a silver beard sprouting on his face.

Finn liked the look. It was reminiscent of the poster of James Dean walking huddled against the rain in Times Square. Or of the Nike poster of John McEnroe reenacting James Dean walking huddled against the rain in Times

Square. And it was eerily similar, Finn thought, to that famous picture of a faintly smiling Jack Kerouac also attired in pea coat and watch cap. Yeah, Finn liked the look. He looked like a man.

But Finn was walking as he admired his reflection in the windows of the Metropolitan Opera, and though he shouldn't have been he ended up being surprised to see himself reappear on the other side of that cement flowerbox, suddenly...pushing a stroller. Ugh! Finn hated the new look. What a shmuck, he thought.

"But I'm Jack Kerouac!" Finn wanted to rail aloud in front of Lincoln Center. "I'm Jack Kerouac!"

On Wednesday morn Finn would again push his son to school in one of those strollers, but the Tuesday night before had turned into the usual cancer fiasco when Danielle returned from her regular visits to the oncologist and neurologist feeling grim and glum. His wife's visits with the doctors were never long, but the wait to see them always was. Plus, the conversations were always so heavy: What was the likelihood her cancer would return? Why were her blood-markers so high? What was the "shadow" that could be seen on her liver on the CAT scan? Would her brain ever gain back the function that had once made her smart enough to join Mensa? Did she need to keep taking the seizure medicine, the chemo pills, the anti-depressants? What about all the side effects? To make matters worse, Danielle said she'd have to return to the oncologist's office on Thursday to get the results of that day's foreboding scan.

Finn did his best to help that night, meaning that when Danielle returned from her doctor visits feeling morose the husband did the one thing his wife wanted most those days: He massaged her feet until she fell asleep. She thanked him profusely, told him how good it felt, but Danielle also told Finn just how sad she was. How she felt like there was no escape. How she couldn't get away from thinking about it all. About the cancer likely still hiding inside her. It colored her everything.

Finn understood, because even if Danielle's disease hadn't yet killed her, it was certainly making a mess of their lives. In the old, pre-cancer days, for instance— the days of co-licking Ivy's nipples, for instance, or the nights of co-fucking a phat-assed Nevada call-girl— Danielle would have loved to hear Finn's anecdote about Maggie's perverted proposition in the park. Finn's wife would have scoffed at it and laughed, but she would have taken it as a considerable challenge, too. You can bet that at the end of a day when a pretty stranger tried to give her husband a blow-job that most sane people would concede he most certainly deserved, Danielle would have wreaked sexual havoc on him, unleashing her entire arsenal of erotic tricks on Finn if only to remind her husband just why it was he never needed to stray from their very own boudoir.

But on the day when Maggie really did offer to suck Finn's cock, Danielle hadn't unleashed any sexual havoc on Finn. None at all. Rather, his wife had actually fallen asleep even before her husband got to tell her the story. Finn understood (it happened whenever he massaged her feet) and didn't hold it against Danielle, but he felt the loss, too, not just of not being on the receiving end of Danielle's entire arsenal of sexual expertise but also the diminishing intimacy between them. Instead of having another adventure with Danielle, another cool escapade, Finn was left alone with the great yarn of Maggie's offered oral sex. It was one more thing they wouldn't share.

Finn had been sitting on the bed with Danielle's feet on his lap, and after Danielle nodded off the husband slid out from under his wife's legs and placed them on two pillows. The elevation, Finn knew, might help reduce the swelling. He brushed a strand of blonde hair away from his wife's face and leaned down to kiss her on the neck. Silently he watched her chest rise and fall with each small inhalation and exhalation. Finn smiled softly. It was the little things, he thought of Danielle breathing. The little things.

On Wednesday morning Finn took his Prince to pre-school, and after kissing the boy profusely at the classroom door he dumped the stigma of the stroller in a hall closet and scurried off to try to make some money. The supposedly easy task of picking up Danielle's seizure medicine (the 300 mg Oxteller pills not available on Monday) turned into the usual health-care cluster-fuck though, and by the time Finn had chased down the missing pills (circling from one Midtown Duane Reade to another, his blood pressure spiking with each unsuccessful stop...) he ended up being late to the atrium.

The David Rubinstein Atrium was a public space affili-ated with Lincoln Center and across Columbus Avenue from it, a high-ceilinged lobby with an indoor fountain, green plants miraculously growing out of its walls, and a two-story high video screen. It was the site of occasional free piano con-certs or dance exhibitions and had a couple dozen tables where people could sit to read or work. For those in the know (George Costanza, we're looking at you), the Rubinstein Atrium also had a number of clean public restrooms on the second floor. The problem was that the place had a limited number of tables to work at, and an even smaller number of electrical outlets around them. If one wanted to plug a laptop in, as Finn always hoped to on the days he worked there, it was imperative to arrive at the atrium as soon as it opened at 9 a.m. Failing to do so meant one would almost certainly get shut out, because as soon as the atrium's doors opened it was routinely flooded with the homeless, who came in both to get out of the cold and, apparently, to recharge their cellphones.

Finn simply didn't understand it. There was nothing else to say. Somehow any number of New York City's home-less also maintained accounts with Verizon, Sprint, and AT&T? They lived on the streets but remained on the grid? Yeah, Finn didn't get it, but that was the reality of the Rubinstein Atrium, and sure enough after the wild-goose chase of chasing down his wife's pills Wednesday morning Finn got to the atrium way too late. The place was already packed with those connected homeless and the other usual army bivouacked there: New York City's elderly. The only empty table available to him was the worst of all worlds, far from the electrical outlets and surrounded on all sides by other tables. Even if Finn managed to secure the spot, he knew he'd be trapped there: The tables and chairs were always jammed so close together, and the aged and indigent ensconced at them always so dilatory or immobile, that maneuvering between the tables was always awkward and unwieldy. It was usually just easier to sit in one place and not go anywhere at all.

While Finn was lucky enough to get that last empty (if surrounded) table, his luck that day didn't exactly change. No sooner had he set his laptop atop it than the security guard arrived at his table, a bit of a smirk on his face and bearing with him an unwanted gift.

"You see *The Times* this morning?" the man asked nonchalantly, offering Finn a folded-over section of the paper of record.

Finn knew something was up. Bo, the guard's name was, a short, thin fifty-something fellow with a head shaved clean and dressed from head to toe in security guy blue. Finn and his son had first become familiar with the security guard the summer before, when they used to ride their scooters across the plaza at Lincoln Center despite the mild protests of Bo and other the guards patrolling there. "No scooting" they would yell as Finn and his son scooted obliviously past— Finn knew they weren't supposed to ride there but simply pretended he didn't.

One afternoon, however, as Finn and the Prince glided their two-wheeled scooters past the dancing fountain in front of the Metropolitan Opera whilst ignoring a security guard's cries, Bo suddenly pulled up next to them on his very own *motorized* scooter. Riding next to the scofflaw Rileys on a contraption that was much speedier than their own conveyances, Bo offered them a bemused look, basically a wordless warning that he was in charge there and they should cut it out with their rule-breaking. The Rileys understood and conceded, riding their scooters on the sidewalks *past* Lincoln Center thereafter or carrying them lawfully across the plaza.

When Finn later began going to the Rubinstein Atrium on Wednesday and Sunday mornings to work, he was therefore not surprised to see Bo manning the security guard desk. At first they just nodded hellos— a recognition that they remembered each other from the previous scooting kerfuffle— but eventually they came to share pleasantries about the world, or at least news about the Yankees and the Knicks and gossip about the various wingnuts who liked to hang out in the atrium. They eventually learned each other's stories, too, Finn telling Bo about his wife's cancer, taking care of his son, and his belief that all that domesticity was hampering his ascent to a future of obvious-if-as-yet-undefined greatness. Meanwhile, Bo told Finn his gig as a Lincoln Center security guard was simply a way to idle away his retirement, the man having hung up his NYPD badge a couple years prior, the old seedy Times Square actually having been his long-time beat.

"And how'd you like that?" Finn had asked.

"A cesspool of humanity," Bo said cheerfully. "Filth and crime and drugs wherever you looked. Pimps and prostitutes on every corner."

He paused, smiling. "I loved it!"

Finn loved that answer, of course, and in short order Bo became Finn's closest confidante. He might have become his closest friend. Or his only one. Other than Danielle, most of the people Finn knew in New York City were his old bar friends and he rarely saw them anymore. Though their relationship occurred solely on the grounds of the Rubinstein Atrium, Bo and Finn talked a lot and had an easy rapport. They were men. They understood each other. They laughed with each other and at each other, so when Bo proffered a section of *The Times* with a bit of a smirk on his face Finn knew something was up.

"Found something that might interest you," Bo said as earnestly as he could manage, looking down at a section of the paper that Finn still couldn't see.

Finn took the paper but looked at Bo's face. It was a mask, revealing nothing. Finn looked down at the article obviously meant for him: *"In Study, Stay-At-Home Fatherhood Leads to Loss of Testosterone."*

Finn grimaced. He looked at Bo, who at that point wore only the faintest trace of a smile.

"Fuck you," Finn said to the security guard.

Bo burst into a great grin. "From what *The Times* says, it doesn't sound like you have enough lead in your pencil."

Just then voices were raised near the largest bank of electrical outlets. A twenty-something girl was arguing with a thirty-something guy about who most deserved to plug his or her iPhone into the single remaining unclaimed outlet.

"Uh-oh," Bo said, nodding to Finn, "Gotta' go. Possible slap fight in Quadrant Four."

Then he strolled away towards the feuding and entitled young Americans, an obvious lack of urgency in his step: After all, it wasn't exactly the crime of the century Bo was off to investigate. Finn, meanwhile, was left to study the *Times* article boldly emasculating him for the viewing pleasure of its many readers: *"In Study, Stay-At-Home Fatherhood Leads to Loss of Testosterone."*

The article, in a nutshell, said that the stay-at-home dad Finn lacked nuts. He had no balls. No cojones. He couldn't get a hard-on, in effect, claiming— or rather claiming scientific proof of the fact— that the more time a man spent with his offspring the less testosterone his body produced. The less of a man he was, basically. The article offered caveats, of course, and excuses too, saying that that lack of testosterone wasn't necessarily a bad thing: Maybe it made those men even better fathers, the article said. It might have made them more attentive parents or better nurturers, in fact.

Finn didn't buy it though. There was no interpretation of "less testosterone" that he was reading as a good thing. He looked around the atrium. Could people see the article he was reading, he wondered? Did they know he was a stay-at-home dad? Did they too think he was impotent?

Finn sighed. He knew Bo had just been joking with him; he knew that Bo didn't think he wasn't a real man. He got the feeling, in fact, that the ex-cop might well have respected Finn for taking care of his family the way he did. But, seriously, Finn wondered, looking down at the newspaper article that questioned his very masculinity in front of millions of readers, was there no end to the insults, the slights, the affronts? Would they never stop?

Not that day they wouldn't, that was for sure. For the next couple of hours Finn worked diligently away at the small job he despised, a chore he reviled but couldn't refuse: writing content for K-12 standardized tests, that being the last tiny bit of work he could get from an industry that had employed him for twenty-odd years but that he'd then publicly condemned in a *New York Times* op-ed piece. Finn really hated the work, for myriad reasons: First, he was philosophically against the idea of massive, multinational, for-profit companies making important decisions about American schools, of course. Second, he was disgusted with the pittance he was being paid to do the job, in effect about a tenth as much as he used to get before he become *persona non grata* to almost everyone in the business. And third, he couldn't believe after publicly quitting the testing industry in such spectacular fashion he was then forced to go crawling right back to it when his wife got sick, begging everyone he knew to forgive his dramatic lil' public condemnation of the industry and please throw him whatever scraps they could. For the most part his former colleagues didn't forgive him— or even answer his phone messages/e-mails, for that matter— although one or two solid friends did mercifully throw him a pathetic bone or two.

Really hating the work, however, Finn kept at it because his family needed the money. Plus, what else could he do? Burn shit down? Jump off a bridge?

The work that day, however, was not even the worst of it for Finn. Far from it, in fact. Around lunch-time he forced his way through the packed tables and chairs to visit the loo, but then when trying to make his way back to his surrounded table Finn was aghast to see coming through the atrium's Broadway entrance a parade of men pushing strollers: Mary and the Pips! Finn panicked, shoving his way through the remaining packed tables of elderly and homeless between himself and his own spot before he grabbed his laptop and planned his escape. A quick look about, however, revealed the sad fact that Finn had nowhere to go: He was surrounded. The atrium had only two entrances, one from the east and one the west, and while the parade of men with strollers were coming from the Broadway side a tour bus worth of squealing teenagers on cell phones was pouring in from Columbus. Finn was trapped. There was no escape from the approaching Mary and the Pips.

Finn's shoulders slumped in inglorious defeat, but before he surrendered completely he had an inspired idea. Nodding towards Bo, who just happened to be looking right at him from the security desk, Finn grabbed his laptop bag and dropped to the floor. He threw his things under his now empty table and scooched under there with them, pulling the chair he had been sitting on and two others behind him as a barricade to the outside world.

Finn knew he might look ridiculous, but he didn't care. He knew that someone might see the empty top of his table and attempt to sit there, thus discovering the huddled Finn below, but he still didn't care. Finn didn't really care about anything at that point other than avoiding Mary and the Pips. He'd suffered enough already.

"Mary and the Pips" were what Finn called the Gotham Stay-At-Home-Dads (SAHD) Club, an organization he'd had the misfortune of briefly being a part a couple years before. Danielle had suggested Finn join as a means to help the Prince make friends and a way for Finn to hang out with what his wife assumed would be a bunch of "like-minded guys." Danielle, however, had been wrong, Finn came to find out. Very, very wrong, in fact, as Finn realized he was far from simpatico with that bunch of humorless guys he thought of not as SAHD dads but "sad dads." As far as Finn could tell, the primary purpose of the Gotham Stay-At-Home-Dads Club was not for either the kids or their fathers to socialize but instead as some sort of civil rights organization, a group that seemed to imagine themselves a collection of idealistic do-gooders heroically fighting for the rights of those poor men who were stuck at home masturbating to Internet porn each day as their kids napped and their wives toiled away at the office (Finn shouldn't stereotype, he knew, but based on a sample size of one that was his general understanding of stay-at-home dadding).

As far as Finn could tell, Gerry— the earnest leader of the group who Finn thought of as "Mary," much the same way some bitter days he thought of himself as "Lynn"— and his minions believed the stay-at-home dads of the world were being sorely, sorely mistreated by American society, and that was a blatant injustice those freedom fighters did not intend to let stand. They "had a dream" basically: A dream that one day men could push baby-strollers through the streets without being stigmatized (polite applause); a dream that one day diaper-changing stations would be found not only in women's public restrooms but also *men's* ("huzzah!"); a dream that one day men could, as women were already given the right to, breastfeed in public (yes, that one might have been complicated, but Finn imagined it was only a matter of time before Mary and the Pips appeared in front of him wearing some sort of jerry-rigged male milkers which allowed the fellows to deliver breast juice to their kiddies the way the Grampa DeNiro did in one of those *Focker* movies). In fact, it was because of this group's extra-vigilant vigilance regarding the rights of stay-at-home fathers that a national boycott of Huggies diapers had been levied the previous year, what with the incredibly insulting TV ad that the heartless, small-minded, discriminatory company had run implying men sometimes didn't change their kids' diapers soon enough because they too often got caught up "watching the game."

Blasphemy, Mary and the Pips screamed when the ad first came out. Sacrilege! An affront! It was making Rosa Parks sit in the back of the bus all over again!

Finn never actually saw the ad run, but he couldn't imagine it would insult him. No diaper company could insult him regarding his fate in the world any more than he already regularly insulted himself. Finn was not, in other words, a particularly militant stay-at-home dad: He could change a diaper with the best of them— he just didn't feel the need to proclaim it from the mountaintop.

In fact, Finn thought, the fewer people who knew about his plight the better. That was why he hadn't participated in the Huggies boycott— well, he'd not bought any Huggies, that was true, but only because he preferred Pampers— and why he continued to ignore Gerry's continual e-mail requests to join the organization at their various play dates, picnics, marches and protests. It was why he'd ignored Gerry's most recent e-mail entreaty begging Finn to join that very day's stroller parade as it made its way to the TV studio on Manhattan's west side, where the Gotham SAHD club would be featured on an episode of "The Wendy Williams Show." Gerry had written that he really hoped Finn would not only join the stroller parade but that he would anchor it.

Sure, Finn thought. Let me be the caboose to your little stroller train. The ass of it maybe. Or, really, he thought, the ass-hole.

Finn's decision to officially break ties with Mary and the Pips occurred after what he called The Incident. It happened one morn when the Gotham SAHD club was having a mass play-date in the playroom of a new building in Morningside Heights where one of the group's dads lived, all the fathers and their children loitering about on the floor in the middle of that day playing with plastic toys or drawing with colorful crayons. It was only a couple months after Finn had started hanging with the group, but he already had his doubts: Their ridiculous tendency towards political protest had already become abundantly clear (how soon before some splinter group broke off from the Gotham SAHDs to fight the particular horrors of being a Caucasian SAHD, Finn wondered? It was only a matter of time, he thought. Only a matter of time...). Finn also couldn't help but notice the guys' only mild interest in the upcoming Super Bowl. Who were these dudes, he thought?

But it all went south for Finn— real south, and real fast— that morning when one of the fathers was describing the dinner he'd made for his family the night before, a delicious-sounding quiche whose contents the dad said included serrano ham and gruyere cheese. Mmm-mmm, Finn thought! Sounded scrumptious, he thought.

So Finn said— and he regretted the words the *second* he blurted them out— to the father/cook, "You'll have to give me the recipe."

For Finn, time stopped. Silently, he gasped. He couldn't believe the words he'd just uttered. "You'll have to give me the recipe"? Like he was some 1950s housewife in an apron talking to a neighbor over the back fence?

Finn felt sick to his stomach. He felt faint. His equilibrium was lost, his balance shot. Finn's very understanding of who he was hung by a thread. "You'll have to give me the recipe"? Finn had never regretted any words so much.

Even more surprising was the response Finn's horrifying question engendered.

"Of course," the father/cook replied, "I'll e-mail it to you."

And that was it. Not another word was said by anyone in the group. As a whole the Gotham SAHD Club acted as if a man asking another man for a recipe— when neither of them was a chef, mind you!— was not only acceptable, it was unremarkable. As in, it didn't need to be remarked upon!?!

Finn couldn't believe it. He shuddered to think what would have happened had he asked most of the men he knew— his many old soccer teammates, for instance, or his brothers, or bar friends like Boogie and Don, or the security guard Bo even— for their quiche recipe. For their *quiche recipe*! Lordie, the ribbing that would have ensued! The questions about his sexuality that would have rained down!

When not a single such word was uttered by the members of the Gotham SAHD Club, however, Finn knew he was done with them. Those men— nice guys, every one, as far as Finn could tell, and universally good parents to their children— were simply not the kind of guys Finn wanted to hang out with. They weren't the kind of guys he wanted his Prince to be raised around. Finn couldn't explain it exactly— what, he liked the sort of guys who regularly teased him, belittled him, challenged his manhood?— but from that point forward Finn & the Prince travelled the island of Manhattan by themselves, a couple of lone wolves making new friends at new playgrounds every day.

From the point of The Incident forward, Finn ignored the e-mails from Mary and the Pips and avoided their get-togethers, too, which is how he found himself hiding under a table in the David Rubinstein Atrium that Wednesday morning. Not surprisingly, however, as Finn huddled in shamed silence a pair of black shoes and blue slacks soon appeared next to the table he was hunkered below.

"Sir," the bemused voice of Bo could be heard.

Finn ignored him. Did his pal really need to needle him right then?

He did.

"Sir," Bo continued, "I'm sorry but no sleeping in the atrium."

Finn stuck his head out just enough to see the security guard's face but not far enough to be seen by anyone like Mary and the Pips.

"Fuck off," Finn mouthed silently at him.

"You got problems, man," Bo laughed, an assertion Finn simply shrugged at before leaning further back under the table.

For the next minute Bo straightened the tables and chairs in the area near where Finn hid. When he returned he leaned down to look Finn in the face.

"The dudes with strollers?" Bo asked.

"Yup."

"They're gone." He held out a hand.

Finn took the hand. He stood up and straightened himself out. He put his laptop and bag on top of the table again.

"What was up with that?" Bo asked.

"Stay-at-home dads group my wife wanted me to hang with."

"Oh?"

"They didn't have any problem with me asking another man for a quiche recipe."

Bo shuddered. He literally shuddered. "Oooh," he said.

Finn smiled. Bo understood.

For the one brief moment of Bo's understanding reaction Finn thought his day had taken a turn for the better, but that shining light of hope was brief indeed: No sooner had Finn watched the last of Mary and the Pips exit the atrium on to Columbus than he saw a new parade of strollers entering through the same door, each of those baby conveyances being pushing by a fit woman in workout gear, each of those women doing some sort of hybrid calisthenics as they pushed, a whole lot of high leg kicks and deep knee bends and reaching for the sky with their tight lil' arms as they went.

Finn couldn't believe it. He thought he might be sick. Could his day get any worse, Finn wondered? So with no other choice, Finn did the only thing he could: He turned to pick up his things from the table, looked Bo square in the eye, and nodded at him.

"If you'll excuse me," Finn said politely, before dropping again to the cold, hard floor of the atrium. He scooched under his table a second time and pulled the chairs back in, returning to the cave of shame from which he'd just been so briefly released.

There were things Finn was embarrassed of in his life, no short list of them really. The incident with Janie Flynn haunted him still. The failed penalty kick remained an albatross around his neck. Paying for sex with prostitutes in Paris and Amsterdam, Bangkok and Tokyo was nothing to be proud of. And a love affair with a married, pregnant woman hadn't exactly been something to write home about. But of all the humiliating moments in his life, all the ignominies, the only one that really made him cringe, the one he could barely bring himself to think about, was Strollercize class.

The whole thing had been Danielle's idea, of course.

"You should take a Strollercize class," she'd foolishly said when Finn had first taken on the role of stay-at-home dad. "You push the baby in the stroller while working out in the Park. Ivy said it was fun and good exercise."

Finn, never the smartest guy to begin with, then immediately imagined a half-naked Ivy, clad only in the tiniest tight workout gear, stretching on Poet's Walk, her spectacular ass perhaps up in the air or bent over a bench in some sort of erotic athletic pose— and next thing Finn knew he was signed up for Strollercize class. While it probably needn't be said, he was the only man so enrolled.

When Danielle later asked Finn how things had gone after his first (only) Strollercize class, Finn declined to answer. He waved his hands at her, shaking his head repeatedly, saying only "no, no, no, no, no, no..." When Danielle insisted, Finn refused. He was adamant. He would not talk about it, he said. He vowed never to talk about it, in fact, so what exactly happened that afternoon somewhere between the Boathouse and Belvedere Castle and the Great Lawn would always remain a mystery to Danielle. It might have been the only secret Finn ever kept from her.

Bo sat at the chair closest to Finn. "The women with the strollers?" he asked.

"Yup" came Finn's disembodied answer from below the table.

"An exercise class?"

"Yup."

"Don't tell me you are in that class."

"No comment."

"Don't tell me you were ever in that class!"

"Not talking about it," Finn said.

"Do *not* tell me you were in that class!"

"Not anymore."

"What, you couldn't keep up?" Surely Bo said it as a joke.

Finn leaned forward from his sitting position and met Bo's gaze. He shrugged and patted his beer belly. "Not anymore," he said.

Bo offered a bemused smile. "Wait," he asked, cocking his head at Finn, "are you certain you're really a man?"

Finn leaned his body back against the metal support that held up the table he was hiding under. He closed his eyes and smiled a rueful smile.

"I was," he said. "I'm quite certain I used to be."

Strike Three (1985-2009)

"I'm Jack Kerouac"?

Yeah, yeah, because Finn had always fancied himself a writer, of course. Maybe even a "Writer" with a capital W. (Had Finn's literary aspirations not yet been made clear to the reader? Even with all the man's solipsism? His self-aggrandizement? His blaming of others for all his problems and his lack of a real job? His predilection for prostitutes and drink? Your Omniscient Narrator thought it was all so obvious.)

But it was true. Finn thought of himself not only as a writer but likely a literary lion: He saw himself as Hemingway reborn; Henry Miller redux; Bukowski reincarnated. Mostly, however, young Finn saw himself as the second coming of Jack Kerouac. He thought the similarities between them were eerie: Both were men; both were men who liked cats (!); both were New Englanders; and both were thwarted jocks (Kerouac forever disappointed an unsympathetic coach had kept him from becoming the Columbia football star he believed he should have been, while Finn blamed someone—anyone other than himself, really— for his not turning into the soccer icon he felt destined to be).

Plus, when feeling rotten about himself Finn even noted that he and Kerouac shared certain negative characteristics as well: Both drank too much; both weren't that good with women; and both were bad parents (Finn clearly not as bad as the s.o.b. Jack, of course, who refused to even acknowledge his only daughter's existence for the first nine years of her life, but there were still occasions— like the recent morning the pissy Finn yelled at his innocent Prince—

that Finn couldn't help but see the ugly parental resemblance between he and Jack).

But other than the outward similarities, did Finn have any reason to see himself as another Kerouac? Between his early twenties and his death (of drink) at age 47, Jack Kerouac produced an entire oeuvre, basically a whole new genre of confessional-spontaneous-spiritual-sexual-soul-searching works, not to mention a seminal piece of American Literature in *On The Road*, a novel that many read as the voice of an entire generation. Between *his* late teens and middle forties, on the other hand, Finn Riley had written one well-received personal essay for a college composition course and had a short op-ed published in *The New York Times*.

It wasn't the same, Finn could admit, but neither did it seem so far apart to him: Ballpark, Finn figured. Six of one, half a dozen of the other, really, as far as our hero was concerned.

Finn's unwavering belief in his own literary genius resulted from that one well-received personal essay. It had been 1985 and Finn a freshman at a Montreal university when the essay he wrote about "home"— about his parents' general store in his tiny Maine hometown, all flowers-in-the-flowerboxes and warped, wooden floors and his mother's traditional Christmas cookies, it was— had wowed the class: When he had finished reading it aloud various co-eds looked at him anew, now suddenly all googly-eyed, while his professor (the man once an editor at *The Montreal Gazette*) showered Finn's work with praise and later told Finn that he expected to see him "in print."

That single phrase— "I expect to see you in print"— kept Finn going for the next twenty-five years or so. It was like a shiny gold nugget he held in his pocket, to be pulled out and caressed and studied whenever he felt down. It made him think— regardless of what shitty place he lived or crappy job he worked or half-assed relationship he was in— that, no matter what, Finn was destined for something bigger. He had an ace in the hole: "I expect to see you in print," the professor

had said (and the man once an editor at *The Montreal Gazette*). That short phrase— seven simple words— confirmed
Finn's belief in his own importance, uniqueness, and overall
wonderfulness and conferred upon him what Finn believed
to be the mantle of greatness.

So did Finn do anything with his extant talent? With
all that promise and belief and expectation? Not immediately. Immediately following his college graduation Finn
went with a friend to Europe, in about three months blowing
(on beer and baguettes, train tickets and hookers) the five
grand his mother and father had just given him (weren't the
Pilgrim Parents proud of that investment! Weren't they
proud!). With his trip to the Continent over, however, and no
job having miraculously arrived on his doorstep, no literary
agent chasing him down or publishing house offering a book
deal based on promise alone, Finn found himself in the early
1990s living back in Maine, bunking down in his childhood
home with his childhood parents, the young man having par-
layed four years of city living in cosmopolitan Montreal and
a bachelor's degree in English (his, uh, native tongue) into
the very job he'd had before going off to college, running the
cash register at his parent's general store (a proper Horatio
Alger tale it was!).

Four unsatisfying years in Maine later— Finn couldn't
exactly remember what happened during that time, although
he vaguely recalled a girlfriend he didn't much care for, lots
of tennis-playing with the bunch of middle-aged hacks who
lived in the area, and a great deal of liberally helping himself to the free (for him) contents of the general store's walk-
in beer cooler— Finn decided to move to Iowa. Iowa City,
Iowa, in fact, home to the University of Iowa and its famed
Writer's Workshop.

Finn wasn't going to the Workshop per se, because he'd
not even applied to it. Still, he knew he had to get out of
Maine, because by Year Four living there post-college every
time he drove by the big oak tree outside his parent's general
store Finn had to remind himself not to swerve directly into

it— it was like that John Irving novel, *The Hotel New Hampshire*, when those morose brother and sister characters with suicidal tendencies had to constantly remind each other not to throw themselves from the top floor of the building where they lived.

"Keep passing those open windows," the sad siblings regularly warned each other.

"And don't smash your VW head-on into that fat tree," Finn had to tell himself every day in Maine, which was about when he knew it was time to go.

Finn figured in Iowa City he'd get around to applying to the Writer's Workshop, but it never really happened. He figured he'd have to write something extraordinary to get in but he never really did. In fact, he didn't really even try, our young Finn apparently subconsciously adhering to that old saw that trying and failing might be worse than not trying at all.

Still, Finn did have a great first sentence for a novel, that he knew: "*Young Shawn was shackled with a crushing ennui.*"

That great first sentence was as far as he ever made it with the book though. Finn knew what the novel would be about— the trials and tribulations of a protagonist who although young and white and male and American and healthy and well-off and attractive and athletic and talented and loved still never felt completely, you know, *satisfied* with his life— but even he was willing to admit the tome might be missing something. The real meat of the book, as he imagined it, was the struggle of "*Young Shawn*" to overcome the cross he had to bear— that being the "*crushing ennui*" of modern American life, remember— but it seemed to Finn that maybe that wasn't *quite* enough for a whole novel. Maybe it was more of a novella, he thought, but in any case Finn never wrote much more.

Instead for more than a decade he enjoyed the leisurely life of an Iowa City townie, playing soccer and reading books and drinking beer and chasing but mostly not catching all the pretty co-eds abounding about town. He worked a litany of sad little jobs, the bunch of them the likes of which would have made Charles Bukowski proud: file clerk, bar back, census-taker, test-scorer. He had the same interest in all of them (that being none at all), but through no fault of his own it was that last job as a scorer of student standardized tests that became young Finn's "career."

From Day One he hated the job, mostly because he was philosophically against standardized testing: It lacked "humanity," he thought. Philosophical stance or not, however, Finn did manage to work in the testing industry for the next twenty years or so. At first he did it because that simple-if-tedious job supported his Iowa City life, paying the rent and keeping Finn flush in paperbacks from Prairie Lights bookstore, pizza from Pagliai's, and pints (or, really, pitchers) of Joe's Place beer. He continued to do it because— again through no fault of his own— Finn found himself getting promoted again and again, with those promotions then coming more and more money and, even better, more and more cool business trips.

For years he spent months at a time on the road opening up corporate test-scoring centers, living on expense accounts as he spent long spells in hotels in Detroit and Tucson, Minneapolis and Albuquerque, Seattle and Jacksonville, Chicago and Phoenix... With the passage of time those standardized tests became more and more important and the work he was doing more and more dubious (if not downright corrupt) but, still, Finn kept at it, at least for another quick decade or so.

Why not, he thought? He had nothing better to do. It was a job. It paid the bills. It was not illegal.

But was Finn happy about his career choice? Not so much. Was he glad to have forgone the literary path he wanted to follow, instead taking up a job whose few merits included the fact it was "not illegal"? Nope. Was he thrilled to be making a living in an industry that he wholeheartedly believed had no right sticking its ugly corporate nose into the business of educating the country's kids? Nuh-uh. Was he proud of himself? Far from it.

Still, the disappointment Finn felt in himself was fighting a losing battle with the rewards the gig offered, that being money (lots and lots of money) and travel. Finn loved to travel, especially on someone else's dime, loved seeing new places and eating at new restaurants and meeting new people/women. Whenever his niggling disillusionment tried to climb its way out of his kvetchy gut, in other words, Finn was normally able to choke it right back down, mostly with the help of free martinis (Grey Goose, straight up, olives) and gratis slabs of steak (not to mention the company of random pretty women, who Finn discovered weren't that hard to come by when living the carefree life of the business traveler).

Looking back at those years then, Finn didn't necessarily recall his disenchantment with himself as much as a million good memories, the sort of recollections that would have filled up the pages of his diary if Finn was the sort of guy to keep a diary: In Tucson, driving through the saguaro cacti of the hot and dry Sonoran desert before a long climb up Mt. Lemon, there enjoying a quick view of its snowy slopes before idling the day away sipping gin & tonics in the ski lodge's piney bar; in Florida noshing on alligator bites and in Arizona snacking on rattlesnake; in Detroit drinking altogether too much Maker's Mark with another of his swank downtown hotel's random guests, that being the Kangol-clad Hollywood superstar Samuel L. Jackson, a guy whose voice and laugh, Finn discovered, became ever more delightful the more bourbon one drank; in Minneapolis one evening eating a brook trout for dinner only after yanking it from the well-stocked stream coursing through a section of the floorboards of the restaurant's dining room; in Chicago bedding a busty co-worker who agreed to Finn's lascivious proposition only when he agreed to impregnate her (!) *in the future* if— on the off-chance, she said— neither she nor he were married and happy by the time they were 35, a vow Finn bravely if insincerely made that night mostly because he was well into his cups (Maker's Mark again the culprit that evening) and also because he figured it highly unlikely he'd even know the woman five years hence, when her scary, scary 35th birthday would be looming.

And then it was 2009, Finn having half-heartedly "pursued" a career path that moved him from his Shangri-La of Iowa City first to Austin, Texas, then to Princeton, New Jersey and finally to New York City . Finn had been at it for about twenty years, that job he didn't much care for, working in an industry he was philosophically against, and though he had tried to quit many a time he always kept going right back. The money was always too good, the travel too much fun, the women too easy to come by. It was like the gag Silvio liked to play on *The Sopranos*, when that fictional mobster impersonated another fictional mobster, Michael Corleone, who in *The Godfather 3* famously bemoaned the difficulty he faced in escaping his station as mafia don.

"Just when I think I'm out," Silvio would say as Michael, "they pull me back in."

And every time Finn tried to quit, they'd pull him back in.

"Would you be interested in a couple months work in _____," someone might ask, and next thing he knew Finn was flying out first-class, supping on T-bone steaks at Cattleman's Steakhouse in Oklahoma City; or slurping down fresh, local oysters at the Seattle Public Market; or sucking down cold bottles of Dos Equis beer at the bar of Tucson's Hotel Congress.

But by 2009, Finn had had enough. Enough, he thought! It was time to get back to his real job— his passion, even— that being his calling as a "***Writer.***" By then Finn even had what he was quite sure was a great second sentence for his novel: "*The cross young Shawn had to bear also doubled as a credit card.*"

Perhaps hard to understand out of context, Finn was nonetheless certain the sentence worked, its complicated meaning somehow alluding to the fact that the cross "*young*

Shawn" had to bear— that being his plight as a young and white and male and American and healthy and well-off and attractive and athletic and talented and loved human being, you'll recall, a station in the world that nonetheless made it hard for him to ever, you remember, be completely *satisfied*— also meant the guy could pretty much never go hungry: The world was too obviously tilted in his favor.

Subtle, Finn thought! Complex even. Mature. He was really on to something big, Finn knew. The novel was beginning to pick up steam!

("Bullshit" your Omniscient Narrator wanted to cough. "Bullshit!" Just how long was this book going to take to write?)

So in order to really cut his ties with the testing industry— to blow up all those bridges, in fact— Finn went rogue. He quickly penned one day an editorial highlighting the utter folly of entrusting decisions about American public schools to a for-profit industry and e-mailed it off to *The New York Times*. Two days later *The Times* agreed to publish Finn's first real writing effort in about twenty-five years, and the next week he saw himself "in print" for the first time on the editorial pages of perhaps the most famous newspaper in the world. Finn wondered if maybe his old writing professor saw the op-ed, but he had his doubts: The man lived in a foreign country after all, not to mention the fact he'd already been a senior citizen when he taught Finn's freshman comp class more than two decades before. Whatever high hopes the guy (a former editor of *The Montreal Gazette* he was, remember!) might have had for Finn ending up "in print," he'd probably taken them straight to the grave.

For Finn, however, that first great writing success was bittersweet. He was proud, yes, but also pained. To begin with, he knew his public excoriation of the testing industry really did mean it was the end for him: Sure, he was philosophically against testing, but not working in the industry any more also meant no more corporate junkets, no more free first-class travel or expense-accounted fine dining or long stays in luxury hotels. It meant meeting no more pretty women in dark hotel bars. Finn might have wanted to pretend he didn't care, but he knew he would miss it.

Worse, however, about "finally" getting published was that it proved what Finn might have known all along: That he really did have what it took to be a writer. That he actually had wasted all those years in standardized testing just because he wasn't willing to take a chance at prose. That he truly was a trifecta of fucked-up, having maybe blown his dream of writing for a living (the guy *was* well into his forties already) the way he'd formerly blown his chance at loving Janie Flynn and blown his chance at becoming a soccer star.

Yeah, you couldn't have convinced the man otherwise: When it came to the three things he'd wanted most in the world, our young hero absolutely believed in his heart of hearts that the mighty Finn had struck out.

East Village Parents Unite!
(Wednesday Eve, 2013)

Before he could wreak any vengeance, the Curmudgeon Avenger had to make dinner.

After spending the better part of the day working at the atrium— and after suffering the indignity of hiding under a table from the successive embarrassments of first Mary and the Pips and then the Strollercize class— Finn raced to his son's pre-school at 3:00 pm because he really missed his Prince. For all the public humiliations Finn imagined he suffered as a stay-at-home dad, he was still never so stupid as not to know what a joy it was to be with his little boy. So many of their days together— at Central Park and the High Line and Tompkins Square— were about nothing other than shared snacks and learning to climb ladders and racing down slides and chasing each other in circles. They were nothing but adventures. Nothing but fun. Nothing but laughter. Nothing but love. And Finn knew no one had ever loved him the way his son loved him. He knew he had never loved any-one— though he might have kept this little tidbit from Danielle— the way he loved his Prince of New York.

"My boy!" Finn smiled at the pre-school door, grabbing the Prince and smothering him with kisses before bench-pressing him up and down in the air in what Finn called his "Daddy Elevator of Love."

"What should we do today?" Finn asked, breathing heavily but almost certain of the answer.

"Ice cream!" the boy squealed, exactly as his father expected.

So Finn strapped his son into the stroller and took him on a tour of all his favorite places, starting with the ice cream truck always parked by the great globe outside the Trump Hotel & Tower at Columbus Circle. Finn was serious about his son's eating habits, so he made sure the Prince ate a wholesome snack of organic raisins and unsalted cashews before they arrived for their pre-dinner (gasp!) dessert, but there he then bought the cones they each always had: chocolate ice cream with chocolate sprinkles for the father, vanilla ice cream with rainbow sprinkles for the son. As much as his father always feigned horror at the idea, the Prince then pressed his cone into Finn's, delighted to see the ice cream and sprinkles from each ending up smushed on the other.

"Oh no!" Finn gasped.

"Ha!" the Prince laughed, happy as ever to get some of his father's chocolate on his vanilla cone.

Next they went into the Time Warner Center to visit the two huge statues there, bronze replicas of a portly naked bald man ("Daddy" the Prince always laughed) and, fifty yards away, a phat-assed naked woman ("Mommy!" he giggled). Heading homewards they visited the lobby of the Dream Hotel on 55th street, the doorman making way just as soon as he saw them turn the corner at Broadway because he knew where they were headed, father and son making almost daily stops there to view the huge, tubular aquarium reaching from the floor of the hotel's lobby all the way to its ceiling, Finn liking to push his son round and round that watery cylinder as they followed various colorful tropical fish on their ceaseless circular circuits of that marine habitat. Then they made a point of passing the Carnegie Deli on 7th Avenue, not to join the line of suckers queued up there to pay $29 for a pastrami sandwich as much as to stare at the huuuuuuuuuuge cheesecake always placed in the front window, a dessert option the Prince had not yet tried but that he hoped one day to enjoy.

"There it is, Daddy!" he yelled, lasciviously eyeing that luscious cake. "Is today the day?"

"Soon, son," Finn said, nodding his head up and down. "Soon....."

At the Albemarle's front door they were met by Lawrence, not to mention his usual inane question— "Daddy day?"— a query which Finn simply ignored that afternoon because he was in a hurry: The Curmudgeon Avenger had places to be.

In Apartment 2A, Finn quickly diced up a fruit salad of apples*, pears*, strawberries*, and bananas* (* all organic, of course, every single piece of that fruit); steamed some broccoli (which, quite miraculously, just happened to be one of the Prince's favorite foods); and then whipped up one of his favorite recipes, chopping chives*, mincing tomato*, slicing goat cheese* and frying up Sunday morning bacon* (* yeah, yeah, we know, Finn, all of it was *organic*), before mixing it all together and beginning to bake it with eggs into what Finn liked to think of as his "world famous" quiche.

His *what*, you might be thinking?!? A *quiche*, you might be thinking?!? *Finn*???

Oh, yes, Finn loved a good quiche. *Loved* one. The dish was one of his favorites, frankly, and he made it for his family about once a week. Why not quiche, Finn thought? Its merits were myriad: a nice eggy quiche was delicious; it was relatively healthy, too, especially when filled with vegetables and constructed of certain* ingredients; plus, the food was also easy to handle, meaning the father could pack a slice into his son's lunchbox the next day and be certain his boy was enjoying a healthy meal at school. Yes, there were many, many reasons an earnest father might make such a meal for his family.

But, no, no, Finn might not have necessarily wanted to advertise his fondness for the food— he didn't feel the need to romp around Midtown Manhattan, for instance, announcing to the world that he'd just been draped in an apron, slaving in the kitchen over a hot stove while he whipped up a lil' ole *quiche*, for example— but neither was the stigma of the dish so strong that it would keep Finn from serving such a fine, fortifying meal to his family. If his wife and son wanted a nice quiche for dinner, in other words, Finn would give them a god-damned quiche, thank you very much, regardless of that entrée's emasculating reputation or not!

No one put Finny in the corner, in other words! No one kept Finny from doing what was best for his family!! No one at all!!!

Not even himself.

Over dinner Finn gently reminded Danielle that she'd agreed to bathe and bed the Prince again that night so that he could go downtown, and though she claimed not to remember any such agreement— okay, Finn would admit it, he'd slyly coaxed his wife's acceptance out of her the night before only when she was in a sleepy stupor of foot-rubbing delight— Danielle still assented. In the years of her cancer battle, Finn had spent most days taking care of the house and family and most nights sitting on the couch, blankly watching TV with a can (or two) ((or three)) of 24 oz. Coors Light, so Danielle had no problem with Finn's sudden interest in going out. Finn's dedication to his family was well-established, and his return unquestioned, so Danielle didn't mind if her husband might have suddenly wanted to blow off a little steam. She seemed even a little amused by it, although "perplexed" may have been a better word to describe her feelings that night when the wife saw her husband heading to the front door in an outfit that was, at least for him, a total anomaly: brown dress shoes, khaki slacks held up by a struggling brown belt, a button-down blue shirt and poorly-knotted yellow tie. Except for the shoes, the entire ensemble looked at least a size or two too small on the man.

"Job interview?" Danielle asked, knowing better.

"Not exactly."

Danielle waited.

"Duty calls" was all Finn said.

His wife smiled. "Righting more wrongs?"

Wasn't she something, Finn thought!

"Indeed."

Finn kissed his wife and son good-night— he kissed them a number of times each, in fact, alternating smooches between the two of them until both were laughing and giggling and telling him to stop— before heading off to his self-appointed appointment at the Earth School in the East Village. Finn had first become acquainted with the Earth School during the long period (2006-2008, let's say) before marriage and fatherhood when his life primarily entailed playing pick-up soccer at the fields on Chrystie Street and idling his time away at the bar of 7B.

Stretching from Fourth to Sixth Streets, the red brick Earth School stood only a block from 7B, and many afternoons from his barstool Finn saw through the open windows a parade of parents and children heading up and down Avenue B on their way to and from the school. At the time Finn had no thoughts about having his own children— neither wanting children nor not wanting them, frankly, as much as just never thinking about kids, not really being able to at that time because his own intense focus remained absolutely laser-like right then on just one thing, that of course being what was best for Finn, Finn, and only Finn— but he did like seeing the students going up and down the street. Children, he thought, and parents and old people, made a neighborhood whole.

While Finn knew of the Earth School before then, it was in 2008 that he really fell in love with the place. His ardor resulted, unfortunately, only after what was almost a terrible incident on the sidewalk outside the school, when one day a random sex offender who just happened to be passing by at the time of the last bell saw a child he liked the look of and made a haphazard grab, actually trying to haul the boy away. Fortunately the attempted abduction was unsuccessful, not because of anything our hero might have done— though Finn was only a block away at the time, sitting with a pint of Stella in hand and watching Manchester United play Champions League soccer— but because the Earth School parents who witnessed the event responded with a bit more, uh, "enthusiasm" than might have been expected from a progressive school community noted for its liberal leanings.

The Earth School had a reputation as one of the city's most touchy-feely public schools (the students had recess a couple times a day, studied art and music a couple times a week, grew vegetables in a rooftop garden and celebrated the equinoxes in front of the Hare Krishna tree in Tompkins Square Park), but when the mothers and fathers waiting to pick up their children from school that day saw the kinky kidnapper try to nab one of their kids, they responded less like peaceful revelers at a music festival than angry bikers knocking heads outside the Hell's Angel clubhouse just around the corner on 3rd street. They unleashed a tremendous ass-kicking on the guy, in other words, a brutal beat-down of his sad-sack ass.

To hear the *New York Post* tell it, as soon as the "beastly bastard" laid a hand on the child, the Earth School community responded with extreme prejudice, acting immediately, angrily, and en masse:

Karen Ramsay, a fifty-year old mother with hair bleached blonde, was first to act. When she heard the boy cry out, she knew the man who'd grabbed his arm was all wrong. Climbing atop the six-foot tall base of the flag pole where she was sitting with her son, Ramsay hurled herself through the air towards the sucky sex offender. Screaming, with her arms spread wide, and flying through the air, the woman was said to have been reminiscent of a comic book hero.

"She looked like Superman,'" said Mick Mullaley, a recently retired New York City firefighter who'd been headed to the Earth School that day to pick up his own kindergartener.

Though flexible, lithe, and strong from a lifetime of yoga, Ramsay weighs less than a hundred pounds, so when the flying banshee of a mother struck the pukey pe-dophile from the sky she didn't quite k.o. him. The graspy groper did at least lose his grip on the grabbed child though, who was instantly swept up by two other quick-thinking Earth School moms (one a curly-haired redhead who scoots to school with her three kids from the Finan-cial District each morning, the other a crew-cutted African-American from Brooklyn known for always tout-ing the benefits of "essential oils"), those two women sandwiching the child snugly between them in a maternal cocoon of protection and affection and rushing him back inside the safety of the Earth School's walls. When Ram-say lightly landed on the a-hole abductor he was only staggered, although after righting himself the cretinous creep's next step towards what he might have hoped was escape instead lead him directly into the firefighter Mul-laley's fist.

"It wasn't the best punch I've ever thrown, because I was holding my son in one arm and pushing the empty stroller with the other," Mullaley said. "I had to make a quick decision, so I let the stroller go and hit him smack in the nose with a right jab."

(Notably, and unfortunately, when Mullaley's empty stroller then rolled off the sidewalk and into the street it was immediately struck down by a passing Uber driver, an Uber driver who couldn't even be bothered to slow down, for that matter, as he coolly crushed flat the hero fireman's child conveyance and then sped away.

"God-damned Uber!" the ex-firefighter scowls. "I hate 'em. Their motto oughta' be 'Uber: When you want a ride but lack the balls to hail a cab...'")

Jab or no jab, Mullaley's punch in the nose was plenty powerful, spinning the stupid snatcher right back from where he came and into the path of Earth School PTA co-president Paulinho Ronaldo and his wife, Renee.

A professional chef who just happened that day to be carrying in her purse a heavy wooden spatula, Renee Ronaldo quick-drew that heavy wooden spatula like a gunfighter with a six-shooter and as swift as a mongoose lambasted the lurid lunatic directly on his cheek.

Ramsay winces when she recalls that blow.

"Oh, you know that hurt," she laughs with Mullaley. "Sounded like the worst slap you ever heard."

But at that point the foolish fiend's troubles with kitchen implements had only just begun, because as he wheeled away from Renee Ronaldo's wicked wooden whack the pathetic perv stepped directly into the sightline of Big Tim, everyone's favorite Earth School cooking teacher. Big Tim is a preternaturally tall man with a pate shaved clean, and while normally the mild-mannered type he did not take kindly to that debauched devil's attempt to steal away an Earth School student.

"Not cool" is all Big Tim says about the incident today. "Not cool."

Big Tim's disapproval of that lewd loser's lame attempt to snatch one of "my kids" was epitomized by the stunning blow he delivered, as the sick scumbag spinning away from Renee Ronaldo's spatula smackdown stepped directly into the path of the frying pan Big Tim wielded from on high.

"That thing looked like a friggin' UFO," PTA co-prez Ronaldo says of the black frying pan Big Tim just happened to have been carrying out of the school. "It was huge and dark and seemed to cover up the entire sky."

"And the sound it made…" Mullaley begins with awe in his voice.

"When it hit that sicko's head…" Ramsay continues, her eyes wide

"It was like Big Tim had rung the biggest gong there ever was…" Ronaldo finishes. *"I think they heard the pealing down on Grand Street."*

Big Tim's cast-iron k.o. leveled that vile villain, sending him sprawling onto the sidewalk while nearly knocking him out cold, at which point the entire Earth School community descended upon him, eliminating the possibility of the beastly bastard's escape by basically having a school gathering directly upon the obnoxious ogre's grotesque head. One Earth School father (a vaudeville magician called *"Cardone the Ultimate"*) held down the sick sex fiend's left arm, while one Earth School mother (a militant lesbian activist and infamous cable-news talking head) pinned down the right. An Italian photographer, a Puerto Rican parent coordinator, a Korean stay-at-home mom, an African-American school safety officer, and a West Indian nanny sat atop the moronic monster's chest and legs. A transgender woman who the year before had been a cross-dressing man sat on the sidewalk and hiked up her denim skirt far enough to wrap her powerful thighs around that idiotic imbecile's neck, maybe choking away his breath just a little bit, while a New Zealand-born United Nations aid worker with a daughter in kindergarten at the school held his two snarling Irish wolfhounds at bay (those dogs knew a freak when they saw one) while also loudly offering his own diplomatic advice on dealing with that weaselly whack-job.

"Git 'im by the balls," the Kiwi U.N. man was screaming, *"Git 'im by the balls."* (A phrase that is <u>not</u>, come to find out, <u>not</u> the official motto of the United Nations.)

By the time the authorities arrived, the crime scene was secure, the victimized child having been returned safely to his mother and the putrid perp delivered consciously (though just barely) to the police.

"I was never so proud of our school," Ramsay says. "When we were threatened, we came together as one, immediately and unquestionably, male and female, gay and straight, black and Asian and Hispanic and white."

"I just wish I'd hit him harder," Mullaley adds.

"I don't know what that guy thought he was getting into at the Earth School," PTA co-prez Ronaldo laughs. "But what he ended up finding was nothing but a rainbow coalition of revenge."

"*A rainbow coalition of revenge*"!!! Finn loved it! He loved the *New York Post,* for one thing, but from the sound of it he loved the Earth School, too. The place was diverse; cared about the things Finn would have cared about if he had a child (play, the arts, gardening, the seasons); and revealed a true tight bond of community. So by 2013, when Finn did have a child, his very own Prince of New York, he always knew exactly where he wanted the boy to go. Other parents at the city playgrounds may have been fretting about where to send their own kids to kindergarten, but Finn fretted not: He always knew his son was destined for the Earth School.

The problem was that by 2013 the Earth School was on the verge of being closed, or so Finn had recently read in a story in *The New York Post.* Apparently the school's administration was at odds with various governments— including each of the city, state, and federal ones, it seemed— because the decidedly progressive Earth School community was unwilling to force its students to follow certain government mandates. Which mandates, you might ask? The ones making it a requirement for all American students in grades 3-12 take a seemingly endless array of possibly-pointless but definitely-profitable *standardized tests.*

As if the hair on Finn's neck didn't stand up when he read those words!

"Blimey," he thought to himself when reading the offending phrase. "Hoisted on my own petard!"

The *Post* said the Earth School community had railed against the Department of Education requirements that its students needed to take those tests— they'd held angry protests and sang inspirational songs and wrote bitter op-eds, that is— but in the end their impassioned civil disobedience had proved largely fruitless. The school may have once been able to defend itself from a dissolute child molester, but in the face of mindless government officialdom and (let's be honest) the for-profit testing industry that had once enriched Finn, the Earth School was out of luck: Its kids *were* going to take those tests *or else*. The bureaucracy couldn't be beat, it seemed, and according to the *Post* a pallor had fallen over the school regarding its fate.

"It pretty much seems over," said a forlorn PTA co-President Paulinho Ronaldo. "I don't see how we can get out of this without some kind of miracle."

Fortunately for Ronaldo and the Earth School community, however, the Curmudgeon Avenger had just begun work in the business of miracles.

The Earth School's showdown with the Dept. of Ed.'s testing regime was occurring Thursday morn, when its students would either take or not take that disputed test, but that Wednesday evening before the school was coming together for a final protest/candlelight vigil/uprising at 7 p.m., a soiree the Curmudgeon Avenger had plans to attend— he'd not RSVP'ed but you couldn't keep the guy away.

Finn took the "E" train south from Midtown, then the "L" train east, before disembarking at First Avenue and 14th street to gear up at a local Duane Reade. The Curmudgeon Avenger believed in disguises, whether just an ineffable persona like the character of Satchel Paige that he'd donned to undertake his onslaught of that fuckin' lil' Funkiberry or the semi-official (if fully felonious) NYPD uniform he'd worn to illegally but righteously impersonate a New York City traffic cop. The purpose of the disguises were less to hide Finn's identity than just to offer him emotional support— to hide him from himself perhaps, as Finn was acting in a way that could otherwise be seen as very un-Finn-like— and that Wednesday eve was no different in that there was also a theme: Poindexter.

At the pharmacy Finn purchased the cheapest reading glasses he could find, a pair with plain, metal rims and small, rectangular frames; a roll of cloth Band-Aid tape; one black Sharpie magic marker with a thick-ish end; a packet of ten ballpoint pens; a clipboard and sheaf of lined, white paper; and one large bottle of Zippo lighter fluid. The pocket protector he'd been hoping for— it had been a long-shot, Finn knew that— was nowhere to be found, perhaps last sold in about 1982.

Finn first wrapped the middle of his new reading glasses with a thick layer of white cloth Band-Aid tape, not because they were damaged in any way but simply because he liked the look. Then from his pocket he pulled out the ID card he still had from his brief career as a low-level clerk in the NYC Department of Education's Office of Accountability. Finn took a single thin strip off the roll of white tape and placed it over the "Riley" on his old DOE ID card, with his Sharpie marker then inking in the thick, square letters C, H, E, and N where the R, I, L, E and Y had once been. "Finn Chen," the card would read.

The guy couldn't help himself: He thought it was funny!

Then Finn hiked up his khakis, tightened his belt, straightened his tie, donned his new (taped) glasses, hung the (doctored) ID card around his neck by its lanyard, placed the lined white paper on its clipboard, and lined up all ten ballpoint pens in the left breast pocket over his heart. The pocket protector would have been nice, of course, but it wouldn't necessarily be missed. Checking himself out in the bathroom mirror of the Duane Reade men's room, Finn liked what he saw: He looked like a nerd.

A nerd with a big bottle of lighter fluid in his back pocket admittedly, but a nerd nonetheless.

Hoping not to be recognized, Finn kept his head down when he passed 7B on the way to the Earth School— it wasn't exactly the time for another Boogie reunion, right?— and saw a large crowd gathered on its front steps. Hundreds of people there seemed to be, a commingled mass of every conceivable East Village and Earth School ilk: forty-something white guys wearing various types of jaunty headgear, their skulls bedazzled with every kind of creative facial hair design imaginable; grim-faced and steely-eyed Asian parents, the looks on their faces indicating a distrust of their Caucasian co-parents and their political protests nearly as powerful as their suspicion towards the New York City Department of Ed; thirty-something white women garbed in flowered dresses or peasant blouses or velvet pantaloons, their hands already clenched into fists of rage and their sing-songy voices fully prepared to chant; quiet African immigrant families and feisty local Puerto Rican ones; anarchist Brooklyn parents who'd come over the East River bridges fully ready to help the shit hit the fan.

It was nearly seven p.m. and dusk had fallen on Avenue B, but the crowd remained illuminated by the nearby streetlights and the small, white candles everyone held. Atop the steps in front of the school's entrance stood four people, who Finn guessed as the unidentified school principal plus Paulinho Ronaldo, Karen Ramsay, and the ex-firefighter Mick Mullaley. Finn knew nothing of the principal, simply assuming (correctly) that that's who the somber-looking woman was, but he remembered those other heroes from their pictures in the *New York Post* during their fifteen minutes of fame at the time of the 2008 attempted abduction/ass-kicking.

Finn was slightly star-struck by the sight of that tremendous trio and briefly even thought about hitting them up for autographs, but the Curmudgeon Avenger didn't have such time to dillydally. If there was one thing the Curmudgeon Avenger had learned, after all, it was that there is no time like the present.

To the left of the school's main steps was a ramp leaping down to a pair of open doors. It was from that door that the

Earth School's custodian normally dragged out the school's trash (which Finn knew from his time in the neighborhood), so it was down that ramp the Curmudgeon Avenger boldly went. Just before he entered the doors, however, out came the janitor, a youngish, barrel-chested African American man with a head full of dreads. When he first saw the khaki-clad, clipboard-wielding Curmudgeon Avenger, the man's eyes went wide— whether from guilt or surprise no one will ever know— before he calmed himself.

"Help you?" the custodian suspiciously said.

"Finn Chen," the Curmudgeon Avenger began, pointing abruptly to the NYC DOE ID card hanging around his neck. "I need to see the tests."

"The tests?"

"The tests, the tests," Finn replied, feigning impatience the way he imagined an obnoxious school administrator might. "Don't be coy here. The tests that have caused this mob to gather."

Finn nodded back at the crowd over his shoulder— all the while acting as if he owned the place and had every right to be there— before stepping around the janitor and passing straight through those possibly-verboten double doors. The man quietly followed.

"I'm from the Department of Education's Office of Accountability," Finn said to him (a place that really did exist), "the sub rosa sub-office of Internal Affairs." Finn wasn't exactly sure what "sub rosa" meant but thought it sounded good, while the rest of it was a bald-faced lie, anything to do with "internal affairs" being no more than a fiction Finn was able to come up with only because he'd watched altogether too many episodes of *Law & Order SVU.*

Finn tapped the DOE ID card hanging around his neck and slowly, confidently nodded his head up and down. "For security purposes, I need to see those tests."

When the custodian led him to a basement room and unlocked the padlocked door, Finn was surprised by what he found. When working at test scoring centers around the country, he'd always been entrusted with overseeing the scoring of hundreds of thousands of student tests, enough to pack full innumerable cardboard boxes and fill entire warehouse rooms to their ceilings. The Earth School storage room where the custodian led Finn, however, was completely empty except for two open cardboard boxes piled on one dolly. Poking through them Finn found the state tests that were to be administered the next day and their corresponding multiple-choice scoresheets. He was puzzled.

"How many students go to this school?" Finn asked.

"Uh, about 350, I think."

"Grades, what, k-6?"

"Yup."

"So probably a couple hundred in grades 3 and up taking these tests?"

"I guess," the custodian shrugged.

"And those are all the tests? All of them?"

"From what I was told..."

Finn was used to working with a much greater number of tests, so when he'd envisioned the night he'd expected more. He'd hoped for more fuel for his fire, so to speak, because the Curmudgeon Avenger had hoped his mission that night might not just spark a small revolution but that it would unleash a veritable conflagration of civil disobedience, an impassioned inferno of populist upheaval that might blaze across this great land and ultimately save America's glorious public schools and their brave students from the terribly tyranny of the god-forsaken, good-for-nothing, immoral, unethical, venal, vile and corrupt standardized testing industry that had so long employed Finn.

Grandiose, our Curmudgeon Avenger continued to be, in other words. Not one to think on a small scale was he.

"They'll have to do," Finn said, nodding one last time at the custodian, tapping the ID card hanging around his neck with a knowing smile, and then pushing out of that basement room the dolly with its two cardboard boxes of tests and score sheets. Finn pushed it through the basement, out the double doors, up the ramp and into the crowd. As he made his way towards the bottom of the steps in the front of the assembly, he could hear the principal begin to speak.

"When we started this school twenty years ago," she began, "the East Village was a different place. There were no Starbucks, no supermodels living in the neighborhood, no cupcake shops on every corner. What there was on every corner was drug dealers. And gangs. Crime. Empty crack vials up and down Avenue B."

The crowd buzzed in support and remembrance. Even Finn was nodding his head up and down, although in truth at the time of the Earth School's inception he'd been living in Iowa City, quite possibly the whitest and safest town there's ever been.

While still listening to the principal's speech, Finn carried the two boxes up to the top of the steps. He nodded confidently towards Ronaldo, Ramsay and Mullaley as he did so, and though those three had no idea who Finn was they assumed— given his assuredness, his shiny yellow tie, and what looked to be some sort of official ID card hanging around his neck— that the man belonged up there.

"When we started this school," the principal continued, "we hoped to provide a safe haven for the children of this neighborhood, a place where they could learn and grow in a loving environment away from the danger of these streets— "

She paused, obviously having a hard time controlling her emotions.

"— and when I think that there might not be an Earth School next year— "

Her struggles continued.

"— when I think this wonderful place that we've created out of such an unforgiving environment— "

Tears had begun to flow down her face.

"— might not be here next year— "

"No" people in the crowd were yelling. "Never!"

"— I just, I can't, I, I, I— "

The poor woman couldn't go on, beginning to sob uncontrollably, not knowing what to with herself until Mullaley, the ex-firefighter, came over to console her, hugging her as she bent her face into his shoulder.

The crowd was on the verge of turning ugly, Finn could tell. "Boo" they were yelling. "Shame!"

Because no one else was doing anything, the Curmudgeon Avenger thought he might. (Remember, no time like the present.) Nodding towards the unmoving Ronaldo and Ramsay, Finn stepped to the front of the steps. He held his two hands high in the air to quell the yells of the crowd.

"My name is Finn Chen," he said loudly but swiftly, stifling a smile while racing through the name due to its utter ridiculousness. "And I work in the New York City Department of Education's Office of Accountability."

"Boo!" came a yell from the back, some yutz in a fedora and goatee. "Boooooooo!"

"Boo!" others echoed. "Booooooooooo!"

"What's his name?" Finn heard someone on the right ask.

"Vincent, I think," answered a Puerto Rican abuela in the front row. "I think he said his name was Vincent."

Vincent, Finn guffawed to himself. *Vincent!* Sometimes the planets just align for you, he thought— and stifling a smile was beginning to become an almost impossible task.

"Where did he say he works?" someone else asked from the left.

"The office of counting," the abuela replied. The woman was beginning to swell up with pride: She had all the answers!

"It's Vincent from the office of counting" was thus the message that began to be relayed through the crowd. "Vincent from the office of counting" Finn heard over and over again. While he just barely managed to maintain a straight face, Finn couldn't recall the last time he'd had so much fun: *Vincent from the office of counting.*

"The guy's from the office of ACCOUNTABILITY," came the correction from another guy, this one all purdy in a beret and soul patch.

"That's the god-damned testing department!" muttered a third dude, himself resplendent in a coon-skinned cap and Van Dyke. "Boo to that!"

"Boooo!" the crowd echoed. "Booooooo!"

Finn glanced behind him to see that the initially confused looks worn by Ronaldo and Ramsay were becoming increasingly more distrustful and unpleasant, while the ex-firefighter Mullaley wore a mean mien that mostly implied he wanted to punch Finn right in the face.

Point of fact, Mullaley then leaned towards Ronaldo and Ramsay, nodded at Finn, and actually said "Should I punch him?"

Finn held a hand up towards the former fireman and quieted the crowd again.

"Yes, I'm Vincent from the Office of Accountability," he said with a smile, "which you could call the office of testing."

"Booooooo!" the crowd bellowed. "Shame!"

"We know that you have no interest in these standard-ized tests." With the brown dress shoe on his right foot Finn nudged the two cardboard boxes. When the crowd gleaned that the very tests that were threatening their school's exist-ence were right there, it turned even more sour.

"Fuck those tests!" yelled a sweet-looking mother in the back.

"Fuck those tests" the crowd began to chant.

"Please," Finn asked, holding up his hands. He won-dered if maybe he'd bitten off more than he could chew with this crowd, but he soldiered on. "I'm here to tell you that we've heard your complaints. We've heard you...that *I've* heard you..."

This speech was beginning to seem vaguely familiar to Finn.

"— And I want you to know the people who want you to take these tests—"

Oh, shit, Finn thought, remembering.

"— the people at the New York City Department of Education—"

"BOOOOOO! OOOOO! OOOOO!!!!"

"— will soon hear from all of us here!"

A deep and angry roar echoed from the crowd, just like the one President George W. Bush had heard when he used that almost identical phrasing twelve years before from atop the smoking pile of rubble that had once been the World Trade Center. Yeah, Finn had just cribbed his own little speech from what was surely the finest hour of the baby Bush's otherwise feckless presidency. Whoops.

Whether anyone recognized Finn's stealing Bush's 9/11 speech or not, the response he heard from the crowd was rabidly enthusiastic.

"Burn, baby, burn!" was the Earth School community's surprising mantra, suggesting to Finn a course of action that he'd imagined he'd have to bring up to them.

Burn, baby, burn? Already, Finn thought? The Curmudgeon Avenger had expected a little more resistance, had thought he might have to coax the audience a little more, but then again he thought, why not? Maybe he'd done enough speechifying already? No time like the present, right?

The Earth School community continued to chant, so needing no more encouragement the Curmudgeon Avenger in one fell swoop unholstered the large bottle of Zippo lighter fluid from his back pocket and liberally doused the two cardboard boxes in front of him. He then pulled from his front pocket a packet of matches from one of the nation's finest (and costliest) steakhouses, one of the many souvenirs packs Finn had acquired over the years whilst criss-crossing the country in the name of commerce.

Finn lit one souvenir match and used that to ignite all the others. To a rumble of approval, he held the enflamed packet up into the sky, and then he dropped it atop the soggy boxes of standardized tests at his feet. Completely soaked with lighter fluid, the cardboard boxes burst immediately into flame, a fiery red light that lit up the chanting crowd both literally and figuratively. How the Earth School community roared to see those boxes burn!

"'This meeting can do no more to save the country,'" the Curmudgeon Avenger muttered to himself, a phrase any student of history would know was exactly what the patriot Samuel Adams declared in 1773 just before unleashing his Sons of Liberty to wreak havoc at the Boston Tea Party.

From behind him Finn heard the ex-firefighter approach and speak.

"You put me in a pickle here, guy," Mullaley said, his hand on Finn's shoulder. "I want that stuff to burn, but I *am* a firefighter."

The former member of New York's Bravest then looked around and considered the entire school environment.

"Nah, concrete steps, brick walls, no wind," he nodded to himself, "We'll be fine. No worries."

Mullaley smiled, patted Finn on the shoulder, and stuck out his hand to shake as Ronaldo and Ramsay approached with arms outstretched themselves. Both were smiling, but the Earth School PTA co-prez did wear on his face a puzzled look.

"Great work," he grinned to Finn. "But remind me again, just who are you?"

Who was he? Who was he is right, our hero thought. Was he Finn Riley? Finn Chen? Vincent from the office of counting? But then he remembered.

"They call me the Curmudgeon Avenger," Finn smiled, shaking those last two hands before slipping down the school's front steps and heading up Avenue B to escape into the wilds of Tompkins Square Park.

Intermission

THE SUICIDAL EFFICACY OF MANHATTAN BRIDGES

If you wanted to off yourself by jumping off a New York City bridge, it seemed pretty clear there was really only one way to go.

Right off the bat you could eliminate any number of the options, for reasons either logistical or philosophical. To begin with, you'd only go over the side of a bridge that had pedestrian access: It's not like you could get someone to give you a ride up there and drop you off— you didn't want to hang that guilt trip on someone for all time, did ya?— while driving yourself and then jumping out of your car would be maddeningly inconsiderate. Seriously, did you want to be one of those people who abandoned his or her vehicle on a bridge, blocking an entire lane or two of traffic and bringing the daily commute to a complete stop? Did you want to keep everyone else from getting home on time just because you were having a bad day? You may have had your problems in the world but that still didn't mean you needed to be a complete dick to everyone else.

Next, some bridges were simply not tall enough, and plunging off them into the murky water below would only result in your splashing around like some asshole. Finally, any bridge not attached to Manhattan was obviously out: You didn't want to go out small, you wanted to go out big, the way you imagined you'd lived big, so any span connecting only those sad outer boroughs obviously didn't interest you at all.

For the same reason, you had no intention of crashing and drowning into Newtown Creek, because— even if in the vicinity of Manhattan— where the fuck was Newtown Creek? Similarly, you didn't intend to die by plunging headfirst into the Harlem River, as you had only good recollections of your two visits to that neighborhood: once embarrassing some hapless defender in a game up there by dribbling a basketball between his legs, another time dropping into Sylvia's for soul food and there enjoying your first taste of chicken and waffles. You didn't want to ruin those good memories, right?

The Robert F. Kennedy Bridge, née the Triborough Bridge? Enough with the dead Kennedys already. Hell Gate Bridge? On the way to the after-life, you figured the less said about Hades, the better. Rikers Island Bridge? You didn't need that bad karma following you into eternity, did ya?

The George Washington Bridge? You knew it had its attributes certainly, including easy access to death right over the short walls of its pedestrian walkways. Plus, you knew the bridge was tall enough to do the trick, as more than a dozen people a year died taking that plunge. But, really, did you just want to be another one of them, another sad jumper, no more than one more faceless statistic in a long line of faceless statistics? Not you, thank you very much. Plus, of course, the biggest problem with that big ole' bridge was that hurling yourself over its side meant spending your last seconds on Earth with a birds-eye view of New Jersey. You'd purposefully avoided "the Garden State" (wink, wink, nudge, nudge) for most of your life, so there had to be a better way to go than including its presence in the last milliseconds of your consciousness.

The Ed Koch Bridge, formerly known as the 59th Street Bridge or The Queensboro Bridge? As the "Queensboro Bridge" it was sung about in the opening montage of *King of Queens*, and was Kevin James' fat face really the visual you wanted to take to the grave? You doubted it. Even worse, you knew— as did anyone who truly loved New York City— the 59th Street Bridge most from its being referenced in *The Great Gatsby*: "The city seen from the Queensboro Bridge is always the city seen for the first time, in its first wild promise of all the mystery and the beauty of the world."

Fuck! "...its first wild promise of all the mystery and the beauty of the world." Really? Whatever kind of selfish asshole you might concede you'd turned out to be, you knew you didn't want your last act on Earth being the kind of asshole move that would despoil such beauty as that little bit of Fitzgerald's prose.

So one of the big three it had to be then, as you'd figured all along, those massive spans linking mighty Manhattan to Brooklyn: The Brooklyn Bridge, the Manhattan Bridge, or the Williamsburg Bridge.

At first glance you might have thought the Brooklyn Bridge would be the place to go, given its iconic status and all, but the obstacles were way too many to overcome. To begin with, the vibe of the Brooklyn Bridge was all wrong for doing yourself in, more of a party cruise than any spot you'd want to sink quietly away into Davy Jones' locker: Vendors were everywhere, hawking key chains and kitchen magnets and pencil & ink drawings of old New York; innumerable padlocks bearing cutesy messages ("Dax ‹hearts› Mary," "Jose & Irene 4eva") were randomly attached to the bridge's many fences and stanchions; and hordes of tourists abounded, at every step another school group or tour bus worth of people clicking selfies with their cell phones or even snapping real photos with their old-school cameras, all those happy folks joyfully living their lives and amazed with their gosh-darned wonderful visit to one of New York City's most famous landmarks.

You thought the atmosphere up there, in other words, was more conducive to being talked out of a suicidal swan dive than actually following through on one. You couldn't help it, thinking that most Brooklyn Bridge "jumpers" didn't really have what it took. Amateurs, you considered the lot of them.

Plus, you knew its logistics were all wrong, with its pedestrian walkway being built in the middle of the expanse making it almost impossible to even get close enough to the bridge's edge to take a flying leap. The only way to really get yourself in position for such a dramatic half-gainer would be to cross over to the side on top of one of the thin, steel girders built across the lanes of automobiles flanking both sides of the pedestrian walkway, meaning you'd have to be as nimble as a house cat or a "teenaged" Chinese gymnast as you unsteadily crept your way over the moving cars passing slowly just ten feet below. A greater likelihood than your actually making it all the way across one of those thin girders would be your tumbling off and landing on one of the cars inching along below, meaning you'd likely smash some poor sap's windshield whilst breaking your head only a little bit, probably just enough to get you sent to a nearby hospital but not the Great Beyond. Talk about a shmuck!

To make matters worse, whether or not you actually made it across such a girder to the Brooklyn Bridge's edge, you'd unquestionably be seen by all the drivers in the cars down there, not to mention by the hundreds/thousands of tourists you'd just been sharing the pedestrian walkway with, meaning any hope you had of going out with some sort of quiet dignity would immediately devolve into your becoming a sideshow spectacle instead. "Jumper!" you imagined some asshole yelling breathlessly, with an attendant ripple of excitement then racing through the crowd as they watched you teetering and tottering up there, everyone pointing and gawking and staring as you tried to get near enough to the water to just do it, the very sort of focus on yourself that you didn't want right then, didn't need right then, an embarrassing, self-aggrandizing hullaballoo it seemed to you that you most certainly would like to avoid before finally, mercifully dropping down, down, down for the Big Sleep.

So, the Williamsburg Bridge then? You knew very well that latter-day Williamsburg isn't the Williamsburg it used to be: Yes, the Hasidim still swarm, but Henry Miller doesn't live there any more, as they say. Rather, you'd seen the "Fourteenth Ward" that literary lion once so bracingly wrote about turn into little more than the famous set of the television show *Girls*, an HBO "comedy" so appalling that it actually made you pine— could you have ever imagined the day would come?!?— for the past glories of *Sex And the City*.

Logistically, the Williamsburg Bridge was also a definite no-jump-go, as its pedestrian walkway was elevated and enclosed in the middle of the expanse, meaning walkers had virtually no way to ever get in position to death-hurdle a side wall. Worse about that span was that even if you made it near enough to the water to try to plummet into it, unless you jumped immediately you knew your drop into the abyss would oh-so-quickly turn into some sort of sad & sick social media frenzy, with all those Millennials teeming like cock-roaches on that bridge greedily grabbing their trusty ole' iPhones for the chance to hopefully snap a quick pic of your unseemly demise, to speedily snap a selfie of smiling them in front of— Jesus, they hoped they got the shot!— you plum-meting down into eternity in the background behind. You knew for sure that if you tried to kill yourself on that Wil-liamsburg Bridge some wise-cracking asshole would have the video online probably before you hit the water, that good-for-nothing punk crossing his un-calloused fingers and praying that this was the time he was finally gonna' go viral with his Snapchat film/Facebook post/Instagram stills of sad sack you going definitively off into that sorry good night.

How long, you figured of that god-forsaken "Billyburg" Bridge, before there would be some suicide flash mob in the very spot where you'd just been hoping to drown your de-mons? How long? No, that bridge seemed more appropriate for a nonchalant murder— hurling some hirsute hipster over the side, let's say— than a dignified suicide.

Thus leaving you, at last, with only the Manhattan Bridge. Logistically, you knew that the Manhattan Bridge was a dream come true, with a pedestrian walkway on both the north and south sides but very little traffic (either foot or bicycle) on either. You knew at night, in particular, those walkways were virtually abandoned, as empty as darkened graveyards. While automobiles did cross the Manhattan Bridge, those cars were on the inside of the train tracks and couldn't really be seen from the pedestrian walkways, meaning you would have a little privacy on that span. Subways did pass closely by (the B and D trains, the N and Q), but even if some straphanger saw you up to something interesting on the Manhattan Bridge they would be in no position to do anything about it. They wouldn't get a chance to film you, for example, to try to talk you down, to laugh at you, or, most likely, to simply stand there gawking at you, mouth all agape.

Seven-foot fences of chain link had been constructed on the pedestrian walkways, apparently to keep anyone from "falling" over the side, but you knew that anyone with even the slightest bit of gumption could have made it over those. An old man could have done it, you knew. An old woman even. A couple quick steps and you'd be up and over the top, easy-peasy, you had no doubt.

Conveniently, on the other side of the chain link was also a metal railing, a thick tube painted a faded blue, meaning if you managed to get over the chain link you could pause there, could rest there, you could stand and enjoy the view or even sit down on that very spot to have a minute or two to yourself. The view of downtown Manhattan would have been spectacular (obviously you'd jump from the south side, you figured, with its inarguably better vista), with the Freedom Tower hovering over both you and the skyscrapers of the Financial District. Just to the south you'd be able to enjoy an epic panorama of the Brooklyn Bridge, the South Street Seaport, and the Statue of Liberty in New York Harbor beyond.

On one end of the Manhattan Bridge was downtown Brooklyn, where a couple blocks into that borough you knew you could get a fat slab of cheesecake and a juicy pastrami on rye at Junior's Delicatessen. On the Manhattan side of the bridge was Chinatown, unknowable Chinatown, on the inscrutable streets around East Broadway nothing but six-story brick buildings with metal fire escapes; colorful graffiti decorating the laundry-lined roofs and Chinese symbols filling every window; open markets on every corner selling exotic fruit and stinky fish; seedy brothels down darkened alleyways for those who knew where to look. You could practically smell the opium down there, you thought. You could feel the presence of the ghosts of the old Five Points slum, you thought. Old New York on both ends of the bridge, in other words.

To summarize, in simple terms of pro/con the Manhattan Bridge definitely came up roses:

RELATIVE MERITS OF MANHATTAN BRIDGE FOR THOSE WITH SUICIDAL TENDENCIES

	YEA	NAY
ACCESS BY FOOT?	✓	
APPROPRIATE HEIGHT?	✓	
MANHATTAN-BASED?	✓	
IN ANY WAY AFFILIATED WITH NEW JERSEY?		✗
SAD REMINDER OF UNMATCHABLE PROSE STYLINGS OF AMERICAN MASTER?		✗
FESTIVE ATMOSPHERE? HORDES OF TOURISTS?		✗
UNTOWARD ASSOCIATION W/ TERRIBLE HBO SHOW *GIRLS* OR ENTIRE GENERATION OF SOLIPSTIC MILLENIALS?		✗
REDOLENT OF PASTRAMI, OPIUM, AND OLD NEW YORK?	✓	
GOOD VIEW?	✓	
Final Answer?	✓	

In conclusion, yes, if you really wanted to off yourself by jumping off a New York City bridge, it was pretty clear that there was really only one way to go...

...Such, at least, were the thoughts on the matter of one Finnegan Daniel Riley.

...Now Back to the Show!

IV.

Cancer (Thursday, 2013)

Thursday afternoon put an end to the fun and games.

The Prince didn't have pre-school on Thursdays, so Finn and his son usually had big adventures that day. That morning they'd headed far downtown towards a playground that was part of Hudson River Park, on Manhattan's west side, a place they'd never visited but that Finn had heard great things about. It was a city park that maybe had amusement rides? Kayak rentals? Rock-climbing walls? It was just the sort of place Finn & the Prince had to see.

They took the "1" train all the way south, nearly to the Financial District. Coming out of the subway in Tribeca and seeing Walker's immediately upon stepping into the light, Finn couldn't help but think of John F. Kennedy, Jr. Finn knew, mostly from *Page Six*, that that neighborhood was the one JFK Jr. had once called home and that that bar had been his local watering hole— at least, of course, until the Kennedy scion pulled that whole Icarus routine and ending up joining the lengthy list of his doomed family members already residing in Valhalla (or, actually, he'd pulled the *reverse* Icarus routine, what with the Kennedy prince not flying tragically close to the sun but calamitously close to the Earth). Finn shuddered to think of JFK Jr.'s watery demise— and he shuddered even more to consider he'd just been imagining a dead prince.

Bad karma, Finn thought to himself. Bad karma.

Heading west towards the Hudson River, Finn and his son scooted. The Prince had always been good on a scooter, although until recently Finn had only allowed him to ride in enclosed areas: Central Park, the plaza in front of Lincoln Center (at least until the security guard Bo intervened, that is), the pedestrian walkways along the East River. Places where there was no other real traffic, no danger. Places where his son would not get mowed down, in other words.

But the boy was three years old by then, and particularly adept on his little two-wheeler, so Finn had begun to allow him to scoot on the sidewalk with him. Finn did have his own two-wheeler, too, a purchase he'd made only to shadow his son on the streets as he was otherwise fully aware just how ludicrous a paunchy, bald forty-something might look whilst riding a boy's toy. On the other hand, Finn knew, scooting places with the Prince did mean no more stroller, too, so there was that.

Perhaps surprisingly, neither Finn nor his son wore a helmet when they scooted. Initially Finn had bought his boy that piece of protective gear, but the Prince had been averse— vocally averse, that is, screaming "bad Daddy, bad Daddy!" at the top of his lungs when he'd first put on the "itchy" thing— so Finn figured it wasn't worth the trouble. He wasn't that worried though: The Prince was an expert on that scooter, so it was easier to imagine there wouldn't be any tragic crash. Plus, even though Finn couldn't help constantly fretting about his son, he didn't want to be one of those parents that was so over-protective that his progeny ended up living his whole life not willing to take any risks, so the father was doing his best to pretend it wasn't that big a deal for the two of them to scoot about with heads bare. After all, like everyone his age liked to say, "we" used to bike or sled or skateboard around when we were kids and none of us busted our skulls open, right? For the most part, Finn thought that was true, too. (Was Finn otherwise too over-protective of his boy? Inarguably. But that still didn't mean he wanted to be.)

The final reason Finn wasn't all that bothered with his son's scooting about with his noggin un-helmeted was because wherever the boy rode his father was literally inches behind him at all times, pretty much always within arms' reach, Finn not really being able for even one sec to enjoy those rides with his kid because he spent the whole time fully focused on possible threats, always on high alert in order to maybe pull his son out of harm's way, to rescue him from speeding cars or cracks in the sidewalk or rabid dogs or falling air conditioners or all those inattentive pedestrians mindlessly staring at their fucking magical iPhones.

Finn was quite relieved, in other words, whenever a scooter ride was successfully completed, as he was relieved that day when he and his son managed to safely cross the West Side Highway and arrive at their playground destination: Pier 26. As promised it was spectacular, a newly-constructed city park jutting out in the Hudson River that had a playground, a climbing wall, a skate park, a mini soccer field, even a mini-golf course. There were not, as far as Finn & the Prince could tell, any "amusement rides," but the place was a keeper nonetheless. At the end of the pier was a clear shot of New York harbor, where Ellis Island loomed large, while right above them soared the nearly-completed Freedom Tower, all seventeen hundred and seventy-six feet tall.

Father and son raced from one end of the pier to the other a number of times, reveling in the warm spring day. Finn was actually able to relax at that point as only pedestrians were allowed on the pier and concrete walls enclosed it, meaning no one was going to get run over or plunge over the side and drown in the choppy water below. The Rileys decided to play mini-golf later but first headed to the playground, with Finn buying a coffee from the concession stand before settling on a bench while the Prince made fast friends with another young boy, the two of them immediately giving each advice on how to master the rock wall even though neither of them seemed able to get so much as one foot up.

Finn exchanged nods with the other boy's father, sitting about three benches away, but appreciated that the man didn't seem to want to talk. That was cool with Finn, too, as he wasn't in the mood right then to get into a whole big thing about what those two grown men were doing in the middle of a workday taking care of a couple of little kids. Sometimes that was the sort of thing that was just best left unsaid.

Atop the Freedom Tower Finn could see tiny construction workers plugging away on the highest floors, perhaps only the top five not yet enclosed in glass. Finn flashed back to his father-in-law telling him that he'd worked down there on the southern tip of Manhattan way back when the World Trade Center had first been going up. He remembered the old man saying that from his parking lot he'd watched the finishing touches being put on the WTC and he remembered the day it opened for business "for good."

While usually averse to using his cell phone in public— surely because he recalled the days when it was considered impolite to have loud conversations in front of other people who were not engaged in those conversations— Finn got his out and dialed.

"'Ello?" the old man answered.

"Hey, Dad," Finn said, still not all that comfortable using that term with a man he'd not known eight years before. "It's your son-in-law."

"Hey, kid," Finn's "Dad" replied. "What's up? We still on for today?"

"We'll see you at our place, yeah."

"Ok, so what's up?"

"Did you tell me you used to have a parking lot downtown?"

"Yup. Pier 26."

"No shit."

"Yeah, why?"

"Guess where I am right now?"

"I dunno'."

"I'm with your grandson— "

"— Yeah? Howsa my boy?— "

"— Good, good— "

"— Aright, good— "

"I'm with your grandson, in a brand new city park. The place has a skateboard park, sand boxes, a rocking climbing wall—"

"— Yeah? —"

"— Down here on Pier 26."

"Aaaahh!" Finn's father-in-law suddenly growled. "That place shoulda' been mine, ya know!?"

Finn knew. He'd not known it was Pier 26 exactly, but on more than one occasion his father-in-law had told him that in the 1970s and 80s he'd run a parking lot on a pier in downtown Manhattan, a lucrative business— "lotta cash," the old man had said ruefully, shaking his head in retrospect, "lotta cash"— that he'd lost only when the city reclaimed it via eminent domain. The city needed the pier in order to house U.S. Navy ships during the gala birthday party being thrown to celebrate the 100th anniversary of France gifting the U.S. the Statue of Liberty, which although perhaps a nice gesture at the time a hundred years later ended up costing Finn's father-in-law one extremely profitable, cash cow of a parking lot.

He never forgave the French either. "God-dammed frogs," the old man would say.

His father-in-law's full-time job at the time had been as a mechanic for the city Department of Sanitation, so how he ended up in the parking lot business was never made clear to Finn. Neither would it be, as all "Dad" ever said about that was, with a chuckle, "oh, kid, I can't tell you that." In fact, much about the side businesses Danielle's father was involved in those days was never made clear. For instance, Finn never knew why Danielle said her father sometimes took a baseball bat to his "business" meetings (corporate softball game?). He never knew exactly how the man got his hands on a second, then a third, parking lot on the Upper East Side, or a check-cashing joint in Hell's Kitchen, or a used car lot in Brooklyn. He never knew what his father-in-law and his cronies might have been up to one fine day at that cash cow of a parking lot that made them consider jumping into the

Hudson River and "swimming for it," as the old man said, when a phalanx of NYPD and FBI sedans suddenly flooded their front gates that morning.

His father-in-law had told Finn that in those days he always thought they were being watched from the pier next door. He said he felt that behind one its many mirrored windows there were eyes upon him, which had ultimately turned out to be true.

"It was scary to see all those cops," Danielle's father told Finn, "But they were there to arrest the armored truck drivers who parked in my lot. They was supposed to be emptyin' out the parking meters but I guess they was skimmin' 'em. Loading the coins into the trunks of their cars."

"I mean," he laughed, the relief still palpable some forty years later. "We wasn't doin' nuthin' wrong, but— "

Even the hayseed from Maine that Finn was never bought that.

Still, Finn liked to think of his father-in-law back then prowling the streets of dirty, gritty, and crime-ridden 1970s/1980s New York City, the very New York City Finn had come in search of but may well have missed out on. Finn had seen a picture of Danielle's father at the time, standing on his pier: A short Italian-American with a bit of a pot belly, his balding hair slicked back, wearing a leather jacket over a wife beater, on his face a small smile that without much effort could be read as menacing. "Dad" looked a little bit like early-Tony Soprano, Finn thought, and a whole lot like a kid from Maine's worst nightmare about a slick New Yorker up to who-knew-what no good. Finn was proud to think of it though, that this man he shared holidays with had not just survived New York City's mean streets but that he'd thrived on them. He'd ruled those streets, it seemed. Bossed them even.

Finn knew New York City would never really be his— he was from Maine, after all, and had lived all over America before he ever even got there— but it made him feel good to know that his son had, through Danielle and her family, such strong connections. His Prince of New York had blood ties to the city. He had deep roots. It was symbiotic, Finn thought of what was going down on Pier 26 that day, like the circle of life, he and his son about to play mini-golf on the very spot where four decades prior the boy's grandfather had barely escaped prosecution by the feds. Yup, the circle of New York City life: Hakuna Matata, baby.

Finn's reverie was broken only when he heard his son's excited call.

"Daddy," the boy yelled, "I can see the Statue of Liberty!"

Finn focused to see his son now atop the rock wall— just like that, he'd climbed it!— the boy pointing out into New York Harbor, where Lady Liberty stood tall.

Finn was so happy for his son. The boy's daily routine included visits to places— like Sheep Meadow in Central Park, or the plaza in front of Lincoln Center, or this playground in the shadow of the Statue of Liberty— where tourists from around the country and globe flocked. Regular stops in his son's daily life were places people around the world aspired to see. He was happy, Finn was, that his son was enjoying the sort of upbringing, the sort of life, of which others only might dream.

And Finn loved to see his boy atop that rock wall, loved to see him laughing with a new friend, just plain loved him. They were so lucky, Finn knew, both he and his son.

Still, idling on a park bench and drinking a cup of coffee in the middle of a spring day, Finn couldn't help but feel— the emotions appearing fully-formed in his heart through no conscious decision of his own— that he wasn't living *his* life. He felt like he was just watching. He felt, seeing his son frolic on the playground, that he was simply on the sideline of the boy's life, rooting for him and supporting him and loving him as the Prince followed *his* life's path. And Finn couldn't help think, when considering Danielle and her cancer battle, that he was simply on the sideline of his wife's life, too, rooting for her and supporting her and loving her as she fought like hell just to keep going on. He couldn't help it: Finn felt like the water boy. He felt like a cheerleader. He felt like someone in the stands watching other people's lives take place on the big stage.

As for the things that Finn had always wanted? Finn personally? He didn't do any of them. He felt like he didn't have time for anything. He certainly didn't have time for himself, not when there were dog diapers to be changed and quiches to be cooked and soiled dainties to be laundered.

Finn didn't write; maybe he never had but he still didn't. He didn't play sports. Christ, the last athletic endeavor Finn had been involved in (if it could even be called that) was when our hero scored a tremendous "goal" at Adventure Playground two days before by decapitating that big ole' rat with a tremendous left-footed blast, but since it happened Finn had been hobbled, limping and lurching around the city with what seemed a bum left hip. While once Finn used to play hours and hours of soccer a day, now one swift kick suddenly did him in? Given as much as that joint was still hurting, Finn's days as a jock sure did seem to be done.

And sex? Finn wouldn't say that he had *no* sex life. He sometimes still made Danielle come by talking dirty or going down on her. Danielle sometimes still made him come with her hand or her mouth. But they rarely ever fucked any more. The sex on Monday afternoon had been their first intercourse in what seemed like forever, and even at that it had not been like before: When once their fucking had been lusty and vigorous and hard, since his wife's cancer and hysterectomy their sex had become subdued, reserved, restrained. Finn felt, like when fucking Danielle on Monday, that he had to be careful with her. He had to be cautious. He imagined, taking his wife slowly from behind, that she had a bottle of nitroglycerin balanced on the small of her back, so that if he moved too fast, shifted his body in any way, jostled his wife even a little bit, the whole thing would be over. It would all blow up. Finn didn't want to be ungrateful, didn't mean to complain, but it all would have been so much easier if Danielle hadn't once liked to fuck so rough.

Hell, the last time Finn had had vigorous sex with his wife it hadn't even been with his wife. Rather it was the time the year before when she'd dragged him to a dusty brothel at the end of a dirt road in Pahrump, Nevada, a sad little spot where they'd engaged in a messy ménage with that phat-assed "whore" (the whore's word, remember), a rendezvous that had disappointed Finn—

((Excuse me, your Omniscient Narrator would like to interject: Could it be.... could it be?!?!... that this Finn character is about to launch into some laundry list of complaints about the time his wife "dragged" him to a legal brothel for a "messy ménage with a phat-assed whore"? Seriously?!?! One might suggest that seeing the visit as any sort of chore— that gosh-darned time poor ole Finn's harridan of a wife made him fuck another lady!— could definitely be characterized as viewing things a teensy, weensy bit "glass half full." Yeah, one might have been able to find at least one or two henpecked husbands across this great land who would have been willing to climb up on that horse that day without finding all that much to bitch about.))

— a rendezvous that had disappointed Finn, we were saying, mostly because that whore woman was not Danielle. Finn had chosen her from the line-up (yeah, they actually did that) in large part because she looked, with her blonde hair and high ass, the most like his wife, but it took no more than a few sentences out of her mouth to remind Finn that golden tresses and a round patootie did not turn every woman into the woman he loved. Nope, for all her physical attributes that phat-assed whore was still most certainly not Finn's phat-assed Danielle.

That's not to imply that Finn didn't fuck the whore. Of course he did. He set them up on the bed, his beloved Danielle and her disappointing doppelganger, on their hands and knees, their heads down and asses up. Finn massaged both their bottoms, trying to enjoy the strange butt of this woman for whom they had paid, but nonetheless kept finding himself drawn back to his own wife. Extremely excited, Finn tried to put his hard cock into the woman he married, but when it was clear that it pained her he instead slid himself easily into the professional sex worker. But stroking in and out of that strange woman, Finn reached for his wife.

"Danielle," he whispered excitedly, "Danielle," until his wife got up on her knees and made her way over to him on the bed, pushing up next to him as her husband fucked another woman. Danielle's two breasts sandwiched his shoulder, her two legs straddled his hip. She put a hand on Finn's ass and kissed his head and neck.

"Fuck her harder, honey," she whispered. "Fuck her so hard, like you used to fuck me."

Finn gasped, fucking the other woman but pulling Danielle closer. He smelled her hair and her body, inhaling her. He kissed her neck, her cheek, her shoulder, her hair. He kissed her on the mouth and kissed her on the nipples. He kissed her anywhere and everywhere he could reach as he fucked the other woman, but it still wasn't enough. He wanted Danielle. He was desperate for her.

"Fuck me," his wife whispered into his ear, one of her hands on his ass and one on his chest, the soft hair of her pussy rubbing up against his leg. "Fuck me, baby…"

It was one of the best sexual experiences of Finn's life, and one of the worst, with its hot elements— the first trip to a brothel, the threesome aspect of it, the shuddering orgasm— ultimately paling in comparison to the unpleasant emotion the scenario uncovered, namely that since his wife's cancer diagnosis their lives were so very different, that no matter how game Danielle was, how sexy or adventurous, the husband still felt like he couldn't get close enough to his wife anymore. He felt like he couldn't reach her. There was always something between them, a buffer or a bumper, and even if what was between them might have at first appeared to have been a good thing— a woman bent over to get fucked by Finn, for instance— all it really turned out to be was something separating him from Danielle. It was the only thing Finn really felt at the end of that sordid/sexy incident, an emptiness that there was now always something keeping them apart.

Finn's reverie was broken only when he heard his son's frightened cry.

"Daddy," the Prince yelled on Pier 26, pointing up at the Freedom Tower. "It's falling!"

The terror was immediate. Even twelve years after 9/11, it was impossible for Finn to be so far downtown without remembering the planes exploding, the people jumping, the towers falling. Without remembering the dust-covered survivors trudging uptown like ghosts.

Finn explained to his scared son that the Freedom Tower wasn't really falling, that it was just an optical illusion, that looking straight up at the tall skyscraper with the clouds moving behind it simply made it look like it was toppling down although it really wasn't.

"You have nothing to worry about, hon," Finn told his son, who was quickly convinced and headed back off to play, leaving in his wake just a father with a sense of impending doom, a premonition of disaster. But Finn couldn't help it: There'd been a shadow over his days ever since he heard about the shadow on Danielle's liver.

A couple hours later, after having dropped the Prince off with the in-laws at the Albemarle, Finn held Danielle's hand in the oncologist's office. More than once in the previous three-plus years of Danielle's cancer battle had the husband and wife sat through similar visits, and though some of those trips to the doctor's had gone poorly none had ever taken a turn quite so dire as this.

"How long?" Danielle whispered.

Dr. Aly had never even been willing to entertain the question. He'd always said the point was moot because Danielle had options. There were surgeries to do and chemotherapies to try and even experimental trials to participate in. Dr. Aly was always reluctant to put a time limit on Danielle's life-line because he never believed her fight was lost.

"How long?" she asked a second time, her voice wavering.

Dr. Aly had not been willing to answer that question when he diagnosed the forty-one year old (and five-month-pregnant) Danielle with Stage IV colon cancer because he said there was a possibility she could live right into a ripe, old age. The statistics were certainly not in her favor, he admitted— with only 6% of Stage IV colon cancer patients being alive five years after diagnosis, the statistics were most definitely not in her favor— but in Danielle's case Dr. Aly said all hope was not lost. The initial tumor in her colon could be easily resected, he said, and fortunately her cancer had also metastasized the best way it possibly could: The only other evidence of disease in Danielle was a tumor that had spread to her liver, and even that tumor was luckily in a place where it, too, could be cut out.

As Dr. Aly predicted, surgeons were able to easily resect the tumors in both Danielle's colon and her liver— not to mention deliver a healthy-if-premature baby boy Prince the same day via Caesarian section, mind you!— so any question of "how long" seemed to be irrelevant: As of that day at least the woman was cancer-free. Then, when Danielle suffered through six months of intense chemotherapy intended to root out any hidden disease, she begun to have small seizures as a result of all that platinum being pumped into her blood. She needed an elective hysterectomy to get rid of a bunch of the organs where recurrent cancer liked to attack. She even had a blood clot in her leg and a bowel obstruction in her belly that each threatened her very life, but not once was Dr. Aly willing to entertain the idea of how much time Danielle might still have on Earth. They simply were never at that point, he always said.

Even when the cancer came back eighteen months later Dr. Aly wasn't ready to talk time. No, he admitted, it wasn't that great that the disease had recurred, especially because its reappearance meant that the most effective chemotherapy for colon cancer had not defeated Danielle's strain, and especially since the two new tumors in Danielle's liver where precariously close to an artery and thus could not be removed surgically. Still, Dr. Aly said, he hoped those two tiny liver spots could be dealt with via cryonic embolization, meaning basically that they'd freeze the little fuckers to death, which is exactly how that second round played out. Then Dr. Aly put Danielle on what he said might be her best hope, an experimental chemotherapy in daily pill form that may have had nagging side effects— memory loss, mood swings, muscle fatigue, exhaustion— but was also believed to be effective. In Danielle's case that turned out to be true, at least for a couple years, that is, and thus Dr. Aly had not yet ever felt the need to entertain the question of just "how long" Danielle might have left, not even one time.

Not until that Thursday afternoon, that is.

"I'm sorry," he began, quietly explaining that Danielle's CAT scan was very bad. Danielle didn't just have one new tumor in her liver, he pointed out, she had many. In fact, what had looked like a "shadow" on her liver had actually been a constellation of innumerable cancerous spots, a nebulae of death they basically turned out to be. Worse, Dr. Aly continued, there was spread into Danielle's abdomen, too, lots of spread for that matter, with all three people in that oncologist's office that day understanding exactly what it all meant: With too much cancer in Danielle's body to remove surgically, and with no more chemotherapy options left for her to try, realistically it was over. At that point it was only a matter of time.

"How long?" Danielle had whispered.

"I want to try to get you into some trials," Dr. Aly began, "There's one out of—"

"How long?" Danielle interrupted, her voice getting stronger.

Dr. Aly's shoulders slumped slightly. "I'm sorry," he said.

"How long?" she said, her voice firm, looking the man directly in the eye.

"Not decades," he nodded, trying to be positive. "Probably years."

"Months?" Danielle wasn't fucking around anymore.

"Probably years," Dr. Aly said.

"Probably?"

"I'm sorry."

The Wooing & Winning of Danielle Rigoglioso, Part I (2006-2008)

How rough had Danielle liked it? Rough.

It was in 2006, back when Internet dating still retained the last vestiges of stigma, that Finn found Danielle online. She'd posted a personals ad at Nerve.com, a web-site that if not about straight- up sex— AdultFriendFinder.com it was not, nor even the "Casual Encounters" section of Craigslist— at least targeted the libidinous. The content on the site was mature, in other words, filled as it was with naked pics and dirty writing, although Finn couldn't help but notice a bit of the holier-than-thou to everything on there; the prose, he saw, would always have been characterized as "erotica," never porn (lots of Anaïs Nin excerpts and the like is what he was saying), while the naked photographs of pretty people were always filmed through what seemed a gauzy haze. Yes, Finn could see the folks at Nerve.com were serious about their sex, that they thought they were producing a periodical more akin to *Playboy* (Meaningful interviews! Stories from real writers! Dignified nudes!) than *Penthouse* (Labia!). Not so much smut as "art" was the way they surely saw it.

It wasn't that Danielle's ad on Nerve was singularly fantastic either, as Finn responded to *a lot* of ads in those days. *A lot* of ads. For the most part his online efforts to meet women were to no avail though, because the women on the Internet were so clearly in the catbird's seat: They sat back and got approached, sifted through dozens or hundreds of e-mails from interested admirers, while the men of the Internet had to somehow prove themselves extraordinary, better than all the rest of their slobbering, desperate brethren. It was all so unfair, Finn thought, so unfair— which was another way of saying he had little luck in the world of online dating. Two months of such hard work had resulted in only one New York City rendez-vous for the man.

Surely the problem was that the dozens and dozens of notes he zipped off every day to possible paramours were forgettable, even their writer knew that, short and abrupt and sadly desperate little missives that their author didn't bother to waste his time on because he assumed they were doomed to fail anyways. Most of the time, in fact, Finn's e-mails to online women were no more than cut & paste jobs, a reality he knew was a mistake but that he couldn't be bothered to do much about: What was the point, really?

When Finn saw someone he liked online— and, let's be honest, the bar was pretty low there, any woman "he liked" being any woman between about 20 and 50 years old and able to locomote, although even that last requirement wasn't written in stone— he whipped off an e-mail to her and waited. Occasionally he got replies, but for the most part those replies weren't legit, largely being either prostitutes on the make or some kindly Nigerian reminding Finn of a guaranteed financial windfall. If Finn ever did get a reply from what seemed to be an actual human (an actual female might have been too much to hope for) asking to see a photograph, when he sent a pic that mostly seemed to bring an end to any budding correspondence. Finn tried not to think about what that meant, that some woman (yeah, let's say it was a woman) who might have had at least the possibility of an interest in him shelved that interest just as soon as she saw his pic: Didn't exactly fill the sails with confidence, eh?

But if Danielle's ad wasn't the only one Finn responded to, it was one of the few that he *really* responded to. Occasionally something about a woman's profile was so intriguing that Finn bothered to write back earnestly, to pen some long e-mail full of clever asides and witty ripostes that implied (or sometimes flat-out stated) his intelligence, his worldliness, his mastery of the English language, and, nonchalantly, the fact he could certainly afford to take a woman some place nice. Even those masterpieces, however, normally resulted in nothing. Radio silence. Damn you, Internet, Finn thought.

Danielle's ad had initially intrigued Finn because of its preternatural cool. The woman who'd written the post clearly didn't need a man. She might have wanted one, the ad said, but she'd live without one. She wasn't going to fall all over herself to get her hands on just any Tom, Dick, or Harry.

"I meet plenty of men," Danielle's ad began, "just not the right ones."

She continued by providing her vitals— age, race, job, marital status, etc.— and described herself as "*blonde*" and "*told I'm pretty.*" Where she really hooked ole' Finn, however, was when she said she was searching for a "*nice guy*" who was also "*a man in the bedroom.*" She wasn't just looking for some dude for sex, the ad said, but that the woman in question hoped to find someone whose real-life company she might enjoy and who also might, in the boudoir, not happen to mind "*holding me down,*" "*pulling my hair,*" and "*forcing me do what he wanted.*"

When he read that a jolt of electricity went through Finn— or, more specifically, a jolt of electricity shot through his groin. Finn had been impressed with the ad, with the easy cool of the woman (she exuded the opposite of desperation), her obvious intelligence, and the fact her post was perfectly punctuated and immaculately written. (Yes, grammar was an aphrodisiac for Finn. A maddeningly large number of things were, in fact.) Finn knew even before he got to the exciting end of the ad that he dug this woman, so when she suddenly turned pervert on him our hero ended up in love.

"Shit!" Finn thought to himself. "I can hold! I can pull! I can force!"

Finn then cracked his knuckles and really got down to it, artfully composing a long e-mail reply to the woman who

wrote that scintillating ad that showed him to be cosmopolitan and well-traveled, well-read and conscientious, funny
and kind, educated and an excellent writer, not to mention
similarly inclined sexually.

"And regarding your erotic interests," Finn concluded
his e-mail, "rest assured that your particular peccadilloes are
mine, too, that though I am a nice guy— in fact, I love pup-
pies and babies— in the bedroom I am not: I will hold you
down. I will pull your hair. And I will make you do what I
want."

The e-mail was spectacular, Finn knew. A work of art.
A billet-doux for the ages, in fact. He read it a couple dozen
times, at least, tweaking a word here or there but mostly just
marveling at his own great skill. Finally, almost sadly, he
hit the SEND button, hoping to get a reply but mostly worried that this woman he had so much hope for might not
recognize the e-mail for the genius it entailed. How Finn
prayed his sublime work would not fall on deaf ears!

If Finn had initially liked Danielle's ad, he loved the
woman herself even more the next day when she wrote back
to say how "funny" and "smart" she found his message. He
had his doubts when she asked to see his pic— "here we go
again," Finn worried— but he crossed his fingers and sent
one.

It was a picture of his recent trip to East Africa, a photograph of a head-shaved Finn squinting into the face of the
sun while sailing a dhow in the Indian Ocean. He wore a
jaunty smile on his face and some kind of skirt wrapped
around his legs, Arabic-style. Finn had always liked the
photo, had thought it exuded some kind of devil-may-care
attitude on his part (Jesus, the man was casually wearing a
dress!), had imagined even that showing him alone in a small
ship sailing solo near the Equator he'd looked a bit like a
pirate. Obviously, given the negative/neutral/non-existent reaction the picture had previously engendered from every
woman he'd sent it to, no one else was getting the buccaneer
look, but in any case Finn was happy with the photograph.

He was even happier when "Danielle" wrote back the next day, telling him her name and saying not only that she liked the picture but that she thought Finn looked "sexy." Even better, Danielle wrote "You look like a pirate!," a compliment that may not have seemed like high praise to anyone else who'd spent any time on the high seas but that nonetheless pretty much sealed Finn's romantic fate for the rest of time. The woman had exquisite taste, Finn thought— she was utterly *discerning!*— and, unlike Groucho Marx's famous claim to not want to join any club that would have him, Finn always looked fondly upon anyone who happened to look fondly upon him.

It was only when Danielle sent back her own picture that Finn lost heart. The picture showed a thirty-something, blue-eyed blonde, an exceedingly attractive woman who also managed in only a head-shot to look sophisticated and intelligent, mysterious and libidinous. Her sparkling blue eyes were a god-damned limpid pool, Finn thought, absolutely spectacular, confirming his worst fears that there was no way this woman could be real. She was too good-looking, he thought, too god-damned good to be true. There was no way this woman both existed and liked him, Finn figured, and he instead assumed that either 1) the pic was a fake sent by some less attractive blonde; 2) the pic was a fake sent by some slobbering, overweight, hairy dude; or 3) the woman in the photo was really a man, a chick with a dick as they say. Damn you, Internet, Finn thought!

The irony, of course, was that even as Finn was worried some "woman" might be in the process of pulling a duplicitous "Catfish" on him, Finn himself was fully engaged in pulling his own sneaky "Catfish" on that very same woman: After all, Finn had enthusiastically replied to the personal ad of someone in search of "*a man in the bedroom*," and that, let's be honest, was a characterization of our hero that could only be made literally. Yes, Finn had a penis, and, yes, he'd been in a bedroom with a woman with said member before, but, no, it could never have been said he'd ever figuratively acted like "*a man*" in any of those bedrooms, at least not in the way that personal ad clearly desired. Finn had never once been Rhett Butler in the boudoir, in other words, not one time even coming close to uttering a "Frankly, my dear, I don't give a damn" and then blithely taking what he wanted from his sexual partner. Nuh-uh. Nope. Never happened.

In fact, in his romantic life Finn had proven to be far from sexually assertive over the years— his milquetoast bona fides having been fully established in Janie Flynn's bedroom way back when, as you recall— pretty much never once doing any single thing with a woman without first getting her clear, distinct, indisputable verbal "okay." For Christ's sake, the first time Finn had ever kissed a woman without her explicit permission had been all of a month prior to meeting Danielle, when at the end of his only other online rendez-vous— a polite but tepid affair that turned out to be— Finn had held open the taxi door for his date and then leaned down to kiss her lightly on the lips. The woman hadn't minded even though there hadn't been any spark between them, but as she rode away never to be heard from again the almost 40 year old Finn almost wanted to celebrate: He'd kissed a woman on his own! He'd done it! He'd really, truly done it!

But in his whole life had Finn ever *held a woman down* in a sexual situation? *Pulled her hair? Forced her to do what he wanted?* Heavens, no.

Still, Finn had replied to Danielle's ad because he was willing to try, and say what you would in terms of relative "Catfishes" Finn was certain that his perhaps slightly exaggerated implication that he liked to be a, quote/unquote, "*man in the bedroom*" still paled in comparison to the possibility that Danielle might, at the end of their first date, suddenly spring a dick on him, right? Finn sure thought so.

But a first date happened. Finn had offered to meet Danielle anywhere she wanted, on her "home turf" he'd said to make it easier for her, but the wise New York woman that Danielle was knew never to give up any such information about herself to some random online suitor. Instead Danielle agreed to meet Finn where he wanted, so it being one of the days of the week he suggested the bar 7B.

When he saw Danielle walking towards him that evening, Finn knew he was in trouble. The woman (from the way she sashayed and from the curves of her hips Finn was now convinced Danielle wasn't secretly packing) was every bit as attractive as her photo had implied, plus she strode nonchalantly through the streets of the East Village like she didn't have a care in the world. She wasn't scared, in other words, nor at all intimidated, by a neighborhood that in those days most of your finer people still largely stayed away from. Danielle had aplomb, Finn could see, had confidence, and he began to really doubt that his usual dating dog and pony show— a witty aside here, an amusing travel anecdote there, a deep and meaningful look to wrap it all up— was going to have any sort of effect on what Finn could tell was a real-life, grown-up woman. He was definitely worried he was punching above his weight class on this one.

Never mind that Finn found Danielle walking down Seventh Street to be spectacularly attractive. Her straight blonde hair was parted in the middle and hung down to her shoulders, her eyes those god-damned limpid blue pools. Her pillowy lips were colored red, but not any bright red or cherry red, more of a blood red, a darkish sort of deadly hue that Finn thought had probably only ever been seen before on a suburban goth chick or a real-life vampire. And she was dressed from head to toe in black, a sleeveless blouse up top, crisply creased pants down below, and on her feet high-heeled black leather boots with silver stiletto heels.

Seriously, Finn thought of the sexy spectre approaching him, this was the woman he was going to boss around in the bedroom? Her? He mostly felt like whimpering.

Brief though it turned out to be, the date went well. After taking a seat at the bar with Danielle, Finn ordered them each a drink: a hair-of-the-dog Captain Morgan & Coke for him, then the same for Danielle when she demurred to Finn's alcoholic expertise. Because he had no other plan, Finn then launched into his usual dating spiel, a routine he was happy to see was having the desired effect even with the impressive Danielle: She laughed at his witty asides. She was interested in his amusing travel anecdotes. And she even returned the meaningful wrap-it-up look Finn sent her way.

The whole thing was going very well, Finn thought, no question about it, even before Danielle mentioned that she'd been to 7B years before, back when she'd lived in the East Village in the early 90s. Finn's heart fluttered when he heard that. She'd lived in the East Village in the early 90s? Talk about your New York City bona fides! It began to go even better, Finn thought, when Danielle nodded towards the bartendress Janine— a busty redhead wearing snakeskin pants and platform heels— and nonchalantly said, "Hot, huh?" Yeah, Finn's cock fluttered when he heard that one, dancing a bit of a jig in our hero's pants. "Got ourselves a bit of sex fiend here!" the talking cock celebrated. It was only when Danielle said that she wasn't much of a drinker that any part of his body protested.

"Loser!" Finn's liver lamented. "Dump her!"

When Danielle wrapped up their short soirée— they'd only scheduled an introductory drink after all— by saying she needed to get to the West Village to see a friend perform in a play, Finn offered to walk her there. It was both a charming gesture and an evil plan on his part, for though neither Finn nor Danielle had much alluded to sex during their drink Finn was planning on what he figured was a come-on for the ages: He was going to plant a big, wet kiss on this nice, smart woman whether she wanted it or not. My god, Finn thought of her licentious personal ad, you couldn't say she hadn't asked for it!

They left 7B and crossed the street, walking along Tompkins Square Park towards Avenue A. Their banter was friendly and flirtatious, and Danielle really seemed to appreciate that Finn was going to walk her across town.

"Most men in New York would never do any such thing," she said.

"Oh yes," Finn nodded with a smile, "I'm different." He'd been walking on Danielle's right side, closest to the park, but at that point he switched sides, moving behind her over on to her left. Danielle looked back when he was behind her, slightly nervous but also slightly intrigued. Finn said nothing but gave her a confident smile.

"What are you up to?" she asked.

"Nothing," Finn answered, taking that moment to put his right hand on Danielle's left arm to turn her towards him, putting his left hand on Danielle's right hip and stepping into her, using his body to push her one step, two steps back into the park's wrought-iron fence, pressing his body into hers as he leaned down and deeply kissed her. She liked the kiss, yes she did, and Finn liked it too, that one long, wet, tonguey kiss basically the lusty equal of every other kiss Finn had ever had his in his entire life, combined.

He stepped away from her, utterly alive. Finn didn't feel like he had an erection— he felt like he *was* an erection. He laughed, cocking his head to the side, with the back of his hand wiping his wet lips dry. Finn imagined at that moment he might have looked like a brute but, he thought, probably a good brute at that, a young Marlon Brando say.

Danielle hadn't moved an inch, still leaning back against the fence.

"Wow," she said, her eyes wide, which Finn took as an invitation to rejoin the embrace, this time kissing her deeply while putting his hand behind her head to pull her close, kissing her neck, dragging a thumb over a nipple, cupping his hand between her legs to squeeze her pussy through her pants (whilst also, hallelujah, confirming the absence of a dick), before turning Danielle around and pushing her up into the fence, grinding his hard cock into the firm flesh of her ass. Finn kissed Danielle's hair and cheek and neck from behind, tightening his grip on the two iron poles on either side of her, pushing her into the fence and restraining her there with the constricting of his arms and legs.

"No," Danielle said, and though Finn had never felt such a thing before— he hadn't even known it was possible— he heard her "no" as a "yes." The point was confirmed by the fact that Danielle's "no" was accompanied by her pushing her bottom back into his crotch, grinding her ass into his cock, her disingenuous verbal "no" obviously thus proving to be more theatre than truth.

"No," she said softly, almost pleadingly, but Finn could hear in the submissive tone of her voice that what she was really pleading for was more.

"Yes," Finn whispered into Danielle's ear, dropping the register of his voice to what he thought was sexy, domineering. "You're mine now, and I can do whatever I want with you."

He could feel her give in to him, curling herself into his body.

"Mine," he whispered.

It was the single hottest thing Finn had ever been a part of, although, in all honesty, he wasn't exactly sure what to do next. They were out in the open, on the street, both facing a jungle gym in Tompkins Square Park (a playground where unbeknownst to them in just a handful of years their son would one day gambol and play), and Finn had never been the sex in public sort of guy. What, he was gonna' lay Danielle down on the tire swing and take her right there? Instead he stood behind her, saying nothing, holding her in place, kissing her softly if also pressing his erection into her bottom.

Minutes passed. Cars drove down Seventh Street. Pedestrians walked quickly by. Finn and Danielle stood together quietly, comfortably. They fit.

"No," Danielle said shyly, making a half-hearted but fully fruitless attempt to escape Finn's arms while also subtly rubbing her body back into his.

"Don't move," he whispered to her in a voice he hoped was deep and sexy, making the sort of threat he thought she might like. "Don't move or I'll pull down your slacks and take you right here."

Finn heard a giggle.

"My 'slacks'?" Danielle asked with what he could see was a smile. "You're gonna' take down my 'slacks'?"

No good, Finn thought? "Slacks" wasn't the right term? What then, "pantaloons?" What did Finn know about ladies' fashion? Who was he, Ralph Lauren?

"Oh no," Danielle was acting all frightened. "Please, sir, don't take down my *slacks!*"

She was mocking him! Was this how these things went? Danielle sassed him and then he put her in her place? Is that how she liked it? Okay, Finn thought, two could play this game.

He pushed Danielle up harder against the fence, squeezing her tighter, and leaned his mouth right up against her ear.

"Watch yourself, woman," he whispered huskily, "or, so help me God, down come those trousers."

How they laughed!

Three nights later, after a friendly follow-up drink at a nearby sushi restaurant that confirmed both that Finn and Danielle really did like each other and really, really desired each other, their Internet dalliance reached the only initial conclusion it ever could, with Danielle bound on the bed in Finn's studio apartment, her wrists tied her behind her back and her ankles duct-taped together, Finn sneaking up behind her with a serrated knife in one hand and the romantic intentions of hacking right off her back the Victoria's Secret baby-doll negligée and matching thong he'd just gifted her in order to "assault" her (no, that wasn't the right word)....to "penetrate" her (nah)...to "make love" to her (yeah, that was it!) with the enormous black dildo he held in his other paw, a big ole ebony shlong, it might be said, that the Caucasian-cocked Finn believed deep in his heart could in no way actually be "life-sized."

To say Finn was not prepared for what went down that first night was putting it mildly. After all, our hero had always been notoriously passive around women (see ***Flynn, Janie, 1987***), in his entire life never actually enjoying fruitful sexual relations with a lady without pretty much receiving a written invitation first. To seal the deal in the sack, Finn had always basically needed to be escorted in the same way those guys at the airport used flashlights to usher 747s up to the gate (yes, in this scenario Finn & his cock are being represented by a jumbo jet...). As reported previously, however, sometimes even an explicit invitation wasn't enough for the guy to get laid (***Ibid***).

Plus, so indoctrinated was Finn in the gender-war dynamics of the early 80s, such a fine student of its lessons was he— remember, 1) women are people, too, and 2) no raping!— that not only did Finn unfailingly adhere to that old saw "'No' means 'no,'" he lived in paralyzing fear of it. Prior to Danielle, when it came to interacting romantically with women Finn started at "no" and worked his way back from there. In fact, not only had young Finn steadfastly believed that a woman's "no" meant "no," he was under the impression that her "maybe" probably meant "no" while we were at it, and it wouldn't have taken all that much to convince him that her "yes" really meant "no," too, for that matter.

Neither did it help in his attempts to find true love/get laid that Finn also pretty much just didn't get women. He was a smart enough guy but also a guileless one, so the subtle semantics of love were lost on him. Non-verbal communication? Body language? Coyness? It all flew right over his head. Just a couple years prior to finding Danielle, for example, Finn met a woman at a hotel bar in Seattle, but because she rebuffed his initial advance (Finn: "Can I buy you a drink?", Nice Woman at Bar: "I'm married.") he dully believed sex between them was forevermore off the table. He thought the woman wasn't interested even though she then spent the rest of her night with Finn, laughing at his jokes and (eventually) drinking his offered drinks; even though she started a risqué conversation about what she saw as the merits of online pornography; even though she later accompanied Finn to a nearby strip joint, there sitting on his lap and telling a gyrating ecdysiast mid-lap dance that she and Finn were a couple of randy newlyweds; even though she then accompanied Finn back to his waterfront hotel suite in the middle of the night, ostensibly to get a gander at "that view of yours."

Not being completely naïve, Finn was pretty sure he knew what it meant that this tipsy, filthy-mouthed, porn-loving woman had found her way to his room in the wee hours, but then when she rebuffed what even Finn would have conceded was an extremely forward *second* advance (Finn: "How 'bout I come over there and give you a little kiss?", Nice Drunken Woman in His Hotel Suite at 2:30 AM: "I'm married."), he believed her. He actually believed her, apologizing profusely for his impolitic behavior before tucking his tail between his legs and scurrying off to the loo.

Finn had sex that night in Seattle pretty much in spite of himself, only after the woman finally sent him a message so explicit that even Finn was unable not to glean its meaning. His clue? After the pit-stop to his hotel room's bathroom— during which time Finn was drumming up the courage to tell the woman it was probably time for her to get going, what with the state of her matrimonial bliss and all— Finn returned to discover his visitor now splayed naked on his couch, wearing a sweet smile but not so much as a stitch of clothing, a turn of events that allowed our young Sherlock to deduce— regardless of his possible paramour's persistent protestations otherwise!— that this "married" woman might have been intercourse-interested after all. Maybe, Finn thought looking down at the nude nymph laying supine on his divan, just maybe she really did want to be more than friends.

So, for Finn suddenly to be in the position of being a "man in the bedroom" like he was supposed to be that first night with Danielle... of theoretically doing whatever he wanted to her... of even proceeding without her "voiced affirmative", as it were...in fact in continuing to keep having his fun even as she begged him to stop and cried real tears and fought him like some Russ Meyer hellcat of a woman!! ....well, that wasn't Finn's basic nature and it did something to him, something that wasn't necessarily a good thing either. It might even be said that it broke some part of him (okay, a lame part, sure...), and while it probably wouldn't be accurate to say that our young hero was "traumatized" by the events of that night, Finn certainly would have conceded that he found it "harrowing" to be forced to force himself upon Danielle in the way she quite clearly wanted. Just harrowing.

At one point, for example, Finn had pinned the naked, wriggling Danielle face down on to his bed, using the leverage of his extra eighty pounds and larger muscles to easily subdue a woman he could nonetheless see was quite strong for a girl. But then as he prepared to send his turgid cock down the path previously blazed by that big black dildo, from outside his bedroom window Finn heard the loud, and close, keening of an NYPD siren, an auditory alarm that Finn would have admitted surprised him right then not even a teensy, weensy bit. He knew it! He was off to the Tombs, Finn figured. Off to Riker's. There was no way a man could treat a woman like Finn was currently treating Danielle without getting arrested. And Finn *got* it: He was guilty. Doing some of the things he'd been doing to Danielle— not rape per se but certainly in the rape ballpark, Finn would've said— he'd wanted to call the cops on himself. Alan Alda certainly would not have approved, that was for certain.

Which was all true, except for one small thing: Finn liked it, guilt or not. At some point, in fact, Finn might have suggested that a coup had occurred in his head, a mutiny or a revolution perhaps, and for maybe the first time after a lifetime of being cock-blocked by his very own psyche Finn's angry "little" phallus was finally calling the shots. He was at last in charge. He'd taken over, truly taken over. (*So preva-*

lent is his presence in the pages of this little tome, your Om-niscient Narrator might suggest, that perhaps it's time to actually name that chatty little cock, "Liam" perhaps as a nod to Finn's family lineage.) In the end, Finn would have said, when it came to being a man in Danielle's bed, "Liam" knew exactly what he was doing. "Liam" couldn't be stopped. "Liam" wouldn't be stopped. "Liam" wasn't taking any pris-oners. "Liam" wouldn't take "no" for an answer.

But did Danielle like it, everything that went down the night of that first threesome between her & Finn & Liam? Early on, before the night devolved into the sort of violent frenzy that might have been found in a sub-basement of one of the châteaux of the Marquis de Sade, Finn had given Dan-ielle every opportunity to stop. To get away. To put an end to their erotic games. He'd not been so dull as to ask her again and again "is this okay?" or "is that okay?", as the old Finn most assuredly would have, but he subtly asked her questions, and she clearly provided answers, that made it obvious eve-rything was okay between them, that the show must go on. One answer: For a couple of hours in Finn's apartment that night Danielle's pussy was a salty swamp of visible, sticky wet, and while Finn knew that arousal alone did not imply consent— told you he'd been faithfully listening to Gloria Steinem back in the day!— he might also have argued that that vaginal seascape wasn't exactly implying any "no thank you" either. Additionally, after he'd viciously/delicately cut that Victoria's Secret baby doll off her body as part of that whole amorous charade of her faux rape, Finn made it a point to lay the steak knife he'd used directly next to Dan-ielle's dominant right hand, and since that tough-as-nails New Yorker *didn't* grab the kitchen utensil to cut him and flee? Well, if that wasn't a pretty clear sign of "tallyho", Finn didn't know what was.

Plus, the woman came. She came and came, in fact, her body the laboratory on which the mad scientist Finn success-fully experimented that night. Eagerly, earnestly, he whirled about, pushing buttons, pulling levers, mixing potions, doing everything he could to please Danielle, to satisfy her— so even if there were restraints, there were orgasms; even if there was pain, there was pleasure for her, so much pleasure (...or so it seemed to Finn).

Finn's belief that Danielle was okay, or more than okay, with all that went down between them was confirmed as they lay together in his bed at the end of that first night. When it was over, Danielle nestled into Finn's side, her two legs wrapping around his one left leg, one of her arms wrapped around his head and the other over his chest. She snuggled her face into Finn's neck. Danielle was exhausted, on one hip a bruise where Finn had held her too hard, on both nipples small scratches from a couple of clamps mistakenly ripped off, on one wrist a burn from a rope pulled too tight (so much for the knot-tying skills he'd learned in the Boy Scouts , Finn couldn't help but think).

It wasn't just that Danielle was nestled in beside Finn either, as many a new lover might have been, but that she seemed to be trying to get as close to him as possible, practically burrowing her way in. He felt like she was desperate for him, like was hanging on him the way a koala clings to a eucalyptus tree, finding in him her safety and succor. It seemed to Finn that what he had done to Danielle, or maybe what he had done *for* her, was not just what she'd wanted but what she'd needed in some place way deep inside her. Finn wouldn't have claimed he knew what it all meant— Danielle's apparent desire for pain or fear— but he knew that he liked it.

And, yes, Finn liked the sex they'd just had, but even more was that when it was over he liked that Danielle clung to him, that she hung off him in a way that suggested he was vital and necessary. Finn might've liked the analogy of his eucalyptus tree to Danielle's koala, except for one little thing, and that was the one big thing that Finn didn't feel that night like an average, leafy tree; he felt like a fucking California Redwood. Before that night Finn had never felt so big, so strong. He'd never felt so true to himself. He'd never felt so much like a man.

And because Finn was not dumb, he got what that meant, too, that in saying he'd never felt so much like a man on a night when the kindest thing that could have been said about him was that he'd perpetrated only a pretend rape, that certainly raised questions even for Finn about what it really meant to be a man. It didn't matter right then though, Finn thought while looking down at the warm woman snuggled beside him. That night wasn't the time to talk gender-politics, he realized: Sometimes a lion just needed to roar.

But before she fell asleep in Finn's arms, Danielle muttered one final thought about their first night together.

"Oh, this is gonna' be fun..." she whispered in a sleepy stupor. She giggled to herself. "Gonna' be fun..."

And she was right, too. For years and years what happened between Finn and Danielle *was* fun— truly fun, deeply fun, fundamentally fun— at least until that one dark night in the not-so-distant future when the pregnant Danielle started bleeding from her ass.

Sheep Meadow Drone
(Thursday Afternoon, 2013)

The Curmudgeon Avenger wanted blood. No, that wasn't true: Finn wanted blood.

In the beginning the Curmudgeon Avenger had been no more than a lark, a bit of a clown even, appearing fully formed as he did from Finn's head like Athena bursting from Zeus' skull, in effect some fantastical genie popping out of a bottle of cinnamon schnapps. Finn had reveled in the fun that "clown" provided though, as well as admired that unlike him— a guy whose raison d'etre had always seemed no more than politesse— the Curmudgeon Avenger didn't hold back. His alter-ego didn't stand on the sideline; he didn't hem and haw and lollygag about; he acted and took stands that Finn respected: Launching a broadside against a corrupt industry that was enriching itself at the expense of American schools? Well-played, sir! Scaring straight a bunch of ne'er-do-well drivers who'd previously cared more about their own schedules than the safety of their fellow citizens? Kudos to you! And physically attacking a god-damned, good-for-nothing frozen dessert shack? I salute you Curmudgeon Avenger, Finn thought.

But after that Thursday afternoon visit to the oncologist's office, as everything had changed for Finn so had it changed for his psycho sidekick: No longer was anyone kidding around.

The cab ride home from Dr. Aly's had been sad that day, staggeringly fucking sad, and the only time the husband and wife felt anything but grief was when Danielle joked through her tears that she wanted "my Mommy." But, in fact, maybe the only solace Danielle had that day was that her mother and father were waiting for her at the apartment with her son, meaning she would immediately be surrounded by her whole family as she tried to process the terrible news. Finn understood, although he couldn't say that he felt the same way. He didn't feel the need to see any family at all. Rather, Finn wanted to go out. He wanted to go out and annihilate.

"I need to walk," he whispered into his wife's ear when they got out of the taxi in front of the Albemarle, and, not surprisingly, his wife understood.

"I know," she tried to smile through the tears. "I'm sorry...."

It was the one thing she'd kept saying to him on the ride home: She was "sorry," she repeated to Finn again and again, so "sorry."

Frankly, it enraged him. His poor wife was going to die and she felt bad for *him*? She felt guilty about what she had done to *him*? Life was so fucking unfair, Finn thought, and he wanted to smash stuff. Finn wasn't sure what he wanted to destroy, but he knew he wanted to destroy something. Fortunately the week before the Curmudgeon Avenger had made a note, one that he was more than happy to share.

"Last Thursday," he whispered inside Finn's head. "Sheep Meadow."

Like every Thursday there had been no pre-school for his son that day, so Finn and the Prince had had a great adventure in Central Park instead. Father and son rented a row boat at the Boat House and floated across the Lake. They climbed together to the top of Belvedere Castle. They kicked a soccer ball back and forth on the Great Lawn and then had a leisurely picnic lunch. The Prince had an hour's worth of turns on the slide at Billy Johnson Playground (although his father had to repeatedly remind himself not to think about what might have happened to poor Billy Johnson...). They sat on adjoining white steeds on the Central Park carousel and rode it around and around, one, two, three times. And finally, near the end of the afternoon, the Prince chased the

bubbles his father blew across the great expanse of Sheep
Meadow, the obliviously happy boy doing his best to— but not
quite managing to— avoid the sunbathers laying all about
the grass on the season's first really nice day.

Finn's intentions in taking his son for that wonderful
day in the park had been pure, but it wasn't pure chance that
they arrived at Sheep Meadow in the late afternoon, with the
sun high in the sky and the sunbathers everywhere. In truth,
Finn enjoyed seeing all those women in bikinis. Perhaps a
touch less admirable about his intentions right then, Finn
also enjoyed talking to those women if in wildly chasing his
beloved bubbles Finn's obliviously happy son just happened
to bump into one of them. Finn would apologize and shrug
innocently, all "what can ya do with a kid like this?", wishing
it was otherwise but also conceding it was pretty much impossible to ever get his little angel to pay any more attention.
For the most part anyone the Prince disturbed immediately
forgave the gorgeous, tow-headed, blonde-haired, blue-eyed
boy, however, and subsequently forgave his apologetic father,
with the end result of all those fun & games being Finn managing to enjoy a minute or two of friendly chatter with any
number of near-naked, sun-baked, beautiful women whom
he otherwise wouldn't have had the reason, or the cojones, to
talk to.

Finn's evil plan to engage in innocent banter with random women seemed to be bearing fruit the previous Thursday
when, just after his Prince scurried past, a woman in what
seemed an agitated state leapt up from her seated position on
a towel on the grass. Finn hurried over to offer the woman
his half-serious/half-disingenuous apology, but on the way
he couldn't help but be impressed: It wasn't just that the
woman was young and pretty and wearing a bikini but that
she seemed to have a theme, too, to Finn's eye an entire 1940s,
post-World War II motif going on. Her bathing suit was a
two-piece, but it looked like it belonged on Betty Boop, big
and blue with a white belt, with designs modestly adorning
what could have been its most risqué parts (between the

breasts was one large bow, for example, and over the butt cheeks another), while the bikini bottom and bikini top, combined, were large enough to nearly completely cover nearly all the woman's bare skin from shoulder to thigh— her midriff was barely visible between the two. "Demure" it could certainly have been said of the bikini, but "classy" too. On her feet the woman wore wide, strappy heels, and over her eyes large, wide, round sunglasses. Her hair, naturally, was elaborately curled, with parts pinned back, the entire outfit evoking for Finn the image of some heroic American nurse in the South Pacific. Think Kate Beckinsale in *Pearl Harbor*, in other words, more than Bo Derek in *10*.

Only in New York, Finn wanted to yell! Only in New York...

Before our hero could launch into any such complimentary spiel to her, or even before he could offer his half-hearted apology, the woman ignored the father and son completely to launch what seemed a tirade into the sky.

"They're watching me!" she screamed, pointing up.

With her outburst Finn initially figured he and the Prince had stumbled upon nothing other than another New York City nutter, one more in the long line of whack-jobs that gave the city character and, let's be honest, helped make it great.

"Look!" she yelled while grabbing Finn's arm, pointing behind him. "Over there!"

When Finn looked up he didn't expect to see anything, imagining that whatever figment of this woman's fevered imagination was up there was surely only visible to her. When his eyes focused, however, Finn did see something in the sky above the Sheep Meadow, and it was a something that pissed him right off, too. Making long, languorous sweeps of the sky high above the lawn but then occasionally swooping low and hovering just above what Finn quickly surmised was only the prettiest of girls wearing the skimpiest of bikinis, was one of those god-damned, good-for-nothing remote-controlled drones, those stupid little flying toys armed with cameras which allowed absolutely anyone to spy on absolutely anyone else whenever they god-damned felt like it.

"Whhhheeeeee.......!" Finn heard. "Whhhheeeee..........!"

That stupid little drone above Sheep Meadow wasn't just swooping around and spying on the nubile sunbathers either, but was also evincing from its pathetic little motor a high-pitched squeal, a whiny wail or a keening shriek, as it were, a disgusting little sound that seemed vaguely reminiscent to Finn before he realized, oh yes, that's the sound of common decency and the expectation of privacy being violently ass-fucked.

"Whhhheeeeee.......!" Finn heard. "Whhhheeeeee.......!"

It wasn't just that there was a single camera in a single drone that annoyed Finn so. It was that there were cameras everywhere now. Just a week before Finn had ignored the work he was supposed to be doing to have himself a "me" Wednesday— "All work and no play makes Finn a dull boy," he would have argued at the time!— but he couldn't really enjoy it too much because everywhere he went that day, there he was: As Finn walked down Broadway towards Times Square at 11 A.M. he stopped into a bodega to buy himself a nice cold tall-boy can of Coors Light in a small paper bag, but then when looking up from the cash register he saw himself on the screen of the store's closed circuit TV, a middle-aged man not doing any work in the middle of a work day but instead at 11 A.M. buying himself a nice cold tall-boy can of Coors Light. Talk about a buzz kill. A half an hour later he looked up from his table at Five Guys on 42nd street to see himself— déjà fucking vu, eh?— on that store's CCTV, a fattish, stressed-out guy with high-blood pressure not daintily enjoying a garden salad like he should have but chowing down on a double-cheeseburger and fries. It almost made Finn lose his appetite. (Almost.)

Immediately thereafter he was in a nearby movie theatre hoping to enjoy a nice matinee when Finn saw himself not on their closed-circuit TV but somehow, in a video game? Yeah, Finn didn't get it, but walking across the empty lobby

he looked at one of the first-person shooter games sitting
there— finally, Finn thought, someone is *finally* addressing
the absolute dearth of shooting opportunities that exist for
this country's youngsters— and saw himself, somehow, on the
screen of that game. It wasn't his reflection on the screen,
mind you, but he was actually being filmed by the game,
somewhere on it a camera pointed at him so that on the
screen Finn saw the video image of himself walking alone
across the lobby, with the added bonus, of course, of a bulls-
eye graphic tracking his every step, implying that Finn
wasn't just being filmed without his permission but that he
was also being targeted by a hidden assassin.

Good times, good times.

Speaking of intrusive photography equipment, every
time he sat down at his very own computer Finn couldn't help
but notice the one dead, glassy eye of its very own webcam.
While Finn appreciated the benefits it provided (the Prince
being able to Skype with the Pilgrim grandparents, for instance), he'd also read that those cameras could easily be
taken over and controlled by hackers. That meant every time
he sat at his laptop to work or play, Finn did so with the
vague feeling he might be being watched. You try to enjoy
some relaxing Internet porn, Finn bitterly thought, when
just at the moment of glorious release your brain is suddenly
swamped with the idea that someone is secretly spying on
you, that sad-sack you— pants around your ankles, dick in
your hand— is some joke, a laughingstock, right then being
sniggered at by one Internet hacker or another, likely some
pubescent punk in Azerbaijan or the like.

Even if his computer wasn't spying on him, Finn knew
it was tracking him, making note of every website he frequented and every viewing predilection he had, if only to
later "helpfully" make recommendations of other similar
sites he might like to visit or other similar purchases he
might like to make. That might have theoretically seemed
like a good idea, but the suggestions his computer most frequently made to Finn pretty much implied his only interests

where European soccer and MILFs, with the apparent hours and hours Finn must have spent each day on those two pastimes not necessarily being something he needed to be reminded of. Meanwhile, after *once* quickly looking online for a gas cap for his father-in-law's Jaguar Finn could never again visit Facebook without being swamped there by ads for auto parts for English luxury cars, Jaguars especially, Mark Zuckerberg and his ilk apparently having alerted the entire Internet that that was the sole market Finn was interested in.

It's not like Finn was any Luddite either. He wasn't against all new technology. He just believed that all those new means to keep an eye on everyone (cell-phone SIM cards, for example, and IP addresses, MetroCards, ATM cards, closed-circuit TV cameras, motherfucking toy drones, etc. etc., all that shit that allowed anyone to know where anyone else was at all times...) came at the expense of privacy, secrecy, adventure. On his first trip to New York City in 1990, for example, Finn had made a point of walking down Manhattan side roads and back alleys as a way to get a flavor for the city's mean streets, a brave but foolish choice which at one point led to him being chased through midnight Chinatown by a couple of skulking teenagers (whether they were thugs out to rob him or kids trying to scare him for the fun of it Finn would never know, as he opted instead to run like the wind towards the bright lights of Canal Street). But had those "thugs" caught Finn and knifed him that night, leaving him dead in the street, in his wake Finn at least would have left an enigma. His motivations would have puzzled. What had their son been doing that night, the Pilgrim parents would have been left to wonder? Had he been trying to score drugs, his friends might have asked? Had he been looking to buy a gun? Searching for Szechuan beef? Trolling for prostitutes? Shopping for a mini turtle? No one would have ever known Finn's intentions or desires; they never would have found an easy answer to the difficult question of why Finn ended up in an unknowable section of an unfamiliar city as the clock was about to strike its midnight witching hour. In his sad death then, Finn would have at least left behind mystery and intrigue— which for a dead guy might've been better than nothing.

But if the modern Finn had a heart attack and dropped dead on the modern streets of Chinatown on his last visit just a couple of weeks prior, between his phone calls and subway rides and credit card charges it would have taken the NYPD all of about ten minutes to piece together the entire narrative of Finn's entire last day. Next thing he knew, some wily detective would've been announcing to the world Finn's ultimate itinerary, releasing the devastating details that Finn's last stops on Earth had been a TCBY and The Eastern Garden, making clear to the whole world the humiliating reality that the last couple of things Finn ever did before departing this mortal coil were to enjoy a refreshing snack of frozen yogurt and get a soothing hand-job at a Korean spa.

"I just don't understand it," the Betty Boop bikini'ed babe was saying back at the Sheep Meadow in regard to that sniveling, squealing, spying drone, "Who would so such a thing?"

Finn had already spotted the guy, about three hundred yards away on a rocky outcropping on the eastern side of the grassy meadow, near an exit that would allow him to escape off towards the carousel and Wollman Rink if it came to that. Holding the remote-controller, the shmuck looked exactly as would be expected of such a creepy perv: a bearded, middle-aged white guy with a pot belly, sunglasses, and a floppy, bird-watching sort of hat atop his head, a t-shirt tucked into long pants and a fanny pack hanging below his belly, what looked to be Birkenstocks on his surely gnarly feet.

Classic loser outfit, Finn thought to himself, before looking down to make sure he wasn't too similarly attired.

"Seriously," the Betty Boop bikini'ed babe continued, "Why would someone do such a thing?"

Well, she lost me there, Finn thought, as the perv's motivation in making a spy tape of a bunch of pretty sunbathing women was the least mysterious thing Finn could imagine. While he couldn't be sure of the exact details of the entire plot— whether that freak was going to look at the film on his computer itself or print out screen shots to wallpaper his entire creepy room, Finn didn't know— there was no question where this entire scheme was going to conclude: The sex fiend was going to end his day staring at bikini'ed girls and whacking himself wildly off, obviously.

Finn didn't begrudge the man that. If he was being perfectly honest, Finn could admit that he himself had more than once done the occasional whacking off to the images in his head of various of these sunbathing beauties, although at least Finn would have said he'd kept it "old school," having the common decency not to announce those intentions to the whole world. Plus, he'd used only his brain, not any stupid camera, meaning none of the women Finn had ever talked to and then masturbated to had necessarily suspected that the nice dad they were chatting with would likely soon be dirtily despoiling their memories with his hand down his pants.

"I'd like to knock that thing right out of the sky," the Betty Boop bikini'ed babe said next , a suggestion the Curmudgeon Avenger had duly noted and reminded Finn of the very next week.

When the cab from the oncologist's office dropped them off at the Albemarle on Thursday afternoon, Finn escorted his wife to their front door and made his escape. He skulked off to the outside stairwell and found what he was looking for— from underneath the stroller, the Maasai war club, two feet long of shiny ebony carved to kill— before rushing out of the Albemarle and up Broadway. The weapon he had stuffed down one leg of his khaki shorts, and while a few inches of its two foot length were visible below the hem Finn knew it didn't matter: He was middle-aged, white and portly, wearing a brand new Iowa Hawkeyes t-shirt. To the outside world the man was innocent of *everything*.

At Columbus Circle Finn didn't even slow down while being accosted by the usual yearning vendors— young men of various nationalities trying to hawk him bicycle rentals and pedi-cab rides and horse & carriage tours, plus a gaggle of newly-arrived African immigrants suggesting that they could show Finn all the secret spots in a Central Park he visited nearly every day with his son— instead plowing towards the Greyshot Arch on the back way to Sheep Meadow. A couple of hundred yards into the park Finn remembered that he needed a disguise— well, he remembered that the Curmudgeon Avenger needed a disguise, although in truth right then Finn wasn't sure exactly where he ended and the C.A. began— so he fought his way back through the crowds of tourists loitering about on that warm day until he could see the statue of Columbus atop his obelisk near the park's entrance. There ignoring the hot dog stands, and the halal trucks, and the smoothie shacks, and the souvenir tables packed with pictures of old New York, Finn found what he was looking for: tchotchkes. He bought from a Middle Eastern souvenir seller an extra-large t-shirt adorned on its front with a picture of John Lennon wearing a New York City t-shirt, an over-sized pair of sunglasses with bright yellow frames and the year "2013" emblazoned across the top, and a foam replica of Lady Liberty to be worn on his head, her torch standing all proud and tall like an antennae above Finn's left ear.

A day when he was told his wife was dying was never going to be Finn's lucky day, so the man wasn't surprised when he arrived at Sheep Meadow in that ridiculous outfit to find that the debauched drone operator and his intolerable toy were nowhere to be seen. And while Finn was ready right then to give up on everything, on his whole life it seemed, he wasn't ready to give up on the idea of smashing that fucking little drone into pieces. Instead Finn leaned back against the Sheep Meadow's low, chain-link boundary fence and waited. Finn recognized that it was a beautiful day— he could see puffy white clouds, a sky of pure blue, greening grass, etc.

etc.— but to his eye a pallor had been cast over everything. A darkness. Nothing could be good or would ever be good again, he thought. He saw in the park only change and loss and death. He felt only despair.

Up Central Park West Finn saw the majestic Dakota, and while he'd always thought the melodramatic architecture of that historic apartment building was creepy cool, that day it came across to him only as strange, eerie, inhuman. Through the trees just north of Sheep Meadow Finn could see the pristine green grass of the Park's last remaining croquet fields, manned that day by only two old geezers dressed in the purest of whites. Normally Finn got a kick of those fields and those players, imagining them a link to a bygone New York City, maybe a better New York City, the good old days perhaps. Finn even got the feeling sometimes, if he ever saw on old man and an old woman playing together out there, that maybe the two were Holden Caulfield and his little sister, now grown old but still hanging on. But that day Finn saw nothing cute any more about the croquet, nothing charming, realizing the old people out there weren't representative of anything, being absolutely decrepit really, on the verge of dying they were, just the sad end of a soon to be extinct era. If those players weren't yet corpses, Finn could see, they were still no more than ghosts.

South of Central Park Finn saw the changing skyline of New York City. The Essex House— whose iconic red neon lights had hovered atop many of the historic photographic nightscapes the young Finn had enjoyed of New York City— was now being towered over by some bland monstrosity, being almost completely overshadowed by a soulless grey spaceship of a building nearly twice its size. The new building did not look livable, Finn thought. It did not look lovable. It looked like no more than a cryogenic chamber, the sort of cold scientific atrocity that might have housed the great Ted Williams' severed head.

Towards the east Finn couldn't see any of the Plaza, not even the flags fluttering atop it, being blocked out as it was by the park's blossoming trees. And while that legendary hotel— the place where Eloise had tea, and where Fitzgerald drank— remained invisible to Finn, hovering above its absence was a clear shot of a Trump Tower. Then to the park's west, another Trump Tower, all the good shit in New York City seemingly being replaced instead by these offenses, one edifice after another being constructed to honor the worst of New York, the worst of America, really, a bombastic blowhard most famous for bad hair, tooting his own horn, and belittling others. Finn couldn't wait for the day when that buffoon's fifteen minutes of fame finally faded. People weren't going to fall for that clown's bullshit forever, right?

Perhaps Finn's favorite site in all of New York City was the Chrysler building— that Art Deco masterpiece on the east side that evoked for Finn all the greatness of the city's Don Draper past— which that day he couldn't see at all from his spot in the Sheep Meadow. The building was almost completely invisible to him from there, even its iconic top, all blocked from sight except for the tippity-tippity-top of the building's spire. But being able to catch a glimpse of that building's tallest point wasn't exactly cause for celebration either, as it looked to Finn that day like no more than the sharpest shard of a splinter, a sliver of silver pointing angrily up, maybe an evil stiletto getting ready to stab someone in the neck— Finn could just see the blood spurting everywhere.

Death, he thought, everywhere death.

"Whhheeeee.........." Finn heard the drone before he saw it. "Wheeeeeeeee.........."

And five minutes later it was done.

First, Finn saw the drone flying high in the sky. Seconds later, he saw its deviant captain walk through an opening in the fence on the far side of the Sheep Meadow, taking up what must have been his normal spot on the rocky outcropping there. Leaning against his own fence and still disguised as the stupidest of tourists, Finn scanned the grass to see where in Sheep Meadow the disgusting drone operator might be most interested, and he discovered that the greatest concentration of sunbathers was just off to his right. Finn also saw there what he took as three twenty-somethings wearing tiny bikinis and taking endless selfies of themselves, the trio of girls carrying on near-nakedly and concupiscently as they preened and pouted for their very own iPhones. Think "Girls Gone Wild," in other words, more than *Breakfast at Tiffany's*.

Finn wouldn't have argued that those young women weren't gorgeous, but in his mind they lacked a little something, too. Clothes, he might have said. Certainly élan, at least as it had been represented the week before in his Betty Boop bikini'ed friend. But regardless of Finn's impression about how idiotically those girls might have been acting, he also surmised that the three of them would prove to be manna from heaven for the "man" with his flying machine. It was clearly them that he and his stupid little contraption would be gunning for.

Sure enough, as Finn hobbled towards those girls— adding an extra limp to his step to imply he was an old tourist as well as a feckless one— the drone swooped in and swooped down, hovering just above the heads of the three scantily-clad women. Unlike the classy lady the week before, these girls weren't upset by the presence of a spy plane ogling them— rather, they seemed to love it. They jumped up and down in front of the drone just above their heads, their jiggly nubile bodies nearly falling out of the tiny strings modestly covering them, and waved at the winged toy, blew kisses at it. They seemed to be having the time of their lives, not seeming to consider that someone was basically peeping-Tom them, and not caring at all about what that someone might later do with any pics he took.

While Finn didn't understand why those young women didn't care about the drone filming them without their consent, he didn't care that they didn't care. Instead— as the debauched drone dude must have been licking his lips in anticipation of the onanistic orgy he was imagining for himself later that night— Finn stepped around the three cavorting girls and leapt up into the air, with all his might swinging the Maasai war club he'd just unsheathed from his shorts and smashing it full-on into the whining little toy, hooking the bulbous end of that weapon over one of the drone's wings and pulling it violently to the ground. Falling to his knees Finn held the keening machine down with the Maasai club in one hand before then grabbing it firmly by the frame with his other.

"Aaaaarrrrggggh," Finn roared, all William Wallace in his *Braveheart* glory, "Aaaarrrrghhh!"

The girls behind him were suddenly screaming in terror. They might not have known exactly what was going on, but right then those young women were operating under the idea that Finn was mad. As in, crazy mad.

The drone's frame was square, with a whirring rotor still spinning around on each of its four corners, and it had a camera mounted in its middle. That camera was the first thing Finn smashed to bits. He grinned to himself as he did so, smiling darkly, before raining blows down on that smashed camera again and again and again. The toy's engine was still wailing, its rotors still spinning, but with four quick shots— one to each corner— Finn shut the machine down for good. Finn rained blows down, raining them down, the dark wood of his ebony war club obliterating the sad little machine, absolutely annihilating it, tiny bits of plastic flying everywhere. Again and again Finn smashed it, hoping not to just break it but to beat it out of its very existence, to turn back the clock to a point in time when there weren't little drones flying around and spying on people, when there weren't traffic cameras on every street corner, when there weren't the technological means to track every single step of every single person through their cell phone use and Metro-Card use and credit card use... He wanted to smash that drone back in time, Finn did, back to a slower time, a better time, a time when there was no such thing as colon cancer.

Finn stood up. He could feel the sweat pouring off his forehead, could feel the crazy racing of his heart. He realized the foam Statue of Liberty decoration he'd been wearing had fallen off his head, while the over-sized yellow sunglasses with the year 2013 emblazoned on their top were at that point then hanging off only one ear. Finn unhooked the shades and tossed them to the ground. He looked up, suddenly realizing that the Curmudgeon Avenger was unmasked and Finn undisguised in the middle of Central Park on a warm May day, the "two" of them having just violently attacked a stranger's property for the public viewing pleasure of dozens and dozens of picnickers and sunbathers.

Finn didn't care.

"He's coming," a twenty-something guy said, and while at first Finn thought the dude might have meant the police he actually looked up to see approaching the drone's owner, that paunchy pervert looking animated at best, agitated at worst, as he got closer and closer, then only about a hundred yards away and waddling fast.

Finn didn't care.

He tossed the shattered drone at the feet of the three young women, two of whom he noticed were right then filming him on their iPhones.

Finn didn't care.

"You're welcome," he said. Then he turned towards the approaching creep, raised his Maasai war club high in the air, roared like a lion, and charged.

Avenue A-hole (Friday, 2013)

In the end, that degenerate drone operator did not turn out to be so dumb. Yes, the perv in the park had his fair share of inadequacies (e.g., his depravity, his lack of common decency, his incredibly poor fashion sense) but when the fellow saw Finn running at him on Thursday afternoon— Finn roaring and sweaty, red-faced and bug-eyed, a hulking ex-jock wielding some weird weapon over his head— the sicko spy-plane pilot had the good sense right then to high-tail it out of Sheep Meadow just as fast as he could go. The guy basically speed-waddled his way towards the closest exit, quite sensibly realizing at the sight of the charging Finn that he didn't really care all that much any more about what might have happened to his winged toy. And although Finn chased the creep off that grassy expanse, when the sicko went right— hoping to escape off towards the old Tavern on the Green apparently, like Rick Moranis didn't quite manage to do in (the original) ((the classic)) (((the one and only))) *Ghostbusters*— Finn veered left, opting instead for the wooded path that would lead him back along the fence and through the trees towards the carousel.

Finn hadn't wanted to catch the guy. He'd demolished his stupid toy already— what, he was going to smash the shmuck's skull, too? Plus, between his sweating, his heavy breathing, and the sharp pain he could feel in his chest, Finn knew he needed to slow down. He needed to take a break, so he stepped off the trail and wandered into the trees, eventually finding a spot to sit at the bottom of a large oak. Finn could hear people everywhere— revelers in Sheep Meadow, ballplayers at the softball fields, children laughing as the carousel twirled— but surrounded by trees he sat quiet and alone. With his heart aching in a bustling city of millions, Finn was completely alone.

It was not an easy night. By the time Finn returned home from his annihilation adventure his in-laws were back home on Long Island and his Prince was asleep. It was only Finn and Danielle then, wrapped up together in an endless night so dark. They cried for her, they cried for him, and they cried for their Prince, the baby boy they'd once believed might be Danielle's savior but then who turned out not to be. Mostly they cried for him, Finn and Danielle did— they were despondent about Danielle but mostly they cried for their poor, poor motherless child.

Things were a little better the next day. The sun did come up, in fact, and though they'd not specifically addressed the topic the night before, it was understood: The Prince wasn't going to pre-school on Friday, Finn wasn't going to the atrium to work, Danielle wasn't going anywhere. The family would be together, so after breakfast they hopped into the mini-van Danielle's father had lent them— no one was exactly sure how the old man had gotten his hands on such a mini-van, but they also knew enough not to ask— to head downtown. Down 54th street Finn drove east, the Prince first excitedly pointing out to his parents the statues he could see in the garden of the Museum of Modern Art, before they hung a right on Fifth Avenue to head south.

"Rockefeller Center," the Prince hollered from the back seat.

"Empire State Building!" he yelled farther down.

"Flatiron Building!" he pointed. "I saw it first!"

"Our own little tour guide," Danielle smiled proudly.

On the Lower East Side Finn hung a right from Houston on to Essex, and then another on to Rivington, parking the car in an empty spot right in front of his destination: Economy Candy.

"Whoa," the Prince muttered, marveling at the bulk sweets filling its windows. "Look at that."

Finn smiled. He'd never been that big a fan of sugar for his boy— and don't even remind him of the articles he'd recently read about how it might lead to *cancer*— but Finn wanted to have a special day with his family, so Economy Candy was the first stop.

Before getting out of the car though, Finn had a chuckle to himself regarding the spot directly across the street: The Hotel on Rivington (or, for those in the know, THOR). Finn had to laugh, because it was in a room there where a number of years before he and Danielle had put on an aborted sex show for a couple of married tourists, when after nonchalantly scrolling through the Craigslist ads one lazy Saturday Finn stumbled upon a pair of honeymooning newlyweds who, although "nervous first-timers," claimed they might be willing to spread their wings sexually as "voyeurs." Basically, those rubes wanted someone to come to their hotel room to fuck in front of them, which was an idea that the exhibitionist Danielle agreed to almost before Finn had even finished reading her the ad.

"Why not?" Danielle said. "Let's go."

So go they did, Finn and Danielle bringing their rough-sex dog & pony show on the road from Midtown to the Lower East Side that day, greedily performing for those tourists the beginning of an ersatz rape, a sex act that in itself seemed to be more terrifying to those aghast out-of-towners than titillating— clothes being ripped off Danielle, her wrists bound— even *before* Finn got hurt, when in a graceless attempt to mount Danielle's chest to titty-fuck his beloved Finn overextended his left hip, pretty much dislocating the joint and causing him to collapse on to the sightseers' hotel bed in paroxysms of pain, our poor hero thus not consecrating his love for Danielle with a cum-shot to the cleavage in front of a pair of random strangers but with the man instead wailing in agony, flopping about like a fish out of water, screaming bloody murder regarding their innocent love-making gone terribly awry.

Finn looked at Danielle and nodded towards THOR.

"Remember that place?"

His wife smiled. "I told you to stretch."

At Economy, Finn pointed out to his son all the sweets he remembered from his youth, treats that were seemingly becoming obsolete even in the 1970s but that were thriving in Economy Candy to that day: button candy to be plucked off a long roll of white paper, rope licorice, stick candy, rock candy, fire balls, candy cigarettes (or, as Finn couldn't help but think of those sugary fags: carcinogens squared!), not to mention in the front windows of the store innumerable boxes of bulk penny candy. He highlighted for his wife and his son the store's tin ceilings, its antique Coca-Cola advertisements all over the walls, and the taped radio broadcast of a Jimmy Durante vaudeville show playing over the store's loudspeakers. Finn couldn't help it: He loved Economy Candy. It reminded him of better days.

After filling their faces with various sweet treats— mostly Charlestown Chews for the father and son, something called "halvah" for the long-time New Yorker, Danielle— the family climbed back into their mini-van and drove off towards the East Village, parking there just past 10th St. on Avenue A. Danielle headed off to visit Ingrid, her best friend and former college roommate, to share with her the terrible news. She said she'd meet her boys later at Tompkins Square, which is where Finn and the Prince would be enjoying the playground, assuming, of course, that the local rats had had the common decency to vacate the premises that morning.

No rodents were anywhere to be seen when father and son arrived at the playground, so the Prince joined another boy building castles in the sandbox, but even without any vile vermin scuttling about Finn saw trouble: Across the way some guy was using the tire swing like a catapult. The guy wasn't actually hurling his kids through the air on purpose, but he was spinning the tire swing so fast— with a couple large teenagers riding it, mind you— that Finn couldn't shake the feeling it wasn't going to end well. Those teenagers were flying in speedy loops while hanging on for dear life, laughing uproariously, yes, but the tire itself— attached to a metal frame by three chains, coming together at one steel plate on its top— must have been nearly six feet in the air as it spun its frenzied, dizzying circles. The whole contraption was about forty yards away from the sandbox, so it wasn't any threat to the Prince, but Finn just couldn't helping thinking it all boded ill. Those kids looked so heavy, Finn thought, the tire so small, its speed so fast.

He considered going over and mentioning to the guy— a thirty-something African-American male pushing a couple of teenaged African-American males— that maybe he ought to tone it down a bit, ya know, take it a little easy, that maybe that device wasn't made to hold such big kids or spin so swift? Finn thought about doing so but he didn't, first of all because no matter how you sliced it interrupting someone else's play-ground fun with words of warning could certainly be construed as "causing a scene." At least it was "butting in," an idea that was virtual anathema to any native New Englander. The other problem was that Finn no longer lived in the neighborhood, meaning he wasn't necessarily in any position to tell someone else how to act down in the East Village. Seriously, how would any such scene have played out— a middle-aged white guy soberly offering some unsolicited advice to a younger black guy about how to behave in pub-lic— but as the living embodiment of gentrification? No thanks to that, Finn thought in the direction of that crazy black guy, and good luck to ya'...

"I know you!"

Suddenly standing in front of Finn in the Tompkins Square playground was none other than Mick Mullaley, re-tired New York City firefighter and Earth School dad, puncher of perverts and star of at least one *New York Post* story. Mullaley was looking at Finn, smiling.

"I know you," he repeated.

Finn raised an eyebrow at him, waiting.

"Earth School the other night," Fireman Mick paused. "You're the...."

Finn waited, half-smiling, pretending that the two of them were having a good time at this little game.

"....The Smudgey Defender?" the retired firefighter laughed, not sure what Finn had called himself on Wednesday night but pretty sure it hadn't been that.

Finn shook his head, shrugged his shoulders, aiming to look confused.

"...The Courageous Pretender?"

Finn waited.

"...The Pudgy Revenger?" Mullaley laughed. He was certain he knew who Finn was but equally certain that he couldn't remember what the guy had called himself.

"I'm sorry," Finn said, trying to look sympathetic at Mullaley while also feigning complete and total innocence.

"C'mon, man," the ex-firefighter laughed. "I know you!"

"Wait..." Finn began, deciding that they were having fun after all. "You don't mean...?"

Mullaley looked at him with smiling eyes, waiting, waiting. He knew he was right!

"...The Curmudgeon Avenger?"

"That's it!" Mullaley roared. "The Curmudgeon Revenger! I knew it was you!"

Finn liked the guy. He was completely without embarrassment. He'd not even been close in remembering Finn's nom-de-guerre, but the guy didn't care. He knew only that he remembered Finn and, apparently, was happy to see him again.

"That would be me," Finn smiled, holding out his hand. "Or you can call me Finn."

"Mick," Mullaley said, shaking.

Mullaley then explained that he was in the park that morning because it was his young son the Prince was playing with in the sand. The former firefighter went on to tell Finn he had that four-year old boy in the sand, yes, as well as another fifth-grade daughter at home, not to mention a couple of thirty year olds kids living out there on Long Island that had resulted from his first whirl on the marriage go-round.

"Shit!" Finn said, both amazed and frightened by the idea.

"Got a couple of little grandkids out there, too," Mullaley laughed. "Sometimes you'll see me out here with all six of 'em...Kids, grandkids, the whole bunch..."

"Wow," Finn said, imagining the stresses of a household like that, trying not to even think about the chores involved when dealing with multiple kids, multiple generations. "How do you manage?"

"What are you gonna' do?" Mullaley smiled. "My wife's working so I take care of it."

"All of it?"

"Someone's gotta' do it."

"You have a babysitter? Housekeeper? Au pair?"

"A what?" Mullaley asked. He wasn't being patronizing. He was just confused. Why would he need help? "I take care of it all. What else am I gonna' do?"

It's not like Finn hadn't always known he was a bit of whiny bitch, but that conversation with the retired firefighter certainly helped confirm it. Mullaley seemed to suffer no stigma at all regarding the idea of a man pushing a child in a stroller. He apparently had no problem with changing multiple diapers and wiping manifold noses or drying many tears. He just did what he had to do. Perhaps having spent his life running into burning buildings to save others meant the man wasn't overly troubled with what others thought of him; it was like he gave no thought at all to the idea of what it really meant to be "a man." He just did what he had to do.

"Wow," Finn said, amazed with the guy's laissez-faire dadding attitude but still treading a little lightly when he brought up what he considered touchy subject. "So *you* are a stay-at-home dad?"

"A stay-at-home dad?" Mick laughed out loud. "I'm never home. We're always out, to the park or school. Music class. Krav Maga. I'm never home..."

An asshole, Finn thought of himself. Such an asshole.

Finn's bout of intense self-loathing had to be brought to an abrupt halt, however, when the two fathers then heard a deep thud, a noise perhaps most accurately described as the sound of a watermelon exploding. The last time Finn had glanced at the tire swing the teenagers were off it but the thirty-something guy was winging the empty tire just as fast as he could, spinning it around and around, the thing screeching in circles while flying about at about the height of a man's head. When he heard the loud "thud" Finn immediately glanced into the sandbox to check on the Prince's safety, and after seeing his son still blithely playing there he turned his focus back towards the swing: There, of course, he saw the empty tire wobbling, heard its shrill chains squeaking, and watched the thirty-something black guy collapse to his knees, his face covered with what looked to Finn like nothing other than blood.

Long story short, the guy died. He died even though the ex-firefighter Mick Mullaley immediately rushed to his side and even though an NYFD ambulance pulled up to help just minutes later. It was all to no avail though. As far as anyone could piece together, the man had been struck directly in the face by the very piece of playground equipment he'd been playing with, his decision to swing that rubber tire in a manner it had certainly not been intended thus ultimately boding quite ill for the guy. A story in the *Post* the next day explained that those tire swings did not consist of simple rubber wheels but wheels reinforced inside with a circle of solid iron, therefore explaining how the guy might've unexpectedly— especially to him probably, Finn thought— ended up first with a broken skull, and then dead. D-E-A-D, dead.

Finn was sympathetic to the guy's plight, for sure, and he didn't want to say "I told you so," but he also couldn't help thinking to himself, well, you know, "I told you so." Finn hadn't known about the reinforced iron, no, but that the guy's swingin' shenanigans were not going to end well was not a circumstance that could have been called unforeseeable. In any case, Finn adhered to some pretty strict park rules, one of which was that if anyone ever died on the playground it was time to call it a day— everyone could agree at that point the fun was pretty much over, right? Meanwhile, if Finn had been feeling like he was living his life in the shadow of the Grim Reaper, watching the New York City Fire Department pull a white sheet over the head of a fellow human being who'd just been cavorting on the same playground as Finn and his Prince pretty much confirmed the idea.

Yup, Finn thought, it was time to get the fuck outta' there.

Finn and the Prince scooted back in the direction of the mini-van on Avenue A, agreeing along the way that they could go for a nosh and thus stopping to sit on the high stools near the kitchen in Tompkins Square Bagel. There they shared a pumpernickel bagel with butter and a blueberry smoothie, watching the shop's proprietor— a dour-looking old New Yorker who never smiled, a 50-something white guy dressed from head to toe in white Crocs, white pants, white t-shirt and white apron, a solid black Brooklyn Nets ball cap atop his silver-haired head— dropping uncooked bagels into a kettle to be boiled and then with a five-foot tall wooden spatula shoveling them into the massive oven to be baked. While Finn liked the bagels served in Tompkins Square Bagels, he also approved that they were actually cooked on the premises. It was a good old-school vibe, Finn thought, as he pointed out to his boy the whole process of how those bagels were constructed, cooked and sold.

After finishing their snack Finn decided to tool around the neighborhood in the mini-van for a bit, hoping a soothing ride might help his boy nod off for a nap. He grabbed the Prince and the scooters and carried them across the street to the mini-van, where Finn snapped his boy into his car seat and covered him with kisses.

"Stop it, Daddy," the Prince was laughing, "Stop it!"

The father wouldn't though; he would never stop.

Finn popped open the back of the mini-van to load up the scooters, gratefully noticing at that point the two feet that

existed between his vehicle and the sedan parked behind it—
less space and the back of the mini-van wouldn't necessarily
have opened. Then he hopped into the mini-van, put it in
reverse, and backed up, using the reverse camera on the dashboard (a wonderful piece of new technology, the decidedly
non-Luddite Finn thought!) to see himself inch closer and
closer towards the sedan behind him. Seeing himself on the
dashboard camera getting within one inch of that car, Finn
turned his attention forward, put the mini-van into drive,
and prepared to pull out of the spot only to see his progress
forward immediately thwarted by a jackass on a Vespa who
sped into the small space between Finn's vehicle and the one
parked directly in front of it.

Finn paused. Was that idiot stopping there, he wondered? Finn had parked right up next to curb, and he knew
he had absolutely no space behind him right then, so if the
clown on the Vespa was going to park there in front of him—
all of about one foot away— Finn knew he'd never be able to
get out. And the thing was, when the buffoon on the Vespa
had pulled in Finn had actually been in the process of pulling out of the spot. He'd actually been physically moving the
mini-van right then, so didn't that mean Finn had the right
of way? Wasn't the fool on the Vespa supposed to have waited
for him to finish moving before swooping in to try to Bogart
that space?

The guy was certainly parking though, popping down
the scooter's kickstand and hopping off the silly little machine. At that point Finn beeped his horn ever so slightly at
the guy, no more really than teensiest, tiniest blip of a beep,
the smallest sound Finn thought he could make on the car
horn whilst also announcing to the jackass on the Vespa that,
oh, yeah, by the way, you've blocked my way here.

The guy looked up all bellicose— yes, he was driving a
wee Italian scooter, the look seemed to imply, but that didn't
mean he was someone Finn could fuck with. Finn was half-
amused by the idiot, and he held up his own hands. What's

up, Finn meant to ask? I can't get out now! You've blocked me in!?

The guy scoffed, gave Finn some kind of dismissive one-handed wave before looking away. For whatever reason Finn remained amused by the whole scenario, so instead of getting mad he rolled down his window to playfully accost the intruder. Finn was seeing himself right then as a real New Yorker, a guy who stood up for himself and didn't get bossed around. It was fun, Finn thought, plus he knew his son was watching from the back seat.

"Dude!" Finn yelled at the guy through his open window. "Dude, I was in the middle of moving and you blocked me in."

The guy repeated his disinterested, dismissive wave.

"Dude! You can't try to park in a spot someone else is already in!" What would the guy have to say to that, Finn wondered? Clearly he had him there.

In some weird accent the guy answered. "Fuck you," he loudly said.

Suddenly Finn wasn't having fun anymore.

"Fuck you," the guy repeated, this time adding some kind of odd, possibly Italian arm gesture, a gesture that no matter how you took it could not be read as any sort of friendly greeting.

Finn looked at his son's innocent face in the rear view mirror and he wasn't having fun anymore. For the first time in his life, he began to get out of his car to have an altercation with another driver. Finn recognized that these incidents occasionally went badly— as in someone-ending-up-dead badly— and he in no way intended to have one of those incidents. After all, his son was watching.

"Dude, please," Finn said to the guy, who was thirty-something and spectacularly coiffed, adorned with some sort of Mephisthophelean haircut and facial hair combination that he'd obviously given a great deal of thought to and spent a great deal of time on. "I was literally in the process of moving out of that space when you blocked me in. Can you just move enough for me to get out?"

"Not my problem," the guy said in some sort of guttural accent, a foreign inflection that seemed northern European to Finn but that he still couldn't exactly identify. He knew it wasn't German (not glottal enough, nor anti-Semitic) and certainly not French (neither submissive enough nor accompanied by a waving white flag) so Finn figured the guy to be Dutch perhaps, or Belgian, maybe Flemish (whatever that meant, Finn thought?)

"I had the right of way," Finn continued, more astounded than angry that a guy who clearly wasn't even from New York was acting like such a prick in New York. "I was already moving when you blocked me in?"

Mostly Finn didn't just understand how long the guy was going to keep up being so impolite, so unaccommodating.

"Not my problem," the punk blandly repeated. "Get back in your mini-van and go back to the suburbs, old man..."

"The suburbs?" Finn laughed. "My son was born on First Avenue!"

But Finn was beginning to get annoyed. His son was in the car so he didn't want to have a fit, but, uh, really?

"I'm just asking you to be decent," Finn said.

The guy said nothing, just shrugging his shoulders without even looking at Finn. He made no move back towards his scooter.

"I've got my son in the car and I just want to get out." Finn walked back to the mini-van and got in, impressed with himself that he'd had such a show-down with the guy but also happy that it hadn't ended badly. There'd been no fight. There'd been no real scene.

Finn put the mini-van in drive and looked at the guy, who looked up and seemed to have a change of heart, at that point nodding at Finn and waving him forward in an apparent effort to help Finn get out of the spot. Finn pulled the wheel all the way left, and though he couldn't imagine he could get by the Vespa without hitting it he followed the guy's instructions and inched slowly forward. Although the mini-van was pulling hard left, it sure looked to Finn like it would hit the scooter in front of him, but its rider was waving him forward, with Finn following his directions inching forward until— unsurprisingly, Finn thought— at about one mile an hour the mini-van bumped the Italian scooter.

"I knew it," the dunce on the Vespa screamed, then pulling his iPhone from his pocket and waving it about, filming everything in sight. He pointed it at the mini-van's license plate, at Finn behind the wheel (and thus, correspondingly, at Finn's son in the back seat), at the site of the "accident" between car and scooter. "And now I've got you. I've got it all on film, too!"

The young man could have made few decisions right then more ill-advised than pulling out an iPhone and pointing it at Finn. It wasn't just like waving a red flag in front of a bull— it was like waving a red flag in front of a bull in the middle of a goring rampage.

Finn began to get out of the mini-van very slowly. He turned to smile warmly at his son, who smiled warmly back. The father then turned to approach the guy, who held his phone in Finn's face and filmed away.

"It's all on tape," he was shrieking now, his guttural voice having all of a sudden gone high. "It's all on film, and everyone saw it."

It was New York so no one was paying any attention of course. No one had seen anything.

"Seriously," Finn snarled, "you need to film this? This is the exchange you want to record for posterity?"

"They saw it," he squealed, pointing his iPhone towards a couple sitting ten feet away at a sidewalk table at Flinders Lane, the Australian coffee shop. The couple looked up oblivious. "Us?" one of them said. Another guy standing at the take-out window there hadn't even bothered to turn around.

"I saw it," Finn heard, and turning around he stood face to face with the proprietor of Tompkins Square Bagel, the crusty old guy that Finn innately liked due to his fine, old-school bagels. The guy was standing there in the middle of Avenue A in his whole baker outfit, dressed head to toe in white, while in his hand he held upward, like a pitchfork, the five-foot tall wooden spatula he used to put bagels into the oven.

"I was looking out and I saw you get boxed in by this scooter idiot," the Tompkins Square baker nodded towards the half-wit with the Vespa, whom he then addressed. "You should've waited for this guy to move."

"Bullshit," Finn heard from behind him again, this time in a voice that was vaguely high-pitched and vaguely familiar. Turning around Finn saw that the back of the guy he'd seen buying coffee at the Flinders Lane take-out window had been none other than his old pal Boogie, as wildly Afro'ed as ever and still hanging on to his cane.

"I saw the whole thing," Boogie continued, nodding towards Finn, "and Grampa here doesn't know how to drive. The scooter guy is innocent!"

Boogie winked at Finn when he finished talking, and actually mouthed something towards him. "What?" Finn asked, approaching Boogie.

"I got ya'," Boogie whispered into Finn's ear. "Who's your nigga' now?"

He smiled at Finn, just having a good time. Finn tried to smile back. He leaned up towards his friend's ear and whispered, one short sentence: "Danielle's dying."

Probably faster than anyone ever thought possible of a guy who walked with a limp and a cane, Boogie grabbed his walking stick like a club and swung it wildly over Finn's shoulder, just over the spectacular coiffure atop the head of the ducking troglodyte Vespa driver.

"You scumbag!" Boogie screamed, "Move your sissy-ass bike right now!"

Finn held Boogie back, thanking him. Oh, Boogie, Finn thought. There was a friend!

He turned back to the scooter guy with the iPhone. "Please just move your bike so I can take my son—"

Perhaps the guy didn't understand English very well, but at that point he certainly didn't decide to be decent. Instead he kept filming and squealed at Finn, nodding towards his son in the back seat of the mini-van, "Fuck you and that fucking brat—"

That the punk deserved to be punched was indisputable, so Finn punched him. And although Finn, Boogie, and the bagel baker had never shared a word amongst themselves before— they were not a team of any kind— as soon as the jackass on the Vespa uttered the word "brat" the three men were like a well-oiled machine, working in perfect cohesion: The baker stepped forward with his five foot long wooden spatula and slid it through the open back window of the mini-van, putting it right in front of the Prince's face before turning it on its side, completely blocking from the boy's view any sight of his father. Meanwhile, Boogie quickly approached the boy in his car seat and told him through another open window, hey, turn around quick, wasn't that just SpongeBob Squarepants walking through Tompkins Square Park? Boogie immediately got Finn's son to turn his attention away from anything that might have been happening in front of the car to instead look at what might have been happening in Tompkins Square out the back, Finn's fine friend then continuing to engage Finn's son in an animated conversation about that animated character, the little yellow goof who amazingly, Boogie said, turned out to be both his and the Prince's favorite.

And Finn punched the guy. He'd never punched anyone before, never really even thought about it. As an educated, well-off, white, American man living around the turn of the twenty-first century, it was hard for him even to imagine a reason why he might have. What, the Red Sox lost? Someone tried to steal his girl? Someone had cut him off in traffic? Please, Finn thought.

But the guy said "fucking brat" about the son Finn adored, so Finn punched him. He punched him hard, too, real hard, every bit of athletic understanding Finn had ever accrued in his entire life coming together in that one punch— every bit of knowledge about weight distribution and the transfer of power that occurred when one threw a baseball, kicked a soccer ball, swung a tennis racket— all the force of Finn's 225 pound body, all the pain of years of living with cancer and in the shadow of Death, all of it came out of Finn's right fist in that one single blow.

But between the guy's utterance of the word "brat" and Finn's fist beginning to fly forward, if he wasn't mistaken Finn could see in his peripheral vision coming up Avenue A none other than Fireman Mick Mullaley, pushing a stroller.

The guy was everywhere, Finn thought!

"Yo, yo!" Finn could subliminally hear from Mick as the power of the punch was building, making its way up his legs, through his torso, and into his right shoulder. "Courageous Revenge Man!"

The way he wanted the power of a soccer shot to come together in his foot at one single point when he kicked the ball, Finn felt the strength of his entire body come together into his right fist as it neared the guy's skull. Deciding not to break his nose— too squishy, Finn thought, too bloody— he instead struck the scumbag from the Vespa in the right eye, Finn's right fist pronating slightly to fill the punk's eye socket without necessarily squishing that all important orb (Finn didn't want to blind the guy, only crush him). His follow through was perfect, the transfer of power sublime, and the Vespa cunt collapsed like a sack o' potatoes. That spectacularly well-coiffed scooter rider was knocked out cold, and he would have dropped directly on to the street if he'd not instead fallen straight into the arms of, of course, Fireman Mick Mullaley.

"Wow," Finn said aloud, thinking of the guy's immediate and complete capitulation. "Must've been French after all..."

"What the hell, man?" Mullaley laughed, automatically assuming his new pal Finn was innocent of that whole to-do. "He deserve that?"

"He deserved it," the bagel baker said, pulling his wooden spatula from the car, nodding at Finn, and crossing back over the street towards his shop.

"He deserved it," Boogie said, reaching in to rub the Prince's head before nodding at Finn, smiling grimly, and turning to walk back towards his home.

"He deserved it," Finn told Mick, "Called my boy 'a fucking brat.'"

"Fuck him," Mick snarled before laying the loser on the ground. "I oughta' punch him."

Finn smiled. Talk about a friend!

Mick shook his head though, smiling. "Courageous Revenge Man, you've been kicking some ass around here, haven't ya?"

Finn shook his head. "Wasn't the Curmudgeon Avenger."

"No?" the former fireman asked.

And it hadn't been, of course, not at all: Finn's costumed crusader had nothing to do with that whole mess. His C.A. had no dog in that fight, as it were. Rather, the whole thing had been Finn. Just Finn. He'd gotten into a traffic altercation and cold-cocked a guy for all the world to see. Finn had, no matter how you wanted to slice it, caused a scene.

The cracks, in other words, were beginning to show.

The Wooing & Winning of Danielle Rigoglioso, Part II (2006-2009)

From the first night it had been pretty clear, pretty quick that Danielle was the girl for Finn. "The One" he would have even called her, had he actually ever been looking for just one.

Finn wasn't just impressed by Danielle, he was almost cowed by her. She lived her life like she'd walked down the street towards 7B that first day, brave and bold, her head up, her eyes forward, shying away from nothing. Danielle seemed the most independent person Finn had ever known. The most fearless. Nothing seemed to upset her. Nothing fazed her. She met every gaze, returned every word, joined every debate. When one day a cab driver whistled at her, Finn watched Danielle approach the man and ask him what was up: Could she help him? His answer? A blank stare. As always, Danielle walked away uncowed, unimpressed. Maybe the only time Finn ever saw Danielle really be affected by something was when he was wreaking sweet havoc on her in the bedroom— yet another thing to make Finn feel good about himself.

When they weren't in bed those first days/weeks/months, Finn and Danielle were usually sitting at a sidewalk table at Maison, the French restaurant around the corner from the Albemarle on 53rd street. There they nibbled on mussels and frites and enjoyed their particular vices, Finn a couple of cocktails and Danielle a couple of fags (some days one or two cigarettes, other days a pair of her gay male theatre friends). They learned each other's whole stories those days, too. Finn went first, hoping to entertain Danielle with a picaresque tale about what he pretended was his exotic past (living across the country, travelling the globe...), making a point nonetheless to gloss over what he saw as his many obvious failures: his failure as a teenaged lover, his failure as an athlete, his failure at even an attempt to be a writer, the pathetic reality of his long cynical career in an industry he despised. For the most part Finn ignored all those cold hard truths about his life because he figured the less said about his obvious inadequacies, the better. Very quickly Finn ascertained that Danielle was incredibly smart and perceptive, so he didn't want to do the woman any favors and assist her in coming to what Finn thought would be the eventual and obvious conclusion that she could do better. Let Danielle figure that out herself, Finn figured whilst staying mum.

Danielle filled Finn in on her whole backstory, too, the birth in Queens, the childhood on Long Island, the undergraduate and graduate degrees from NYU and the decades living on and around Manhattan. Danielle told Finn that she'd wanted to live in New York City since she was twelve years old, when one day she'd gotten so annoyed with her mother that she walked to the local train station and climbed aboard an LIRR train, heading for what she hoped would be a new life on her own in the big city. Fashion, Danielle said she thought. She'd work in fashion. At fifteen she began setting up a table on the sidewalk outside her father's Upper East Side parking garage to deal three-card monte, ultimately proving to have enough of both the hand-eye coordination and the balls to make hundreds of bucks a day at the game. At seventeen, while on vacation with her parents in "the islands," Danielle finally succumbed to her mother's endless requests one day that she speak French to the handsome waiter by looking the young man in the eye and exclaiming, "Je veux que tu me baises contre le mur."

I want you to fuck me against the wall.

"See," her mother laughed obliviously, "that wasn't so hard, was it?"

No, Danielle nodded, it hadn't been that hard, although she did then have to spend the remainder of the meal studiously ignoring both the cheerful chirping of her mother and the eager ministrations of the young man now providing for Danielle and her parents what must surely have been the greatest service ever provided to an American family visiting the Caribbean.

Danielle told Finn she had degrees in philosophy and theatre, plus a lapsed membership in Mensa (which Finn was impressed by, Danielle's embarrassed caveats aside), and that she was a professor at the New School. No one ever said Finn wasn't a smart guy (he read the newspaper from front to back almost every day, in fact), but he still would have been the first to admit that when it came to Danielle's career, Finn was at a loss: Danielle taught philosophy, emphasizing Heidegger and Hegel and Foucault, and the, quote/unquote, "science of logic," not to mention something called "syllogism." They were people and ideas that meant almost nothing to Finn; he heard and understood the words, yes, but in his brain: Blank. Cobwebs. (Syllogism? Nope, he didn't get it at all, only the fact that it sure did sound like a whole lotta' fun!). Finn simply could not wrap his head around Danielle's career no matter how many times she attempted to explain it, our hero instead just smiling at her blandly, feigning understanding.

Notwithstanding those extra IQ points of hers, Danielle and Finn fit intellectually as well as they did inguinally. Neither, for example, could quite finish the *New York Times* Crossword puzzle alone, but combined, they could complete that entire grid: Finn helped Danielle with all the answers she would otherwise never have had a clue about (regarding past Super Bowl champions, the Top-40 music charts, and every single iteration of MTV's *Real World*), while Danielle provided for Finn all the ones he couldn't have come up with in a thousand lifetimes (regarding classical music, early Woody Allen movies, and 19th Century French philosophes). If not a match made in Heaven, Finn and Danielle were at

least a match made in New York City, the two of them a commingled couple of educated, agnostic/atheistic, far-left-
leaning whites. Without even much trying Finn and Danielle came to realize they agreed on most things: Both, for
example, believed gay marriage and abortion should be legal
while assault rifles and standardized testing should be
banned. They weren't Jews, so the new couple wouldn't have
quite ticked off all of the boxes of "The Worst Nightmare" of
your average pick-up-drivin', rifle-totin', tobacco-spittin',
red-state redneck, but Finn and Danielle would nonetheless
have proudly conceded that, yes, they were a couple of col-
lege-educated, god-less, ultra-liberal New York City hippies.

The ease with which they became a happy couple was
only threatened by one thing: The fact Finn really had no
idea at all how to be any "man in the bedroom." Prior to Danielle, Finn did his best to be a nice guy towards any woman
he was interested in, hopefully impressing upon her the fact
that he was not any rapist or serial killer, just a sweet, funny
fella' who would also be agonizingly attentive to the sexual
satisfaction of his lady partner first and foremost, getting to
his own base sexual desires much after that fact; in other
words Finn would do his best to never, ever bother any poor
woman with his silly, stupid, superficial dick. Frankly, he
apologized for its very (rigid) existence.

Danielle wouldn't have gone for that, obviously, so Finn
needed a new plan; he needed to figure out exactly what it
meant to be "man" in Danielle's heart. From her initial post
on Nerve, Finn knew (cue *The Sound of Music*) a few or her
favorite things, and during their first sexual interludes he
made sure Danielle got what she wanted. Hair-pulling?
Check. Holding her down? Check. Forcing her to ... Check.
Like clockwork, Finn did them all. But other than that, he
came up blank.

Then when Finn's Internet research failed him— go
ahead, Google "man in the bedroom" and see what you get—
he realized the only way he could find out what Danielle

wanted was for her to tell him. So, during their initial get-ting-to-know-you conversations Finn as nonchalantly as possible peppered Danielle with the kinds of questions that he hoped would lead to the kind of answers that would specifically tell him how to treat her. Finn listened to her, really listened to her, this woman whose beauty had smitten him, whose brain had wowed him, and whose preferred per-version seemed to Finn like just about the most thrilling thing he'd ever heard about in the entire god-damned world.

Finn occasionally made notes of things Danielle said to later investigate them: He Googled the philosopher "R. Toad" whom Danielle had recently referenced before managing to realize she'd likely been talking about the French playwright Antonin Artaud. He rifled through the stacks of Kim's Video on St. Marks Place to find the movies she said she loved (Quentin Tarantino's *True Romance* highest on the list, plus a remade *Thomas Crown Affair*, not to mention some recent Ang Lee). He crept through the stacks of The Strand with a bunch of prurient books that might prove relevant to them (*The Story of O, The Collected Works of The Marquis de Sade*). At some point Finn realized he was preparing for his ensuing get-togethers with Danielle the way he'd once crammed for college final exams, which wasn't a bad way for him to think of things since he so desperately wanted to ace their next dates.

He was edified by some aspects of his research and con-fused by others. In reading *The Story of O*, for instance, Finn felt deep in his bones what might be right about a relation-ship between a man and a woman when the woman wanted to feel owned. He was less certain what he felt, on the other hand, about some of the works of the Marquis de Sade: An occasional paddling of a naughty bare-bottomed laundress, that intrigued Finn, yes, but he assumed he and his new par-amour could both agree that de Sade's inveterate forcible sodomizing of his (male) manservant was not all that cool, right? Finn and Danielle were anti-buggery, right? Right?!?!

Finn got why Danielle might have loved the newest *Thomas Crown Affair* (how sexy was that stairway scene!) but was at a loss understanding why she so loved *True Romance*. Yes, the love story between Clarence and Alabama was exhilarating, but did Danielle's fondness for the movie imply that she also wanted a drug-dealer of a boyfriend? A john? A gunslinger? Finn understood Danielle to be a liberal, educated New Yorker so he couldn't quite wrap his head around the fact she was so taken with such a vicious, blood-spattered film. Additionally, Finn understood why Danielle was so moved by *Lust, Caution*— when the male lead hauls his female lover across the bed and takes her there roughly, yup, Finn got that!— but he also had his doubts and questions. In that movie, the female member of that steamy couple is fucking the male member whilst also still planning to assassinate him, which made Finn question whether or not Danielle might have had ulterior motives with him: Was she was possibly a psychopath, he worried, a Black Widow perhaps, maybe some praying-mantis-wannabe who intended to fuck Finn first only to bite his head off after? Who knew? They had met on the Internet after all.

But in the early days of their love affair Finn and Danielle just fit: They liked each other and had fun together, both in the bed and out of it. When Danielle wasn't teaching and Finn wasn't freelancing away at his awful standardized testing gig, they visited bars and restaurants, went to the movies and frequented New York's many theatres. At old-school cinemas like the Ziegfeld and the Paris Theatre they saw artsy flicks like *Pan's Labyrinth* (Finn: "Huh?"), while on 42nd street Finn and Danielle joined the hoi polloi in watching fantastic Hollywood shlock like *Borat* (Finn, laughing uncontrollably: "Help me, I think I'm having a heart attack..."). While Finn wasn't gay he did love a spectacle, so he had no problem at all joining Danielle in her weekly trips to various Broadway and Off-Broadway (and Off-Off-Broadway) shows, where over the years they saw Mary Louise Parker play *Hedda Gabler*, Daniel Radcliffe in *Equus*, and Brian

Dennehy in *Desire Under the Elms*. The far-left-leaning, uber-hippies fell in love with each other all over again during one fantastic performance of *HAIR* in Central Park— dancing together on the grass as a warm rain poured down from the darkening skies above— and enjoyed around the city various performances of the New York International Fringe Festival, too. While Finn and Danielle decided they definitely wanted to see the comic masterpiece of puppetry that was *Avenue Q*, for whatever reason they also decided they would only see it if they won the daily lottery at the theatre of dirt-cheap tickets (a little known fact about New York City theatre that Danielle had to teach Finn), but, alas, that day never came, and as many times as they participated in the lottery they never saw that show. It was one of their few disappointments together.

From the beginning Finn and Danielle had their sexual adventures (and misadventures), too, both inside their bedroom and out. The problem— if one wanted to call it that— was that Danielle had "the kevorka," what scientists (or at least Kramer on one episode of *Seinfeld*) called the "lure of the animal." She was, in other words, indefensibly desirable. Danielle was an attractive woman, shapely and blonde, but even she wouldn't have said she was the most attractive woman around (certainly not when the "around" where she lived was the megalopolis of Manhattan). But more than her looks was the fact that Danielle exuded sex. Maybe it was simply pheromones, or maybe it was the fact she would look people directly in the eye and boldly hold their gaze, but every day any number of innocent bystanders in the street or on the subway or at Starbucks would be blandly thinking of their work day or their daily commute and would unwittingly, upon seeing Danielle, suddenly be imagining nothing but a warm pink pussy, a firm round ass. It could not be stopped.

Once the lovers were enjoying a cocktail at the Flatiron Lounge on 19th street, for example, when a free round of drinks was suddenly delivered to their banquette.

"From the lady," their waiter nodded towards a hulking Latina in a sport coat standing at the bar, a woman who shortly thereafter lumbered over and took a seat next to Danielle. She introduced herself as an NYPD detective from the nearby 10th precinct house and then made clear, without a great deal of subtlety, that what she was really interested in was getting her meaty paws on Danielle's sweet ass.

"No offense to you," she nodded to Finn, raising her glass in a toast.

Finn raised his glass right back, as the lady cop had been kind enough to buy him a fresh tumbler of Maker's Mark *and* because what was happening at that banquette was far from insulting to him: That woman simply found Finn's woman irresistible, which Finn couldn't help but think— following some transitive power of eros, he was— made *him* irresistible, too.

Danielle, meanwhile, sat silently, a subtle smile on her lips. Finn got the feeling she was watching the negotiation between he and the lady dick much the same way Dian Fossey had studied her gorillas in the mist: Just what were these monkeys up to?

Eventually it was decided that the nice lady cop would not be getting her meaty paws on Danielle because— and let's be honest here— Finn had no interest in any sort of sexual scenario that included the fat Latina while the fat Latina was correspondingly not too thrilled about any sort of ménage that included the fattish Finn.

Another time Finn and Danielle were having a snack at the bar of David Burke Townhouse on the Upper East Side and chatting with a random couple of married out-of-towners when the husband— perhaps emboldened by the considerable number of glasses of red wine he'd been pounding down— slid an arm around Danielle and made it clear that he and "the wife" sure would be delighted if she and Finn headed back to their hotel to engage in some swingin' hijinks, to enjoy, in other words, the ole' switcheroo. While in theory Finn liked the idea he had to put the kibosh on it because— again, let's be honest here— it wasn't a fair trade: In the exchange, the drunken husband would have gotten his grubby little hands on the sumptuousness that was Danielle while Finn would have had to settle for no more than the guy's friendly but bony-assed wife.

Nuh-uh, Finn thought. No thank you, he thought, instead straightaway dragging his Danielle home to bed by himself.

Had he been paying any more attention, Finn might have recognized that even if he was theoretically in favor of all those sexual shenanigans— threesomes and wife-swapping, oh my!— when the opportunities arose he nonetheless seemed to be consistently demurring, instead retreating home to the Albemarle to enjoy his Danielle on his own. But as self-awareness was far from Finn's forte, another night he suggested the happy couple head down towards Madison Square Park for a visit to the legendary sex club Le Trapeze, an idea Danielle okayed pretty much before the syllable "-eze" had slipped from his lips.

"Why not?" she said, game as ever, "Let's go."

It seemed like a good idea at the time, as they say, but in the end that swing club visit played out the only way it ever could have— and the only way that Finn, deep in his heart, surely knew it would: No sooner had Finn and Danielle darkened the club's doors than the Lifestylers milling about there descended upon the new couple, those old pros instinctively sniffing out the new girl's kevorka and culling her from the herd, hauling her off to a divan in the corner and falling upon her like starving vultures to fresh carrion. Finn, meanwhile, more than a little surprised with how swiftly these events were all going down, found himself sloughed off into another corner of the room, quickly coupled up there with a Italian-American housewife from Jersey who seemed less interested in getting it on with our horny hero than regaling him with her encyclopedic thoughts on the relatives merits of the elementary schools of Montclair.

Sexually, the visit to Le Trapeze was a bust, for both of them. Danielle was an adventurer so was glad to have had the experience, but she didn't end up being too thrilled to discover that the world of swing clubs may have been the last bastion of good manners on Earth. Danielle wasn't against such courtesy, of course, but for a woman who liked her sex like a barroom brawl the idea of five or six kind people graciously asking her if they could softly tickle her or tenderly caress her— "Would you mind, sweetheart, if I were to lick your labia?"— was the very opposite of the sort of thing that might have rung her bell. Danielle had been looking for a man in the bedroom, you might recall, not a gentleman.

Finn didn't particularly get off on his visit to Le Trapeze either because it was there that he discovered he was impotent. (*A lie, Liam interjects! A bold-faced lie!*). "Impotent" probably was not the right description for the condition of Finn's cock that night— perhaps "selectively erect" does it more justice— as he *was* able to maintain a hard-on whenever he found himself in Danielle's presence. However, in any other woman's presence— whether that Chatty Cathy of a Montclair mom, or the skinny black girl with dreadlocks from Brooklyn, or the admirably big-assed wife from Spanish Harlem— Finn wielded only an embarrassed smile and a limp dick. The problem, he realized, was not that he was really impotent but that he was suffering from a sort of sexual heliotropism, meaning Finn was like one of those flowers that followed the sun across the horizon over the course of the seasons. The man, in other words, only blossomed when within the warm rays of his girlfriend's love: Finn could only get hard for Danielle.

While his general limp-dickedness might have been cause for embarrassment for Finn, the sad situation turned out more wonderfully than he might ever have hoped: When Danielle figured out what was happening to her beau at Le Trapeze, she responded as if it was the most romantic gesture she'd ever seen. That in a swing club— a place where pretty much everything goes (after politely asking for permission, of course), where a man had free reign to rein in whatever ass he could get his hands on— that Finn only wanted only *her*, to Danielle it was a declaration of love. It was like a modern-day, X-rated version of John Cusack holding up the boom-box in the rain. Danielle apparently could imagine no poetry more poignant, no prose more profound: The man in her bedroom was her man alone.

Finn and Danielle left Le Trapeze that night sexually unsatisfied but more in love than ever, and by the time they reached the Albemarle lil' Liam had come roaring back to life (*a matter of simple loyalty, he sniffed*) and their love took its usual turn: Just inside the front door of apartment 2A Finn pulled Danielle to the ground and tore the clothes off her ...pushing his huge, hard self into warm, wet her... taking her rough and fast... and when it was over Danielle snuggled into Finn, her cuddly koala bear burrowing into his immovable California Redwood. They slept all night right there on the floor. They slept like babies.

The only time there was ever any real trouble between Finn and Danielle those early years was the one time he tried to fly too close to the sun: Finn considered broaching the idea of an open relationship with Danielle. (Wait, hadn't the man just admitted to being "selectively erect," basically only being able to have sex with *her*? Yes, but that was after the man first admitted to lacking "self-awareness," too, hence this cockamamie idea.) Finn was no moron, and he knew very well he'd never find anyone better than Danielle, anyone more absolutely perfect for him than her. No way. But Finn also couldn't help thinking that, you know, maybe he'd just like to sleep with another nice lady or two. Just spread his wings a little bit, explore a smidge, use some of those freshly-learned "man in the bedroom" skills in some other nice woman's bedroom as well. No big deal, right?

Not to Danielle, it wasn't.

The idea had been knocking around Finn's heads for several months, but before he ever even got around to saying anything Danielle sensed something was up.

"What's happening, Finn?" she asked one night. "You've been distant."

"No, nothing, honey," he smiled, shaking his head. Finn realized that was his chance, the moment he'd been waiting for, but he couldn't do it. His idea was too bold. She'd never understand. What woman would ever willingly agree to such a thing?

Danielle looked at Finn. Or maybe she looked through him. With a Mensa-level intellect and nerves steely enough to coolly deal three-card monte on the streets of New York City at fifteen years old, Danielle looked at Finn and saw right through him.

"What?" she asked. "You wanna' date other people?"

Finn didn't know if he blanched on the outside, but inside he blanched.

"I'll date other people if you wanna' date other people," she said.

Finn had never been a religious man, but he was always grateful for what happened next. Whether it was a sign from God or Buddha or Mohammed or the Great Spirit, he didn't know, but as soon as Danielle called his bluff and said she was willing to date other people Finn saw the light. He had a revelation, an epiphany, a fantastical flash-forward like some Dickensian Ghost of Fucking Future that revealed to him what life would be like in an open relationship with Danielle: Basically, Finn would be stuck home alone looking at Internet porn while waiting in vain for any one of the many women he'd contacted on Craigslist to get back to him, while Danielle would be out on the New York town again, the belle of the ball once more, agreeing to dates with construction guys who whistled at her on the corner, tenderly holding hands with various earnest hipsters as they sat through readings at the Bowery Poetry Club or listened to jazz at Joe's Pub, going to Knicks' games and red-hot Broadway shows with the various hedge fund managers and doctors and lawyers who regularly hit on her all over the city. Finn blanched, suddenly realizing that he'd seen this movie before and definitely didn't like the way it ended.

"Date other people?" Finn said, pretending to be shocked. "What are you talking about?"

By the next night Finn had himself an entirely new plan altogether, and when he saw the blonde beauty in a sheer nightie lying beside him in bed reading Paul Bowles, Finn knew it was time to act. It was time to be a man, so he rolled over and tried to seduce the woman he loved. Finn took the novel from her hands and kissed her profusely, pushing her legs open with his own and pinning her arms above her head.

"What are you doing?" Danielle asked with eyes wide, the innocent ingénue.

"I've got something for you," he whispered.

"I can feel."

"No, something else."

"Yeah?"

"Something bigger."

"Ohh," Danielle whispered, wiggling beneath him. "Yeah?"

"Yeah."

She waited.

"I decided it was time to plant my seed."

"You what?!" Danielle's eyes hardened. The ingénue was gone, replaced again by the tough-as-nails New Yorker she had always been.

"To inseminate you."

Danielle did not look happy. Oddly, Finn had thought she would look happy, but in reality she was staring daggers at him. Finn had never thought the phrase "staring daggers" made any particular sense, but right then he was beginning to understand.

"What are you talking about, Finn?" Danielle looked angry, and she started to struggle, but Finn had made sure at the beginning of this seduction that he would be in a position to hold her down. Weight and strength and leverage were all in Finn's favor right then, so Danielle wasn't going anywhere.

"I decided it was time to knock you up," he said. "To mark my territory. To make you mine."

Danielle stared darkly at him.

"To impregnate you," Finn clarified, as if she hadn't already got it yet. He realized things weren't really going so well but decided to say more. "Congratulations!"

Danielle fought, wriggling and struggling and trying unsuccessfully to get out from under him, fruitlessly trying to remove her arms from his grip. Finn didn't let go, but he was impressed with the fight in her. He had to admit to being a little surprised though, because frankly he'd expected his proclamation to be met with a bit more enthusiasm. However, the only enthusiasm Danielle really seemed to have right then was an urgent desire to escape.

She looked Finn right in the eyes. "I'll scream," she said.

Finn smiled at that, because the Albemarle had been built a hundred years before and its walls were thick. Yelling certainly would have been a futile gesture. Still, the intensity with which Danielle was trying to fight Finn off, the earnestness with which she seemed to be trying to get away in order to *not* have his baby, gave our hero pause: He'd really thought that deigning to award Danielle with the privilege of his progeny was going to have led to a bit more celebration on her part.

"Who do you think you are, Finn?" she asked.

Not surprisingly, Finn was willing to give up the fight a lot more quickly than Danielle. He loosened his grip on her wrists a bit. "Uh," he answered. "Your man in the bedroom?"

Danielle said nothing.

"Your man?"

She looked into his face and said nothing.

"Fine," Finn said, defeated, rolling off Danielle. "Fine."

For a couple minutes neither said anything. Finn lay on his back looking at the ceiling, while Danielle lay on her side, looking away.

"Don't you think this is something we should've discussed?" Danielle eventually asked.

"Whatever," Finn replied, as petulant as a forty-something man might be.

"I'm not saying I don't want to have a baby with you," she said later, still facing away from him.

He said nothing.

"Finn?" she said after minutes had passed.

He stared at the ceiling a while longer and didn't say anything.

"Finn," she whispered. "Look at me, Finn."

Without wanting to give in because he was still feeling pouty, he glanced quickly over at her. She still faced away from him, laying on her side, but she was looking back over her shoulder. When Danielle saw Finn look, she subtly pulled the sheer nightie up over her bare bottom, wordlessly confirming with no more than a flash of her ass that, yes, it was time to be starting a family together. Finn may have wanted to ignore Danielle but by then it was too late, the siren song of her haunches already playing in his heart.

Two days later Finn and Danielle betrothed themselves to one another in front of a justice of the peace at New York City's City Hall, and two weeks after that Danielle came out of the bathroom one Sunday morning with a stunned look on her face and a home pregnancy test in her hand, a home pregnancy test sporting two visible lines. When Finn saw it he laughed aloud.

"Victory is mine," he crowed, grabbing Danielle and hugging her, covering her face with kisses as he spun her around.

"All mine," he said, putting her down.

"I'm yours," she whispered into his chest.

Finn dragged his fingers over her breast and then down to her pussy, cupping it with his hand. "Mine," he growled into her ear.

He pulled the hand up over her belly, placing his open palm softly over where he imagined his baby might be.

"Mine," he whispered sweetly into her ear.

He put his hand over her heart and kissed her on the lips. "Mine," he said.

"All yours," she said again.

And it was true, too. As husband and father, all of it was Finn's now, *all* of it: the woman, the baby, and all their mutant genes...

Eggs Benedict Roulette
(Friday Night, 2013)

"Drink?" Mick asked.

It was two minutes after Finn had kayo'ed the kid with the stupid hair, and he stood next to the mini-van on Avenue A rubbing the knuckles of his right hand. The ex-fireman wasn't going anywhere though and seemed to want to get a cocktail.

"Drink?" he'd said.

When he'd punched the guy, Finn had the feeling everything had broken, not just the guy's eye socket but maybe everything inside Finn, too. He couldn't imagine going on, couldn't imagine living anymore, not without Danielle.

"Drink?" Mick repeated.

Finn liked the guy, yes, but he also thought the fellow might've given it a rest right then.

"Uh," Finn began, pointing with an open hand at the punk laying prostrate halfway off the sidewalk and halfway into Avenue A. "I just knocked a guy cold?"

"Celebration drink?" Mick laughed.

It was hard not to like him, Finn thought. Mick didn't take no for an answer.

"Is it even noon?" Finn wondered.

Mick glanced at his watch. "12:06," he said. "C'mon, there's a bar on the other side of the park."

Finn's alcoholic antennae twitched. "A bar?" It didn't seem the worst idea, Finn thought. There were things he wouldn't mind forgetting.

"On the corner of Avenue B, across from the park," Mick said. "The Horseshoe Bar?"

"You don't mean 7B?"

"Yes!" Mick answered with glee. "That's it. I love that place."

Finn shook his head. "A man after my own heart...."

"Right on," Mick smiled.

"What about these kids?" Finn asked, nodding towards his Prince and Mick's napping boy in the stroller.

"My son just fell asleep," Mick explained. "We got two hours."

They both looked at the Prince through the open back window of the mini-van. The boy was wide awake, looking right back at the two of them.

Mick turned sideways and edged closer to Finn, whispering under his breath. "He nap?"

"Usually," Finn answered quietly, talking down towards the ground.

"No nap!" The Prince suddenly called out the window. "No nap!"

The two fathers looked at each other and smiled, both of them knowing full well that nothing signaled a child's need to nap more than his insistence that he didn't need to nap.

"No nap, son," Finn cooed, first struggling to get the stroller out of the back of the mini-van and then opening its side door. "No nap, son. Let's just take a stroll around the neighborhood and maybe get a snack."

"No nap!" The Prince was maintaining as he got strapped into his stroller, and though both Finn and Mick insisted to the boy that he would not have to take any nap, they both knew it was only a matter of time: Any dad worth a dirty diaper knew there was no more soothing soporific to a tired child than the whirling wheels of a stroller, nothing that would knock him out any more quickly than a speedy spin around a green park on a warm, spring day.

"No nap, son, don't worry," Finn said to his Prince, before locking the mini-van and joining Mick in lockstep as the two broad-shouldered, shaved-headed, middle-aged fathers turned and headed south down Avenue A, racing their strollers towards the oasis of the bar on the far corner of the park. Side by side they strollered, baby carriages in front of them, two hulking guys making good time as they barreled down the wide sidewalks around Tompkins Square Park, pedestrians flying like plowed snow out of the way of those two men on a mission. As predicted, after only one twirl around the park the Prince was snoozing, but as they veered left and careened down 7th Street Finn realized the idea of two men bringing their babies into a bar might not be too well-received. It wouldn't have been that well-received back when Finn was a regular at 7B, particularly not even by Finn himself.

"They might not go for this in there, you know," he muttered to his new friend.

"Let 'em try to stop us," Mick growled.

The point was moot though, because no sooner had the two men banged their way through the swinging front doors of Finn and Mick's new favorite bar than the bartendress there saw Finn and shrieked. Dita, it was, resplendent as ever in a sharp Mohawk, bedecked as always in a white wifebeater and black leather pants, her arms and neck and shoulders covered in colorful tattoos.

"Finn!" Dita squealed, hopping up off the stool she was sitting on behind the bar and coming around front to say hello. Dita didn't just say hello, however, as much as she raced forward and jumped into the air, landing on Finn just as he turned away from setting up his sleeping son next to Mick's sleeping son in one of the bar's dark corners. Dita landed on Finn and wrapped her arms around his neck, her legs around his waist. Quite unexpectedly Finn found himself with two handfuls of leather-clad, thirty-something ass. "Firm," he couldn't help but think.

"What the hell," Mick laughed. "I guess you have been here before."

Finn was a little surprised. Frankly, he had no idea he had such a close relationship with Dita. He'd always liked her and enjoyed her company, and he might've even admitted to once having a ridiculous crush on the woman. Still, there had never been any hugging between them that Finn could remember. Finn understood their new dynamic, however, just as soon as Dita spoke.

"I've missed you, Finn," she whispered into his ear. "I'm so sorry about your wife."

It confused Finn. How did Dita know? Even when he realized she was probably only talking about his wife's old news (that she had cancer) and not her new news (that it was only a matter of time), Finn didn't recall ever telling Dita about Danielle. The look on his face must've showed his confusion though, because as Dita climbed off Finn she looked at him and continued.

"Facebook," she shrugged.

Fucking Facebook, Finn scowled. The place where privacy and decency went to die.

Dita headed behind the bar, and when she got back to where Finn and Mick had taken seats at the bottom of the horseshoe she was carrying two of Finn's old go-to drinks, the 24 oz. cans of Labatt's Blue beer. She knocked on the bar. "On me," she smiled to Finn.

"Christ, look at this thing," Mick said of the massive beer can he held in his hands. "I'm supposed to drink this in the middle of the day?!"

Finn clinked cans with Mick. "Why don't you just put on your big boy pants and enjoy?"

Mick smiled and shrugged, lifting the beer to his lips to gulp, leaning his head back and basically pouring the contents of the entire massive can down his gullet, chugging and chugging away. Dita and Finn looked on in wonder as Mick finished the huge beer, wiped his lips, and smacked the empty container back on the bar with a tinny clang. He patted his belly and covered his mouth before burping ever so slightly. "I should be alright," he grinned.

Dita got Mick another drink before returning to her stool at the far end of the bar, with Finn for the first time registering who else was in 7B. On one side of the horseshoe bar were three twenty-something women, quite attractive Finn realized except that all three of them had their heads down, their faces glued to their iPhones. The women were speaking to each other occasionally, although even when doing so they could barely be bothered to look up. The drinks in front of them sat untouched.

Meanwhile, on the other side of the bar sat a solo male Millennial, that guy holding up his own Apple gizmo in order to click a selfie with his only companion, that being a roast beef sandwich that it looked to Finn had come from Sunny & Annie's next door. The kid had just finished framing the photograph— opening the sandwich up into a V so both inner halves were facing out, spreading potato chips on the wrapper in front of them, posing a full pint of beer next to that— before bending his head down and holding his phone up to snap a photo of them all. Finn couldn't believe it: He'd thought it had only been an urban myth and yet there it was, some fucking guy taking a picture of his mid-day meal to post on the Internet, the yutz apparently super avid to update all his online peeps re: the status of his lunch.

Mick must've concurred with Finn's opinion regarding the utter ridiculousness of the guy, because even before Finn had time to point out the lunching loser than the ex-firefighter had slammed the bar with an open palm.

"Drink!" he bellowed at the punk making a memento of his lunch.

The guy, the girls, and Dita were all startled when Mick slapped the bar, but the kid found himself particularly mortified when he realized it was he who was being singled out, he who was being told what to do by some loud, old man at a bar. Mick didn't care though, with a grin holding up the beer can in his hand and repeating a loud "Drink!" For a second the Millennial looked like he might not have appreciated being told what to do by a stranger, but after no more than a quick glance their way did the kid realize he probably wanted to tread lightly re: the two old fathers with whom he was sharing the bar.

"Cheers," the boy said instead, raising up his previously-untouched beer to take the tiniest of sips.

"Cheers," the girls on the other side of the bar also said, each of them meekly raising their own glasses and sipping submissively.

"Cheers!" Mick thundered, smiling all around.

With an eye on their sleeping sons in the corner, Finn and Mick then settled in for a quiet hour of day-drinking. The men said little to each other, the new friends both okay with an easy silence and a cold beer, and Finn's mind began to wander. He looked out the huge windows filling the walls of Avenue B and 7th Street, enjoying the views of a new spring day in the East Village and all the joys that entailed: warm breezes wafting through the open panes, budding leaves and flowers on the greenery in Tompkins Square Park, the return of bare shoulders and naked legs and straining cleavage on the million beautiful women meandering happily down the city's re-awakening streets.

Finn had always loved New York, and he especially loved the East Village. When he'd finally managed to drum up the nerve to move to the city, it was to that neighborhood he'd always intended to go, the place where Kerouac and Ginsberg and Burroughs had once run wild; where the Ramones had rolled; where the homeless had first taken over Tompkins Square Park and then taken on the NYPD. The East Village had once been a place for the creative and the brave, and though Finn felt he might have missed some of it by arriving too late he was still always glad to have made the place his home.

But even more than his neighborhood, Finn knew, the East Village had always been Danielle's. After only one year in the NYU dorms in the early 90s, she'd moved with her best friend Ingrid into a two-bedroom apartment on 9th street & First Avenue, back in those days when it took some real balls to live that far east (the place was also rent-controlled, mind you, thus explaining why Ingrid still lived in the very same pad some two decades later). Danielle had told Finn all about her life back then, all about idling the hours away at the pinball machine in the far back corner of Downtown Beirut; about being pulled around the basketball courts of Tompkins Square Park on roller skates every day by the leashed pit-bull of a neighbor; about riding down the streets and avenues of Alphabet City in the sidecar of a motorcycle of an older man who may or may not have been her boyfriend ("Who knows?" Danielle had coyly shrugged when Finn once asked).

Finn marveled to think of it all, of the life led long-ago by that young girl his wife had once been. He liked to think of her at the pinball machine in Downtown Beirut, dressed as he knew she did in cut-off jeans and t-shirts, on her feet a pair of black Doc Martens. He saw her shapely legs, her long blonde hair in a tight ponytail, imagined a Diet Coke on a table next to her, a Camel Light in an ashtray beside that. Finn saw the look on Danielle's young, eager face, an expression that said, always, "Why not?" She'd always been open to try anything, Finn's Danielle, had been willing to experience anything, that girl even when so young ever so brave.

Sitting at 7B on that warm spring afternoon, Finn though of his wife back then, of the dreams she might have had, the life she may have wanted to live, and he wondered if she'd been happy. He wondered if he'd made her happy, too, but mostly Finn wished he'd known his wife way back then. He wished he'd known her *since* back then, in fact, and raising his beer to his lips it was the only thing he could really think: Finn wished he had more time with Danielle.

The man's plaintive stroll down memory lane was interrupted right then when on the north side of 7th Street he saw a ghost: Danielle. Through the windows of the bar he watched her, walking past the very spot he'd first pushed her up against the iron fence and kissed her roughly so many years before. She wore a perfect spring-time outfit, a strapless yellow summer dress and flip-flops on her otherwise bare feet, on her face large, round, dark sunglasses. She wore no underwear, Finn knew. When he'd seen her getting dressed that morning he'd suggested that though it was supposed to be a nice day those few clothes might leave her cold, but Danielle had smiled knowingly, not uttering a word. Seeing her walk down 7th Street right then Finn understood, because Danielle looked perfect: The sun lit her face and the breeze tousled her long hair; she looked bright and vibrant, young and beautiful and alive. One more time she had intended to be young and beautiful and alive.

With a tinge of jealousy and a tinge of pride Finn watched as Danielle turned her face to smile broadly at the bearded young man walking past her in the other direction. That young fool, of course, didn't even see the pretty older woman smiling at him, being too absorbed with whatever was playing on his smartphone to get that at that very moment he was at least a little bit getting hit on by a passing MILF. Danielle was undeterred by the fact the young man had not seen her, and she continued down 7th Street wearing a subtle smile on her face, the sly Mona Lisa grin that Finn always thought made it look like his wife had a secret. It used to be, Finn knew, that her secret was that his Danielle was willing to jump on whatever joy ride anyone had to offer, but things had changed. When once he'd been proud to be in on it, to know what that subtle smile revealed about the furtive go-ings-on of Danielle's heart, now Finn wished he didn't know her hidden truths: He wished he didn't know that on her right collarbone was a big bump, a rounded protrusion stretching Danielle's pale skin that covered the metal chemotherapy port that had been surgically implanted there so his wife could be filled with infusions of terrible poison; he wished he didn't know she had an IVC filter buried deep in her belly to keep any stray blood clots from randomly killing her, wished he didn't know that her stomach was criss-crossed with surgical scars from the colon resection and the C-section and the liver resection and the elective hysterectomy and the bowel obstruction; he wished he didn't know right then, on that seemingly-perfect spring afternoon, that his beautiful wife was being eaten alive from the insides.

It didn't seem possible, Finn thought: She looked so good.

Finn nudged Mick beside him and nodded out the window. "In yellow," he said. "My wife."

Mick looked, saw her. "Her?" He smiled. "You wish."

Finn did.

Two minutes later the swinging doors of 7B were pushed open with a flash of light. Danielle smiled at Finn and walked over. She put her arms around him and her head into his neck.

"Baby," she whispered.

"Baby," he whispered. "You okay?"

She nodded.

"How was it?" Finn asked, wondering how his wife's visit to the apartment she'd lived in twenty years before might have gone, worried about how Ingrid might have taken the news that her best friend was now counting the days.

"So fucking sad," she said.

They stayed wrapped up for a while, not saying a word. Even Mick, not knowing what was going on between husband and wife, knew not to speak. When she finally uncurled herself from her husband, Danielle looked around the bar where she and Finn had had their first date.

"When I didn't find you at the playground, I knew you'd be here."

Mick leaned forward, answering for Finn. "We just got here this very second," he grinned. "No one's been drinking nothing!"

Danielle laughed at that, and Finn introduced his wife to his friend.

"I don't care what you two are up to," she said to Mick. "But where's my son?"

"You don't care?" Mick asked, a bit incredulous.

"Please," Danielle continued, entirely disinterested that her husband had taken their sleeping child into a bar. "I'm a New Yorker."

"My kinda' woman!" Mick exclaimed.

With a nod of his head Finn pointed towards the corner of the bar, where the Prince's little legs could be seen stretching out of his stroller. Behind him could be seen the second stroller, as well as a second pair of sleeping legs.

"He okay?" she asked about the Prince.

"Asleep," Finn answered. "Mick's son's right behind him."

"We had to teach 'em how to act at a bar sometime," Mick offered with a grin.

Danielle smiled, said nothing. She looked out the windows of the bar.

"My old stomping grounds," she said aloud.

Her husband nodded.

She looked around the inside of the bar. "And your old stomping grounds."

"Yeah," Finn agreed, nodding to the youngsters populating the place. "Not the same though."

"Thing's change," the dying woman said, as unflappable as ever, and if her response amazed Finn, it didn't surprise him: Danielle had always been so much wiser than he.

Dita approached, smiling at Danielle. "You must be the wife," she said. "Something to drink?"

"And you must be the famous Dita," Danielle smiled. "Nothing for me, thanks."

"Famous?"

"My husband may have mentioned you a couple of hundred times or so...."

Mick enjoyed that.

"What?" Finn blushed. "What? I used to like hanging out in this bar is all I said...."

"Yeah," Danielle hugged her husband, kissing him on the lips, squeezing him warmly. "That's what you said, honey...."

Dita and Danielle laughed, the shared camaraderie of two pretty women dealing with a lifetime of foolish men, the pair of them reaching hands across the bar to exchange some kind of odd half-handshake of sisterhood and solidarity.

"Just let me know if you need anything," Dita continued, before turning to head back to her stool at the far end of the bar. Finn and Danielle and Mick all watched her go, each of them thoroughly enjoying the sashaying away of her leather-clad ass.

Danielle nodded. "She is hot though."

"My kinda' wife!" Mick blurted.

Danielle took Finn's hand and walked him over to the corner of the bar where their child slept, and she kneeled down in front of his stroller. The mother looked at her son, her sleeping baby, and reached inside to fix the straps, to straighten the boy's head. She stared at him, and finally with the beginning of tears in her eyes she tried to stand up. The squatting had strained her muscles— while the years of chemo had never taken her hair, it had ruined her muscles— and when Danielle tried to stand she wobbled and stumbled, not falling only because Finn caught and held her.

"You okay?" he held on tight.

"Okay," she smiled, her hand grabbing his fore-arm in a death grip. "I'm fine." She managed to straighten herself up and let herself be led to their seats at the bar.

"Finn," she looked at him. "Is he going to be alright?"

For someone who didn't know any better— Mick, let's say— the question might've seemed innocent enough, a mother asking a father if their child would be okay that day. But with Finn and Danielle things were never simple any more.

"Your boy will be just fine," Finn said, choking his emotions down, pretending that he imagined only smooth sailing ahead for he and his boy. "We'll be fine."

He sat her at the bar and Dita, having apparently seen what happened, brought Danielle a glass of water. "Here, hon," she said.

Danielle sipped, sat.

"It's okay," Finn said. "I'll take you home now."

Danielle shook her head, drank a little more water.

"It's fine, I'll drive you home, hon."

She shook her head again, sipped some more. "I'm meeting Ingrid. She's picking up a script at the St. Mark's Church-in-the-Bowery, and then we're going to the Cloisters Café."

Finn smiled. "Like the old days?"

"Like the old days. Gonna' sit on the patio, sip a French martini, maybe smoke a Camel Light."

Mick shook his head. "You can't smoke there anymore."

Danielle gave him a stern look. "Let them try to stop me."

"Atta' girl!" Mick nodded in approval.

Eventually Danielle said it was time to go. She stood up to say good-bye to her husband's drinking buddy. "Nice to meet you, Mick," she said, shaking his hand, holding on to it far longer than normal. "Don't let him drink too much when I'm gone."

"Of course not," Mick laughed, thinking they were all just having a good time there, not necessarily understanding that he was maybe being asked to do something more than just keep his new friend out of trouble for the day.

Danielle looked Mick in the eye, still keeping her hand wrapped tight around his. "Mick," she said firmly. "Keep an eye on him when I'm gone."

Mick might not have known exactly what was going on, but he suddenly got that he was being asked to help. He nodded earnestly. "Yes, ma'am," he wasn't joking at all any more. "Yes, ma'am."

Danielle raised a hand towards the woman at the other end of the bar. "A pleasure, Dita."

"Mine," Dita answered, blowing Danielle a kiss.

Danielle turned and looked up at Finn, quickly kissing him on the lips. "I love you, Finn Riley," she said. "You take care of my son."

And with that Danielle Rigoglioso-Riley was gone. She turned and pushed her way through the swinging doors of the bar, crossed 7th Street, and headed up the diagonal foot path into the middle of Tompkins Square Park. Through the

windows Dita, Mick, and Finn watched, all of them following a mother walk past the playgrounds where she would
never see her young Prince later frolic and play; past the dog-
runs where her nine year old boy would one day walk his
brand-new puppy; past the park benches where her teenaged
son would one day roll his joints and kiss his girls. Through
the bushes and branches they watched as Finn's wife walked
farther into the park, until her yellow dress, her blonde hair,
and her pale skin all faded away, lost in the blooming flowers
and trees of a burgeoning New York City spring.

"Man," Mick said quietly, squeezing Finn's shoulder
from behind. "I love your wife."

"Me, too," Dita said quietly from her end of the bar.

Me too, Finn thought, watching his wife disappear. Me
too.

*

It was well past midnight and Finn stood on the north
side of 7th Street, deciding into which one of two windows he
would hurl the last of his baker's dozen of Yonah Schimmel
knishes stuffed with rolls of nickels. Finn might've liked to
have said he didn't know how he got there, but that would've
been a lie: All week long he'd been headed to the same dark
place, and breaking a bunch of sweet shoppe windows along
the way with a late-night fusillade of loaded snacks wasn't
any great deviation from that plan.

Twelve hours earlier Finn and Mick had left 7B and
taken their sons to the playground for the second time that
day, and a couple hours after that they were headed back to
their respective abodes. Along the way Finn and the Prince
stopped for supplies— knishes and cookies and nickels, flowers and candy— before jumping into the mini-van and
heading home. At the Albemarle Finn set up his son in front
of *Nick Jr.* and checked in on Danielle, who after a big day
was already asleep in her bed, laying still and silent as a
statue. Finn whipped up a quick dinner of ground pork* ta-
cos (*organic, you'll remember), unsalted sunflower seeds,
and fruit smoothies made of bananas*, strawberries*, and

pineapple*. The father then fed himself and his son before giving the boy a quick bath, entertaining the Prince throughout with a reading of one of his favorites, Robert McCloskey's "Blueberries with Sal." Finn helped the boy out of the bath and into his PJs, brushed his teeth, and lugged the yawning child into the bedroom, laying him there in the big bed next to his mother. Finn kissed the boy's cheeks first and then walked around to kiss Danielle's next, the husband not exactly surprised but still somewhat relieved to feel the warmth of his wife's skin. He then sat on a recliner at the end of the bed and smiled at his son, silently mouthing "I love you" to the grinning boy, until eventually the Prince closed his eyes and nodded softly away.

Finn looked at them both, his wife and his son, snug in a warm bed in their New York City home, but he felt no comfort. He had no peace. The Prince slept deeply, his head back and his mouth open, and while Finn wanted to believe his son's life might unfold into varying degrees of wonderful, it was impossible to forget that innocent boy would soon have no mother. Plus, of course, there was the terrifying bit of news that Dr. Aly had recently shared when he announced to Finn and Danielle that Danielle's terminal cancer was also likely hereditary, meaning the terrible colon-cancer gene that was right then striking her down would probably one day come calling on their Prince, too. The doctor and Danielle told Finn not to worry though, said that even if that was scary information it was still good to know, that maybe that realization would even allow everyone to be extra vigilant with the boy and thus probably save his life, but to Finn all that news did was confirm his feeling that there was no escape, that he *was* under siege, that he really, truly was being stalked by Death. Finn couldn't help himself, and looking at his family under the covers he saw not the two warm bodies of his wife and his son but something more akin to a couple cold corpses sharing one terrible shroud.

Finn had to get out of there, so on the night table on the Prince's side of the bed he placed a plate of rainbow cookies, on the table on Danielle's side a vase of her favorite flowers (tulips) and a box of her favorite candies (chocolate-covered cherries). He wasn't exactly sure how his night might play out, but if Finn didn't happen to make it back the next morning he wanted his family to have something nice. Then, with one final glance back at his wife and his son, the husband and father left, quickly and quietly slipping out of the Albemarle and into the New York night.

Finn walked that evening from what seemed one end of Manhattan to the other, heading north as far as the Great Lawn, south all the way to Chinatown, west to the waters of the Hudson River and east to the East, all night long his heart and his mind swamped with remembrances of what had been his life in New York City. Finn's long march that Friday evening— his long, long solitary march— was part Old Homes Day, part PTSD flashback, on every corner what seemed another recollection or another portent, another memory or another sign. There were nightmares and there were fantasies, bad memories and good, but given the cloud Finn felt he was living under most every reminiscence ended up imbued with gloom for him, infused with grey, tinged with loss or fury or regret. Regarding his New York life, in other words, Finn couldn't see the forest for the trees; he couldn't see the light because of the dark.

On the Upper East Side he stopped for a drink at the favorite saloon of one of his favorite authors, but with bourbon going for $13 a pop Finn got the feeling that even if he were still alive Frederic Exley would no longer drink at P. J. Clarke's. Another drink in Chelsea was equally unsatisfying, as in The Lion's Head the failed writer found sitting at the bar not any long line of literary lions but a gaggle of giggling girls swiping left and right at a ceaseless cavalcade of Tinder profiles. He stopped in to The Corner Bistro for a bite, both because of the place's famous burgers and because Danielle had once frequented the joint, back in the glorious 1990s, but as many times as the bar's doorbell chimed that evening never once did Finn turn to see Danielle walking in.

And never again would she, he couldn't help but think.

In Central Park Finn shuddered in shame to recall that time— never far from his mind— when on the Great Lawn in a Strollercize class full of young moms the fattish father had first keeled over and then passed out from no more than the tiniest bit of exercise. At 30th street he climbed through a construction site and over a chain-link fence on to a closed High Line, trying there to get the feeling back from before the Coming of the Crowds, back to those freezing winter days when that elevated city park was an empty and unknown destination enjoyed only by Finn and his Prince. In Chinatown Finn tried to get lost, tried to find again those abandoned byways where a man could thrillingly get chased through the streets by gangs of young toughs, but those days were done, too, the entire island of Manhattan below 14th street by then having since been blanketed— literally every foot of it— by NYPD cameras.

Near Gramercy Park Finn looked up an office building that housed a viatical life insurance company that had recently bought Danielle's policy, a greedy corporation that had paid the needy family fifty cents on the dollar after Danielle's Stage IV diagnosis had meant her early death was virtually assured. Those bastards called Finn on the 15th of every month, like diabolical clockwork, purportedly to see if there was any change in Danielle's "contact information" while in reality checking to see if they had yet cashed in.

"Sorry to tell you," Finn had snarled at their representative the month prior, "but my wife ain't dead yet."

Then it was after two in the morning and he was standing on the north side of 7th Street, deciding into which one of two windows he would hurl the last of his baker's dozen of Yonah Schimmel knishes stuffed with rolls of nickels. The barrage had begun thirty minutes before, on the corner of Bleecker and MacDougal in the West Village. Finn had been reading a National Historic Register plaque detailing the spot as the former home of the San Remo Café, the Greenwich Village coffee house frequented by pretty much everyone back in the day (Bob Dylan and Dylan Thomas, Miles Davis and Jackson Pollock, Kerouac and Ginsberg and Burroughs et al), when a couple passing NYU students highlighted for Finn all the ways New York City— and the world— had gone wrong.

"OMG," one of those meat-headed clowns said to the other, pointing to a nearby boîte, "have you ever tried their cheese tea? Yelp says it's the best in town...."

Finn grimaced. He wouldn't have said that offending phrase surprised him (which one, "OMG" or "cheese tea" or "Yelp"?), but he grimaced to think of it all, that the Greenwich Village once home to young seekers searching for meaning was now little more than a glorified mall food court, a spot overrun with hyper-connected consumers hunting only the most exotic of noshes or the best of deals. Looking around the new neighborhood Finn wouldn't have been surprised to see an Orange Julius, and while he didn't spy one of those historic abominations he saw something equally execrable: Across the street from what had once been the San Remo Café stood a (closed) dessert outpost called "By Chloe," a business that Finn knew little about and harbored no ill will towards— no ill will, that is, until he saw the advertisement painted on their front door hawking what they were proudly touting as "dairy-free ice cream."

"Finally," Finn thought when he saw that ridiculous sign. "At last we're saved from the scourge of milk..."

That shit didn't fly with Finn right then, but you know what did? A (k)nickel knish, the first of which Finn grabbed from the pastry arsenal amassed in the bag over his shoulder and which he launched from ten feet away right through the front window of By Chloe. Kaboom!

Just steps away was another joint selling what it cheekily labelled "Snow Ice Desserts," and though Finn didn't know exactly what that meant he knew he didn't like it. Ergo, the man (k)nickel-knished that place, too, promptly kabooming its front window as well. Directly across the street from there another business was advertising "tastefully smashed ice cream," a turn of phrase that practically begged our hero to tastefully smash the spot's front window with some kind of pastry bomb, which Finn immediately did. Kaboom.

Around the corner he did the same to another establishment called The Dessert Kitchen and then again to another called The Rice Cream Shop. The first place's only real fault was that it sold desserts at a time when Finn seemed to have a vendetta against them (kaboom!) but the second— The Rice Cream Shop, wink, wink, nudge, nudge— got attacked for a bunch of reasons: First, those fuckers sold rice pudding, which was irksome enough to our hero; and second, on its front window had been painted advertisements for both "vegan gelato" and "acai bowls," phrases that Finn thought each, in and of itself, deserved to be blown up. Kaboom!

All that breaking glass had made a bunch of noise and something of a commotion in those not-quite-empty streets, so Finn decided it was best at that point to high-tail it out of the neighborhood. He headed down Bleecker and veered right, turning south towards Soho and that special spot he felt most drawn to. Going down Sullivan Street Finn passed a restaurant that he didn't think much of, at least, mind you, until his subconscious registered what its sign had said. When it did, however, Finn circled back— as Ferris Bueller had done in *Ferris Bueller's Day Off*, when he turned around to chat up the pretty sunbather he'd just hurdled over— to check out that sign.

Holy shit, Finn thought to himself, reaching into his gym bag and wrapping his fist around the loaded treats waiting there. It really does say that!

Rockin' Raw, the restaurant was called, which Finn could have lived with, but beneath its happening title that place's sign claimed to be selling something described as "Peruvian Creole Vegan Cuisine". "*Peruvian Creole Vegan Cuisine*!!!" Obviously, Finn immediately broke that restaurant's front window with a nosh volley— "Attica!" he yelled

for no reason at all as he lobbed that broadside— and if anyone didn't know why he'd done so, Finn thought, then
frankly that S.O.B. was probably part of the problem.

On Spring Street he headed east, towards his dessert des-
tiny, but before he even got there Finn was slowed by a tiny
closed window that claimed to sell "bite-sized dessert treats."
Nuh-uh, Finn thought. Kaboom.

Next was that spot that had irritated him for years, Rice
to Riches, a business that was the first he'd ever seen dedi-
cated solely to rice pudding (strike one!), included in its
name a fanciful play on words (strike two!), and for fun included in its front windows any number of colorful quips and
verbal delights, things like "finally a rice pudding that
doesn't suck" and "we are fancy but not shmantzy" (strike
three!). When he hurled through the plate-glass front window of that establishment a fastball of a (k)nickel-knish,
Finn grinned with manic glee.

On the Bowery, Finn lobbed a potato pie grenade
through the front door glass of a brand-new 7-11 convenience
store. "Big Gulp this!" he yelled as he did so.

On First Street with a tartlet barrage he broke the glass
of a Chase Bank. Why Chase Bank, one might've asked?
"Fuck 'em" Finn would've said to that.

On Second Avenue he put two fingers to his forehead
and nodded at Moishe's Kosher Bakery, offering a somber
salute to an establishment that had always treated Finn with
dignity and New York City with class. "Respect" he might
have said towards Moishe's if Finn hadn't been altogether so
white.

Around the corner on 7th Street, however, Finn's blood
boiled anew at the sight of Van Leeuwen's, a coffee shop that
with a completely straight face had recently charged him
$9.80 for a hot fudge sundae. Nine dollars and eighty cents!
Nuh-uh, Finn thought. Kaboom!

Just up the block at The Cupcake Market Finn ka-
boomed again— enough with the fuckin' cupcakes, Finn
begged!— before he realized that, just like that, he was almost

out of ammo. His baker's dozen of loaded potato knishes had not gone as far as he'd figured. In fact, he had but one of those starchy quiches left to throw, a reality which proved especially troubling when striding down the north side of the street Finn saw two deserving targets side by side: Butter Lane Cupcakes and The Big Gay Ice Cream Shop.

Finn stopped between the two and considered the merits of each: Which most deserved to get its front window smashed in through the ironic message of a (k)nickel knish, he wondered? Was it Butter Lane Cupcakes, a spot which both sold cupcakes and in addition quite shamefully taught cupcake-baking classes to various *Sex and the City*-obsessed gals in the neighborhood? Or was it The Big Gay Ice Cream Shop, about which Finn had no particular gripe other than the fact the line of people snaking out its door occasionally slowed down his 7th Street commute.

What to do, Finn thought, what to do— evil cupcakes on the one hand, too many idlers in the street on the other— before he opted to be inclusive and throw his final potato bomb straight through the plate glass of The Big Gay Ice Cream Shop: Finn had initially considered *not* breaking its front window simply out of respect for gay rights, but then he realized that treating the possibly homosexual owners of that establishment differently just because of their homosexuality was in fact the very sort of crap that Finn didn't believe should happen in America anymore, and especially not in New York City; that's not how Finn had been raised, frankly, so as some kind of equal-opportunity, *pro*-gay rights movement he ended up throwing the final (k)nickel knish of the batch not into Butter Lane Cupcakes but into The Big Gay Ice Cream Shop, shattering the glass there under its waving rainbow flag.

"Suck on this!" Finn yelled when he hurled that pastry salvo, a phrase that confused even Finn at the time as he didn't know if it came across as derisive or supportive, homophobic or homoerotic. To try to clarify his feelings on the issue, Finn tossed off one last rejoinder at The Big Gay Ice

Cream Shop before walking off towards Avenue A. "Viva Stonewall!"

Finn's worry about anyone misinterpreting his feelings regarding gay rights disappeared just as soon as he turned the corner, however, because there on Avenue A Finn came face to face with— and just after he'd completed thirty minutes worth of destruction, an absolute cornucopia of vandalism, a panoply of spite!— two young officers from the New York City Police Department. Finn nearly froze when he saw them but, mercifully, in the end, everything turned out okay.

How did it turn out okay? Finn was not accosted by those officers and remained untroubled by law enforcement for the remainder of that night not because of the usual reason— his Cloak of Caucasian Innocence and Invisibility— but because when Finn turned the corner onto Avenue A and almost immediately saw those two young cops, they did not see him: They, of course, were both looking down instead, entirely engrossed in the magical goings-on of the electronic devices each held in his hands.

Finn might've laughed, if only right then he didn't find absolutely everything so fucking sad.

*

Finn needed a drink.

He needed a drink because he was out of knish ammo and there were so many more windows to smash. He needed a drink because there would never be enough ammo to smash all the windows that needed to be smashed. But mostly Finn needed a drink because he recognized that the battle was over and he had lost: Undertaking such acts of urban vigilantism, Finn would've admitted, no longer brought him any satisfaction, largely because he'd come to see that there was really no longer any such thing as a "Curmudgeon Avenger." That appellation, Finn had realized, was a total misnomer. Yes, in the beginning, when on a lark Finn had taken on the role of a grumpy old man tilting against windmills, the name had made sense. It had been ironic and cutesy, Finn thought, when he so anointed himself. But with each new battle— or, really, with each new loss of an endless battle against a maddening and frightening new world— Finn realized his alterego was not best described as a "curmudgeon." Instead, a better name for his feckless freedom-fighter would've been one that emphasized how utterly futile the guy's efforts had been. How fruitless and ineffectual. Finn hadn't done anything, he could now see, all his "heroic" stands ultimately proving to be completely in vain: He'd not been able to save his city from gentrifying, had he? Not been able to stop his world from changing, right? Not been able to keep his wife's cancer from ceaselessly metastasizing...

Yeah, Finn could admit it: His vigilante hadn't just been some grumpy old fart grumbling about the state of the world, he'd been someone completely powerless to do anything about it. As an Avenger, Finn would've conceded, he hadn't just been a Curmudgeon— he'd been entirely Impotent.

Finn needed a drink.

Finn needed a drink and was in the East Village so he decided to go "home." Though nearly closing time Finn could see through its open windows that 7B was packed— and it looked packed by so many of those god-damned loud, young weekend drinkers— but it was Finn's bar so he decided to stop. Just inside the front door, however, a bouncer he didn't know stuck out his hand to thwart Finn's progress. He looked Finn up and down.

"ID?" the bouncer asked.

The guy was African-American and short, so very short, maybe only five and a half feet tall, but he had huge legs, wide shoulders, and a massive pot-belly. He looked like a circus strong-man, and at the sight of him Finn couldn't help almost immediately imagining the guy in a unitard, one arm holding up an enormous barbell.

Finn wanted to laugh at his request though. He was being carded to get into a bar? Between his bald head, the silver grizzle on his unshaven face, his fat gut and achy hip and sour attitude, there wasn't a thing about Finn that implied even so much as a whiff of under-21.

"ID?" the bouncer repeated.

Although the place was packed and loud Finn then heard a shrill whistle that the bouncer turned towards.

"He's with me, Vernon," Finn heard from a voice behind the bar, there a smiling Dita still manning the stick some twelve hours after Finn had left her earlier that day.

Finn looked back at the bouncer and raised an eyebrow at him. Vernon smiled right back.

"Sorry, Dad," he said, "just messin' with ya.'"

"Dad?"

Vernon smiled some more. Finn didn't mind though: He'd been called worse.

He stepped past the bouncer and towards the bar, where Dita was studiously ignoring the desperate requests of any number of thirsty patrons to greet Finn. She held her arms open from the other side of the bar.

"Dita," he smiled, leaning in and putting his cheek up next to hers.

"Finn," she smiled, her cheek right up next to Finn's and her arms wrapping him tight.

Just then a dopey twenty-something dude in a baby blue button-down shirt leaned in, almost close enough to join the embrace, and slurred, "Gimme a Cosmo..."

Dita looked at him without saying anything before lifting the soft-drink hose and blasting the guy, dousing his shiny young face with what smelled to Finn like either tonic water or ginger ale.

"Vernon!!!" she yelled, but by then the tiny behemoth of a bouncer had already materialized at Finn's side, the guy apparently having leapt like a leopard off his seat by the front door and up to the bar at the sight of all that flying soda-pop. By the time Dita had called for him Vernon had the aspiring Cosmo drinker in a headlock and was in the process of enthusiastically showing him the door.

"Now where were we?" Dita asked, embracing Finn anew. She wrapped her arms around him tight, so tight. When she finally unwrapped herself from him, Dita looked at Finn with tears in her eyes.

"Boogie told me about your wife," she said. "I didn't know it was so bad."

Finn tried to smile, to fundamentally wave it all of, no big deal, no big deal, nothing to see here... but he was also sure that on his face was some stupid, lame grimace, some blank look of pathetic, helpless hopelessness.

"I'm so sorry," Dita cried, wrapping him up again. "So sorry...."

"Thank you," he whispered to her, real tears appearing just like that in Finn's eyes. "Thank you..."

It was nice, Finn thought, to finally have someone— anyone— commiserate with him. Nice to finally have someone recognize that something terrible had happened to Finn, too, along with to his wife and his son. Even if his wife and son were fucked, Finn thought, so was he. He was fucked, too. That was no lie.

When their hug finally ended, Finn asked Dita how she knew. "Boogie told you?"

"Yup," she said, nodding her head over her shoulder, back towards a mob of people standing almost around the corner on the other side of the horseshoe-shaped bar.

Finn couldn't believe it when he saw it but there they all were, nearly everyone from his old gang: Right in the front was Boogie, as spectacularly Afro'ed as ever, but next to him were Don the erstwhile bartender and his girlfriend the editrix Lucy, plus Rocco the Psycho and Ricky the Brooklyn Bouncer (seemingly back from the dead), even Jimmy the loquacious cheese peddler who having moved to Colorado had just happened to stop in that night on one of his regular cross-country jaunts hawking edam and cheddar and brie. Second-tier drinking buddies were there, too— not Finn's closest friends but people he recognized as regular fellow denizens of the 7B night— including the stand-out

Kansas City actor Sal, the brilliant graphic artist Lance, even the genius Armenian film-maker C.C (to whom one should never, ever mention the country Turkey, trust Finn on that one...). About the only people missing from that great 7B reunion were Sunil (surely still living in London) and Barry the Angry Artist, but Finn was still so happy to see so many of his other old friends.

"Finn!" Don yelled when he spotted him, and when Don spied him the others did, too. Unwrapping himself from Dita's warm embrace Finn was bombarded with "hullos" and "welcomes" from his old boozin' buddies, on all of their faces wide smiles and shining eyes, a bunch of looks so animated that it was pretty clear to Finn that the crew had been at it for a while. No question about it, Finn realized: His friends were *drunk*.

"Finn!" Lucy yelled and "Finn!" Rocco the Psycho repeated. "Finn!" Ricky called and "Finn!" Jimmy echoed. Everyone was holding up drinks at him and waving him over. "Finn" Finn heard again and again, and to be honest, he liked it. It filled him up. It made him feel good.

"Finn!" Boogie yelled, although the look on his face was less warm, less welcoming. Frankly, Finn thought, Boogie looked less happy to see him than he looked scared or nervous.

"Finn! Finn!" Boogie was yelling across the busy bar. He was also pointing his finger past Finn towards something behind him, although the place was so loud it was hard to get what Boogie was getting at. Finn didn't really understand the guy's excited pointing, nor his sudden switch into a person pantomiming the throwing of punches (what was this, charades? Finn wondered).

Finn shrugged at Boogie and held up his hands, just not getting his point, at least not until someone tapped Finn on the shoulder and he turned around. Finn saw no one in particular at that point, just a guy with some kind of ridiculous pompadour and a big black eye.

A big black eye.

"Hey Grampa," Finn's Vespa-riding enemy sneered, "how about—"

So Finn punched him. You could never have convinced Finn that that punk hadn't deserved it: He'd called Finn's son a "fucking brat" earlier that day, meaning, as far as Finn was concerned, that Finn could punch the guy absolutely whenever he wanted, any time, day or night. As far as Finn was concerned regarding the asshole on the scooter, he had absolute punching carte blanche.

So, yes, Finn punched him, not a repeat of that phenomenal right cross k.o. from earlier that day, just a quick left jab directly into the guy's at-the-time un-blackened left eye. As his fist flew forward Finn again decided not to break the punk's nose— too squishy, he thought, too bloody— instead pronating his left fist and filling the guy's left eye socket with a quick left jab. This time the punk wasn't knocked out, but he did fall immediately backwards into the couple large lugs standing behind him, a couple bushy-bearded types in overalls— Williamsburg in the house???— who Finn immediately realized were there *with* the sucky scooter rider. Maybe the guy had recruited some friends and spent the day walking around the East Village looking for Finn (and his son?) to fight? Finn didn't much care, not really, but he also did realize right then that he'd probably just thrown a punch that would start a fight that was going to end up pitting him one against three.

Finn didn't care.

Neither did he need to though, because as soon as that Vespa-riding prick picked himself up from the grip of the pals he'd fallen into, things started happening fast: First, from he couldn't imagine where, Finn heard a bell rung, a sound that perfectly imitated the noise made at the beginning of every round of a boxing match. Ding-Ding! And then a female voice was heard above the din, too, clear and loud, a voice filled with what seemed decades worth of violence and repression and rage. A punk voice, in other words.

The noise of the bell and the voice had both come from Dita, of course, standing right then *atop* the bar. Straight and faithful and true, her arm was pointed directly at Finn. "I'm with him!" she roared, a cry that seemed to come all the way off the fields of battle in *Braveheart*, like William Wallace imploring his troops to fight for what was theirs, to stand up and defend at any cost the place they had always called home.

"I'm with Finn!" she roared.

In the end it wasn't even a fair fight. If Finn had thought he was about to be pitted in a battle of one against three, the actual numbers were more like three against nineteen. To say Finn had the home field advantage in that donnybrook was putting it mildly, because as soon as the douchebag with the bouffant hairdo (and the two blackening eyes) straightened up again that jerk and his two obnoxiously hirsute friends were straightaway swept up into a melee, a whirlpool of hate, Vernon immediately putting the scooter punk into a hard headlock and from everywhere in the bar coming a litany of downtown drunks looking to land a couple of kicks or punches in defense of their local and their Dita. If there was one thing those old drinkers enjoyed, after all, it was lashing out against those "kids today," against the sorts of "men" who spent a great deal of time on their facial hair. In other words, let's just say the Queensberry rules weren't exactly in effect during that brawl, shall we?

Meanwhile, Finn's friends descended upon the fight from the other side of the bar: Ricky led the way, the ex-bouncer no more than a cyclone of haymakers, but behind him Don was wildly swinging Boogie's cane in the air, whipping it about like he was the Count of Monte Cristo, while hot on his trail came his girlfriend Lucy, the brilliant *Times* editrix, who had in her hand a rolled-up copy of the *Magazine*— he couldn't be sure, but it looked to Finn like Lucy about to thump on someone with that periodical the way one might beat a bad dog. Rocco the Psycho was never much of a fighter (ironic, eh?), but he came next in that parade of

Finn's attacking friends, hurling epithets as he went, while behind him Jimmy was rushing forward carrying above his head, if Finn wasn't mistaken, an enormous wheel of cheddar. A second later Finn saw that cheese wheel crack in two over the pompadour of the dainty Vespa rider, which Finn might have imagined would have been the most absurd part of the fight at least until he saw Dita.

Squatting on the bar she held in front of her a tumbler full of what looked like flaming whiskey, and her cheeks were puffed as full as a chipmunk's. Then with one great exhalation, the woman blew forward as hard as she could, from her lips coming an enormous fireball shooting across the barroom, flames that mostly scorched the faces of the three 7B "intruders" who'd had the audacity to go after one of the bar's own, but also a fiery fountainhead that, let's be honest, singed the eyebrows of any number of other innocent people who might have just happened to be standing there; a little unfortunate, most people in the bar would have agreed, but really just the collateral damage of battle.

"East Village in the house!!!" Dita roared, laughing maniacally, in her wild eyes the look of a woman who lived for that shit, punk to the bitter, bitter end.

As the fight tumbled away from Finn, he found himself stepping away from it and back towards where his friends had initially been gathered. There Finn saw Boogie, sitting on a chair by himself, sipping on an enormous blue can of Labatt's. Boogie raised it to Finn and smiled.

"Lover," Boogie said with a smile. "Not a fighter."

Finn grinned, but then he saw it on the bar next to Boogie, what looked like a still-life poised to be painted: a pristine copy of *The New York Daily News*; a full glass of what looked like clear liquor, a vodka tonic perhaps, its ice melted completely away and one slice of dull lemon wedged onto its side; and a candle, its wick still flickering with a tiny flame but mostly melted down, a candle that had clearly been there for a while and that was on its last legs. Finn recognized who used to sit there, and he knew: Everybody had convened that night to say good-bye to a friend.

"Barry?" Finn asked Boogie.

"Barry."

"Liver?"

"Liver."

"Too much drink?"

"What else?"

In a move that wasn't intended to be ironic but could certainly have been seen that way, Boogie then raised his can of beer and held it up towards Finn, toasting to the friend they'd lost who'd drank himself to death. Finn understood though, and he picked up from the bar a bottle of Budweiser— it must have been one of his other friends, Finn figured, and they surely wouldn't mind— and clinked it with Boogie, then taking a sip.

"To Barry," they said. And they drank.

Soon the "fight" was winding down and the bar emptying out. Right then Vernon, with the help of about ten angry old drunks and five of Finn's friends, was actually in the process of evicting the raccoon-faced Vespa pilot and his two lugheaded friends out the back door of the bar, but even that brought Finn no solace: So empty was Finn right then that even the remembrance of punching a Millennial couldn't fill the void he felt.

It was time for Finn to go. He stood up and bumped fists with Boogie. "Gotta' split, brother."

"You just got here, man."

"It's time."

"Okay," Boogie nodded. "Peace, man."

The two hugged.

"Where you off to?" Boogie asked.

"Dunno'," Finn said. "The usual. Throwing myself off the Manhattan Bridge."

Boogie laughed. He was a young man with a limp and a cane, so he was certainly fluent in the language of black humor. "Take me, take me," he joked.

Finn smiled, rubbed Boogie's 'fro. The thing was though, Boogie was probably kidding.

*

Easy-peasy it was not.

In fact, it took Finn Riley two tries to get himself up and over the protective fence built to keep people off the railings on the south side of the Manhattan Bridge. The first time he was climbing pretty easily up— the fence was only about seven feet tall— but when he found himself in position to throw a leg over the top it was his left foot's turn to go. Given how hincky Finn's left hip had been feeling of late, however, how tight and how achy, he knew that wasn't going to happen. No way, Finn realized.

Instead the man had to jump back off the fence and on to the pedestrian walkway to start again, that time beginning with his right foot to be sure that it would later be his right hip's turn to do the heavy lifting. That worked, thankfully, at least until the no longer agile or svelte Finn found himself teetering atop that fence, one leg over and one not, hanging there like some corpulent klutz as the fence wobbled back and forth beneath him, first swinging towards the safety of the walkway and then out across the dangers of the water. Finn had the vague feeling the whole thing might go over— that he was maybe going to pull the entire protective fence over the side of the bridge and into the East River with him— but eventually it stopped its teeter-tottering so he could keep on. Finn did. He held on and finally did it, pushing himself over the fence and finding his footing on the railing below. Finn then turned himself around and leaned his back against the fence, looking south towards the Brooklyn Bridge, at least until he slid down along the chain-link and sat his fat ass on the railing. At last, Finn thought. At last. His feet dangled over the edge, nothing between them and the choppy waters of the East River below except two hundred feet and the pull of gravity, the heavy pull of gravity and imagined relief.

Finn wouldn't have said he was suicidal. He wasn't actively trying to kill himself, he didn't think. Rather, Finn thought he was being a little more Zen about it. He was going to let whatever happened happen. He would take what came. Admittedly, of course, by placing himself on the *wrong* side of the protective barrier that had been built to keep people from accidentally plunging to their deaths over the side of the Manhattan Bridge, Finn was greatly increasing the chances he'd end up drowned. He got that. But he thought that Fate had been making itself perfectly clear regarding its intentions for him— of late it seemed the Grim Reaper was his constant companion, always seeming to be walking lockstep with Finn and his family and his friends— so Finn was prepared to just let it be. To let go. To welcome whatever would be, he thought.

Que sera, sera.

But the view was less wonderful than Finn might have imagined. It was then about four in the morning, New York City illuminated only by electrical light. To Finn's right he could see the Freedom Tower standing tall, eighteen hundred feet of skyscraper built as a "Fuck you" to Muslim extremists, an enormous edifice built to try to help New York forget the buildings that had once stood on that spot, the twin towers that fell to the twin terrors of fire and death. As if anyone could forget. To reemphasize the fact it was on that very spot that thousands of people had suffered a gruesome, terrifying demise, two shards of lights shot up from the ground there, piercing the night sky, two ghost twin towers, a not so subtle reminder for everyone to remember that, really, lower Manhattan would never be anything but a graveyard, a goddamned graveyard.

On the Brooklyn Bridge and FDR Drive cars sped past, even at that ungodly hour— really neither day nor night— dozens and dozens of vehicles careening down the road, their bright headlights leading the way, red taillights trailing behind. In all of those cars Finn knew was another life, other lives, all the different avenues in the world he hadn't had to go or hadn't decided to go. Those cars were full of people he'd never know living lives he'd never imagine, a thought that didn't fill him with optimism over the world's myriad possibilities as much as it filled him with dread about all the things he'd never do or see or know. Over everything that was lost.

Did it even matter if Finn went over the side? Who was he after all? Who was Finn? Just some guy, he thought— or, really, some guy who'd once wanted to be a playboy but who could no longer even really get laid. Some old man— or, really, some old man who'd once dreamt of athletic greatness but who could no longer easily manage even a single kick. Just some asshole— or, really, some asshole who'd aspired to be the next Jack Kerouac but who'd never even managed to write any more than two sentences of any book. Two sentences! That wasn't a novel. It might not even have been a haiku.

Who was Finn? Just some old, asshole, guy— or, really, some old, asshole, guy halfway over the edge of the Manhattan Bridge on the way to a watery grave. Just some old, asshole, guy.

And it was only as a "guy" that he thought of himself, Finn realized, not necessarily even a "man". Seriously, he wasn't really sure how it happened, but at some point Finn had made the career choice to take over a position that for millennia had been almost the literal definition of "women's work"? He'd opted to be a stay-at-home dad? Finn may not have cared what jobs other people wanted to do or not do, but that didn't necessarily mean he wanted to end up being someone's mother. How had it happened, he wondered? How had he ended up in charge of changing the diapers and drying the tears? Had he actually agreed to put the needs of another before his own? Did he really think that was his forte?

It had not even been cancer but indolence that had sealed Finn's fate: When the Prince of New York was about to turn a year old and Danielle seemingly in remission, she was offered an excellent position doing P.R. for a Broadway theatre making more than Finn did at one of the last testing companies that would hire him, so it was without a great deal of thought that they decided to switch. Danielle would go to the office to make the money and Finn would stay home to care for their son.

When he spoke to his boss about leaving, she was impressed. "Wow," the woman said. "Good for you. Some people might feel a stigma about a man taking care of the kids."

"Oh, there's a stigma," Finn laughed. "But it can't be as bad as work."

Hanging off the side of the Manhattan Bridge, Finn wasn't so sure about that any more. To him, pushing that red baby stroller through the streets of Manhattan ended up being every bit as traumatizing as Hester Prynne's scarlet letter. One of the last times Finn had rolled the stroller on to the subway he was aghast at what happened, when a teenaged girl got up to offer him her seat. It was, no question about it, a classy move, an offer Finn simultaneously considered to be both most polite and terribly mortifying. On the one hand, Finn was impressed that a young person had been raised with the good manners to be gracious enough to offer a person with a baby stroller their spot on the train; on the other, he wanted to slink away in shame to think that a young girl looked at him— at someone Finn imagined was a big, strapping man— and thought "let me help that poor guy." Finn had been raised to assist the elderly, the disabled, pregnant women, etc. etc.— really anyone who wasn't as capable as the big, strong man he was— but suddenly as a stay-at-home dad Finn was the helpless one in the eyes of a teenaged girl? When it happened, Finn didn't want to tuck in his tail and run— he wanted to tuck away his dick and run, like the little girl he felt he was.

Then there was Finn's concern about what effect his stay-at-home dadding might be having on his son. Not such a good one, Finn didn't imagine. He recalled a couple years prior, for instance, when the boy was still a toddler, Finn changing the Prince's diaper and discovering a rash. The father then delicately cleaned his son's junk, top and bottom, before deciding he ought to put on a salve. Finn didn't like the look of the angry red rash on his son's balls, so he got out the A&D and massaged it on to his boy's testes, then leaning down to blow those cojones dry. Right about then— as he was softly blowing a warm breeze on to his son's naked nuts— Finn looked up to see the Prince staring right at him. The eye contact between them was strong. Christ, Finn thought, that can't be good. It was a little funny to think of the scenario, Finn would have conceded that, but he didn't see anything amusing about that scene being seared into the Prince's developing brain, the image of an unshaven grizzled old man blowing on his balls. That couldn't be good, Finn didn't think.

Looking over the side of the bridge to the long drop below Finn thought, why not? What did he have to look forward to anyways? Mostly funerals, he thought. Mostly he had to look forward to donning a black suit to attend what would surely be a surfeit of future funerals. Not funerals of distant relatives, either, nor even expected funerals of older relations, but the tragic ones that might befall a man who lost his wife, or a man who lost his child. How long before he would be left alone, Finn wondered, the patriarch of a family that had ceased to be? A solitary man standing solo in a black suit at the head of an empty holiday table. How long? How could letting go and falling away over the side of the Manhattan Bridge be any worse than that?

Finn couldn't help himself, and he reached into his pocket to pull out his phone. Finn had an addictive personality, at all times being pretty much on the brink of a Coors Light bender or an Internet porn binge, but he was at least proud to say he'd manage not to get seduced by the cell phone. In fact, for emergencies only he had only the most basic of models— a flip phone with neither the Internet nor even a camera— but sometimes even with that Finn couldn't help himself: He needed to check for messages.

That night there were none. The screen on his cellphone listed the time as 4:21 AM but showed no messages.

Finn wasn't surprised. Who would have called him or texted him? His wife? Danielle trusted Finn, and whether or not she even knew he had gone out that night she would have trusted that he would return by morning. His friends? Who were Finn's friends? There was the gang from the bar, and he'd just seen them. His drinking buddies, he knew, were really that, people to drink with. They were fun, especially at the bar, and they'd already done their part: When Finn appeared they welcomed him, and when he was in a fight they defended him. But, were they really the kind of people he could turn to in a crisis? What did any of them know about cancer, anyways? About loss and aging and death?

Finn scrolled through the phone's directory, looking at the people whose telephone numbers he had. Maybe someone would help, Finn thought. Maybe someone would offer a hand.

First were a couple names of parents from his son's preschool, nice people but acquaintances at best. Then Bo, he saw, the security guard from the David Rubinstein Atrium, the ex-cop who liked to tease Finn and to whom Finn liked to give shit back. Next was Gerry, a.k.a. Mary, the head dad of the Gotham Stay-At-Home-Dads (SAHD) Club. Then Mick. Who was Mick, Finn wondered, until he recalled the ex-firefighter who had just that day started to become Finn's new friend. He saw his brothers listed in there, one, two, three. His parents, of course, and his in-laws.

It was 4:30 AM but Finn didn't care. He needed to be in contact with someone. Anyone. The other option was to go over the side. He needed not to feel quite so alone, so Finn started to look at the phone directory again, starting at the top. Bo's name he saw first, and he thought about it. The fact was, Finn had never seen Bo outside of the Rubinstein Atrium. Finn didn't even recall how he'd gotten the guy's number. Still, there was something about Bo. Finn got the feeling he was a stand-up guy. He was an ex-cop, after all.

> Bo, You up?
> Finn here.
> I need a hand.

Bo was even older than Finn, so it was no great shock that even at that incredibly early hour the man seemed to be awake. Or, perhaps, Bo was always on call, always ready to go. In either case, he texted back within a minute.

> You!
> I'm not surprised.
> Get arrested?

Finn wasn't surprised either. He could see the smirk on Bo's face. It probably couldn't be helped though, as the two men's relationship had been heavily based on giving each other crap.

But then the phone beeped again.

> Seriously, pal, what ya need?

Finn's eyes began to well up. A stand-up guy, Finn thought. Bo was a stand-up guy. He shouldn't have been surprised though. Ex-cop.

The next name Finn saw in the directory was Gerry. That was a long shot, that Finn knew, but he was grasping at straws. He was grasping at straws, Finn was, so he forwarded the earlier text to Bo, slightly edited.

> Gerry, You up?
> Finn here.
> I need a hand.

Finn had only been a member of the Gotham Stay-At-Home-Dads Club for about three months, and then he'd studiously avoided the group since. He had actively avoided them, in fact, at times hiding under tables so as to not have to see those fellows. To think those guys were going to come running to his side was a pipe dream, Finn knew. A goddamned pipe dream. He wasn't surprised when a minute passed, then another and another, with no reply. Finn understood: It was his fault, nobody else's.

Finn saw Mick's number and thought, why not? They'd just exchanged phone numbers that very day, in fact, but Finn thought, why not?

> Mick, You up?
> Finn here, from the playground and the punch-out and the bar...
> I need a hand.

Either Mick didn't go to bed at night or he got up before the sun, because the response was almost immediate.

> im on my way

Finn actually gasped. His eyes filled with tears, but then he laughed and fired off another text message.

> You don't even know where I am!

Thirty seconds later it beeped again.

> doesnt matter. im on my way.

Finn smiled. Firemen, he thought. New York City civil servants, he thought! Then the phone beeped again, Mick once more.

> ok where r u

Every single beep of his phone made him feel better, Finn realized. There were people out there, people to help, maybe even people who gave a shit or two about him.

He kept looking in the phone directory and next saw his brothers, one, two, three. Nah, Finn thought to himself. Not yet. He'd call his brothers if things got more dire.

His in-laws? Finn laughed to think about that. If he called his father-in-law and told him there was trouble, the man— not even needing to know why— would have been driving towards the city before the phone call was done. He was almost eighty, the old man, but you couldn't stop him. He'd have been driving like the lunatic he always was, tail-gating and passing and honking as he went, probably jamming into his pocket an enormous wad of hundreds with one hand while loading a pistol with the next. He'd have been scouring his brain to remember the old friends who might be able to help in times of crisis like this. And all before he even knew what the problem was, mind you, but you messed with his daughter's husband, you messed with the old man.

Finn's mother-in-law? She would have wanted to help, too, but only after her hair was done. She'd have gotten there eventually, yes she would have, and then you could bet some-one was going to get an earful. In other words, she would have helped in her own special way.

The Pilgrim Parents? The couple from "American Gothic" but with a light coating of snowflakes in their hair? Finn smiled to think of it. If there was a barn-raising; a bucket brigade to fight a big fire at the old town hall; an In-dian attack on the frontier where rifles needed to be stuck out of the stockade and bullets let fly? They were your couple. Not necessarily the first pair you'd want to call if you were starting a stand-up comedy festival, but the Pilgrim Parents were born to aid. It was in their Yankee blood.

If he called and said there was trouble, Finn knew, his mother and father would come. Grimly they would come, hu-morlessly they would come, but inexorably they would come. You could not stop them. They would gas up the car, load it up with supplies— maybe extra gasoline, a couple quarts of oil, some jugs of (tap) drinking water, a bunch of peanut butter and crackers, perhaps a flashlight, some blankets and pillows, an air pump, cough drops, tissues, extra cash, their AAA card, etc. etc.— and drive, drive, drive. If they believed their son was in need, you couldn't stop them: The Pilgrim Parents would have immediately been on their way, their progress inexorable, inexorable, inexorable. They were el-derly now, so maybe one would be lost along the way, maybe even both— the harsh climate, natural disasters, age and in-jury, traffic, even those Injuns' hunkered down in the woods of Eastern Connecticut near the casinos all being obvious threats— but they would never stop. If they were called, the Pilgrim Parents would never stop.

Inexorable.

It wowed Finn to think about that, to know in his heart the lengths his parents would go for him, but he also decided right then not to call his mother and father. Right then that might have been a little more inexorable than he had in mind.

But thinking so fondly of his parents, Finn remembered something else: The year he was in 7th grade his parents took a year off from running their businesses to stay home with the teenaged kids, meaning they were home all day, every day. Worse, Finn's father— a.k.a. the Pilgrim Pop— decided he would make his boys breakfast every day before school, but because the man had come of age during that whole pull-yourself-up-from-the-bootstraps era of American history, he did not go small. The guy had pretty much never cooked a thing in his life before but he definitely did not go small.

Rather, the Pilgrim Pop ensconced himself every day in that pre-dawn kitchen and whipped up every sort of culinary experiment for his children, every morning an attempt at breakfast even more extraordinary than the last, each day another offering in what the man's sons came to call his Eggs Benedict Roulette: Some days of course there were Eggs Benedict, but over time his sons were also fed apple-stuffed pancakes, huevos rancheros, steel-cut oatmeals, banana walnut French toasts, home-made corned beef hashes, shaksuka, the occasional attempted frittata. As god was their witness, one day that father even tried to serve to his teenage sons, for breakfast, a peach soufflé. A peach soufflé, alas, that did not rise, but a peach soufflé nonetheless! Later the boys agreed amongst themselves that none of them could remember ever once having been served over the course of that school year even a single bowl of cereal, a piece of toast, a scrambled egg. Not a one. Never. If it wasn't a kitchen masterpiece, their dad hadn't even given it a try.

When they were older the sons ended up making hay with their father's year of breakfasting dangerously, teasing the old man about the elaborate lengths he had gone. But the

Riley boys knew, too, what else that school year had meant: It meant their father was there. It meant their father was paying attention. It meant their father cared.

Finn's phone beeped again, and then a second time. First Bo.

> Seriously what you need?
>
> I'm here.
>
> You want I send a cruiser?

Then Mick.

> really where r u
> i can help

Finn dropped his head, shaking his head, tears welling up. He was proud to know those two men, both of them: When someone called, they answered. Finn wasn't even their family; he was only nominally their friend (having never spoken to Mick until two days ago!); but when it was time to step up, Bo and Mick stepped up. They stepped up.

Would he, Finn wondered? Had he? At the time of his family's crisis, had he stepped up? Had he answered the call?

Finn thought he had. After Danielle got a more lucrative job and Finn became a stay-at-home dad, he thought he'd answered the call. He changed the poopy britches and took daily trips to the park and taught his boy how to climb the monkey bars. He wiped the tears and went on picnics and helped his son learn to swim. He'd been there every day before and after pre-school; he'd been there on the playgrounds of Central Park; he'd been there at cannoli huts and ice cream trucks all around the city. He'd been there. If his son had trouble, Finn knew, his father had been there.

Christ, he'd even been there when his son's balls itched and someone needed to put ointment on them; he'd been there when someone needed to blow on those balls, Finn had. And that, Finn was beginning to see, had not been anything to be ashamed of; rather, it was a badge of honor, something to be proud of. At the time of his boy's testicular crisis, Finn had been there, right there, up to his elbows in it.

Neither had Finn been afraid to get his hands dirty. Literally. Right after the Prince's birth, in fact, the very first time Danielle was showing Finn how to change a diaper, their bare-assed son began to shit right there on the changing table. With a smile on his face but no diaper on his butt the Prince just began to go. Danielle panicked, and screamed, looking about for diapers or wipes. Finn, however, as smoothly as Derek Jeter had every turned a double play a couple miles away in Yankee Stadium, stepped forward and caught that poop, a sure-handed, bare-handed grab.

Danielle screeched and the Prince smiled while Finn calmly carried those fistfuls of shit out of the bedroom and into the bath, depositing it there in the toilet before cleaning himself up.

When he walked back in the bedroom the Prince was still smiling, an impish little grin, but Danielle was looking at Finn with awe.

"I can't believe you just did that," she said with love in her voice.

Finn shrugged. "Anyone who's ever had anal sex can't worry about a little shit," he explained.

But had Finn stepped up when it was time to help Danielle? He thought he had. When there chores to be done, he'd done them. When there were meals to be made, he'd made them. When there were prescriptions to be picked up, he'd picked them up. Finn wasn't so naïve as to think that he'd been any Mother Theresa, some saint dedicating himself to the well-being of another, but he'd tried his best. When Danielle's feet hurt, Finn massaged them. When Danielle's back itched, Finn scratched it. When Danielle's phat ass was interested in someone being interested in it, Finn remained lovingly devoted.

Finn had tried.

Sitting on the railing on the south side of the Manhattan Bridge and looking down at the choppy water so far below, Finn began to be a little ashamed of himself. What was he doing? Things weren't working out perfectly for him so he was going to give up? He was going to quit? Once the going got a little tough, Finn got going too?

He was a little ashamed.

His phone beeped then, just once. He didn't recognize the number or name at first, and it was a mass text that had been sent to what looked like a hundred numbers, but then Finn began to figure it out.

> Guys, Gerry here.
> Man down.

Gerry. Head dad of The Gotham Stay-At-Home-Dads (SAHD) Club. "Man down."

One of the few "rules" the Gotham Stay-At-Home-Dads (SAHD) Club had was that when the alarm went out, it would be answered. "Man down."

That when one of the fathers called, the other fathers would be there. "Man down."

That when a man needed help, his fellow men would step up. "Man down."

Finn's phone beeped. He could barely see the screen through the tears in his eyes, but he knew what it would say.

> Man down.
> Finn Riley
> 631 721 3971

The text was almost scientific proof that Finn was an asshole, a whiny little asshole, but he smiled through his tears when he saw it. He laughed through his tears when he saw it, his feet dangling two hundred feet above the blackness of the East River. He was such an asshole, Finn thought. Such an asshole.

His phone beeped.

> Finn, Tom.
> Whaddaya need?

And beeped.

> Roger here Finn.
>   Dont know I know you
> but how can I help?

And beeped.

> Whats up?
> What can I do?

And beeped and beeped and beeped, texts from men he vaguely knew and others he definitely did not. The texts kept flying in though, one after another. It was not yet six in the morning but Finn's phone began to beep and beep and beep, gaining momentum with the passing of every second until it was popping off like the latter stages of a bag of popcorn in the microwave. Beep, beep, beep, beep beep beeeepeepeepeee-peeepepepeepeeeep.

He was such an asshole, Finn knew, such a whiny asshole, a lesson the Gotham Stay-At-Home Dads (SAHD) club
were kind enough to teach him along with offering their
help. Finn was amazed with the responses he was getting, absolutely awed by it, moved so much that when he'd asked for
help those men had come running. But he shouldn't have
been surprised: Wasn't that what men did? What fathers
did? Apparently, Finn chuckled to himself, even fathers
with a diaper bag in one hand, a bottle of formula in the
other, and a crying baby Bjorn'ed fully to the chest. They
answered the call.

And what kind of father was he, Finn wondered? He
looked across a great expanse of the East River to the Brooklyn Bridge just south of the Manhattan Bridge, and Finn
thought of his son, his Prince of New York. Finn imagined
his son on the Brooklyn Bridge maybe twenty year hence, his
gorgeous, tow-headed, blonde-haired, blue-eyed little boy
now all grown up, a strapping young man, perhaps on a date
with a sexy young blonde girl (Oedipal, maybe, but that's
were Finn's brain went). He thought of his son and his girl
strolling alone together along the pedestrian walkway in the
middle of the Brooklyn Bridge, the girl maybe in a flowery
dress and the Prince traditional, old-school, maybe even
Beat, dressed in Levi's and a white t-shirt like some Kerouac
redux. Finn imagined his grown-up boy, his twenty-something son— how he ached for his Prince to live to see that
day!— smiling with his girl, maybe linking pinkies in the
most subtle holding of hands, maybe pressing their lips so
softly together. And then Finn thought of them turning
northward, towards the very bridge on which Finn was currently sitting, and imagined the expression on his son's face
changing. He saw a pallor coming over him, thought of the
boy whispering to the girl that it was there that his father
had died. That it was there, on the Manhattan Bridge, not
where some old man had slipped over the edge but where *his*
old man had: *His* old man. He didn't know why his father

had done it, his son would say to the girl. He would never know why.

No fucking way, Finn thought to that, shaking his head. Nuh-uh. No fucking way.

He wouldn't do it. He would never do it. He would never take from his Prince the city he'd bequeathed to him. He would never take from him the Manhattan Bridge, nor the Brooklyn Bridge, nor downtown. His boy had been born on First Avenue, and the city was his. He was the Prince of New York, and he would not have to say good-bye to it because his father had not been enough of a man.

Scanning the New York City skyline Finn saw that the ghostly twin towers were gone, their lights extinguished for the night. To the east the sun wasn't yet coming up over his city, but in the lightening sky Finn could tell it wanted to.

No fucking way, Finn thought.

Finn penned a quick text and sent it to Bo, to Mick, and to the hundreds of numbers that Gerry had addressed.

> Crisis averted, men.
> Thank you!
> Finn Riley

No fucking way, Finn thought.

Sadly, there would be plenty of death in the Prince's future, way too much in fact: The family dog was on his last legs. Big Momma was not a young cat. The boy's grandparents were all approaching their eighties, and the Prince's mother— their Queen— lived her life under a shadow of daily death. Would Finn add to that litany? Would he make the list worse? What kind of father would do that to his son?

No fucking way, Finn thought.

The week before Danielle told Finn she'd discovered their son in the living room attempting to put a diaper on his teddy-bear, George. When Danielle asked him what he was doing, the boy said that all that day he was going to act like "a grown-up man." A grown-up man! When Finn heard it, he'd been proud. He couldn't exactly wrap his head around it, the idea that his son thought being a "grown-up man" meant changing diapers, but somehow Finn felt like he liked it. He felt like somehow he'd done something right: In watching the way his father had acted his son had gleaned that the job of a "grown-up man" was to take care of others. Not so bad, Finn thought.

No fucking way, Finn thought. No fucking way. He stood up on to the railing and turned around, grabbing the chain link fence with two hands.

If cancer came calling on his family again, Finn would be there. If it came after his wife, he'd be by her side, doing his absolute best impression of a California Redwood. If it came for his son— if that god-damned illness came for his angelic little boy— Finn would be waiting. Finn would be waiting, with organic vegetables by his side and the world's best doctors and an Internet's full of information about fighting that heinous disease.

No fucking way was he going over the side of this bridge, Finn thought, because he had too much to do. Too much to live for, so no fucking way. He reached both hands up to the top of the fence, which from his position standing on the railing wasn't much of a stretch. With both hands firmly holding the chain link, Finn crouched down and then leapt up, propelling himself upwards with the force of his powerful legs, in one fell swoop that old jock hurling himself back away from the dangers of the East River and over the fence towards the safety of the pedestrian walkway on the south side of the Manhattan Bridge. He realized in mid-flight that he was about to land on his achy left hip, but Finn didn't care. He knew the landing would hurt but, fuck it, he thought, he would just rub some god-damned dirt on it and walk it off. He'd rub some god-damned dirt on it and walk it off....

Flying through the air Finn thought he could kill himself another time, but right then he had to get home to make his family breakfast. Since it was Saturday, the one day of the week when Finn usually spun the wheel of his own Eggs Benedict Roulette, he realized he'd have to make something special for his Queen and his Prince. He'd have to make something extraordinary, something great. Blueberry pancakes, he wondered? A fritatta? Maybe even a breakfast quiche?

Finn couldn't be sure, not just yet, but of one thing he was certain: The breakfast he would make for his wife and his son, it would be organic. You could bet the fuck it would be organic.

THE END

ABOUT THE AUTHOR

T.S. Farley (a.k.a. "Todd") is the author of the memoir, *Making the Grades: My Misadventures in the Standardized Testing Industry*, and the novel, *The Impotent Avenger*. He regularly writes about sports and comedy for *HUSTLER* and has been published in *The New York Times, Washington Post, Christian Science Monitor, Education Week, Neurology Now, Heart Insight, New York Press, Port City Life, Working Waterfront*, and *The Camden-Herald Gazette*. Todd lives in New York with his wife, his sons, and a Newfoundland named Nana.

Contact at www.tsfarley.com